J__ H____ ____ __ in 1916. He a___r__d'__ b__t__lling *The Sea*
Sh___ No__ ____ ____ ____ ____ __nes of Mark
Hebden and Max H_____, ____ _ sailor, airman, journalist,
travel courier, cartoonist and history teacher. During the Second
World War he served with two air forces and two navies. After
turning to full-time writing, Harris wrote adventure stories and
created a sequence of crime novels around the quirky fictional
character Chief Inspector Pel. A master of war and crime fiction, his
enduring fictions are versatile and entertaining.

BY THE SAME AUTHOR

JOHN HARRIS

A KIND OF COURAGE

A Kind of Courage
Published in 2003 by Redwood Editions
An imprint of Hinkler Books Pty Ltd
17–23 Redwood Drive
Dingley VIC 3172 Australia
www.hinklerbooks.com

Previously published by House of Stratus in 2001

© 1972, 2001 John Harris

The right of John Harris to be identified as the author of this work
has been asserted.

ISBN 1 7412 1119 0

Typesetting: McPherson's Printing Group, Maryborough, Vic,
Australia
Printed and bound in Australia

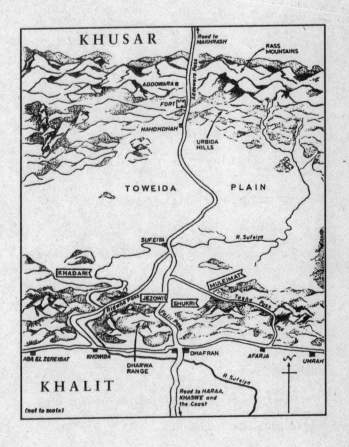

PART ONE

Because of the Treaty

one

1

There was nothing about the hills surrounding the fort to indicate that they were full of eyes, but they all knew they were there, staring down on the little group of grey-white buildings in the valley, watching silently what went on – the passage of mules in and out along the rocky paths, the arrival of tradesmen from the village, the movement of the fleet of not very modern lorries, even the mounting of individual guards, their positions, and probably even whether they stayed alert or dozed at their posts. It had been going on for weeks, though no one in Hahdhdhah had ever seen any movement that wasn't intended to be seen.

As the sun sank and the bright brassiness of the heavens faded to jade green and then to lemon yellow, the hills remained silent, changing with the colour of the sky from drab red-brown to salmon pink and then to gold. 'Hills' was really a misnomer, because they were about as far from the low rolling folds of England, that they liked to remember as hills, as it was possible to be. These heights, though they could hardly be called mountains either, were still ugly eruptions on the face of the earth, in reds, pinks, violets and yellows – never green – dark screes

3

and slopes devoid of vegetation, rising cliff on fantastic cliff, ridge on massive ridge, tower on tremendous tower, until the sharp curving wedge of the summit pierced the sky in a pyramid of baked volcanic lava; layer on layer of precipices, crags, ledges, rocks and cornices, most of them bare of growth, and all of them capable of hiding a man. It was ghostly sometimes, to stare at them, and terrible in the silence they produced. There was no sound from them, not a tree in them, not a blade of grass, and the bastions of rocks seemed sometimes to glow in the sun against the sky, as unreal as a superb stage setting, particularly in winter when the rains came and the approaching storms dragged themselves to shreds among the polished lava pinnacles.

They all knew that every niche overlooking the fortress contained a watcher, wrapped in ragged clothes and holding a rifle – some of the oldest dating back even to the First World War and as dangerous to the owner as to the intended victim – flinty eyes staring down in a constant and never-ceasing vigil.

Occasionally – and everyone in Hahdhdhah knew it was never by accident but just to convince them they were still there – a small group could be seen moving along a ledge of the hills, a small dimly seen file of men; edging cautiously along some path or across a slope, moving slowly so there should be no doubt about them being seen – and that Hahdhdhah existed only because they allowed it to exist.

As the Toweida bugler, Nalk Owdi, a stubby-featured Dharwa, sounded his evening blast in the courtyard, his face shining with the pride he felt in the possession of the gleaming copper instrument he carried and the sound it made, the group of men on the ramparts of the fortress,

4

staring out at the silent hills, were all a little uneasy. None of them was very old and they were all aware of their lack of experience.

Of them all, Sergeant James Fox was the most experienced. Despite the fact that his permanent rank was no higher than corporal, Fox had been in the army for ever – a mechanic, an armourer, an administrator of sorts, a psychologist and an expert fighting man. But for an erratic wildness as a youngster that had lifted him up and thrown him down three or four times, Fox might have been a sergeant-major. He was a brave man, too, but he had been badly wounded in Borneo and, because he had learned that courage was an expendable thing that dwindled just a little more with every injury, he was cautious now and wary – and surprisingly sympathetic towards lesser men. His yellow wily eyes flickered as he listened to the others talking near him, reflective and interested, as became an old soldier concerned with affairs of his superior officers.

One of them, a youngster with a round cheerful face and a large yellow moustache, gestured through the embrasure. He was a newcomer to Hahdhdhah and looked it with his white knees and the pinkness of his nose.

'Go on, Billy,' he was urging. 'Hazard a guess, old boy. How many do you think there are out there?'

Fox saw his commanding officer, Major William Edward Lillywhite Pentecost, stare at the hills, his eyes blank, his smooth, good-natured face thoughtful. He was a slight young man with soft fair hair and pale eyes and a straight nose which showed a distressing tendency to peel in the searing sun. His clothes fitted him neatly but his legs were thin and his knees bony and he wore his shorts longer than regulation to hide them a little. He had stalked on to the ramparts rather like a mild-mannered and disinterested stork.

'Football team,' he said casually. 'At least a football team.'

'No, seriously.'

Pentecost seemed to put a great deal of effort into hazarding a guess. 'Couple of thousand, shouldn't wonder,' he offered. 'Not less than two thousand. Perhaps ten thousand. Perhaps twenty even. Half a million?' he ended cheerfully.

The first speaker stared over the ramparts. 'Kids' stuff,' he said, but his voice was uneasy. 'Long odds, all the same, if it comes to a scrimmage.'

'Perhaps it won't,' Pentecost said.

'Let's hope not,' the youngster with the moustache agreed. 'Just thinking about 'em's enough to give you burning spots on the mind.' His eyes narrowed as he stared again at the hills. 'It really lays our ghoulies on the line, doesn't it? I've heard the bastards are real balls of fire when it comes to aggression.'

'That's what I heard, too,' Pentecost agreed. He spoke with feeling. Like Fox, he was as well aware as anyone that they were outnumbered by the hidden watchers, and that it was a matter of great moment just how aggressive they might be.

Because the fortress of Hahdhdhah was due to be evacuated, and Pentecost knew – as Fox knew, as they all knew – that if those watchers in the hills chose to make it so, their departure could be made not only difficult but well-nigh catastrophic.

2

Despite the howl of protest from the merchants who were on to a good thing with the British presence in the Trucial State of Khalit, despite the wail of woe from the reactionaries in Westminster about the country ditching its friends, the British Government's instructions were clear. The Prime Minister had made them clear in a preliminary order which had been passed via the Khaliti Command at the coast to all outposts in the country. 'After the date of departure no British agent is to be kept in the country; the fortresses of Hahdhdhah, Umrah, Maria, Dhafran, Khowiba and Aba el Zereibat are no longer to contain British Army officers.'

It was clear and unequivocal, and the government of Khalit in Khaswe had been obliged to accept that they could now no longer keep guard over the Toweida Plain, their frontier north of Dhafran. No Khaliti or Toweida Levy could be expected to stand for long with only Toweida officers, and there weren't enough Dharwa Scouts from the grim hills to the south to hold it in their place. Umrah, Aba el Zereibat and Hahdhdhah were to be evacuated and their troops concentrated under Khaliti officers at Afaija, Khowiba and Dhafran. And of the lot, none were so glad to leave as the garrison at Hahdhdhah.

'We are only here because of the treaty made between previous sultans and previous British governments', the Prime Minister had said, and Fox could quote him because every time he thought of his wife in England he found it was printed on his heart in encouraging letters of gold, 'but we are aware of the anachronisms and the strong feelings of nationalism in the Middle East and we are leaving because we have been asked to leave. Pending the finalisation of the new agreement, we have given instructions for withdrawal.'

Fox's fingers strayed to the comforting shape of the revolver he wore in a webbing holster on his belt. Prime Ministers' instructions were sometimes easier to issue than carry out.

His yellow eyes flickered towards Pentecost and he saw him stare at the empty hills again, a small frown wrinkling his brows. There were no sheep up there, and no goats, and no sign of any herdsmen from the village, and the lower slopes were silent with the approaching silence of the night.

Standing on the wooden tower at the west corner of the fort, Fox looked round him, approving of the trivial ceremony of the guard changing in the courtyard just below. Fox liked ceremonial, considering it gave a little swagger to a military life that had become increasingly dull in recent years. Pentecost was aware of his tastes and to please him, Fox knew, he kept a Toweida pony in the stables. It was no bigger than a rat but it gave Fox great joy when Pentecost reviewed his troops mounted.

Looking up, he saw that Pentecost was clearly disquieted by the stillness, as they all were at this time of the evening. Somehow, during the day, when the sun hung in the brassy bronze sky like a molten ball, it didn't matter so much. Then, the very brightness of the sky and the glaring quality of the light gave a certain amount of reassurance. It was in the evening, when the sun disappeared and the hills changed colours – changed shape even, with the moving shadows – that Fox remembered all the stories they'd ever heard of this part of the Middle East – the ruthlessness of the Hejri tribesmen from the Khusar country to the north, their joy

8

at torturing their captives, and their unswerving, unrelenting hatred of anything non-Arab that made their tenure of Fort Hahdhdhah such an uncomfortable one.

Pentecost was thinking of the stories, too, he knew. Fox knew how Pentecost ticked. He had served with him in Aden, Ireland and Dhafran to the south of the Dharwás, and over the years had learned to interpret the flicker of an eyelid and the slightest gesture he made, even before he spoke. Fox was the perfect sergeant, ready with advice if it were wanted, silent when not wanted, but he was also something a little more. He'd been with Pentecost so long, he felt he even knew how his brain worked.

Staring over the wall again, surprised how uneasy he felt, Fox realised that the hills were having an hypnotic effect on the officer. He wrenched his gaze away from them with what seemed to Fox to be a physical effort, and moved to the other side of the tower to stare towards the south across the plain.

The evacuation worried Pentecost. It was common knowledge that Abel el Aziz el Beidawi and his gang of Hejri-Zihouni cut-throats were waiting in the hills among the unseen watchers, and the reputation of Aziz was enough to make the Toweida Levies Pentecost commanded tremble in their uniforms.

Pentecost had worked at the Toweida language, and he knew that the Hejri were a narrow-minded people with a temperament heavily overlaid with defiance. Unlike the Toweidas who came from the plains and were more civilised, they had no arts beyond war. The Khusar country and the Rass Mountains where they came from — known in the south as Bleidas Siba, the country of the lawless — was an area where food was so scarce fat men were rare and even the upper classes looked underfed. The most effective bribe north of the Urbida Hills was a good meal, but despite this, all the Hejri prophets – and there were hundreds of them – had always driven their people north, arguing that they belonged to the wilderness, not to the city. And their unintelligible passionate yearning for freedom had kept them there rather than accept the domination of Khaswe on the coast as the Toweidas had. Most Hejri reims – lean-shanked warriors carrying a rifle and wearing a curved Berber dagger at their waist – would rather have died of proud starvation in the sparse hills than live in comfort in the plain.

They were a race of vast upheavals who continued to convulse both themselves and the area by their politics – even more these days when the border had been for years what passed in the area for quiet. They were a people of instinct, little religion and a great deal of failure. Save in one sphere alone – battle, murder and sudden death, at which they were acknowledged experts. And the best of them all at the game was Abd el Aziz el Beidawi.

3

Aziz el Beidawi had married a dozen times and been wounded twice as often. He was reputed to have slain as many Khaliti and Toweida soldiers with his own hands as he had wounds – to say nothing of more than one white man who had had the misfortune to be in the wrong place at the right time. His joyous love of battle had reduced his tribe to a shadow of its former strength because, in addition to being at loggerheads with the Khaliti and the Toweidas, he was also careful to preserve a state of constant enmity, not only with the Jezowi, the Khadari, the Muleimat and the Shukri, his neighbours along the

Dharwa Mountains to the south, but also with the Hassi and the Dayati, who were his neighbours to east and west in the Urbida Hills and who, when it suited them, formed part of the Hejri nation, one of the two great clans of Khusar.

Aziz was the last of the robber barons. There were no more like him. All the others had succumbed to nationalism, become involved in the production of oil, or gone over to modern methods of war and dressed themselves in olive green or khaki battledress, hung about with hand-grenades. Aziz alone scorned the modern world. Not for Aziz the new standards of the West. He had stuck to the old ones rigidly and, because the tribal systems of the Hejri had never broken down, he had retained an enormous pride in himself and his people.

Unfortunately, this pride did not permit peace, and Pentecost was very much concerned about the dash they were going to have to make across the wide Toweida Plain when the day of evacuation came. None of the lorries was new and they were under-established for radios, both receivers and transmitters, and would have to be prepared for the almost certain appearance of the wild Zihouni horsemen across their path. There was a great deal of the Toweida Plain, and beyond the village of Hahdhdhah, ten minutes' lorry ride away, there was little else until the River Sufeiya.

A flat plateau fifteen hundred feet above sea level, in summer Toweida was a scorching bowl. In winter it was a wind-swept waste, puddled by the rain into a quagmire and frozen by icy winds that came from the north. On the south flank, the land dropped slightly in dusty folds to the Dharwa range, a craggy line of mountains that barricaded the country towards Khaswe and the sea. The road from the coast and the capital of Khalit passed through Dhafran and the narrow Fajir Pass then rose slowly to the River Sufeiya, and wound across the Toweida Plain to the village of Hahdhdhah, the fortress, and the Addowara Pass through the Urbida Hills and the Rass Mountains to Khusar and its capital, Makhrash. At Dhafran it was crossed by the dusty road that led east and west to the frontiers of the sullen sliver of land that made up the Trucial State of Khalit; with Umrah at one end, and Aba el Zereibat at the other, and Afarja and Khowiba between guarding the tracks to the north, all of them out-of-date tollgates built by Victorian soldiers and political agents to hold back the northern tribes – the Hassi, the Dayati and the Zihouni of the Hejri nation, and the Deleimi tribes of Tayur, Hawassi and Dayi, and all the attendant clans and septs that made up the whole murderous Khusar people.

Pentecost had been in Hahdhdhah now for three months, aware always of its uselessness and the strain it put on him. He thought of his wife, occupying a shabby flat down in Khaswe on the coast, separated from him by the need to remain with their two small children, enduring the loneliness and the separation and trying hard though never entirely successfully to keep out of her letters the frustration she felt, the need for him, and the fears of living in a hostile foreign community, waiting only for the day when he was allowed to depart from Hahdhdhah and return to her bed.

And, thank God, he thought fervently, that time wasn't far distant. The evacuation had been hanging over them now for weeks. A provisional date had even been fixed and the removal of stores had already commenced.

But Hahdhdhah was no sinecure. Fox had once suggested that it had been thrown up by a cross-eyed water-carrier with a penchant for treachery, and he was probably right. It was badly planned and badly sited and had been built in the days when it had been felt that a solitary fortress was sufficient to keep a whole countryside in check. It was hideously and hopelessly out of date – a wide but shabby stone-and-wood square surrounding a few thatched-roof mud huts. There were quarters for the men and the native and white officers and NCOs, a store, a gaol and an armoury and four wooden towers to look out over the plain. And apart from a bazaar, stables, stores and a Toweida brothel outside, that was about the lot. Whitewash and sweeping brushes had done wonders with it, but it was still not a place to keep a countryside under surveillance.

It had been built by the present Sultan of Khalit's grandfather – long after the treaty with the British had established the frontier along the Dharwa Hills. In one of his minor wars with the northern peoples, to his surprise he had been more successful than anyone had expected and had thrust his territory outwards, erecting Hahdhdhah Fort as a symbol of his strength and as a warning to the Khusar tribes.

Modern weapons had ended all that, however, and for years Hahdhdhah had been nothing more than a storehouse and training station for the northern units of the Sultan's roving frontier regiments and the Toweida and Juf Levies he used north of the Dharwas – supplying them with the not-very-new machine guns, rifles and mortars which were really all that were of much use among the year-gashed hills and mountains along the border of the Sultanate.

Once, Hahdhdhah had guarded the camel route, but these days camels had given place to lorries, and the flavour of decay which was obvious everywhere on the coast was even clearer in Hahdhdhah, because no one believed in the frontier any more.

The feeling of the approaching end was obvious even in the attitudes of the Toweida Levies who, for the most part, made up the garrison of Hahdhdhah. Stiffened by eighty men of the Dharwa Scouts, reliable Khaliti men from the mountains to the south, the Toweida Levies were neither good soldiers nor enthusiastic supporters of the Sultanate.

'Ethnically, they're as Hejri as the Khusar hill tribesmen,' Pentecost had been told at Dhafran as he had left for the north. 'Only the Sultan's war made them anything else.'

They were shabby, ignorant and dirty; careless with their weapons and even more careless with their hygiene so that when Pentecost had arrived there had been a sick bay full of sullen men.

'They look to me, sir,' Fox had commented, 'as though they're not fit to be commanded by a dustcart driver.'

Pentecost had nodded gravely, unsmiling. From that moment, as he had well known, he had been on his own. Sultan Tafas, down in Khaswe, was far more concerned with other matters and was still desperately hoping that the discovery of oil in his territory might help subdue with a sudden influx of wealth the unruly elements that caused him so many sleepless nights. But, with the aid of two other British officers, Captain George Gould Lack and Captain James Frederick Minto, and three sergeants, Pentecost had managed to bring the hygiene into line, had emptied the sick bay and had even managed to give, by means of drill and a lot of patient good nature, the men under his command a little pride in themselves. Under the high scream of commands from Fox, who was his acting sergeant-major, Sergeant Stone and Sergeant Chestnut, the garrison had actually begun to look like a command fit to be led by a major.

Not that Pentecost was really a major at all. He was actually a junior captain who had been given a temporary step-up in rank on his attachment two years before to the Khaliti army. Under the terms of the treaty, while British troops were not allowed north of the Dharwas into the disputed Toweida Plain, officers and NCOs could be seconded to the border forces, ostensibly for training and instruction, and to help them exert their authority, the appointments carried extra rank. Lack, who was there for no other reason than to superintend the removal of the ageing arms that filled the armoury, and Minto, who had been encouraged to apply for the attachment to Khalit because he had already spent most of his career being sent on courses to get him out of his colonel's hair, were really only lieutenants. Sergeant Fox, Sergeant Chestnut and Sergeant Stone – known as the Holy Trinity or Animal, Vegetable and Mineral – had also been upped in rank to make them the superiors of the native troops they were to command.

Staring at the hills, Pentecost found he wasn't sorry to be leaving. He was a modest, not-too-clever young man who liked to read poetry and modestly didn't consider himself especially brave or even especially good at his job. But, at that moment, despite his anxieties, he was feeling rather pleased with himself. Life had not been worth living in Hahdhdhah when he'd arrived, and his troops had tended to hug the shelter of the walls with the tenacity of men who were fond of life. He had changed all that. Zaid Fauzan, the oldest of the Toweida officers, a grizzled warrior who was a Dharwa, anyway, and claimed to be fifty-three though he was probably sixty-three, was a born soldier, and having at last found someone to follow, he had backed Pentecost up to the hilt.

He and Fox had started football matches between the Toweidas and the Dharwas, and between the native clerks, drivers and store-men and the Hahdhdhah villagers – since they all played in bare feet there was little need for equipment – and Pentecost had even taken the chance of allowing the men into the village. This had particularly pleased Int-Zaid Mohamed, one of the junior Khaliti officers, because his wife came from the area and she'd moved up with her daughter to a house near to the drab huddle of buildings across the plain. In a very short time there had been a marked difference in the bearing of the garrison. Although their uniforms were still falling off their backs and their German leather equipment was never complete, and though Fox, Chestnut and Stone had always seemed to concentrate their efforts only on teaching them how to make tea according to the exacting standards of the British Army, they had become – if not expert – at least sound with their weapons.

Pentecost had deserved his success. And, though he didn't know it at that moment, he was to be presented with an enormous stroke of luck.

4

Hahdhdhah village was a drab place built of mud brick on high earth mounds with a few palm gardens. The narrow streets were shaded with an occasional tamarisk or cypress, and a few melons, marrows, cucumbers, grapes and tobacco were grown, m addition to withered oranges and the inevitable dates. Once Hahdhdhah had been much bigger but, with the constant danger from the north, the families had moved away. Some of the houses had crumbled and some of the palm gardens were neglected, but there were still enough sullen villagers clinging to their scrap of soil to support the fort with eggs, vegetables, goats' milk and fresh meat.

The Toweidas were an indifferent people, however – the very opposite of the leaner northern tribes – and they knew that so long as they expressed no opinions and did no more than charge excessive prices for their produce, no raiding Hejri reim would ever blame them. As a result, the place was a hotbed of spies and Aziz kept men there to watch the movements in the fort.

Since, however, the information about Aziz that reached Pentecost was always sparse, Pentecost himself had fallen into the habit of making a regular visit to the village elders. It was always ceremonial and the headman always offered a seat on his carpets, and coffee or mint tea in the mud-washed huts. But while they talked over the charcoal braziers, Pentecost was able to keep his eyes open, watching for anything that might indicate that Aziz was taking the initiative. And on this particular day, with the evacuation of Hahdhdhah presumably not far in the future, he noticed at once the three lean pale-eyed men standing quietly in the shade of the trees not far from the coffee mortars. Though their cloaks were not black and they kept their tribal beads covered, he knew instinctively that they were Zihouni reims.

It was while he still watched the three men that Fox appeared with the news that there had been an accident.

'One of our chaps?' Pentecost asked.

'No, sir.' In front of the headman, Fox was the picture of punctilio. 'One of theirs. Knocked down. Broke his leg. Bloody fool didn't look where he was driving.'

This had all the makings of trouble and Pentecost drew his breath in sharply.

'Our vehicle?' he asked.

'No, sir.' Fox grinned, knowing exactly how Pentecost's mind was working. 'Village bus.'

Pentecost smiled his relief He knew the vehicle. It moved about as fast as an elderly camel, was appallingly maintained and worn out before its time. Its load invariably exceeded the maximum permitted weight by a great deal, which made it even less manageable on the steep slopes down to Dhafran, and the excess of parcels, boxes, bundles, sacks, bales and trussed goats crammed on top made it into a vast, unstable, up-ended pyramid that wobbled, wavered and wandered as its uncertain wheels and even more uncertain tyres jolted and lurched over the rocky road.

'That's a bit of luck, isn't it?' he said. 'What happened to the driver?'

'He was carried away unconscious.' Fox grinned. 'I think the victim had a lot of friends.'

'And the victim?'

Fox looked sideways at him. 'I slapped a guard over him so they couldn't take him away,' he said. 'He puzzled me, sir. He's only a kid and he told Ali, the interpreter, that he came up from the Sufeiya area to help his uncle grow marrows. Personally, sir, I think he's a bloody liar.'

Pentecost nodded. He had a great regard for Fox's judgement. 'I'd better have a word with him,' he said.

There was nothing about the boy with the broken leg to appeal much to Pentecost. He was inclined to be pernickety about manners and the boy was surly, his thin lips twisted with pain and scorn. He wore a neat braided djellabah and gave his name as Ghani and insisted once more that he was a grower of marrows. One of the Hahdhdhahi market gardeners was prepared to swear that he was his cousin but Pentecost's suspicions, like Fox's, were aroused when the boy was unable to answer, without prompting, questions about his family.

'Think he's spying for Aziz?' he asked Fox quietly.

'That's exactly what I think, sir,' Fox said.

Pentecost nodded. The boy certainly had an arrogant manner that no Toweida possessed, and there was an air about him that seemed to suggest he might be even more than just a Hejri scout.

'Tell 'em we'll take him back to the fort,' he said briskly. 'Tell 'em I'm afraid one of these Hahdhdhahi quacks might set the bone wrongly and we wish to help. Among other things, Mr Minto's taken a pretty solid course in first aid.'

When the interpreter explained to the Toweida who claimed to be the boy's uncle what Pentecost intended to do, he immediately flew into a noisy panic. He would look after the boy, he said wildly. He would see that he was cared for. He was not a poor man and he would fly like the Prophet's horse to fetch a healer he knew who had a knowledge of medicine. Pentecost's smile never slipped.

'Game little beggar, isn't he?' he observed to Fox. 'Hejri agent, shouldn't wonder.'

The Toweida's voice rose shrilly but Pentecost persisted gently. 'I have learned the ways of the tribes,' he said calmly, 'and if the bone is wrongly set, it would not be at all odd for a stupid boy to dig into the flesh with his knife, find it and break it again to reset it. We will take care of him. It is a gesture of friendship between my nation and thine.'

They lifted the boy into the lorry and almost at once the three lean-faced men with the hostile eyes vanished. The crowd closed over the spot where they had stood like water closing over a thrown pebble so that there was no sign that they had ever existed. A few moments later they heard the thud of a horse's hooves.

'One of those hungry-looking bastards has hopped it, sir,' Fox commented.

Like the Toweida, the boy protested loudly but by this time he was so weak with pain he was almost indifferent to what happened to him, and, back at the fort, Minto set the leg quickly. Whatever else there was about Minto, he took the courses he'd been sent on seriously, and he knew what he was doing.

He watched the boy carefully, a shy young man with a stammer that grew worse when he was excited or animated. Like the rest of them, he was with the Khaliti forces because of the extra emoluments that were added to his British Army Pay and because he couldn't face the horrors of peacetime soldiering in Europe. But for all his shyness, he was sharp-eyed and he noticed that Pentecost fussed round in his prim neat manner to make sure the boy was comfortable and properly cared for by the indifferent orderly, in a way he didn't do even for the Toweidas under his command.

'Perhaps Billy's got his eye on him,' Lack observed with a grin. 'It's this randy-making climate. If I don't get a woman soon, I'll be chasing you round the ramparts,

Freddy, old boy. It gets us all. They tell me even old Fauzan's got his favourites.'

Minto smiled uncertainly, never knowing how to reply to Lack's extrovert vulgarity. He even wondered nervously if he could possibly be right about Pentecost because Pentecost was a strange private sort of individual – a very odd pair of boots.

Within a day or two, however, he was reporting his own suspicions in the bare whitewashed cell that served Pentecost for an office.

'I don't know who this kid is you brought in, Billy,' he said, 'but I don't think he's a Toweida at all.'

Pentecost smiled. 'Neither do I,' he admitted.

'He's no pauper, either,' Minto went on earnestly. 'And he's no grower of marrows. He wouldn't know a marrow from a barrage balloon.'

'I don't think he even comes from the Toweida Plain,' Pentecost said. 'I think he's from north of the hills.'

The boy remained in the fortress, not a prisoner but always discreetly watched by a Dharwa Scout to see that he didn't escape. Pentecost was well aware that if he could prove the boy was a spy he was entitled to put him in the dungeon. According to the Sultan's law that he administered, he could even have the boy shot if he felt like it. His word on the Toweida Plain was final, and, though he was nothing more than a mere attachment from the British Army, no one would have quibbled about a thing like that. Hejri spies had been imprisoned and shot before by Khaliti troops anxious to repay a few old debts.

For a long time, nothing happened, and Pentecost found he was waiting for something to happen.

He conducted his affairs quietly, and sent his command about its business, one eye always on the hills, the other on the road across the plain. His orders from the south, in an attempt to avoid trouble, had always been irksome in the extreme. Across the Toweida Plain, they couldn't question any party of less than ten men unless they were armed and off the path. And as the paths were often impossible to discern at a distance and the Hejri clothing made the concealment of weapons always very simple, the danger inherent in this restriction was immense, and Pentecost had lost more than one careless Toweida as a result.

Occasionally he talked to the boy from the village. Occasionally he questioned him. Occasionally the suspicion broke down and the boy's scowl gave way to a wary smile, but still he stuck to his story that he was the nephew of the Toweida marrow-grower and had come north from the Sufeiya River area to help his uncle and to find a bride for himself.

Lack's attitude was full of scorn. He was less experienced in Hejri ways and didn't like Hahdhdhah. 'I'd pull the plug on him,' he said firmly. 'You'll probably find the little bastard'll nip away when you're not looking, and then you'll have put up a black that won't look so hot in your file. Send him down to Dhafran and let them deal with him.'

Pentecost ignored the advice and exactly one week later he was awakened from his sleep at first light by a startled Sergeant Fox.

'Sir, there's a bloody great crowd of blokes outside,' he said.

Pentecost blinked himself to full consciousness. 'What sort of blokes?' he asked gravely. 'Toweidas? Khaliti? A

22

column from Dhafran, perhaps, bearing messages that it's time to shut up shop and go home?'

Fox grinned. 'None of them, sir. They're Hejris.'

'Hejris?' Pentecost sat bolt upright. 'Hejris?' he said again.

When Hejris appeared outside the fortress it was time to be worried. They had plotted, intrigued and murdered for generations to get back the disputed land north of the Sufeiya River and were to be trusted about as far as you could trust a homicidal lunatic armed with a cleaver.

He was reaching for his clothes now. 'What are they doing?' he asked quietly.

'Nothing, sir.'

'Nothing?' Pentecost stared at Fox. For a Hejri to sit outside the hated fortress of Hahdhdhah doing nothing seemed about as normal as a cow circling in orbit.

Fox looked puzzled. 'That's what gets me, sir,' he said. 'They're just sitting there, waiting.'

'What for?'

Fox gave a wry smile. 'We haven't found out yet, sir. We've not really established contact.'

Pentecost lit a cigarette and beamed at Fox in the precise manner of a clever prefect at school talking to a dim small boy. 'Then it's time we did, isn't it?' he said. 'Tell 'em not to go away.'

Fox grinned. 'I'll suggest coffee, sir.'

Ten minutes later, Pentecost had shaved and dressed and was walking to the wooden tower near the great barred gate that was closed every evening at sundown – less to keep anyone from getting in to steal the store of elderly and valueless armaments that were his care and concern than to stop the Toweida Levies getting out to stir up trouble among the Hahdhdhahi women in the village.

Standing on the tower, neat and tidy despite the sudden summons from his bed, he stared across the stretch of open ground between himself and the first rocky outcrop leading to the hills. A line of horsemen was sitting silently beneath a green banner staring at the fortress.

'Armed to the teeth, shouldn't wonder,' he observed to Fox. 'Better rouse the rest of the chaps. My compliments to the officers and ask 'em to meet me here.'

As Fox turned away to send a messenger, Pentecost stared again at the silent line of horsemen just becoming visible in the dim half-light. There was a troublesome breeze stirring the dust into little whirls and he felt grit between his teeth. In the tower near him, one of the Toweida Levies had his rifle through the embrasure, staring at the silent figures, occasionally glancing at the neat figure of Pentecost as he wondered what to do.

Pentecost became aware of Fox reappearing at his side.

'Message delivered, sir,' the sergeant said. He nodded at the silent line about a hundred yards away. 'Nasty-looking lot, sir. What do you reckon they're up to?'

'Perhaps they've called to ask if we'll play 'em at football,' Pentecost said with mild facetiousness. 'Great ones for football, I'm told.'

'The only football they'd play,' Fox said grimly, 'is with our ghoulies.'

Pentecost smiled his small careful smile. Fox was one of the old school of sergeants, wary, cautious and wily in the ways of conniving troops; never one to take any risk, big or small, unless he was told to; but utterly reliable and with the strange sort of honour that existed among the best NCOs of every army in the world, which allowed him to fiddle stores and get drunk but never permitted him to let the side down.

He stared at the silent line of men again. There was a
certain amount of restless movement among them now, as
horses jostled each other. Dark faces stared towards him,
half-hidden by black burnouses. Lean bodies were
swathed in ragged gowns and cloaks of black wool. Dark
thin hands cradled rifles across ornamented saddles.
These were men dedicated in their hatred of all things
Western, and of the Sultan of Khalit in particular because
he was considered a turncoat who allowed Western
officials to tell him what to do. They were utterly ruthless,
and cruel enough to castrate a captive or chop off his
hands or cut out his tongue when they caught him. But
only because they would just as easily and with as little
thought disembowel their own wives if they found they'd
been unfaithful.

'Zihouni,' he observed laconically. 'Black headdress,
black cloak, green girdle. The Black Men of Khusar. The
nastiest of the lot.'

He noticed further movement among the group, then
he realised there was a bunch of horsemen behind the line,
arguing fiercely among themselves, and, even as he
watched, the line parted and one of the arguing figures
appeared before them, sitting silent and alone, huddled in
his black garments, still staring towards the fort, as
though prepared to attack it but wondering just how to
set about it.

Pentecost nodded towards the Toweida alongside.

'Just see that chap's under no delusions,' he said. 'I'm
not having him potting at the gent on the horse.'

'He could do it easy,' Fox grinned.

'That chap out there's as aware of that as we are,'
Pentecost said primly. 'But he doesn't think we will. That's
why he's sitting there.'

Lack had arrived by this time and was staring through the embrasure with Pentecost.

'Ugly bloody lot,' he observed bluntly. 'Straight out of a Khaswe knocking shop by the look of 'em.'

Minto appeared shortly afterwards and they stared at the line of men and the silent figure sitting a white horse in front. Pentecost threw away his cigarette. An idea was forming in his mind.

'Think I'll go out and see what they want,' he said unexpectedly.

Lack stared at him as though he'd gone off his head. 'Out there?' he asked. 'With that shower of night-shirted Khusar pimps? Sometimes, Billy, I think you're not quite right in the head!'

Pentecost shrugged.

'They could knock you off easy as w-w-wink,' Minto said.

Pentecost shrugged again. 'It'd be a rotten bad idea, Freddy, if they did,' he pointed out. He turned to Fox. 'Get 'em to shove up the Bren, Sergeant, and see that everyone's loaded for bear. If anyone does knock me off, see that the compliment's returned three-fold.'

Fox nodded. 'OK, sir.'

'No nonsense, though,' Pentecost said. 'If he's come in peace, let's have peace.' He gave a little sigh, thinking of his vast responsibilities. 'Because,' he added fervently, 'we need peace.'

They watched as the great wooden gates were hauled open a foot or two to allow him to pass through, and he strolled towards the solitary figure on the horse, carrying only a short cane and with no sign of a weapon about his person.

'That bloody man never fails to surprise me,' Sergeant Fox observed to Sergeant Chestnut as they watched the slight figure in the flapping shorts stalking in its neat stride from the fort. 'Would you go out there, with that lot waiting for you?'

Sergeant Chestnut said nothing but it was obvious from the expression on his bleak Scots face that he wouldn't.

As they watched, the man on the white horse set spurs to his mount, so fiercely it seemed to jump into the air. It came down on all four feet in a puff of dust and seemed to leap towards the solitary figure of Pentecost, who stopped and waited, his thumbs tucked into his belt.

The horse halted a yard or two from his peeling nose just when he was expecting to be trampled into the ground, slithering on its heels as its rider wrenched savagely at the reins. Pentecost forced himself not to back away as the horse came up on its hind legs, pawing the air, and dropped with a thud and a jingle of caparisoned equipment.

'Impressive,' he said aloud, more than anything else to keep his nerve steady.

The rider, a striking figure in dusty robes sitting a bright red metal-studded saddle, was wrestling with his spirited mount now, gazing down at Pentecost. A pair of fierce black eyes stared over a scimitar of a nose, then, with a gesture, the rider swung from the saddle and laid his rifle – a modern Mannlicher, Pentecost noticed, that could drill the eye from a chicken at five hundred yards – carefully on the ground behind him.

'There is no need for that, Reimabassi,' Pentecost said in the sharp Toweida tongue he had learned, choosing the

27

word for 'warrior-lord' because it would do no harm to be flattering. 'Dust is harmful. Keep it in your hand.'

The other man stared at him for a moment with arrogant merciless eyes, a little startled by his mild tones, then a fleeting grin flashed across the dark face and he hoisted the rifle under his arm again, butt-foremost as a token of friendship. 'It is better,' he agreed in English. 'They are hard to obtain.'

Pentecost felt a little easier. All the way from the gates his heart had been thumping chokingly in his chest but he had been so certain that this man opposite wished to communicate with him he had been prepared to accept the risk he had taken.

'You speak good English,' he observed.

The other smiled. It looked like a hawk's smile, disdainful and enigmatic. 'It is better than thy Toweida,' he said, and Pentecost nodded agreement.

'Thou art the leader, Bin T'Khass?' the other man said and it was a moment or two before Pentecost recognised the Hejri corruption of his name.

He nodded again, studying the dismounted reim, whom he saw now was a man of fifty-odd years, twice his own age and as lean and hard as coiled springs.

He gave a little bow, acknowledging the name, and the other swept his hands away from himself in a gesture that was half bow and half gesture of welcome. 'I am Abd el Aziz el Beidawi,' he said.

two

1

There had been other occasions in the past when messengers had appeared outside the fort to make some impossible request, and Pentecost had all along half-expected the wild figure on the white horse to be one of the Hejri chieftains, perhaps one of the Hassi or the Dayati leaders come to make some demand of him. But he had hardly expected it to be Aziz himself. Yet, with the idea that was slowly turning over in his mind and had been ever since the boy with the broken leg had been brought in, he found he wasn't entirely surprised. He jerked his shoulders back, and held himself a little straighter. Aziz topped him by a whole head, lean and taut as piano-wire, staring into Pentecost's smooth face as if he were a little puzzled.

'Meha babicoum, Lord Aziz,' Pentecost said loudly. 'Welcome to our door.'

Aziz bowed again. He was a tall strong figure with a haggard, tragic face and a rich booming voice, an unbending feudal warrior – ruthless and strong. He was simply dressed after the fashion of the Hejri, scorning modern battle-dress for the old robes of a Hejri noble, with a black woollen cloak and a copper-dyed Mosul

29

girdle containing a curved Moroccan dagger of gold and enamel. He was straight, spare and still clearly active.

Pentecost knew his eldest son had been hanged by the Sultan of Khalit and the sorrow seemed to show in wide dark eyes that were eloquent of suffering. His nose was thin and strongly hooked, but the mouth between the beard and the moustaches neatly trimmed in Zihouni style was wide and humorous. Beneath the black head-cloth, Pentecost could see he scorned modern styles and still wore his hair braided.

He was a magnificent-looking man who seemed not to mind Pentecost's careful study of him. It was as though he had spent his whole life having people stare at him, and enjoyed the experience. The Zihouni were the master fighters of the Beidawi tribe – indeed, of the whole Hejri nation – and Aziz was a perfect example of their type. From what he had heard of him, Pentecost knew his hospitality was so overwhelming he had never amassed the fortunes of the other chiefs, but, despite this, he was obsessed also with a sense of his own superiority which was really all that kept him at the head of his people.

Pentecost became aware at last of the older man studying him with a puzzled frown.

'You are not what I expected, Bin T'Khass,' Aziz said. 'You are very young.'

'Early nights,' Pentecost said. Then he smiled and lapsed into the flowery language Aziz favoured. 'The men of my race do not dissipate their strength with women.'

'You do not look like a warrior. Western warriors never do look like warriors. Sometimes they are fat. Sometimes' – Aziz looked at Pentecost's slender figure – 'sometimes they are thin. The Americans wear spectacles in battle and have a fondness for ice cream.' He still seemed puzzled, like a wolf wondering which end of the chicken he was about to devour to start on first.

'You know me?' he asked proudly.

'By reputation,' Pentecost said. 'You send the Toweida Levies quaking to bed at night. At least,' he added, 'you did before I arrived.'

'And now?'

'They are afraid no longer. I have made them unafraid.'

'I have heard so.' Aziz stared at him. 'It would be a bloody day for both of us if I decided to take the fortress of Hahdhdhah from your hands.'

'I don't advise it, Aziz el Beidawi,' Pentecost said with a certain amount of self-conscious pride. He didn't really yet believe in his Toweida Levies but it wasn't a good idea to let Aziz know that.

'There are three hundred of you,' Aziz snapped. 'No more. There are many times that number of Hejri reims.'

'We have a few tricks up our sleeves.'

Aziz stared at Pentecost's grave face, his eyes glittering. 'Hahdhdhah is in Hejri country,' he said.

'Not according to my map.'

Aziz gestured. 'Yours is a map drawn many years ago by men in Khaswe who knew nothing of this territory. Toweida is the name of a plain, not a people. Until the Khaliti administrators changed it, this was Hejri land.'

Pentecost smiled. 'Nevertheless,' he pointed out, 'it would be foolish to fight over it. Many young men would die. Not only Hejri reims but Toweida men, too, whether they feel they are Hejri or not. Perhaps you. Perhaps me.'

'Hejri reims are not afraid to die.'

'Neither are Toweida men. Not now. Neither am I.' Pentecost hoped that the lie wouldn't show in his face because he knew his Toweida Levies were very much

31

afraid and he certainly was himself. His wife and two children were waiting down in Khaswe, and the old days of dying for ideals had finished.

For a while there was silence and, wondering what the purpose of the meeting was, Pentecost fished out his cigarette case. From the silent line of men fifty yards away, the butt-foremost rifle and Aziz's affability – the affability of a shark, he thought – it was clear that Aziz had come in peace.

He offered the cigarettes and Aziz accepted one without a word, holding it in lordly fashion for Pentecost to light it. Then, while Pentecost still waited, he looked up.

'My smallest son, Ghani,' he said. 'The little frog of the family with the anger of a singed tomcat.'

Pentecost smiled again, knowing that the suspicion that had been growing in his mind had been well founded. 'The boy in the fort,' he said.

'You have him prisoner,' Aziz said.

'Not prisoner,' Pentecost corrected him. 'He's a child. He did us no harm. He has a broken leg. A lorry. Not one of ours.'

'That I have heard.'

'He is comfortable,' Pentecost went on. 'He is well fed. He is no longer in pain.'

Aziz paused. 'I have come to bargain,' he said quietly and with a strange humility. 'He is the last of my line, the last gift of the One, the Merciful.'

Pentecost stuck his peeled nose in the air and gave him the look he gave the Toweida zaids when they suggested treating with the Hejri.

'I don't bargain with the lives of young boys,' he said stiffly.

Aziz's eyes swung to his face. 'Thou art hardly more than a boy thyself, Bin T'Khass,' he jerked out in surprise.

Pentecost ignored the insult. 'Your son is free to go, Lord Aziz,' he said.

'You do not wish to make demands of me?'

'Not over the broken leg of a boy.'

'Other men would make demands.'

Again Pentecost ignored the comment. 'You have means of transporting him?' he asked.

'We shall carry him.'

Pentecost stared at the hills. 'All the way? By hand?'

'All the way.'

Pentecost shrugged, thinking of the journey and the effort it would require.

'He shall be brought to you here,' he said.

'So be it.'

Pentecost looked into the fierce dark eyes then he bent and drew a mark in the dust with his cane.

'No Hejri reim shall come closer to Hahdhdhah than that line,' he pointed out. 'You are enemies in my territory. There are Toweida zaids in that fort, eighty Dharwa Scouts who have no love for Hejri reims, and two hundred and fifty Toweida Levies who are expected to fire on you.'

'Allah take pity on them.' Aziz grinned. 'I could eat them.'

Pentecost gave a small twisted disbelieving smile, and indicated the line again. 'You have your reims under control?' he asked.

The answer came in a bark. 'No Hejri defies Aziz.'

'It is well, because my men are not afraid to fire and I am not afraid to order them to do so. Keep your reims well back. Only the litter-bearers may approach that line.'

'It is so.'

As Aziz turned away, Pentecost stared alter him and smiled to himself, a little self-satisfied but aware deep down of the sheer luck of the thing. He had always been aware that the departure from Hahdhdhah could well, if the Hejri warriors were in a sour frame of mind, become a bloody shambles. He had voiced his fears to Lack and Minto as he thought of the damage that could be done by a few Hejri sharpshooters determined to make a nuisance of themselves. Always at the back of his brain had been the question, Would they make it? Or would Aziz el Beidawi decide that the operation was a matter of prestige and make a point of showing what a Hejri war-party could do when it got into top gear?

2

The boy vanished and the waiting went on. The sun swung in its slow implacable circle. Despite rumours that the Sultan, Tafas el Taif, in Khaswe, had reneged on his agreement and was now refusing to let the British off the hook, they were not confirmed by any altered orders, and the Khaswe Command's instructions remained. As the days went past, Pentecost's thoughts turned more often and with a new feeling of certainty to his wife.

The last time he'd seen her had been in Khaswe. They had swum from one of the beaches, so happy together they had staggered over the sand, their arms about each other, drunkenly and joyously content in each other's company.

What was the old army joke? he thought. What will you do when you get home? Go to bed with the wife. And after that? Take off my pack. Pentecost's narrow loins ached sometimes at the thought of the eager girl waiting for him in Khaswe.

Then, fifteen days after Aziz's appearance and the departure of the boy, Sergeant Chestnut came running out of the wireless shack, flourishing a buff signal sheet and screeching in his thick Scots accent. 'Sorr, Sorr' – his excitement set heads turning round the whole fortress – 'it's come! It's the instructions for leaving!'

They so made a point of celebrating the signal with their meagre stock of liquor that Lack woke next morning with a violent headache, but they were still euphoric about the thought of release and for several days moved about the place with gleaming eyes. Then the nightly news review from England that Chestnut managed to pick up for them started uneasy thoughts in their heads again. It seemed Sultan Tafas really was having second thoughts. Certainly nothing had been signed yet, and the British Government, caught on the horns of a dilemma, was beginning to issue ominous statements about the withdrawal that could be construed to mean anything or nothing, so they could be proved right later whichever way Tafas decided to jump.

'The rotten bastards,' Minto said as the evening broadcast finished. 'They're trying to s-s-stop us leaving.'

'Those statements don't apply to us,' Lack decided in his self-important know-all way. 'We've already said we're leaving. They must mean withdrawals from other places.'

Minto considered the words they'd heard then he frowned and burst out again. 'There aren't any other b-bloody places,' he said. 'We've already left them all.'

As though to reassure them, however, a date was fixed on the normal link-up with Khaswe that very night –

twelve weeks later on the twenty-first of the month – and, as if to consolidate the fact, they received a signal which seemed to indicate that their very last duty would be to provide an escort for an American oil expert who was arriving to give the Toweida Plain a final once-over before it was too late.

'Let's hope he brings some booze,' Lack said.

3

They were not disappointed. Luke Beebe turned out to be a dark, hairy, good-humoured man who believed in making sure of his own comfort. He didn't particularly want to be in Hahdhdhah because in his bones he felt that the situation in Khalit was dangerous, but he was paid to be there and since he had no choice, he felt he might as well make himself at home.

'Beebe,' he introduced himself as he climbed from the lorry in the courtyard of the fort. 'Lucas Eugene Beebe. Luke for short.'

Pentecost offered his hand. 'Pentecost,' he said. 'Silly name. Most of the chaps call me Billy.'

'OK – Billy.' Beebe felt vaguely flattered. He was a man of working-class birth and he knew about Pentecost. He'd heard in Dhafran that he was upper crust and he knew that upper-crust Britishers still had strange ideas about discouraging familiarity till you'd known them for years. He'd even heard a funny story of a British nobleman who didn't learn the first name of his mistress till he sued her for the return of the jewels she claimed he'd given her.

He stared round him, slapping the dust from his clothes, and lit a cigarette. The sun was glaringly bright and seemed to slam back at him in violent blows that were almost physical as it was reflected from the whitewashed walls. In one corner of the courtyard he could see a British sergeant with mad eyes screaming at a bunch of Toweida Levies in some unintelligible tongue and in another a grizzled Khaliti zaid ticking off items on a list on a clipboard he held in his hand. The heat was so intense it seemed to dry the sweat on his face.

'Some joint,' he observed.

'You can say that again,' Lack commented. 'And if our cup of happiness weren't already soured by it, we're running out of booze.'

Beebe grinned. 'Good job I brought plenty with me,' he said.

He sent his driver to bring his valise and produced a bottle of whisky, and Lack led him triumphantly across to the mess.

'First scotch we've seen for some time" he pointed out.

Beebe raised his glass. 'All we need now are a few dames. What do we do about women?'

'We indent for 'em,' Lack grinned. 'If we're turned down by Stores, we live off the country.'

Pentecost was speaking now. 'You're looking for oil, Mr Beebe,' he said, more as a statement than a question, and Lack grinned. Everyone in Khalit knew of Sultan Tafas' hopes. His income came from the export of dates, olives, canned fruit, mint, saffron and a few assorted minerals, and it was common knowledge that he still hoped to implement it with the discovery of oil. He had had French and American geologists in every corner of his Sultanate for months in a frantic attempt to salve his tottering fortunes before it was too late.

'That's it,' Beebe was saying. 'Oil. And as soon as I've looked, I'm off.'

Where to, he wasn't sure. He liked travel and a hint of danger, so long as it never went beyond a hint, but he'd always managed to avoid trouble before, though he'd almost been caught once or twice, as he'd lingered too long in Algeria, Aden and Jordan. By this time, however, he'd begun to suspect his delays had been deliberate because it was in his character to be a contrary last-minute man.

'I'd advise you to make a start on your programme straight away, Mr Beebe,' Pentecost advised. 'We leave in twelve weeks' time. On the twenty-first of the month, to be exact.'

Beebe shrugged. 'It's a job that can't be rushed.'

'Still,' Lack said, 'toot sweet would be a good idea. The tooter the sweeter, in fact. When they finally get Tafas to fix his cross on the old document, those Khaliti staff johnnies in Khaswe'll probably send us a signal saying "Tomorrow at dawn, boys." '

It took Beebe a moment or two to decipher this speech. When he did he looked at Pentecost.

'What'd happen if he didn't sign in the end?' he asked.

'Trouble,' Pentecost said blandly.

'What sort of trouble?'

'Border war, shouldn't wonder.' Pentecost sounded too nonchalant about it to be true.

'A shooting war?'

'You've got it,' Lack said cheerfully, not believing for a minute a word he said. 'A shooting war.'

Beebe ignored him and studied Pentecost. He intrigued Beebe with his apparent youth. He hardly looked old enough to know how to use a gun.

'What'll you do?' he asked.

'Stop 'em,' Pentecost said.

'Here?'

'Here.'

'Like John Wayne at the Alamo.'

Pentecost nodded gravely. 'Exactly like John Wayne at the Alamo.'

Beebe grinned. 'You couldn't do it,' he said. 'There are only three hundred of you – give or take a few. Aziz has thousands, they tell me.'

Pentecost didn't bat an eyelid. 'We've got thick walls between us,' he pointed out. 'If we played it close to the chest, we might be a hard nut to crack. What about you? If it did come to the crunch, I mean. What would you do about it?'

'I'm an American citizen,' Beebe said at once, as though it were the solution to any and every problem.

Pentecost seemed unimpressed. 'Aziz's reims, alas, might not worry about the distinction,' he said.

Beebe's reply summed up his attitude, the attitude of the whole American nation.

'Aziz isn't going to throw me out,' he said firmly. 'No goddam gook tells me when to leave.'

4

Beebe settled down quickly among them, though his transatlantic sense of humour grated a little at times. He didn't seem to think much of their chances and considered it amusing to remind them of the fact.

Watched by a scout car and a lorry-load of Dharwas, he and his foreman, an Iraqi geologist from Abadan, set to work on the stony plain, digging holes with picks and filling them with small cylinders of explosive which they detonated by wires connected to instruments in their truck a hundred yards away, throwing up showers of dust and filling the plain with a series of thuds that made the air expand and contract.

'You look like a couple of hens searching for food,' Minto said from the scout car.

'We explode the canisters,' Beebe informed him, 'and read the result on the gravimeter. It gives the difference in gravitational force resulting from variations in the densities of the rock layers beneath the surface. The sound wave reflects on the formations below and tells you if there's oil down there.'

'And is there oil down there?'

Beebe gave a slow grin. 'Not a goddam drop,' he said.

Lack began to tick off the days, watching the political situation like a hawk and listening eagerly all the time to the commentators broadcasting from London.

Because British bases abroad had become an anachronism – something that no longer belonged in a world where nuclear bombs existed – the government in London was becoming embarrassed by Tafas' havering. No one wanted another Suez or another Aden situation and they were eager to be quit of the place, but the treaty rights said quite clearly that if Tafas requested a British presence in Khalit then they had to stay. It was something they had been trying to avoid bringing to light for years.

'There's one thing,' Minto said as Chestnut switched off. 'This is the last place we've got. If we withdraw any further we'll be s-soldiering on Clapham Common.'

'I'm all for soldiering on Clapham Common,' Lack said firmly. 'At least there'd be women there. Not like this place. All a woman needs to be a success in Khalit is a cocktail dress and a pair of tits. We'll be going all right.'

Despite his bounce, however, he was still a little nervous. But all the signals that came in seemed to confirm their departure. Dhafran knew the frontier could not be held and though Tafas still hadn't signed anything there were instructions about their route, instructions about what to take and instructions about what to leave behind. Even instructions about the exact time of departure.

'Twelve hundred hours,' Pentecost pointed out 'Right in the heat of the day.'

'We can always start a bit early,' Lack suggested. 'Tom Jeffreys at Aba el Zereibat won't wait till midday, I bet. He's overdue for leave and I've heard his wife's romping around with a blue bod from the Air Force.'

Then, two nights later, four weeks after the departure of the boy with the broken leg, the line of Hejri horsemen appeared once more in the first light of the morning. They had waited between the ragged piles of rocks in front of the fortress, invisible in the darkness until the first glow of the sun touching the mountain tops to the north had picked out their black robes and showed them as a shadowy broken necklace across the violet background of the foothills.

'They're here again, sir,' Sergeant Fox said as he roused Pentecost from sleep.

Beebe, who had heard of the strange meeting between Pentecost and Aziz and hadn't really believed it, turned up out of curiosity to see what it was all about. Pentecost was already by the gate with Lack and Minto.

'How many of 'em out there?' he was asking.

'Not many,' Lack said. 'It's not the ones you can see who matter, though. It's the bastards you can't see.'

Pentecost seemed undisturbed. As he lowered his binoculars to glance at the hills, Beebe studied him. Pentecost fascinated him. He was the arch-type of British officer he'd thought had died out with the First World War – with his book of verse, his fragile manner, his precious way of speaking and his use of outdated slang.

He seemed a little nervous and Beebe gazed into the growing light to where he could just see a green banner and the faint broken line of waiting figures. Their very stillness had an alarming effect and he decided once again that he was glad he was American.

Aziz met Pentecost as before, on foot and with his rifle-butt foremost, but this time he was wearing a long curved scimitar at his waist. The blade alone was all of a metre in length and curved like a sickle, and, Pentecost guessed, sharp and heavy enough in the hands of a strong man to cleave an enemy from crown to navel in one stroke. He decided it was some sign of authority and that Aziz wore it because he had come to talk terms.

'Your son is well, Lord Aziz?' he asked.

Aziz nodded gravely. 'My son is well again, Bin T'Khass,' he said. 'His leg is mending and with help he walks.'

'Tell him it is wiser to remain on his own side of the hills in future,' Pentecost said gravely. 'He is too young to spy for Aziz el Beidawi.'

Aziz's frown deepened. 'He did not spy for Aziz,' he said. 'He spied for Thawab abu Tegeiga, his cousin, who is a hothead and would have swallowed your fort weeks ago if Aziz had allowed him.'

Pentecost had heard of Thawab abu Tegeiga. The little information he received told him that Aziz's rule over the

Khusar nations was not undisputed. Thawab, leader of the Deleimi nation, claimed that Aziz was growing old and that his methods were out of date, and he was reputed to have men behind him who understood radio and the use of explosives.

'He would be unwise to try,' he pointed out.

Aziz was watching him carefully. 'We could wipe your fort from the face of the earth,' he said. He spat into the dust then drew his foot across the spittle so that it was erased. 'So!'

'The words of Aziz break stones,' Pentecost said calmly. 'But Aziz boasts, nevertheless. I know he boasts. And Aziz knows he boasts because he has German glasses that tell him that the fort at Hahdhdhah now is not the fort at Hahdhdhah of a few weeks ago.'

Aziz stared at him, then he grinned. 'Aziz boasts,' he admitted.

'And since the English are due to leave before long, it would be foolish for Aziz to risk the lives of his young men.'

Aziz paused. 'You have heard this?' he asked quickly.

'I have heard it. In messages from Khaswe.'

'I have heard this too,' Aziz said. 'We have radios at Addowara. And Egyptian instructors who inform us of world politics.'

'And when the English leave,' Pentecost went on, 'the Toweida Levies must leave also. They will not stay without us. We shall take them with us to Dhafran, south to the Dharwa Mountains.'

'It is good. We will wait.'

Aziz hesitated a moment then he unbuckled the great scimitar from his waist, weighed it in his hands for a moment, and held it out, resting across his palms, towards Pentecost.

'Aziz trusts thee, Bin T'Khass,' he said. 'Here is a token of his trust, and of gratitude that thou didst not choose to imprison a boy with a broken leg who is too young to understand death.'

'Is this for me, Aziz?'

'I have carried this sword since I was a young man. I carried it in the clean and honourable days before we used grenades and mortars. I part with it willingly, to show my great love for Bin T'Khass.'

Love, Pentecost thought wildly. With a face like that!

He wondered hurriedly what he could offer in return. Then he remembered the monogrammed cigarette case that had been given to him as a wedding gift by his wife and he fished it from his pocket and held it out, laying it across both palms in the way that Aziz held the sword.

'I am no great leader like Aziz el Beidawi,' he said, searching out all the flowery phrases he could find. 'I have no warrior tribes like the Zihouni falling before me and hiding their eyes when I approach. I am a paid soldier and a poor man. This is all I have to offer. I have carried it many years.' He paused then plunged into what he considered a good, honest-to-God lie and left it standing on its own sturdy legs for Aziz's inspection. 'Before me it belonged to my father, whose name I bear. Another paid soldier but an honest man.'

'Did he, too, not look like a great warrior?'

Pentecost thought of the stumpy stiff-legged old man, recently dead, whose independent spirit had prevented him rising to any dizzy heights in the army he had loved. He had closed his eyes for the last time still puzzled by the effeminate slightness of his only son and the apparent indifference to duty in the younger generation, and had gone to his grave still failing to appreciate that patriotism had a different meaning these days and that duty was not set within narrow national boundaries. Yes, Pentecost thought, the old man had looked like a warrior, and he'd have enjoyed being lumped with Montgomery, Alexander and Wavell.

'He looked like a great warrior,' he said. 'He was a great warrior.'

Aziz was pushing forward the scimitar now and they exchanged the gifts shyly. Then Aziz stepped back, his face grave.

'Go in peace, Bin T'Khass,' he said.

'Peace to thee also, Lord Aziz.'

Together they turned their backs on each other and marched towards their own men, Aziz straight and lean and wearing dignity like a cloak, Pentecost unhappily aware of his short stature and trying to make light of it because he was still carrying the heavy jewelled scimitar in both hands before him and he felt rather stupid, and top-heavy enough to be unsure of his steps.

Minto and Lack were waiting just inside the gates, with Beebe. 'What the hell's that?' Lack said, staring at the weapon in Pentecost's hands.

'It's a scimitar.'

'Did the old josser give it you?'

Pentecost nodded and he saw Fox's look of approval.

Beebe's jaw had dropped. 'Say, that's quite a souvenir,' he said. 'I wouldn't mind that hanging over my mantelpiece when I get home. Wouldn't want to sell it, would you?'

Pentecost's look almost shrivelled him. He was warmed by a stupid sense of pride. People didn't collect battle trophies these days but somehow he felt that this vast scimitar would bear pride of place in his household for ever.

5

That was only the beginning. Following the scimitar there were more exchanges of gifts, Aziz's horsemen always appearing in their ragged line as the sun began to lift beyond the hills to throw its light across the Toweida Plain.

A strange kind of rapport had grown up between the haggard old warrior and the smooth-faced young man not long out of school, a friendship that permitted them to make wry jokes about each other and about the fighting qualities of their men. From time to time Aziz asked the date of departure, and Pentecost was able to reassure him that all the necessary signals had arrived and that plans had gone ahead much faster than anyone had expected for the run-down of Khalit as a British base. All it now required was the Sultan's signature and the necessary final word from the Khaliti Government.

'They are the elected representatives of the nation,' he explained carefully. 'As in Britain, they speak for the people.'

'They do not speak for the northern people,' Aziz snapped.

Pentecost shrugged and Aziz went on with a grin. 'Hejri men do not need elections,' he said. 'A leader not strong enough to hold his place at the head of his tribe would be replaced by one who was.'

'Is that how you became their leader, Aziz?'

'That is exactly how.'

'How many men did you murder?'

Aziz grinned again, enjoying the leg-pulling. 'Not many,' he said. 'Not more than two or three dozen of my relations. They were old and useless, though. Is this how Bin T'Khass became a leader?'

'A few elderly majors,' Pentecost explained with a straight face. 'Not more than a dozen. I am not the great warrior that Aziz is.'

It was a strange friendship, between two most unlikely human beings. Pentecost put down its success to the fact that he had managed to ignore the thudding of his heart and hide the flinch of fear when Aziz's horse had first thundered towards him. But, oddly enough, he also actually managed to like the black-bearded old rogue who could have cut him down easily if he'd wished and, before the poor marksmanship of his Toweida Levies, probably have got away with it, too.

Aziz was an entertaining old rogue, but even in his craziest exploits – and he didn't hesitate to boast of them to Pentecost – there was always a factor of hard-headedness. Despite his reputation, though, he accepted criticism with a smile that was surprisingly captivating. Only when they talked of Thawab abu Tegeiga did he become angry and then he shook with passion as he described how the younger man was trying to do away with the pattern of tribal life.

'He seeks to destroy our standards,' he said. 'Yet he has nothing of value with which to replace them.'

Pentecost sympathised. It was a cry he'd heard more than once from his own father, and he was just beginning to reach the age himself when he could see what it meant. The knowledge served to draw him closer.

'When I am old,' Aziz said, 'they will want to do away with me. Even Aziz cannot live for ever. It is written in the

Book. When we have back the Toweida Plain, I shall step down and retire to my lands.'

It was clear life was a heroic thing to him, and any event with which he was not connected was, in his narrow Hejri way of thinking, insignificant. He told tales of long-forgotten raids and forays into Khaliti territory, of his quarrels with the Hawassi and the Dayati and the Jezowi. Sometimes he even sang – in an embarrassingly loud baritone that could be heard in the fort – traditional songs of Hejri and Zihouni warriors. Sometimes he beat his breast as he confessed that he had no control over his tongue and made constant enemies with its use. Yet he was also so sure of himself he didn't hesitate to tell stories against himself, even mischievously to invent legends that could not possibly have been true, and recount appalling libels about the sexual appetites of Thawab or Sultan Tafas el Taif. It was easy for Pentecost to see where his reputation came from. Despite his lies, despite his boasting, despite his cunning, his villainy and his casually held attitude to life, he was honest, humble, direct, and even surprisingly kind.

As it was difficult for Pentecost to see the reason for it all, so it was for Aziz. He believed in Allah, the One and the Merciful. He believed in Mohammed the Prophet, the Book and the Reading which was the core of all knowledge. He prostrated himself to Mecca, praying in a raw primitive faith, and believed in the Chosen of God who had once rolled across North Africa and into Europe almost to Madrid, and his natural enemies were the Khaliti to the south and the Roumis, the white men who were their masters.

Never in his life had the Hejri – old by the standards of his tribe – ever shown any interest in the pale-haired, pale-eyed, pale-skinned peoples, save for the Circassian boys who had interested him in his youth. All his adult life he had believed that the white-skinned races were to be distrusted, yet here he was, smoking the cigarettes of this peeled-nosed beardless young man with the soft yellow hair, and the bony knees of an elderly camel. Here they were, exchanging gifts and confidences, laughing with each other, trusting each other. In all the years of skirmishing round Hahdhdhah, Aziz could never remember holding a parley with anyone from inside, not even when they had wished to collect the dead or wounded from one of their affrays. For a century, Hejri tribesmen had waited in the hills staring at the fort. Hahdhdhah had always been a thorn in their side and it had always been unthinkable that they should treat with its defenders.

Yet, due to the accident of his son being eager to prove himself in his father's eyes, here he was, Abd el Aziz el Beidawi, cracking jokes with this downy-haired prim young man from a country two thousand miles away whose precise mannerisms and slightness of stature would have fitted one of the Hawassi dancing boys.

Two months before, if he'd caught Pentecost in the open he would have shot him without compunction. Yet, because of this minor accident, they had talked with each other normally and without distrust, and to the wonderment of Aziz they had found they liked each other.

three

1

Though Pentecost wasn't aware of it, down in the shabby tortuous city of Khaswe, the commanding British officer, Major-General Alan Cozzens – known to his troops as 'Teeth and Trousers' – had also heard of the strange friendship that had grown up along the northern frontier.

The decaying atmosphere of Khaswe, with the Nationalists waiting to rush in when the British left and the Sultan living under the sword of Damocles, was enough to give Cozzens nightmares at times. The latest information in his possession was that, despite all the reassuring noises from Whitehall, Tafas was going to repudiate the agreement he'd made and demand that they stay. Tafas was noted for his slipperiness and the impermanence of his decisions. He was forgetful, changeable, stubborn, brave, and so secretive it was said his Ministers had to spy on him to find out what he intended. And with the Arab Nationalists flaying him for the presence of the British and ready to throw bombs like confetti if he went back on his word, good news was more than welcome. Especially about Aziz.

Aziz el Beidawi's Zihounis were the notorious Black Men that Lawrence had so distrusted fifty-odd years before and, in their time, they had indulged in sensuality and the grossest kind of murder, treachery and sudden death. Yet, despite their cold-blooded cruelty, Cozzens had also heard that they were strangely poetic in their language, liked music and were given to wearing flowers in their hair, and enjoyed stories of fairies and djinns. But they were also vain, vengeful and venal, and their history was a monotonous record of perfidy, naked treachery and wholesale betrayals, and men of importance in Khusar were still said to sleep during the day and stay awake at night holding a loaded gun. Their whole life was one of warfare and gloom. Every tribe had its enemies, every family its blood-feud, every man his assassin. Hejri and Khaliti didn't mix and never could. They had loathed each other through all their history and there was a story of how, when one of each had been murdered in the Fajir Pass, even their blood had refused to mingle as they had lain together on the stony ground.

In all this hatred, Cozzens found the news from Hahdhdhah deeply satisfying because he was also aware of the restrictions placed on the frontier garrisons in an attempt to keep the atmosphere up there sweet. People like Pentecost were conducting their affairs with one hand tied behind their backs and the Hejris were far from being out of practice. They had never lost interest in murder, rape and looting, and with Abd el Aziz el Beidawi sitting in the hills Cozzens realised he would be quite wrong to imagine they'd lost their old hostility. The last man who'd had to face Aziz had come back broken in spirit and health, but there was a calm self-confidence in Pentecost's reports – almost a smugness, dammit! – that made Cozzens decide that the boy had a kind of genius. He had somehow made contact with the grim old warrior when a dozen political agents before him had failed, and they were now not only on speaking terms, they were actually even exchanging gifts.

As he thought about Pentecost, Cozzens thought also about his wife. Charlotte Pentecost was the daughter of an old comrade from the last war and he guessed she wasn't enjoying herself alone, with her husband two hundred and fifty miles away to the north, sitting on a bomb. She was a pretty young woman with a lively mind and a tremendous zest for living, as attractive as her mother had once been and, judging by two children in three years, just as eager. Cozzens' eyes grew distant with nostalgia, then he coughed hurriedly and rubbed his hand across his face.

'Hm! Hah! Yes!'

'Charlotte Pentecost,' he said aloud, trying to keep his mind on the present when it persisted on straying to the past. He knew she kept herself to herself and never placed herself in a position where any of the brash young officers in the city, encouraged by the heat and Pentecost's absence, might try to take advantage of her loneliness. Yet Cozzens knew she wasn't happy either, because Khaswe was no place for a young woman with two young sons, and he made a note on his pad that it might be a good idea to have her to the next party they held so that she could meet a few other wives of her own age – in an atmosphere of safety away from the dangers of the old town where she had a flat.

Charlotte Pentecost, he wrote in his diary in his cramped square hand. Dinner? Drinks?

He wondered if she'd accept. His wife was known to the Command – most unfairly, because they thought quite wrongly that she ran it – as 'Machine Gun Maggie', and he knew that the wives of many of his officers failed completely to see beyond her hearty facade to the kindness beneath and ducked her receptions.

As he put down the pen, he noticed at the top of the sheet another entry – Bishop of Harwick – and he sighed.

Oh, God, he thought, that bloody man! With his dog collar and holier-than-thou face, the Bishop of Harwick was one of the younger men in the top echelons of the Church and well known to Cozzens for being far more concerned with racialism, aid to backward nations and world starvation then he ever was with the spiritual needs of his own flock. Until he and his friends had started preaching 'Love our black brothers', it had never occurred to the blunt and forthright Cozzens to do anything else. The same applied to backward nations, world starvation and bad housing. Cozzens had been prepared to accept them all, even to offer his mite towards their alleviation, but the Bishop of Harwick had finally begun to convince him that everyone was right but the British.

And the Bishop had now arrived in Khalit on what he liked to call a fact-finding tour, together with Forester Hobbins, who was Britain's arch-protester, member of the Nancy Left, intellectual and leader – from the back – of every assault on the American Embassy that ever took place. With them had come all the hordes of newspapermen who hung on their words, eager to make capital out of well-chosen criticism, among them Alec Gloag, the one television commentator Cozzens actively detested. His clipped Glaswegian voice sent shudders up and down Cozzens' spine as he tore to shreds the reputations of men who, not having the advantage of television's speedy growth, had taken a lifetime to make them. There were others too – Lewis, Garbitt, Hatchard and Diplock – already in Khalit and sending home snippets of news that gave Cozzens sleepless nights as he saw in them provocation for the Nationalists who were just waiting in the back streets of the Khesse district for something to go wrong.

Staring at the Bishop of Harwick's name, Cozzens wished he could send him across the Toweida Plain to Hahdhdhah on an ass carrying a palm branch, which was all he seemed to think was needed to ensure peace. It might have worked for Jesus Christ, the General decided bitterly, but it certainly wouldn't work for Harwick.

And finally, Westminster's representative, a senior Minister of the Crown who was on his way to reassure the Sultan of the British Government's honourable intentions with regard to the treaty but to beg him not to have second thoughts about it because such treaties had long since become embarrassing.

Cozzens had heard that the British Government would much have preferred a more enlightened rule whether they were there as peacekeepers or not, and only the fact that the Sultan's son in Rome refused to return home had prevented a palace revolution.

He glanced at the dates again and grinned maliciously as he decided he might kill several birds with one stone. Rasaul Pasha, the Sultan's Minister for the Interior, had been after him for some time to find out British intentions if Tafas proved difficult. Perhaps he could introduce him to the Government's representative and let them fight it out between them. It might even, he thought spitefully, be enlightening to listen to the ill-humour that would result. Perhaps he could even get Charlotte Pentecost in on it. She was a good talker and pretty enough to take any Minister's mind off his job.

Rasaul, he wrote after Charlotte Pentecost's name. Westminster chap. Maybe even the bloody Bishop, too, he thought sourly. And that gadget, Hobbins! At least it would keep them quiet for a while and might encourage Tafas to make up his mind and sign.

2

Though Cozzens didn't know it, Sultan Tafas el Taif at that moment had just about finally decided not to sign. In the exotic old palace on the headland, furnished with hi-fi and televisions bought with the revenues from American-owned businesses, he and his Minister for the Interior, Rasaul Pasha, were angrily discussing the situation.

The Sultan was an old man who enjoyed the out-of-date comedies of Dean Martin and Jerry Lewis, dreamed dreams of settling all his problems with the discovery of oil, and handled the affairs of his country like a mediaeval monarch. Rasaul was well aware of the British dilemma. With no one to put in place of Tafas they were stuck with the elderly, old-fashioned man who held back the development of his country, only because he was considered one stage better than the fist-clenching young men from the Khesse district or a junta of ambitious colonels.

'I didn't expect to give up the Toweida Plain,' he was saying. 'This Sultanate was carved out by my great-grandfather after the troubles between the British and the Italians in the last century. For my father's work in the First World War the treaty that was made in 1860 was renewed for another eighty years, and because I placed our airfields at the disposal of the British in 1940, they agreed to stretch it for another forty and poured money into the country. Now the Americans are bringing trade. Why should I give it up to the half-wits who get their training in Cairo?'

Rasaul sighed. He knew Tafas well enough to realise that this was all nothing more than the preliminaries to another of his colossal changes of mind.

'Because, sir,' he said patiently, 'if you don't allow the British to go, you will find these same hotheads who got their training in Cairo will apply it to rise as a body and force them to go.'

'The British Army?'

'Sir, the British Army is not the vast organisation it once was. They have commitments elsewhere – too many sometimes and some too close to home. They don't want to stay. They can't stay.'

'They have to stay if I refuse to sign!'

The Sultan stared angrily through the window, hearing the faint wail of a muezzin from one of the minarets silhouetted against the pearly sky. 'La illa Lah Mohammed rassoul Allah – There is no God but Allah, and Mohammed is his prophet.' The tamarisk plumes in the garden below him drooped in the still air and the geraniums made a flare of colour against the white walls. The dusty rose bushes were half in bloom and from the mouth of a stone lion water trickled musically into a stone basin. The garden had an air of faded opulence that went with the rusted metal furniture and the bleached and shabby awnings and the lawns covered with weeds and fallen dates. Beyond, the murmur of the streets and the babble of the bazaars, the water-sellers' bells and the endless 'Allah, Allah' of the beggars were hushed to a soft monotone.

'If the frontier forts are closed down,' he said slowly, stubbornly, 'the frontier will move south of the hills, and once it starts it will never stop until the Sultanate is thrust into the sea.'

'The British would never guard the frontiers, sir,' Rasaul pointed out.

'The treaty says they must.'

'The treaty terms say clearly, sir, that the British will back up the Sultanate and such borders as are agreed with our neighbours. They will never support disputed or artificial ones, and the Khusar Hills were decided arbitrarily in the last century by your grandfather's administrators against the advice of the British and despite the protests of the northern tribes. The British will stand by that clause.'

'The small print on the back of the contract,' Tafas sneered.

'The terms of reference of the treaty extend to the Dharwas, sir, and no further. The British refused to alter them in 1940.'

'They are opting out of their promise.' The Sultan's voice was sulky.

'Sir' – Rasaul's voice rose angrily – 'you and your Ministers agreed to them going.'

'Things have changed since then.'

'I can't imagine them permitting you to back out now, sir.'

Tafas gave a sly smile. 'There are ways of making them,' he said. 'They believe in sticking to treaties even when they don't like them. And I need the northern frontier. I need Hahdhdhah. I need those young men up there who put backbone into my troops.'

3

Standing at the window of his office, Pentecost could see the hills reflecting the yellow glow of the late sunshine, and he shivered a little as he felt the evening chill. Hahdhdhah was high enough in the foothills of the Urbidas to be cold in the evenings and through the night. Sometimes, in winter, even, there was snow, and when snow lay on top of the Rass range just beyond the Urbidas the little fortress could be freezing, and the Toweidas stumped around the place with their heads down between their shoulders, wearing every scrap of clothing they possessed, their faces as long as fiddles. Thank God, he thought, they'd be out of Hahdhdhah – and probably out of Khalit – by the time the next winter came.

From Beebe's quarters he could hear the sound of a radio. Beebe was still with them, still working across the plain, guarded always by a scout car and a lorry, exploding his little canisters, reading his instruments and checking and rechecking his columns of figures. From time to time, a report was sent down to Dhafran for the coast, but as far as they could tell they were all negative and discouraging.

A Toweida near the tamarisk which at noon gave the only scrap of shade to the courtyard that existed started singing to a one-stringed guitar which made a noise like a tortured cat. Pentecost frowned at its barbarity, then he breathed deeply, catching the snuff-dry air in his nostrils, wondering how his wife would have regarded him walking out alone towards a line of tribesmen armed to the teeth. He had described the affair in a letter to her, then thought better of it and torn it up and written again without making any mention of it. Living in the uncertain atmosphere of Khaswe was enough. Already, he knew, his older son was going to infant school in a bus with windows grilled against grenades, and there'd been more than one shooting in Victoria Street, the main shopping centre. It seemed months now since he had shared his wife's bed, and a long time since she had told him frankly that it was time they did something about increasing their family.

He stared again through the window, noticing how the shadows of the few scattered trees near the fortress striped the dusty yellow earth. The trees were unexpected in the bare Toweida Plain and he found himself wondering why they had never been cut down. In all the past assaults on the place they must have been a perfect haven for snipers. Probably some earlier commander, considerate of creature comforts, had planted them there to break the monotony of the view or to give himself a little shade where he could enjoy a picnic during the more peaceable periods.

Thrusting the thought from his mind, he sat down at the desk and lit a cigarette. He was a young man of precise and regular habits and he allowed himself only five a day. Enjoying the first puffs, he considered the situation.

Despite the quietness, he knew it would still be wise to take every care with the evacuation.

He paused, thinking of Aziz. The great curved scimitar hanging on the wall opposite him was a reminder of their friendship. Beneath it now there were a ceremonial dagger and a muzzle-loading musket, its stock inlaid with ivory and mother-of-pearl, its powder horn decorated with filigree gold and silver. Aziz's gifts had been mostly warlike, though lately – as though sensing that they were entering a new period of peace – he had produced brassware and a carpet. His own gifts in return had all been peaceable because you didn't give teeth to a wolf and because the weapons he held weren't his to give. But his lighter had gone – at a later meeting Aziz had complained it had not worked – and so had the silver photograph frame which had once held a picture of his wife. It was probably now in a tent in Addowara or in the hills, holding the photograph of Aziz and Pentecost that Minto, who had also taken a photographic course, had taken of them.

The whole business was becoming rather expensive, in fact, because while Aziz could doubtless take what he wanted from whoever he wanted – merely by issuing a threat or using his strong right arm – it cost Pentecost a lot of money and he didn't have much. Though the first Pentecost, by fighting on the right side at Hastings, had set the family up for generations, a later one had decided for the wrong side at Marston Moor and beggared them and he had had to buy Minto's Japanese tape-recorder and Lack's transistor – even the New English Bible Fox's mother had given her son on his departure overseas, which he'd explained to Aziz as the Englishman's Koran. It hadn't been easy to persuade them to part with things they preferred to keep and only the feeling that they were contributing to their future safety had encouraged them to let them go.

Aziz, he felt, would give no trouble under the circumstances but he hoped that when Tafas finally got round to putting pen to paper the officials in Khaswe would not expect them to get out at such speed so that they would not only lose their dignity but probably also their pants.

Lack appeared in the doorway. 'Beebe sent this,' he said. 'It's not calculated to bring roses to your checks.'

Pentecost took the sheet of paper he offered. Ever since he had arrived, Beebe had been keeping a bulletin on the BBC news he picked up on the big receiver in his lorry with which he contacted his office in Khaswe. He taped it then typed it out and hung it in the little mess they shared, deriving a certain amount of wry humour from presenting them with a running commentary on their own end.

Pentecost glanced down at what he'd written.

Despite the British Government's wishes, the Sultan of Khalit is now insisting that the treaty cannot be repudiated. Conditions have changed, he claims, and while a provisional date has been fixed for the British withdrawal, he now says that under the terms of the treaty he still has the right to insist on a British presence in Khalit.

Pentecost looked up. 'Makes a change to be asked to stay,' he observed mildly.

Lack shrugged. 'They'd never let him off the hook,' he said. 'Not now. A joint statement was issued.'

'Funnier things happen these days,' Pentecost said. 'Diplomacy takes some funny turns.' He pushed the sheet of paper aside and sat for a moment deep in thought. 'What's your opinion of the Toweidas?' he asked unexpectedly.

Lack smiled. 'Well,' he said, 'they were never up-and-at-'em boys but, apart from a tendency to lose their heads when they're excited, they're in fine shape.'

'That's gratifying at least.' Pentecost sat back and, without any further explanation, tossed a file across the desk. 'Stores,' he said. 'I think we'll have to itemise a bit further those we're leaving. That pentolite for blasting, for instance – separate it from the rest of the explosives. It looks prettier and quartermasters like things pretty. Those two old inch-and-a-half Martinis. Shove 'em down. The politicians like to appear generous. Timber, biscuits, grain, kerosene' – he leaned across the desk, his eyes travelling down the list – 'sheets, plastic.' His finger jabbed. 'They're different strengths, aren't they? And sheets, iron, corrugated. They're different sizes.'

Lack laughed. 'When we've gone,' he said, 'the whole bloody Hejri nation'll have corrugated iron loos with plastic windows.'

4

As Pentecost left the office, the Dharwa on guard outside slammed to attention and he returned the salute precisely because his polite mind told him a mere casual acknowledgement was not enough. He was a believer in God, the Queen, the realm of England, and good manners.

Crossing to his quarters, he took a shower, then, dressing in fresh clothes devoid of dust and the stains of sweat, he lit a cigarette, picked up a folding chair and a book of verse and marched in his precise narrow stride to the ramparts. Five minutes later, Talaal, the officers' mess steward, appeared with a bottle of beer and followed him.

If they had done nothing else, the Khaliti engineers had managed to build the fortress over a well, and just inside, on a shelf where it was cool, Talaal always kept two or three bottles of beer for Pentecost. From time to time Lack tried to persuade him that there should be one for George Gould Lack, but nothing – neither persuasion nor outright bribery – had ever persuaded the Toweida to grant him the same privilege, and bitterly he watched as

Pentecost climbed the steps and put down his chair. Lack thought he was a little mad, the way he performed the same ceremony at the same time every day, carrying his little seat up to the ramparts to watch the sun go down. Pentecost was opening his chair now and Lack looked round as he settled himself, to see Talaal just emerging from the mess with a tray, moving with as much decorum as if he were head waiter at the Savoy. Lack would have given his right arm for the same treatment, but without fail he got his beer warm and slapped in front of him with as little ceremony as if he were a new-joined lance-jack in the corporals' mess.

The fact that he was observed by everyone in the fort and that Fox liked to set his watch by his movements completely escaped Pentecost. He was aware that he had the makings of an eccentric, but it didn't worry him greatly. All Pentecosts were eccentrics. His great-grandfather had ridden into battle at the Alma eating raisins because he considered the army rations of the day bad for the health. His grandfather had worn a cotton kilt and sandals through the East African campaign in 1916 because he considered stockings and shorts the worst thing possible for prickly heat and jungle sores. And in the desert in 1942, his father had always been among the more outrageously dressed officers in an army noted for its outrageous dress. They'd always got away with it, whatever their rank – because there'd been Pentecosts in the Army List ever since there'd been an Army List.

As he took the beer from Talaal, he opened his book of verse and stared at the hills. One or two of the Toweidas were kicking a ball around on the square, then, deciding they were hungry, they disappeared abruptly, and the fort became silent. The sentry on the tower moved and

Pentecost heard the clink of his equipment, but otherwise everything was still. For a moment, he caught the sound of high-pitched morse from where Beebe was toying in the back of his lorry, some brief harsh words in Arabic – probably from Cairo or Baghdad – then they were cut off sharply and the place was silent again, in a silence that held a great deal of menace.

Pentecost sipped his beer and stared around him between glances at his book of verse. The light was changing, and the shadows on the hills were changing rapidly from violet to purple. Over in the west, there was a faint pinky glow where the last of the sun still stained the sky.

Nalk Owdi was sounding off near the gate, and down near the MT park Sergeant Stone, talking to himself in a monotonous exasperated fury, was struggling to sort out the plug leads on a lorry which one of the Khaliti drivers had managed to connect in the wrong order. By the living quarters Sergeant Chestnut's clipped Scottish voice lifted in a piercing shriek of disgust. 'You – MacFadyen! Come here! No' tomorrow – the noo!'

Only Chestnut could make a Scottish Highlander out of a Toweida called Mufaddhin but everyone knew that years in the sun had made Chestnut a little mad and the sound of his crazy screech belonged to the background – familiar, safe and secure.

'Yon bastard's no' pullin' his weight,' he was saying bitterly to Stone. 'He'll nae do a bluidy thing I tell him. He can understand but he pretends not to.'

Stone's laugh came up to Pentecost. 'Go on, man! Even I can't understand you.'

Pentecost smiled, then he became aware that the sound of frogs in a gully that led down to the river had stopped suddenly, as though something had moved down there and the alarm had been sounded. The silence seemed to envelop him, and, suddenly restless, he stood up, the glass still in his hand, and crossed to an embrasure.

There was a burst of chattering from a group of Toweidas under the solitary tamarisk then everything was quiet again. His eyes narrowed, he stared at the hills and, somehow, he was troubled in a way he couldn't explain. Out of the corner of his eye, he saw a light go on in one of the windows overlooking the courtyard and he felt almost as if he wanted to say, 'No, not just now.'

He'd heard rumours, some of them brought to him by Fox who picked them up from God alone knew where, some of them by Zaid Fauzan who'd spent his whole leathery life on the frontier and knew the place like the back of his hand. They'd heard that Thawab abu Tegeiga was due to arrive in the hills to the north, with his Hawassi and Dayi and Tayur reims, and that the trouble-makers down in Khaswe had been suborning the Jezowi, the Khadari, the Muleimat and the Shukri, who were supposed to guard the Dharwa passes for the Sultan. If the agitators from Khaswe stirred up trouble there, it might be difficult getting through to Dhafran when the time came.

Pentecost glanced at the hills again. An army could hide itself in the folds up there, and he found himself looking for small things that might show where they were – a layer of floating dust over one of the ridges, a flock of birds disturbed from their roosting. Nothing moved and he told himself he was being unnecessarily edgy. There was no need to be afraid – not while he and Aziz were on their present good terms. Briefly, he saw a flicker of light, which burned and died almost as suddenly as it had come.

Then another, and away over on his left another. Aziz was still there with his Hejris. If Pentecost was taking no chances, neither was Aziz. The mere fact that contact had been made didn't break down the distrust of centuries, and both he and Aziz still sought proof that the other was honest. He wanted to be certain that when they walked out of Hahdhdhah, Aziz would permit them to go in peace. And Aziz would never be certain they were leaving till the last man had left.

Pentecost forced himself to sit down again, a priggish young man troubled by his own thoughts. He knew that Hejris were moving about in the market place in Hahdhdhah village, had probably even been to the gates of the fort with the Toweida traders. Never in a hundred years had anyone ever been able to stop that. All Toweidas were Hejris, even if all Hejris weren't Toweidas, and it was impossible to tell the difference unless they wore their traditional headbands and girdles and the beads that decorated the fronts of their robes.

His eye roved over the land in front of the fort, resting on a clump of rocks fifty yards away, the mud-hut that had been a Toweida brothel, the little bazaar and stables, the patch of trees and long grass where the stream ran down to the river, all places he might have to fortify or clear if things went wrong...

He stopped dead as he saw himself once more nervously thinking of strong points and defences. For God's sake, he told himself, it won't come to that!

Then he noticed that the sound from Beebe's receiver had changed suddenly, and heard a heavy voice blare out, iron-sounding with too much volume, only to die abruptly so that he could just still hear the voice without being able to catch the words.

As he listened it stopped abruptly, as though a switch had been thrown, and he saw Beebe jump down from his lorry and cross to the radio room. A moment later the voice started again, on Chestnut's receiver, and he wondered what was going on.

5

The sardonic expression on Beebe's face increased as the astonishment grew on Lack's. He was almost enjoying himself as he watched his expression change.

'You'd better get Billy,' he said. 'He'll want to hear this.'

Lack was staring open-mouthed at the big receiver that Chestnut had tuned in, on Beebe's encouragement, to London, his face slack, his eyes as round as marbles. On the table near his hand was an empty glass. Minto had a sickly grin on his face and looked like an overgrown schoolboy. Beebe watched them, amused. His heavy beard left him blue-jowled within a couple of hours of shaving, and his eyes, under his black eyebrows, were merry and restless as fleas. Chestnut's thin Scots face looked frigid with rage.

Beebe's big shoulders hunched. 'Go on,' he persisted. 'Fetch Papa.'

Minto, who was almost too young to be certain of anything, knew that the insulting tone of Beebe's remarks was really only a joke, but he had never quite been able to accept that his laughter was not unfriendly.

'Yes,' he said. 'Of course.'

He turned on his heel and left the room. Crossing the square, he could see Pentecost leaning against the embrasure near the tower, a lonely figure against the darkening sky. He ran up the steps and stopped alongside him.

'I think you ought to come,' he suggested. 'Special announcement coming up on the BBC.'

Beebe was bent with Chestnut over the set when Pentecost arrived, and he looked up as he entered.

Lack's face still wore its stunned look. 'They've ratted on us,' he said at once.

Pentecost's voice was suddenly surprisingly sharp and commanding. 'Who've ratted on us?'

Lack gestured. 'The Government.'

Pentecost frowned. 'Would you mind telling me what's happened?' he said.

Lack seemed to shake his head, as though trying to force some sense into it. 'The Government's agreed with Tafas,' he said. He seemed bewildered, as though someone had cheated him over something he failed to understand. 'Or, in effect, they have, anyway.'

Pentecost's eyes glinted. 'I've still not been made aware of what's happened,' he pointed out frostily, and Beebe could see he was growing angry. 'Surely, you learned to make a report more clearly than that.'

Lack seemed to pull himself together at the rebuke. 'Questions at UNO.' He gestured heavy-handedly. 'The whole pack of 'em on our necks. They had to admit Tafas' right to invoke the treaty if an emergency still exists. While at the same time saying what a rotten lot we are to be here, anyway.'

'And?'

'Well, can't you see what's coming? He doesn't have to sign now if he doesn't want to!' Lack's face became thunderous. 'It's sheer bloody cowardice,' he burst out. 'The old bastard won't face up to the fact that times are different.'

Minto was staring at him, puzzled. He was obviously not very clear on politics. 'What difference does it make?' he asked 'We've had our instructions to leave.'

Lack's rage exploded from him at last. 'Don't be a bloody fool, Freddy,' he said. 'Now that they've admitted Tafas' rights, it's kicked the underpinnings from the Government's arguments. Tafas can demand that we stay. And if we do, we'll be staying in Dhafran, too – and in Hahdhdhah!'

6

'Her Majesty's Government' – the well-known voice sounded weary ' – has been accused of failing to meet its responsibilities. It is not a matter of British prestige but of contractual commitments.'

'It's enough to poison the atmosphere of Eden,' Lack growled. Pentecost gave him a quick look that Beebe caught, as though he found Lack's comments pointless and irritating. As Lack became silent again, the heavy voice came through once more.

'The Government has given a great deal of consideration to the Sultan's claims,' it droned on, 'and we shall not be accused of going back on our promises. We cannot deny our commitments and we have been reminded that we have treaties...'

'Oh, my God,' Lack said.

'...and in Khalit foreign agents are using the British military presence to destroy an established régime.' There was a long pause and Pentecost found he was holding his breath. 'If called upon, we cannot let our old friends down. We have been looking into the matter in the light of the Sultan's claim and a responsible Minister will be sent out at once to see what can be done.'

There was a long silence and Beebe saw Pentecost draw a quick breath. Despite the cautious words of diplomacy, they had it at last. They were staying.

'Talks are continuing with Khaliti Ministers' – the speaker was winding up now and, though there was more to come, they were no longer interested – 'and a senior British Minister will be flying out immediately to meet the men on the spot to see how the British presence in Khalit can be made acceptable to the Khaliti people until the present situation changes...'

They heard him out, not speaking, their faces grave, then, as Chestnut switched off, Lack lit a cigarette, flinging the match away furiously.

'That,' Pentecost said in a flat, calm voice, 'appears to be that.'

Beebe had never been a soldier but he felt he had sufficient experience of roughing it to know what men were made of. He had carried his trade to Alaska and the wilds of Canada, to the Amazon and India and Indo-China, all the corners of the world where American trade and American know-how had found its way, and he suddenly felt desperately sorry for these three young men.

'What'll you do?' he asked. 'If you stay, I mean.'

Pentecost lifted his head and as his eyes met the American's he gave him a small private smile that seemed to be full of quiet personal jest. 'Do, Mr Beebe?' he said. 'We shall exercise our calling. We shall fight to the death.'

As he left, Beebe stared after him, suspecting sarcasm. No one said anything and he turned to Lack, wondering if he'd heard correctly. 'He doesn't mean that, does he?'

Lack stared at the door and then at Beebe so that the American realised that Pentecost was as much an enigma to the others as he was to him.

'God knows,' Lack said. 'Probably.'

four

1

No matter how the situation had been phrased, no matter how much concern was caused in Westminster by the circumstances which had been forced on them, nobody was deluded. The British were staying. And, as if it were a warning, the first explosion of anger occurred in Khaswe within twenty-four hours of the Prime Minister's speech.

During the day someone stole the Union Jack from the flag-pole outside the British Information Centre and hoisted a dead cat in its place. No one saw it happen – or so they claimed – and the police swore that they knew nothing, and during the evening the window collapsed as a brick shattered the glass. The crowd tore the interior to shreds and within ten minutes the market was on fire and the place was given up to murder, robbery and arson. Half a dozen British-owned cars were burning in the streets, a British soldier had been shot in the back on the Wad, and three policemen, attempting to disperse a mob near the Ministry of Justice, had been seriously beaten up.

As the Saladin armoured vehicles appeared on the streets and the narrow alleys began to echo to the wail of police sirens, in the bizarre palace on the headland the

71

Sultan nervously discussed the situation with Rasaul Pasha.

'The Defence Force has brought in half a dozen youths, sir,' Rasaul was saying.

'Children,' the Sultan growled. 'It's not the boys and girls from the university I want. It's the agitators. The agents. The people who put the ideas into their heads. The Havrists, the Istiqlal Brotherhood.'

Rasaul sighed. 'Sir, these men rarely find their way into the streets. They're zealots, not seedy little terrorists.'

The Sultan irritatedly tapped a report on his desk. 'This is the fifteenth incident today,' he said.

Rasaul shrugged. 'It's the treaty, sir,' he said. 'The people aren't happy about it. We're walking a tightrope.'

The Sultan stared through the window, hearing the shifting noises of the city beyond the Palace gardens. Out there, down the narrow, odorous alleys of the old city, scattered with vegetable refuse and the droppings of donkeys and redolent with the smell of charcoal and mint tea, men had started to plot against him, he knew. He turned slowly, his shoes scraping on the bright Moroccan tile-work that covered the floor.

'Of course we're walking a tightrope,' he said sharply. 'But what do you suggest? That I go aboard my yacht and head for the South of France like Farouk and a few more and live off my savings dallying with women?'

Rasaul said nothing. Privately he thought it was a good idea. The Sultan was noted for his virility and his interest in young women.

'I'm well aware that there are those in Khalit who're anxious to see me go,' Tafas went on. 'But I don't intend to go. They'll only throw in their lot with Cairo, which wants merely to carry on the war with the Jews. I don't believe in that. I believe in peace!'

Rasaul knew perfectly well that the last thing the Sultan was concerned with was Middle East peace. He was concerned with his own safety and his own revenues, and Rasaul almost had it in him to feel sorry for the British who found themselves in such an unenviable position. If they had gone back on the treaty Tafas was invoking they would have been the object of scorn and derision from their enemies. By standing by it, they were allowing other enemies to raise a storm of fury.

'There are other factors, sir,' he said patiently. 'Our liabilities are in the region of three hundred and fifty million dollars and our assets can't be realised in the open market. There's been pressure throughout the whole area to withdraw funds. The banks are uncertain and people are moving their accounts – even the bordel women from the Khaliba area. And when they think of leaving we should look to our affairs.'

Tafas frowned. Alongside his income from olives, fruit, almonds, saffron, mint and minerals, he drew a discreet revenue from hemp and prostitution. 'I expect the evacuation of British troops to be halted,' he growled stubbornly.

Rasaul decided he was completely out of touch. Sultans, khalifs and kings were no longer currency under the onrush of new ideas.

'It will be, sir,' he pointed out 'In Khaswe. But the British Government's offer of support will never include the frontier. We have a time bomb under us just waiting to be lit.'

Tafas frowned and Rasaul went on. He was no more honest than any other of the Sultan's Ministers and had long since decided it might be a good idea to develop some illness which would necessitate going to his country estate until he could see which way the wind was blowing. When the British left – as they would have to eventually – and the Sultan had disappeared, the people who would inevitably take over would be bound to start looking round for someone with experience to do their work for them, and, having seen his plans wrecked, he was trying to salvage what he could. For once the British Government's interests ran parallel with his own.

'The frontier has only remained quiet for so long,' he pointed out, 'because the northern tribes have been expecting that we shall have to give up the Toweida Plain. If the British stay, we shall be in trouble on two fronts – here in Khaswe and in the north. The British are prepared to look after us only as far as a line running east and west through Dhafran to Umrah and Aba el Zereibat.'

The Sultan jerked his hand irritatedly. 'We can hold the frontier with ease,' he was saying. 'Khowiba. Umrah. Hahdhdhah. Afarja. Aba el Zereibat. All of them. As for the tribes holding the Dharwa passes – the Shukri, the Khadari, the Jezowi, and the Muleimat – we'll worry about them when they make a move. At the moment they're still taking my subsidies.'

'And what about the evacuation of Hahdhdhah, Umrah and Zereibat?' Rasaul asked. 'These were ordered on your instructions and the instructions still stand. Only you can cancel them.'

Tafas gave him a sharp look and Rasaul knew he was still hesitating to do anything definite about invoking the treaty in case it should be the final step which would lose him the north. The day's violence had shaken him and he was wavering again.

'Does General Cozzens feel he has the situation here under control?' Tafas asked.

'I'm seeing him shortly,' Rasaul said. 'He's giving a small party.'

'Will the Bishop of Harwick be there?'

'I hear so, sir.'

'We should declare him and his friends persona non grata.'

Rasaul's expression didn't change. 'It would be difficult,' he said coldly. 'The British set great store by their clericals. A newspaperman or two, perhaps. Even a politician. But not a bishop. He's supposed to be a man of peace.'

'He's stirred up more trouble in his time than a Holy Man declaring a jehad. Perhaps we might arrange for a bomb to be thrown through his window. We could always blame the National Front.' For a moment the Sultan looked hopeful then he sighed. 'What a pity I'm only joking, Rasaul,' he said. 'I think I'd better ask General Cozzens' advice, after all.'

Rasaul's mouth twisted. He'll never remember, he thought. He never did. The Sultan's memory was as legendary as his havering.

'What about the press, sir?' he asked.

'What about them?'

'They are asking for an interview.'

Tafas' shoulders hunched doggedly. 'I'll talk to them later,' he said. 'For the moment, I expect they know how to look after themselves.'

2

He was right, and at that moment they were crowded into one of the private bars of the Intercontinental Hotel, waiting for General Cozzens to wind up the little talk that the switch of policy at the Palace had made necessary.

They had been badgering his staff for some time now, demanding to know what was happening, and his conference was an attempt to explain. He wasn't succeeding very well because it was impossible to explain something he didn't yet know himself, and the Khaliti Command, unable to pin the Sultan down to anything, was lying low and offering neither help nor press conferences. The press had turned up en masse, the foreigners making sour cracks at the British, all a little edgy and excited because they knew that trouble was brewing, and angry because that morning they'd been in the way of the troops and been rounded up on Cozzens' orders and marched to safety. Some of them were even feeling spiteful and were after Cozzens' blood.

There were men – and women – representing the sharp American magazines that so caught the urgent spirit of the States, crisp, bloody-minded, sparing with words but cramming everything into blunt square paragraphs that pulled no punches when it came to criticism. There were the French writers and the slick photographers of Paris-Match determined to get a few of the gory pictures that they put across so well. And all the crowd from London – the Express, the Telegraph and The Times, and all the agency boys, to say nothing of the television teams. The situation was made for disaster and they were anxious to show a few pictures of smoking motor cars and motionless figures sprawled across the pavement for the delectation of the British public with their before-dinner gins.

Alec Gloag regarded them with a jaundiced eye. He'd more than once posed a small boy with a petrol bomb when it wasn't possible to get close to the in-fighting, more than once helped to stir up a crowd for his own purposes and to titillate his public, and could always write a commentary to go with it that was nicely tinged with sarcasm. There was no one better at it than he was.

He had already talked to the Bishop of Harwick and his companion in indignation, Forester Hobbins, professional protesters both of them, always concerned with someone else's agony at the other side of the world when it always seemed to Gloag that there were plenty of agonies in England that could use their names.

'Britain has no right to keep its troops in this part of the world,' the Bishop had said in the interview Gloag had taped.

'These people are entitled to work out their own salvation without any help from us.' Hobbins' attitude had been even more unequivocal. 'I wouldn't lift a finger to save a single British soldier. They have no right to be here and they should protest.'

Gloag had listened to them sourly. A fat lot of good it was asking a British soldier to protest, he thought. Soldiers didn't have that right and most of them, he noticed, curiously didn't have much time for the Hobbinses of this world, who, while coming to watch with triumph their departure from the squalid little settlements they had protected with their flesh and blood, didn't hesitate to demand VIP treatment.

Gloag could still remember how the Bishop had refused to walk a hundred yards from the aeroplane that had brought him to Khalit, to the ferry that would carry him across the harbour, and could still recall the bitter expression on the face of the major who had had to give up his car for him. Privately Gloag thought it was because the Bishop, since the attempt on the life of the Pope, had realised that even churchmen were no longer immune to murder, and suspected there might be assassins hidden in the crowd.

Despite the fact that he'd photographed thousands of demonstrations and thousands of protesters, amateur and professional, Gloag had little admiration for them. It was no longer a brave thing to protest. Once, a man who had the courage to stand up and shout against authority had been on his own and likely to be rushed off to prison. Nowadays, protesting had become a national sport and there were so many of them at it, it no longer required much courage. Gloag was disillusioned even with his own brand of disillusionment.

Cozzens' little lecture was coming to an end now. It hadn't achieved much. It was only stating what the Prime Minister had already stated – that the Government had been forced by Sultan Tafas into second thoughts about Khalit – and the newspapermen were at him now, crucifying him as they hurled questions at him.

'If British troops stay here in Khalit,' he was being asked by a big Frenchman who spoke perfect English, 'by what right would that be?'

'By right of the treaty signed originally in 1860...'

'Over a century ago!' someone shouted.

' – recreated after the First World War' – Cozzens struggled on to the end ' – and recreated again in 1940. That is the right.'

'What about the Khaliti who might have your men pushing them around?'

'What about my men who are going to have to endure a bit of pushing round themselves?' Cozzens snapped back with a show of spirit that Gloag privately applauded.

He got to his feet while the journalists about him were drawing their breath for the next attack.

'What about the outposts at Khowiba, Umrah, Hahdhdhah, Aba el Zereibat and Afarja?' he asked. 'They are, I understand, surrounded by Hejri and Deleimi warriors who consider they are on their soil.'

The bastard knew his stuff, Cozzens thought bitterly. 'What is the question?' he asked aloud.

'I understand they contain British troops.'

'Not British troops. Khaliti troops.'

'Officered by men from the British Army. What about them?'

Cozzens drew a deep breath. 'My information is still that all British officers are to be returned to the coast,' he said. 'The outposts will be brought in first. That order has never been rescinded.'

'And the Khaliti troops?'

'According to my information, they are to be brought in also. Umrah, Hahdhdhah and Zereibat are being closed down to shorten the Sultan's lines. Later, I understand, they will be reopened.'

'That'll be the day,' someone at the back said.

'What's your view, sir?' Gloag persisted.

Cozzens frowned. 'I'm not in a position to offer a view,' he said. 'The frontier's the Sultan's problem. I can give no opinion on something I know nothing about.' And something I'm never likely to learn about either, he thought bitterly. The Sultan had never been in the habit of telling him much even if he remembered. 'I command in Khaswe. The Khaliti army, at present commanded by Brigadier Wintle, at Dhafran, controls the frontiers.'

'And if the Hejri decided not to trust the Sultan?'

Cozzens sighed, hating the job he had to do. 'The officers in command at Hahdhdhah, Umrah and Aba el Zereibat,' he said, 'have already received their instructions. I have received no orders contrary to those I already hold, and have received no signal that I am likely to receive such orders. The evacuation south of the northern garrisons will therefore, I imagine, continue as originally planned.'

Gloag almost pitied Cozzens. He was playing him like a fish on a line. 'My information,' he went on, 'is that Aziz el Beidawi himself is up near Hahdhdhah with most of his men.'

'If that's your information, I'd like to know where you got it,' Cozzens snapped back. Sometimes the bloody newspaper and television people had more money to spend on information than the army itself! 'In any case,' he ended, 'I have every confidence in the officer in command.'

Gloag ignored his burst of anger. He had been about to point out that confidence didn't count for much when there were a hundred of the enemy to every one of you, but he suddenly lost patience and sat down. In his cynical way, he could keep it up for hours if necessary, but he was growing bored. He glanced across at his cameraman who held up a thumb to indicate that he not only had General Cozzens answering questions but he also had Alec Gloag asking them, which, to viewers in England, was probably much more important. While they had never heard of General Cozzens. and couldn't care less what sort of show he put up, the performance of Alec Gloag was a matter of great moment to the elderly ladies who followed his programme in Bath, Cheltenham and Tunbridge Wells.

As another of the Americans got to his feet with the scrape of a chair, Gloag wondered how best to set about his programme. He had plenty of shots of burning cars and shattered shop fronts in Khaswe, and some good footage of youngsters running from the police. He had the Bishop of Harwick with the breeze blowing his thinning hair about his eyes and Hobbins holding forth on the moral courage that was so lacking in the Government It was still incomplete, though. Having got the British public aware of the garrison at Hahdhdhah, they'd be watching for what happened to them – as if they were watching Watford in a cup-tie against Chelsea – asking themselves if the lost cause was going to come off, and he found himself wondering if he could somehow get permission to go up to Hahdhdhah before it was too late and, if so, if he could get a promise from Aziz el Beidawi, in return for some footage of film, of a safe passage back. He wondered, in fact, what Aziz was thinking about it all, and what the situation was at that moment at Hahdhdhah. He'd heard they were still playing football with the natives.

3

As Sergeant Fox blew his whistle, the Toweida Levies trooped off the dusty field below the fort, followed by the triumphant Dharwa Scouts who, as usual, had won.

There was a lot of cheerful boasting from the Dharwas and sullen responses from the Toweidas, who somehow never seemed able to produce either the energy or the skill to beat the aggressive little hillmen. The Dharwas could knock them into a cocked hat at everything, whether it was weapon-handling or sport or merely knocking back their liquor and chasing the women.

'Toweidas play football like camels in rut,' one of the Dharwas said loudly, and Sergeant Fox, scenting trouble, manoeuvred himself to a position between them and started shoving the cocky hillmen back into the fort while Zaid Fauzan's heavy fists thudded on the heads and shoulders of the Toweidas.

Several groups of villagers had turned up from Hahdhdhah to watch the match, with the civilian clerks and drivers and a few of the wives and children from the fort. They enjoyed football and went berserk when a goal was scored, turning somersaults and loudly offering from the touchline to fight the losing side. As the surly Toweidas trailed back, the drivers and clerks started a game of their own with the Hahdhdhahi, kicking the ball about with more enthusiasm than skill with their bare leathery feet, then Fox noticed that one of the men from the village approached the Hahdhdhahi who was playing in goal, who immediately shouted something to his full-back and set off towards the village at a trot. Soon afterwards, the full-back left, too, and before long most of the villagers had disappeared, only a few of the young boys remaining. The match never got beyond the stage of a kick-about and, eventually, even the boys cut it short and disappeared abruptly, leaving the clerks and drivers angry, hot-eyed and frustrated.

It was a curious incident because the Hahdhdhahi liked the game and many of them fancied themselves at it enough to get hold of European football magazines. Fox stared after them, a referee without a match, wondering how much it was connected with the political events in Khaswe. Rather to their surprise the cancellation of all the instructions for departure they had received had not yet arrived; and they were beginning, tremulously at first but gradually with increasing confidence, to feel that the powers in Khaswe had decided, with the outbreak of violence in the capital, that British officers would be of more use on the coast and were prepared to consolidate by withdrawing from the frontier.

Day after day had gone by yet still the expected order to stay had not arrived, though Fox had long since become aware of the growing tension north of the Dharwas and that the word Istiqlal – Independence – had begun to turn up on the walls of Hahdhdhah village. In addition, a man had been found by one of the Civil Guards, the tough village policemen of the frontier, with a stick of gelignite in a highly volatile state and circular metal discs drilled in the centre which could well have been the base plates of grenades. Fox knew very well what that meant and as the clerks and drivers trailed away to their quarters, he spoke quietly to one of the Dharwa storekeepers who nodded and set off after them.

Not long afterwards, Fox presented himself at Pentecost's office, still in football shorts but wearing his uniform jacket and cap to make the visit official. He slammed up a salute that shook him from head to foot. He believed in saluting.

'Hello, Jim,' Pentecost said, using Fox's first name as he sometimes did in the privacy of his office. 'Have a cigarette.'

Fox accepted the cigarette and sat down at Pentecost's suggestion.

'I think you ought to know, sir,' he began. 'I have a feeling there's something funny in the wind.'

'Such as what?'

'You watched the football match, sir?'

'Yes. From the tower. It's a pity the Dharwas always win. It doesn't help the Toweidas' confidence.'

'Notice what happened afterwards, sir?'

Pentecost frowned. 'No,' he admitted. 'I didn't. I saw the drivers and the storemen start a match with the villagers but I expected it to be the usual shambles of bad temper and sulks, and decided to let it go.'

'It never finished, sir.'

'It didn't?'

'No, sir. The villagers broke it off. They went home.'

Pentecost frowned. 'Something wrong?' he asked.

Fox gestured with his cigarette. 'Nothing I saw, sir, but I got Jemal Zeidkha to make a few enquiries. It seemed the villagers had been warned to get home because there was trouble brewing.'

'Trouble?'

'That's what they said, sir.'

That night, as usual, Pentecost took up his position on the rampart and stared uneasily towards the hills. Fox's report didn't surprise him. He had noticed that the daily cart of fresh vegetables from the village had been growing later each day and that day hadn't arrived at all. He'd already decided that that was ominous in itself and somehow it seemed more ominous still with the incident Fox had reported.

As he considered the situation, Lack appeared behind him and leaned alongside him in the embrasure.

'Something worrying you?' he asked.

'Here and there,' Pentecost said mildly. 'Talaal tells me no vegetables found their way here today. Perhaps the Hahdhdhahi have been listening to the radio, too.'

'If they haven't, the Hejri have.' Lack frowned. 'They've been down in Hahdhdhah threatening the villagers. Beebe picked that one up this morning on his way back. He stopped to buy fruit.'

'I'd rather Beebe didn't wander around Hahdhdhah alone,' Pentecost said. 'Tell him, will you?'

'You know what he'll say: I'm a civilian. I'm an American citizen. I can do as I please.'

Pentecost stared at the hills again, almost as though he'd forgotten Lack.

'I've decided to call in the Civil Guard,' he said suddenly.

Lack's eyebrows rose. 'Oh? Why?'

Pentecost gave a little smile. 'Let's say I want to inspect them.'

Lack thought of the tough scruffy policemen of the Hahdhdhah Command who kept the villages in order with the weight of their fists and the threat of their weapons. 'They've never been inspected before,' he pointed out.

'Then it's time they were.'

Lack frowned, never quite able to understand the working of Pentecost's mind. 'You mean you want them all?'

'All! – And while we're at it, I think we should do something about those vegetables that didn't appear. I thought we might send someone down to round them up.' He paused, then gave Lack a radiant small boy's smile. 'You, for instance.'

Lack looked shocked at the idea of someone of his rank performing such a menial task.

'Can't one of the sergeants do it?' he suggested.

Pentecost shook his head. 'I'd rather you went.'

Lack shrugged. 'OK,' he said. 'Don't think I'm dodging it – if that's what you want. Suppose the bastards don't want to sell?'

'I suggest that you take Sergeant Stone down there with Int-Zaid Mohamed and twenty men to encourage them. Leave Mohamed outside with the men – we don't want him visiting his wife and getting himself knocked off down an alley.'

'Wouldn't it be better to take Hussein? He hasn't got a wife down there to visit.'

Pentecost smiled. 'It won't worry Mohamed. I've noticed that when he's parked outside, his wife always nips out and visits him.'

Lack frowned, wondering how it was that Pentecost seemed to know everything worth knowing about everyone. He'd never noticed the movements of Mohamed's wife when he'd visited the village. 'OK,' he said. 'Mohamed it is.'

'Take Stone in with you to do the arguing,' Pentecost went on. 'If the excuses are genuine, make sure the supplies come back with you. If they aren't genuine, get Stone on the job.'

Lack was inclined to make light of the missing vegetables. 'Won't they turn up tomorrow?' he asked.

'They might not.'

Lack frowned. 'Billy,' he said, 'are you gathering stores in case we have to stay here?'

'I'm just fussing perhaps,' Pentecost conceded mildly. 'But it's a great thing in a soldier – fussing. All the best soldiers are born fussers.'

'Do you think something'll go wrong and they'll make us stay?'

'We've been given no indication that they're thinking that way,' Pentecost said. 'Our orders are still to leave on the twenty-first.'

Lack nodded. 'You'd expect some sort of provisional instruction if they were going to change it, wouldn't you?' he said.

'You would indeed.'

'Then what's with all this about the vegetables?'

'I just like my greens,' Pentecost said evasively. 'That's all. But while you're at it, you might to-and-fro a bit and see if you can spot anything.'

Lack was looking uneasy now. 'You think there's something in the wind, Billy, don't you?' he said.

Pentecost was still non-committal. 'Got to keep the Hahdhdhahi up to snuff, haven't we?' he said. 'Got to let 'em know we're not relaxing or they might be encouraged to do something naughty on the twenty-first.'

4

Lack was not the only unwilling one. Despite his wife's presence, Int-Zaid Mohamed seemed to show no enthusiasm for the job either – any more than the Toweida Levies who were usually cheerful enough about a chance to see women. They marched out briskly, however, making a good show, and Pentecost watched them from the rampart above the gate. He turned to Fox. 'Let's have the sentries doubled, Sergeant,' he suggested. 'And tell 'em to keep their eyes open.'

Fox gave him a curious look, then he saluted and turned away.

'Billy's worried,' he observed to Sergeant Chestnut as they passed on the parade ground a moment later. 'He thinks there's trouble in the offing.'

'Och, charming,' Sergeant Chestnut said sourly. 'Bluidy charming! Yon's all we want.'

Lack didn't enjoy his stay in the village. The headmen were polite, even effusive, and as usual offered him coffee and a seat on their carpets. He refused, though he knew quite well that Pentecost would have accepted and, perched primly on a dusty cushion under the fretted woodwork of the coffee house, would have remained chatting cheerfully, drinking coffee or mint tea off the charcoal barriers and nibbling sweetmeats while still managing somehow to conduct the search that Stone was undertaking at that moment. Pentecost had the gift of being polite even to a murderous-looking Hahdhdhahi and completely in touch with his job at the same time. Lack decided he wasn't cut out for searching hostile villages.

Behind him, the women were beating their washing by the stream and the labourers and farmers were tending the meagre earth beyond the houses, where their withered oranges and olives and dates grew. But he had also noticed strangers standing in doorways and in the shade of the few dusty trees, and he suspected they were tribesmen who had filtered down in the night from the hills to stir up the trouble he was encountering now. He even suspected they had guns with them and, as his back tingled at the thought, he wished to God he was within the safety of the fort.

He decided he'd been a damned fool to volunteer for this duty with the Khaliti army. He'd been growing bored with Germany at the time and had felt that Khalit might be a good place to get in a little not very dangerous active service that would enable him to lord it over the newcomers in the mess when he returned to civilisation.

He hadn't allowed for a dangerous switch in policy and he certainly hadn't expected to be posted to a God-forsaken spot like Hahdhdhah.

He heard the crash of Sergeant Stone's boots behind him and turned. Stone was always the most militaristic of the sergeants. He was a short thickset man with a stiff blond thatch and he always conducted himself as though he were on parade with the Guards outside Buckingham Palace.

'All ready, sir,' he announced.

'What have we raised?' Lack demanded.

'All three carts of vegetables and grain.'

'Much trouble?'

'No, sir. But it's my opinion the bastards didn't want to let us have 'em.' Stone looked at Lack curiously. 'What's Mr Pentecost up to, sir? Why are we getting so fussy? We're still leaving on the twenty-first and we've got enough tinned stuff to keep us till then.'

'Major Pentecost,' Lack said glumly, 'like God, moves in a mysterious way.' He slapped his boot with his cane. 'Mohamed seen his wife?'

Stone grinned. 'Yessir. Vanished into one of the Toweida huts for ten minutes. I reckon it was long enough.'

Lack shrugged. 'OK,' he said, 'let's go. And, since there was some difficulty in getting the bloody stuff, let's have the Toweidas under Mohamed behind us, between the carts and the village, and you and I in front in the car so that the bastards can't bolt. We don't want any twisted knickers this trip.'

Back at the fort, Pentecost eyed the vegetables with approval. 'What was it like in the village?' he asked.

'Bloody nasty,' Lack replied feelingly. 'You could feel it. There were a bunch of bods down there who were never Toweida. They had Khusar stamped all over them.'

'Armed?'

'Nothing I could see. Though my back was tingling all the time. I reckon they've been intimidating the headmen. I heard a few snide remarks.'

'They know about the Sultan's new attitude?'

'Oh they know all right.'

Pentecost nodded. 'You might be good enough to ask Beebe if he'll drop in on me when he's a moment.'

Beebe didn't have a moment just then and he made no effort to provide one. It didn't really suit him to take orders from a young man who looked as though he ought still to be in diapers, and he finished what he was doing before strolling over to Pentecost's office. Outside the door he met Minto emerging.

'How's Billy?' he asked.

Minto grinned. 'Navel still central,' he said.

Beebe paused and lit a cigarette deliberately because he knew that Lack and Minto always made a point of putting out their own cigarettes before entering. One always did put out one's cigarettes before entering the commanding officer's sanctum sanctorum and one continued to do it even when the commanding officer was only a jumped-up captain with a face like a Botticelli cherub.

The action gave him surprisingly little pleasure, however. Pentecost had always been scrupulously polite and friendly towards him. His manner always made Beebe feel more important than he was and he realised that it sprang from a gift for making each of them feel he was their only friend. It was charm, Beebe knew, but he also knew that it wasn't a false or superficial charm; but something very real that came with breeding, something Lack would never have, for all his boisterous bonhomie, and he guessed it came through his family, from centuries of caring for other people.

As it happened, Pentecost didn't even notice he was smoking. He simply waved him to a chair, pushed a packet of cigarettes across the desk to him, and finished signing two or three papers before looking up.

'Sorry to keep you waiting, Mr Beebe,' he said with a disarming smile.

Beebe moved uncomfortably in the chair, to his own surprise keeping the cigarette below the desk where it couldn't be seen. 'Understand you want to see me,' he said.

'That's right.' Pentecost paused, rubbing his peeling nose before he spoke. 'Like a drink? I have a little left.'

'No thanks. Not for me.'

Pentecost didn't press him, and leaned back in his chair.

'You'll be fully aware of the Government's new policy towards Khalit, Mr Beebe,' he said. 'In fact, it was you who drew our attention to it.'

'Sure, I heard it on the radio.' Beebe was conscious of the studied formality of Pentecost's address. Lack and Minto seemed to have got over their surprise at having an American among them and gave him his Christian name but Pentecost still stuck to the stiffer title.

He eyed Pentecost warily. He was fidgeting with a book on the table and Beebe caught the title. The Cavalier Poets, for Christ's sake. The idea startled him at first then somehow he realised it went with Pentecost.

'Have they told you you've got to stay?' he asked.

Pentecost smiled. 'Not yet, Mr Beebe. Not yet. I still have my fingers crossed.'

'Will they?'

'So far we have no reason to think they will. For some reason that's beyond our ken, the Khaliti Command seems to be giving up the frontier.'

'Either way it's a lousy deal they've handed you.'

'It's nothing new,' Pentecost replied. 'We have to earn our keep.' He seemed a little shy, as though his sense of duty were something to be ashamed of in front of others. 'However, I do agree with you and I'm making a point of putting it all down on paper. Just in case something goes wrong and they start blaming us.'

Beebe stared at him. He seemed to have a strange solid belief in his own ability, as though his family traditions made sure of that. It was an odd self-satisfied attitude which was also, at the same time, self-effacing, because he seemed to feel that, with his background, it wasn't necessary for anyone else to appreciate his worth.

He was a funny little cuss, Beebe thought, puzzled as always by him. Pentecost – even the goddam name suited him! Vaguely prim, very correct, dainty, even the right overlay of religion that best suited his type of soldier – 'Oh, Lord, if I be too busy this day to remember Thee, do not thou forget me.'

'How about your wife?' he asked. 'What'll she think if you have to stay?'

Pentecost smiled. 'She's a soldier's daughter,' he said. 'She won't argue.' Though he wasn't so sure about it when he considered it. Soldiers' daughters weren't so stiff-upper-lip as they had been, because they were a great deal better educated and more realistic these days.

'I'd like to meet her,' Beebe found himself saying.

'I'll see that you do, Mr Beebe,' Pentecost said warmly. 'When we get to the coast. She's a pretty girl. You'd like her.'

Beebe found himself smiling and suddenly thought with surprise, goddammit, the sonofabitch's twisting me round his little finger!

Pentecost seemed to sense his irritation and came to the point quickly. 'Have you thought of your plans?' he asked, and Beebe became blunt and brusque again, feeling he'd been led up the garden path.

'They remain the same, I guess,' he said shortly. 'When I'm through I go.'

'Have you considered getting a bit of a wriggle on? Despite the absence of orders, Mr Beebe, circumstances have changed and I thought you might prefer to go a little earlier than you originally planned.'

'I guess I'll go when I've finished.' Beebe was still feeling that he'd been too ready to be friendly.

Pentecost smiled, undisturbed by his stubbornness. 'As you wish, Mr Beebe,' he said. 'That seems to be that then. Perhaps when you've time, you'll let me have it in writing. I should hate anyone to accuse me of keeping you here against your will. Or neglecting to get rid of you when I should.'

'Aw, hell…!' Beebe began angrily, but Pentecost looked up, a faint twisted smile on his face.

'They might, Mr Beebe,' he said.

He picked up his pen again and Beebe rose, aware somehow of a curious dissatisfaction with the interview. It had been his intention to run it his way, but it had been Pentecost who had kept the initiative all the time, despite his surly defiance.

He set off towards his own quarters still feeling faintly offended, then his cigarette began to burn his fingers and as he stopped to light a new one from the butt, he remembered Aziz and wondered what he was thinking about the new situation.

5

The coffee-hospitality was over. Thawab abu Tegeiga and his Deleimi were in a hurry. They were all young and most of them favoured shirts and trousers to the flowing robes of their elders, and Aziz stared at them with scorn on his thin features. Behind him in the shadows, the women chattering over their duties, the tinkling instruments and wailing flutes, the snake-charmers, the beggars and the dancers that always followed the camps went unheeded. Thawab had appeared at Addowara as the light went out of the hills, unasked and unwelcome, ignoring the green banner that stated it was Aziz's territory.

A few of the older men with him still wore the dyed cloaks or the traditional headcloths of their tribe, but all of them were armed to the teeth with rifles and pistols. All in all, Aziz had to admit, they were a younger group than those who stood behind him – more up to date and more urgent.

At their head, in the firelight that caught the colours of a woven rug and the burnish of copper cooking utensils, stood a small dark-faced man with the icy eyes of a fanatic. He wore the red Tayur cloak and black headdress of the Deleimi nation. Aziz knew him well. Majid the Assassin he was known as, and he knew that if Thawab gave the word Majid would shoot him dead and be willing to pay the price of his crime with his life.

By his side, as though he sought his protection, Thawab himself waited, like a cat, sleek and comfortable, his face cheerful. But Aziz's expression didn't melt. Though Thawab was only thirty-five, he was already putting on flesh. He liked to indulge himself too much and, despite his religion, Aziz knew he drank whisky when no one was looking. He wore Italian suits and shirts away from Khusar and there was a hard-featured Egyptian belly-dancer in a house in Makhrash.

Not that his sex life troubled Aziz much. He had a girl himself in his tent in the village, a Hassi from Gara, one of the mountain villages, a wild creature whom he kept for his old age, for dalliance, not for love. He dressed her in a Hejri cloak of blue brocade held by a jewelled haik pin, bangles and necklaces of gold coins and gold and silver baubles, and an elaborate bead headdress with a medallion between the eyebrows. It hid the hair and the ears but, when worn with little else but a filigree necklace and Berber earrings, could always excite the old man. She was anointed with perfumed oil and painted her toe nails and finger nails on his orders, and he had decided that when he moved back to Makhash she would go with him.

But everyone knew about her, as they did not know about Thawab's Egyptian. Thawab was soft-centred, a hypocrite, with ice in his veins, condemning all things Western while enjoying them himself, wearing his battledress to impress and not because he went into battle.

Thawab liked to laugh when he wasn't occupied with plans, short, strong, fair-skinned, and popular, and his people thought him a farseeing man. Aziz didn't. Neither did he trust him. He considered him insincere and ambitious and knew he made friends arbitrarily and was full of caprice. Even the simple humour that his followers noticed was false because always, even as he was careful not to stir Aziz to too much anger, he watched out of the corner of his eye for the opportunity that would give him political leadership of the Khusar peoples.

'My young men,' he was saying, 'tell me that Aziz el Beidawi has allowed himself to be tricked by his blond young friend from the fort.'

Aziz said nothing. He knew Thawab's men had been down in Hahdhdhah for some time, listening and watching, and he knew they made remarks about his friendship with Pentecost, comparing the young Englishman with the Circassian boys who had pleased him in his youth.

'They tell me,' Thawab continued, 'that the English Government has had second thoughts on their treaty with Tafas.'

'I have heard this, too,' Aziz replied warily.

'They tell me they will uphold the treaty after all. You have been telling us that the Englishman promised you they were to leave Toweida land.'

'The Englishman promised me nothing,' Aziz growled, despite his reputation fanatically faithful to those he considered his friends. 'He is a paid soldier, a mercenary, who must do what he is told.'

Thawab's mouth twisted with disdain. 'It is odd that the Lord Aziz treats with a mere mercenary,' he said.

Aziz's scimitar of a nose went up. 'There are some mercenaries I would rather treat with than great chieftains,' he growled.

It was a sharp dig and Thawab knew it was directed at him. He decided not to respond in kind.

'We were promised Toweida,' he said. 'If we are not given it, my young men insist that we take it.'

'And will Thawab be in the forefront of the attack?' Aziz asked slyly, knowing perfectly well that it had never been Thawab's habit to expose himself much.

Thawab smiled, but it wasn't a friendly smile. 'Soon the Dayi men will be here, with Ghalim, my cousin. They will join my Tayur and the Hawassi, their allies. There will be enough of us to defeat the wishes of Aziz.' He moved restlessly inside his clothes. He seemed to be summoning his courage. 'My young men tell me that Aziz grows too old to lead the Hejri,' he went on. 'And that when a man talks with the enemy instead of destroying him, he has reached the age when he should retire to his lands and grow cucumbers.'

Aziz's hand reached for the rifle. 'Thawab is eager to dispute my strength?' he asked quietly.

Thawab smiled. 'I am not eager,' he admitted. 'I am reporting what my young men say. My cousin Ghalim tells me that the Dayi think the same way.'

'Your cousin Ghalim is in your pocket. He is Thawab's tongue. When your young men stand up to me face to face and tell me they are more capable of leading than I am, when your silken skin has as many scars on it as mine has, then I will step down. Until then I am the leader of the Khusar peoples.'

'Thou art an old fool, Aziz,' Thawab said softly.

Aziz rose slowly to his feet but Thawab was already moving away, and Aziz was aware of the clear hostility in the eyes of his followers. There was a murmuring behind him, too, that told him that there were some even among the Hejri men who felt like Thawab and believed they would even now be cheated of the Toweida Plain.

Thawab turned and spoke over his shoulder. 'Thou art an old fool, Aziz,' he said again, more confidently. 'My father told me so. "Take no notice of Aziz," he said. "Leave him in the forefront of battle and he is happy, but don't trust him with the cares of the council. He has not the head for it." '

As he finished speaking, Thawab turned quickly. A few of his young men waited behind, in case any of Aziz's men tried to avenge the insult, then they too turned and left.

Aziz stared at the empty door of the tent, his eyes hot, his mind seething with rage, his breast hollow with the anger that was consuming him. Despite what he had said to Thawab he had not heard of the change of attitude in England and he resented the fact that he had received the news in this way from Thawab. He felt he had been made to look a fool. His face began to work and he found he was shaking with passion. He saw his followers edging away.

'Get me my horse,' he shouted in an explosion of rage. 'Get – me – my – horse!'

6

'Sir –' Pentecost sat bolt upright in bed as he felt Fox's hand shaking his shoulder ' – His Nibs is here again.'

Pentecost drew a deep breath. He had been expecting this for days. 'Aziz?'

'The man himself, sir. Sitting there, with his boys, in the darkness. You can just see 'em from the tower.'

Pentecost paused for a moment, then he nodded. This one was going to be tricky, he told himself. 'I'll be there,' he said. 'Have you told Mr Lack and Mr Minto?'

'Do you want me to, sir?'

'I think you'd better. And turn out the chaps.'

Fox stared at him. 'You going out there, sir?' he asked.

Pentecost had stripped off his pyjama jacket now and Fox studied his slender frame. 'Why not?' Pentecost said.

Fox stared at him for a second and was aware of a great feeling of affection for this young man whom he treated vaguely as a cleverer younger brother. He was well aware of the tension that had been growing around Hahdhdhah since the Prime Minister's speech.

'If you like, sir,' he volunteered impulsively, 'I'll come with you. Make a bit of a show. Best bib and tucker and so on. Bags of swank.'

Pentecost turned to look at him. His body was ashen in the light of the lamp because, since his fair skin burned easily, he never dared sit in the sun without his shirt like the other men in the fort. In the middle of his face, his nose glowed redly.

'Would you, Jim?' he said softly. 'Would you do that?'

The way he said it twisted Fox's heart. He was no sentimentalist but he trusted Pentecost and at that moment he seemed desperately lonely. He nodded.

'Yes, I would, sir, if you wanted me to.'

Pentecost smiled. 'Thank you, Jim,' he said. 'I didn't know you cared.'

Fox grinned and the frail sentimental moment passed easily because of Pentecost's facetiousness, when it might easily have left them awkward and wondering what next to say.

'All the same,' Pentecost said, 'I'm going to refuse your offer despite the thought behind it. It's me and Aziz. It always has been and that's the way it's got to stay. If he saw anyone with me, he'd have to bring someone, too. Face! Anything you can do, I can do better. You know the way they think. And that would prevent him speaking freely.'

'I understand, sir.'

'He'd have to be diplomatic. He'd have to remember that everything he said would be carried back to the Hejri and, probably, held against him later. After all, he's only their leader because he's the toughest or the craftiest. If they could quote his words at him, he might find himself in a sticky situation. And I suspect he's probably already in a sticky situation. Just as we probably are.'

When Fox had gone, Pentecost finished dressing and shaving, taking care to be precise. As he stared at himself in the mirror he wished he were a more martial figure. There had been no gilt's for a long time now, and the hills had seemed more silent than ever, and they had been aware of hostile eyes among the tradesmen who arrived to sell their wares in the fortress. He suspected that everyone, and especially Aziz, was waiting to see what would happen at Hahdhdhah. They had read the signs and now Aziz had come down personally to find out the truth.

They were both out on a limb, he decided. He, on account of a stubborn old man in Khaswe who was insisting on sticking to the last full stop and comma of his treaty with the British because he could see no sense in giving up territory; Aziz, because he was being jockeyed by Thawab and had to produce the goods he had promised.

Pentecost sighed, suddenly aware that they couldn't both win.

He finished bucking on his belt and walked out into the morning light. Lack was standing near the gate with Minto, and they both looked a little nervous. Faizan and Zaid Ghalib were watching them, with Int-Zaids Hussein,

Mohamed and Suleiman standing behind them. Beebe was there, too, swarthy and bear-like, a faint cynical stare on his face.

'Give him m-my love,' Minto said facetiously in a voice that was unexpectedly high-pitched. He cleared his throat. 'If he's come to ask us for cocktails, tell him I've got a date.'

'I hope to God he's not brought any more gifts,' Lack grumbled. 'You're not having my electric razor for the old bastard.'

Beebe's eyes flickered between them. All Lack's big talk washed over his head as though it were meaningless gibberish, and Minto he regarded as a boy still wet behind the ears. Pentecost he wasn't so sure of, but the chaffing still seemed stupid. They'd probably be calling silly remarks to each other, he thought, as Aziz's tommy gunners blew them to shreds.

He watched as Pentecost adjusted his uniform.

'Got your popgun?' Lack asked.

'No.' Pentecost gave him a wry smile. 'I'll chance it without.'

'Tell him we still appear to be leaving on the twenty-first, and have no hostile intentions,' Lack went on. 'Tell him I have no hostile intentions, in fact, towards anyone.'

Pentecost's mood changed and he straightened himself abruptly. He glanced round. A group of Dharwas and a few of the Civil Guards who had appeared for the 'inspection' he had ordered were watching him, their eyes wide in their dark faces. The gate opened slowly.

'After you, Cecil! It's all yours!'

Beebe watched from the rampart as Pentecost walked slowly across the dusty patch of ground towards the waiting line of horsemen. This I've seen before, he thought on television. John Wayne. Walking out to meet the Indians. It just isn't real. It just doesn't happen. It was too corny to be true. Anybody who could get on with the murderous old rogue beyond the rocks could get on with tarantulas.

As he halted by the group of boulders which had become their meeting place, Pentecost saw Aziz clap spurs to his horse. As it leapt away from the man carrying the green banner and halted beside him, Aziz made no attempt to climb from the saddle.

'I come in anger, Bin T'Khass,' he shouted, his thin face drawn. 'I come aware of treachery!'

Pentecost stared up at him, keeping his face expressionless. 'There has been no treachery on my part, Aziz,' he said mildly. 'Though I am aware that Khusar men watch me in the village of Hahdhdhah.'

For a moment there was silence as Aziz's tragic eyes rested on his face. 'Thawab's spies,' he said contemptuously, then he went on loudly, his voice bitter with reproach. 'My young men tell me,' he said loudly, 'that your Ministers do not intend to act with honesty.'

Pentecost remained calm. 'I have heard nothing, Aziz,' he said quietly.

Aziz stared at him, his eyes flashing. 'Cannot your Queen remove these men?' he demanded more quietly.

When he had set off down the scree slopes of the Urbidas to the plains, his brain had been full of the worms of rage, but now, faced with Pentecost's calmness and transparent honesty, he was unable to say the things he had wanted to say and found himself seeking to blame someone else. 'Cannot your Queen remove them?' he asked again.

'My Queen doesn't do that sort of thing, Aziz.'

'Then why is she Queen?' Aziz shouted. 'You should have a king! Men should not be ruled by a woman! They are no good at ruling!'

'She doesn't rule, Aziz,' Pentecost explained.

'Then why – ?' Aziz frowned and dropped the subject. 'Thou hast lied to me, Bin T'Khass,' he said harshly.

'I have not lied,' Pentecost pointed out. 'I told thee the facts. These facts still exist.'

'My young men tell me the English intend to uphold the treaty they made with Tafas el Taif and that the soldiers will not leave the fort.'

'I have heard nothing about staying, Aziz,' Pentecost persisted, raising his voice to make himself heard through the older man's anger.

'It is a bad treaty,' Aziz snorted, still trying not very successfully to be ill-tempered in front of Pentecost's friendliness. 'No man in Khalit wants it. They wish to rule themselves, not to be ruled by the British.'

'The British don't rule Khalit,' Pentecost pointed out. 'They simply support the Sultan under the treaty.'

Aziz's head jerked. 'The Sultan is no longer popular,' he said. 'Like us, the Khaliti wish to elect their own leaders. The days of hereditary government are done.'

Pentecost gave a slow, quiet smile. 'Your father was hereditary ruler of the Hejri, Aziz,' he pointed out gravely.

Aziz stared at him, then he grinned. 'Thou art no fool, Bin T'Khass, for all thy youth. That is so. But I am strong enough to lead them in the way they wish.'

'When you are old, will you not make your son ruler of the Hejri?'

Like Beebe, Aziz felt vaguely that his words were being chosen for him. 'I shall make him ruler of the Hejri,' he said sharply. 'It is up to him to remain ruler.'

'Thawab abu Tegeiga might think differently.'

Aziz's smile faded. 'Thawab abu Tegeiga always thinks differently,' he growled. 'Thawab abu Tegeiga is the cheating son of a camel. He and his young men drive me. They insist we take back what is our own. They know there is nothing can stop them if they so decide.'

'Only me, Aziz,' Pentecost said quietly.

Aziz eyed him warily. 'Thou art a great warrior, Bin T'Khass, but even thou art not that great.'

'Thawab might be surprised.'

Aziz paused again. Clearly the old man was troubled by the news that had been brought to him.

'Thou hast heard nothing of this decision to hold Hahdhdhah?' he asked more calmly, sincerely eager to be reassured.

'Nothing,' Pentecost said.

'That is good.' Aziz looked earnestly at him. 'Could not thy duty allow thee to leave?'

'My duty is to stay here until five noons from now. My duty is to hold Hahdhdhah until then against the Hejri, and if necessary against the whole Khusar country, against Thawab, even against thee, Aziz.'

Aziz looked uncomfortable. 'Toweida is my people's birth-right,' he said sullenly.

'Toweida will be yours five noons hence.' As he spoke, Pentecost watched the old man, guessing at the harsh words that had been spoken over the coffee in Addowara village and the tents in the Urbidas.

'I understand your problems, Aziz,' he went on and the old man gave him a twisted smile.

'I am glad this new friendship we have found, Bin T'Khass, is not to cease. I do not wish to part as friends to become enemies.'

'Nor I.'

The old man's heart jumped. Pentecost reminded him uncomfortably of his dead son. 'I shall always think kindly of thee, Bin T'Khass,' he said impulsively. 'Whatever happens.'

'And I of thee, Aziz.'

Aziz sighed. 'If your Ministers do not give us Toweida, I fear there will be much bloodshed.'

Pentecost shrugged. 'So be it.'

Aziz stared down at the young man in front of him. 'It is the will of Allah,' he said slowly. 'Thou art an honourable man, Bin T'Khass. Aziz is well aware of this. One cannot talk with men without becoming aware of these things.'

Pentecost bowed slightly.

Aziz was silent for a moment. His face was working but his anger had dissipated. 'If there is treachery, Bin T'Khass,' he said at last, 'I must fight. Even against thee.'

'I understand all this.'

'If it comes to war, it will not be possible to hold back my young men.'

'This I understand also.'

Aziz stared at Pentecost from the saddle, his mouth twisted.

'Allah protect thee, whatever comes.'

'God be with thee, too, Aziz.'

For a moment longer, Aziz gazed at Pentecost. Then the horse whirled as he clapped his spurs against its haunches; and as he reached the line of horsemen, its ends curled inwards like the horns of a bull, and they swept behind him as he headed for the hills.

For a long time, Pentecost stared after them, blinking at the dust they had stirred up which was blowing into his face. Then he turned round and slowly headed back towards the fortress.

7

'…All grain, rice and foodstuffs beyond what will be needed for the journey to be left. Weapons to be removed, together with all mechanical, electrical and radio equipment, and all ammunition and explosives. Timber, corrugated iron, iron piping, rush mats, plastic sheets may be left…'

'Toilet paper?' Lack asked sarcastically.

Pentecost looked up. 'That, too,' he said, frozen-faced.

While they talked, Beebe was scanning his instructions. 'The first party,' he read, 'will leave at 1100 hours under Captain Lack. It will consist of half the lorries, each manned by a driver and two guards, the cooking equipment and one of the armoured cars. The lorries will contain the women and children and civilian workers, and include the vehicle of Mr Beebe. They will carry half the mortars and machine guns, both light and heavy, and half the ammunition for all weapons. The Civil Guard will march behind. Bugler Owdi will accompany this party.'

He looked up at Pentecost sitting at the other side of the desk, small, smooth-faced, self-assured – a spruce little figure who looked as though he ought to have been editor of a woman's magazine rather than a soldier.

Beebe's eyes fell again to the sheets he held in his hand. 'The second group, under Captain Minto,' he read, 'will leave at 1130 hours and will consist of one lorry, 150 men of the Toweida Levies, and 40 men of the Dharwa Scouts. They will carry their weapons, forty rounds of ammunition and rations for three days. The last group under the Commanding Officer will leave at 1200 hours.

This group will consist of the remaining Toweidas and the remaining Scouts, marching in a formation to be decided later, the second armoured car and the rest of the lorries containing the remainder of the weapons and ammunition. Weapons and ammunition in all groups will be stowed so as to be easily accessible. A radio watch and a sharp look-out will be kept at all times. In case of trouble, a red Very light will be fired. If a Very light is seen, groups will close up on it and wireless communication will be opened immediately.'

Beebe looked across at Pentecost who was waiting patiently for him to finish reading, his elbows on the desk, his hands together in the form of a steeple, his finger tips neatly under his chin. He looked pleased with himself.

Beebe gave him a puzzled look. The orders he'd drafted were sound enough and seemed professional even to Beebe. Pentecost had prepared for all emergencies and had worked out a formation that would enable the first group to be in Hahdhdhah village before the last group left the fort. That way, Beebe realised, if Aziz decided to be difficult, they could hold a passage through the village until the last party arrived. Yet if there were shooting or treachery, they would still have one foot in the fort and could call back the lot if necessary.

Lack and Minto had finished reading now. 'Bit cautious, aren't you, Billy?' Lack asked.

'You never know,' Pentecost said calmly.

'But, hell, all that about splitting up the weapons and having everything ready. Thought you and Aziz were like that.' Lack held up two fingers.

'Just precautions, actually,' Pentecost said mildly. 'We'll be meeting Wintle at the other end of the pass.'

'Think the Civil Guards ought to be in the first group?' Lack asked. To Beebe he seemed to be trying to show off his knowledge and experience.

Pentecost didn't bat an eyelid. 'Yes,' he said. 'They can keep an eye on the women. The women are used to them. They're a bit scared of 'em, too,' he added. 'And that's no bad thing.'

Beebe thought of the forty or fifty scruffy-looking men in shreds of khaki uniform assembled in the courtyard. They had been arriving for some time now and, despite their general air of slovenliness, he had to admit they looked tough customers. They were reputed to dislike the Hejri as much as the Hejri disliked them.

As they finished speaking, Beebe stepped forward. 'I can't have my equipment in the first group,' he said abruptly, 'I shan't have time.

Pentecost looked up. 'Couldn't you hurry, Mr Beebe?' His voice sounded sad and reproachful, and Beebe suspected he was being manoeuvred again.

'I guess not,' he said firmly. 'I'm dealing with explosives and precision stuff.'

'Surely you could pack it beforehand?'

Beebe stared back at Pentecost, determined to remain his own man and take orders from no one.

'Mine's last-minute stuff,' he said. 'I need all the time I can get. Even an hour.'

Pentecost stared at him and Beebe had an uncomfortable feeling that he could see through the excuse to the meanness of spirit that had prompted it. 'Very well,' he said, not arguing. 'I'll arrange for your vehicle to go with my group.'

Lack spoke. 'Couldn't we leave at first light?' he asked.

'My orders say midday.'

'What's an hour or two when we're giving the place up?'

Pentecost surveyed Lack expressionlessly. He was still not convinced that they were giving the place up. Deep down in his mind, he suspected that somewhere something had gone wrong and he was sufficiently a professional soldier not to transgress against instructions in case circumstances arose whereby they were later flung in his face.

'I bet Tom Jeffreys at Zereibat won't wait till midday,' Lack said. 'And Howard at Umrah won't be out on a limb.'

'We're rather more out on a limb than either of them,' Pentecost pointed out quietly.

'But hell, Billy – !'

Pentecost sighed. It was not his duty to query orders, even if he suspected them. It was his duty to do as he was told. Exactly as he was told. Whatever he might think in private.

'Midday,' he said firmly.

five

1

It was a pity that General Cozzens' cocktail party coincided with the arrival of orders – both for him and the frontier. He had been expecting them for some time, half-hoping they wouldn't be what he feared and wishing to God that the Sultan would finally surface and let everybody know what he intended.

But the Sultan had wavered on and on until the last moment, congenitally unable to commit himself to something which might be politically dangerous, economically disastrous and bad for prestige, and had left it so late his intentions had become well-nigh impossible to carry out. When the orders finally arrived Cozzens didn't feel like holding a party at all.

Then, however, he remembered Charlotte Pentecost. If nothing else, he decided, it would give him the opportunity to talk to her in a way that would be less alarming than if he made a special call on her or summoned her to see him. And, in all honesty, he felt he could hardly send one of his aides with a duty like that.

'We'll go ahead with it,' he told his wife. 'But we'll keep it simple.'

His wife noticed that he looked tired but she knew he wouldn't want to be troubled by any concern for his welfare from her. They had been married a long time now and were beginning to look forward – most of the time unspeakingly because they were both a little afraid of it – to a retirement in which they would probably both be bored to tears.

'Right-ho!' she said. She was not a pretty woman and never had been but, like Charlotte Pentecost, she was a soldier's daughter and many years before she and Cozzens had been swept away by the warmth and the moon and the fact that there had been more men than women in one of the British Red Sea bases. When they had wakened up to reality, Cozzens had found himself with a wife who was lumpish and loud-voiced, and she had found herself married to a man who was not at all the romantic figure she'd expected.

She knew they were regarded as a funny couple and they were both well aware of the nicknames that had been given to them by the young officers of Cozzens' staff. But, rather to their surprise, they had both found that in each other they had got a better bargain than they'd ever expected. And now, Cozzens spent most of his time silently worrying that some fool would throw a bomb through their drawing-room window when she was arranging the flowers, while she spent her time in a mute fear that one morning when he started his car someone might have planted a plastic charge behind the facia board.

2

The Minister from London was big, fleshy and pink, as though he took great care with his health but rarely obtained any exercise, and at that moment he seemed overworked to the point of having a driven look in his eyes. Watching him with his enigmatic dark glance, Rasaul managed to feel sympathy for him. The Khaliti Ministers wore the same look, after days – weeks now – of trying to persuade the Sultan to make his decision.

The Minister was dressed for the part, in evening dress with the red ribbon of an order across his shirt front and a small cluster on his lapel of miniature medals won between 1939 and 1945. He looked like a Minister, Rasaul had to admit – a Minister of the arrogant northern country which still hadn't entirely grown out of the humbugging ways it had developed when it had had its empire. Cozzens, too, was playing the part. He was dressed in the blue bum-freezer jacket of a hussar regiment, with a gold-braided waistcoat and skin-tight overalls, and looked exactly what he was – an elderly cavalry officer trying to put on a show.

It didn't convince Rasaul much. Behind the soldier's expressionless visage he saw irritation, anger and bitterness, and he knew from reports that Cozzens had put on a spectacular display of fury when he had received his instructions. It had been followed by a flurry of orders that had placed about the streets the groups of soldiers who had stopped him three times on his way that evening, stern-faced young Britishers a little puzzled by the volte face of the Khaliti Government and a little nervous about what it meant to them in terms of life and death.

'I take it your orders have all been issued,' the man from Westminster was saying.

'Indeed they have,' Cozzens replied with a briskness he didn't feel. 'The Sultan's instructions are being transmitted to Dhafran at this moment, to be passed on to

Umrah, Afarja and Hahdhdhah.' His eyes flickered as he stopped speaking. And just in time, too, he thought sourly. One more day and they'd have been too late.

'Since the Sultan has made his decision,' the Minister went on, 'it's up to us all to see that his requests are carried out. His subsidies will be re-negotiated, of course, with the Shukri, the Jezowi, the Muleimat and the Khadari peoples guarding the Dharwa passes, and we'll try also to arrange something with the Hejri and the Deleimi.'

Cozzens just hoped to God that the Shukri and the Jezowi and the Muleimat and the Khadari would be willing to accept renegotiated subsidies. He hadn't for a moment the slightest doubt that the Hejri and the Deleimi would reject out of hand any offer that was made, but they needed the passes to make the border safe. If the passes through the Dharwa Mountains were closed the whole of the Toweida Plain was in jeopardy.

His face expressionless, he listened to the chatter with hatred in his heart for Sultan Tafas. Plans had been brought for new married quarters for Khaswe – from estates to blocks of flats – all with air conditioning, refrigerators, schools, churches, shops, cinemas, beach clubs, bars, all for the men who were to hold Khalit for the Sultan – in the firm belief that the employment they would bring to Khaswe would endear the British to the Khaliti people. And Whitehall-itis had already got rid of the pamphlets with the basic Khalit-Arabic phrases for 'Get lost!' and 'Hands up!' and replaced them with new ones which included 'Good morning' and 'How are you?' For once they were being asked to stay and the British Government was trying to look wanted.

The Minister was moving away now and Cozzens reached for another drink.

'I hope the Minister made everything clear?' he said to Rasaul.

The Khaliti made a face. 'Only too clear. I just hope it won't be as bad as I expect and that you have enough troops.'

Cozzens felt embarrassed. 'I expect my government's drumming up more men,' he said. 'But it's not easy these days with commitments elsewhere. They can't possibly arrive before the month's out.'

'What about Hahdhdhah then?' Rasaul asked.

Cozzens turned and glanced uneasily about him for Charlotte Pentecost. She was talking to his wife who had had instructions to keep her busy until Cozzens was ready to talk to her.

'I can do nothing for Hahdhdhah,' he said stiffly.

As Rasaul moved away, Cozzens lit a cigarette to collect his thoughts, brushed off an American businessman who was anxious for a résumé of the situation, and the wife of one of his colonels who was eager to be pleasant to him for her husband's sake, and crossed to Charlotte Pentecost. His wife saw him coming and rose.

As she moved off, her face a mask of cheerfulness she didn't feel, her husband dropped on to the settee in the seat she had just vacated. She saw him pat Charlotte Pentecost's hand and offer her a cigarette, and she sighed, wondering what awful lies he was going to have to tell her and how good he was going to make them sound. He had never been very skilful at telling untruths, she knew.

Cozzens also knew how bad he was at gilding the lily and as he lit Charlotte Pentecost's cigarette he was

114

wondering how he could tell her the truth and still give her the impression that her husband was in no danger when he was.

'Never very good at these affairs,' he said in an intimate, friendly voice as he stuffed away his lighter. 'Hate small talk. How's your father, Charley?'

'Finding the New Forest a little dull,' Charlotte Pentecost said. 'He was never a man to take easily to having nothing to do. He's thrown himself into good works, but I think he's bored stiff by the elderly ladies and the vicars who make up the committees he works on.'

'Got that coming to me before long,' Cozzens said. 'Not looking forward to it very much. Mother?'

'Much the same.'

Charley had heard about her mother and Cozzens, but she was giving nothing away.

'H'm! How's Billy?'

'The usual. He never seems very downhearted in his letters.'

'Remarkable chap,' Cozzens said enthusiastically. 'Knew his father, too. Not so professional as Billy.'

Charley crushed out her cigarette and faced Cozzens squarely. For some time she had been wanting to know how long her husband was to be in Hahdhdhah and, now, with Cozzens indulging in euphoric nostalgia, seemed as good a time as any to find out.

'I miss him,' she said as an opening gambit.

'I'm sure you do,' Cozzens said, realising that she was offering him the opportunity he was seeking.

'I'll be glad when he's back at the coast.'

'So will I, Charley.'

'Will it be long, do you think?' she asked.

For a moment Cozzens puffed at his cigarette. This was the sixty-four-thousand-dollar question, because he had been very firmly instructed that there were to be no involvements on the frontier, no matter what happened.

'Between you and me,' he had been told, 'we've been pushed into this business, by a few not very far-seeing officials in the past who failed to leave any get-out clauses for emergencies like this. We had to accept it.'

Cozzens became aware of Charley watching him closely. 'I hope it won't be too long,' she said, grinning engagingly, 'because there are too many of your bright young men who are suffering from the heat and the impression that a grass widow's easy meat.'

Cozzens sighed. 'Things have changed, Charley,' he said. 'But they'll get him back as soon as they possibly can.'

She looked quickly at him, and his heart jumped abruptly as he noticed how much like her mother she was.

'But I thought they were marching out tomorrow,' she said. Cozzens swallowed. 'So did I, Charley,' he said. 'But that was before the Sultan finally made up his mind and formally requested help.'

Her eyes hardened and for a moment she was silent, then she went on in an unsteady voice. 'You mean he isn't coming? Is that what you mean?'

'I'm afraid that's exactly what I mean, Charley.'

'Oh, God!' she said abruptly, and she spoke with such misery it twisted Cozzens' heart.

'I'm sorry, Charley.'

'But I always understood –'

'Billy's a soldier. So am I. We have to do as we're told. And you've heard all the bangs going off in Khaswe. We've rather got our hands full.'

'You mean he might have to stay up there for a long time?'

Cozzens gestured lamely. 'He might. He's quite safe, though.'

She looked at him with an expression of pure hatred on her face. 'I'm not worried about his safety,' she said coldly. 'I'm worried about me. Us. It's all right for that dreadful old man in the Palace to insist on our staying in Khalit but has he thought what situations like this mean to families? It's no wonder soldiers' wives are always subject to nasty little innuendoes about sex. It's no wonder so many of them get neurotic and go off the rails. I need my husband. I need him alongside me. And I don't mean just at cocktail parties, either.'

As she stood up and turned away, Cozzens rose quickly, too, trying to pretend he hadn't just been snubbed. He put out his cigarette and fished for another, catching sight of a bat outside in the garden beyond the embroidered Rabat curtains. It was swooping among the tamarisks and cypresses, and he watched it for a moment. Then, as he jerked his jacket straight, the windows seemed to leap in their frames and, almost with the rattle of the glass, he heard the heavy thud of an explosion nearby – heavier than any he'd so far heard. Undoubtedly it was something big going up.

Oh, God! he thought. Off we go again!

3

There were four Khaliti operators in the radio room at Dhafran, each equipped with a receiver, transmitter and headset, and the first bomb that went off wiped out the lot of them and all their equipment in one blow, leaving them sprawled among their chairs, their dead staring faces stuck like pin-cushions with the splinters of bakelite.

The second bomb exploded in the headquarters block and then there was a series all going off together – in the MT park, the telephone switchboard room and the officers' mess. The thud of the first explosions brought the officers to their feet with a jerk. They were just sitting with their last drinks before bed when the mirror suddenly leapt from the wall and broke into pieces, and the mess waiter was on his knees in a wreckage of tables and chairs, pawing dazedly at the shattered glass from the bar with bleeding fingers.

As they dashed from the ante-room they saw that the front doors of the mess had been blown off their hinges and that the hall was a shambles of trampled glass, torn carpet, and broken palms. There appeared to be three dead men in uniform there, one European and two Khaliti, their bodies shockingly lacerated.

'Oh, Jesus,' someone said. 'They got Philip! He was telephoning his wife in Khaswe. For God's sake, shove the carpet over him!'

The Khaliti doctor was already on his knees by one of the mess waiters. He was sitting with his back to the wall and appeared to be cradling a shattered pot plant which had been blown from outside clean through the doors. His eyes were open but he made no complaint.

As the doctor got down to work the other officers picked their way past him, snatching at webbing and belts as they went. Outside, the air stank of smoke and there was a car burning by the headquarters building which appeared to be on fire. In front of it lay the guard, minus a leg, twitching and screaming in a way that hurt eardrums still recovering from the pressure of the explosions. Already the sound of a fire-engine was striking across the livid parade ground.

While they were still trying to decide where to head for first, the Brigadier appeared from his quarters. He was a tall man no longer young and no longer a British officer, thin as a lathe with a gaunt ravaged face that looked as though it were made of tanned leather. Jeremy Wintle had been in places like Dhafran for most of his life – so long, in fact, even the Hejri and the Jezowi sang ballads about 'Owinda-el' around their fires. He knew whom he could buy and whom he could bribe with promises of power or revenge upon ancestral enemies, and he was addressed always and with respect – even by his enemies – as Reimabassi, Warrior Lord. Nothing surprised him. Not even bombs.

'What in God's name was that?' he demanded calmly.

'The bastards must have planted explosives, sir,' someone said. 'Though Christ knows how.'

'Who's that under the carpet?'

'Philip, sir. He was in the hall telephoning his wife in Khaswe.'

'Always was a bit abrupt on the telephone,' Wintle growled without intending to be smart or funny. 'Someone had better put me in the picture.'

It was difficult, because no one else was in the picture, either, and they were still trying to explain when a British sergeant appeared in a car. He looked shocked.

'Sir – sir – !'

'Spit it out, man,' Wintle snapped. 'What happened?'

'Bombs, sir.'

'Where?'

'Headquarters block, Sir! Door blown in. Man killed there. Guardroom! That one nearly got me, sir. MT park, sir! Sergeant Waterhouse, Int-Zaid Zufril and two of the Scouts killed there.'

Wintle frowned. 'What about the wireless shack?'

'That as well, sir. There's nothing left of it.'

'Blast!' Wintle had been sending urgent messages to the radio room at the Palace in Khaswe for weeks now and was badly in need of replies. He turned to one of his officers. 'You'd better get it working again. Pretty damn' quick, too! We're expecting the Old Boy's instructions from Dhafran.'

'About Hahdhdhah, sir?'

'And Umrah and Zereibat. I've been warned to expect them. The old fool must have finally and officially decided to give up the Toweida Plain. I've been advising it for weeks.'

As the officer vanished, Wintle turned to the sergeant. 'Telephones?' He was known for not wasting words.

'Cut, sir. The bomb at headquarters smashed the switchboard.' Wintle turned to the remaining officers. 'Malpass, run field telephone wires to all necessary points. And get a temporary switchboard connected up.'

'Sir!'

'Ahbub!' A short Dharwa zaid stepped forward. 'Get down to the MT park and see what you can make of the shambles.'

'Yes, Reimabassi.'

'Dec –' Wintle turned to the medical officer kneeling on the floor ' – can you get some of your people down to the guardroom and these other places? Storrs, see what you can make of the radio shack and let me know. See if you can find out what the position is. We must have everything working again and all traffic cleared. Those chaps on the frontier start off at midday tomorrow, and I want their channels working in case of trouble.'

4

All morning they had seen little groups of Hejri warriors moving about the few tree-grown spaces where the winter rains collected off the sides of the hills, and there had been a great number of pin-points of light in the hills the night before. The last Toweida tradesmen had brought news of strange horsemen in Hahdhdhah village, and Pentecost knew they were Hejris waiting to sweep into the fort as soon as the last lorry was clear. They were lying low, though, and he was puzzled because it wasn't a Hejri habit to lie low and he had expected them to be nearer and more demonstrative. Nevertheless, he knew they were still all round him in the lower folds of the hills, waiting for that final exultant rush that would prove to them for good and all that the Toweida Plain was Hejri once more.

Aziz's celebration would be quite an affair, he thought. He sat in on a diffa once with Wintle when he'd been in Dhafran and he could still remember the servants staggering through the crowd into the vast white woollen tent carpeted with Berber rugs, carrying the rice and meat on a huge silver tray. It had had an inscription running round it in flowing Arabic letters – To the glory of God, and of Allah, His prophet, and in trust of mercy at the end – and it had been full to the brim, edged with rice in a mound eight inches wide. Three grown lambs had been slaughtered to make a pyramid of meat in the centre such as the honour of a chieftain demanded, and surmounting the lot had been the heads, the ears out flat and the jaws gaping to show the cooked tongues and the long incisor teeth between the purple lips. It had been placed in the space between the guests while a stream of servants brought the copper bowls in which the cooking had been

121

done and ladled out the rest of the meat, the entrails, the yellow fat and the brown twists of muscle and skin.

They had taken their lead from the chief – 'In the name of God, the merciful, the loving kind' – then they had set about it, occasionally dipping their fingers into it and plunging their burnt hands into their mouths to cool them. Wintle had thoroughly enjoyed himself, Pentecost remembered, though he himself had been faintly disgusted by the whole thing, by the way the Khaliti had torn up the meat with their fingers and kneaded the rice into little white balls and flicked them into their mouths with the thumb, stuffing themselves until their movements had grown sluggish and they had sat gasping for breath.

Although his precise manners had prevented him enjoying the obscenity of over-eating, he almost wished he could have been present at Aziz's party. He hoped the old man would enjoy it.

He certainly intended to enjoy his own celebration with Charley. A few drinks and a meal at the Intercontinental, a bottle of bubbly and a large brandy each, maybe a bit of smoochy dancing to the Egyptian dance band, with Charley draped over his shoulders, her cheek against his, her body hugging him so that he could feel every curve and indentation of it against himself. He half smiled. He knew how it would end. It had happened before.

Suddenly, without a word, she'd grab his hand and pull him outside, and they'd hail a taxi back to the flat. She'd have her shoes in her hands as he unlocked the door and she'd be throwing her clothes across the room and searching with her lips for his mouth even before he'd slammed it behind them. That ought to be quite a celebration, too, he thought.

For a while, he'd thought they weren't going to get away with it. Every day for the past week he'd been expecting the wash-out signal on the evacuation to come through – specially after the speech the Prime Minister had made – and the fact that they had got away with it had made their celebration the night before an occasion to remember. Lack had been grey-faced and bad-tempered as he'd left the fort, unable to make up his mind whether he was glad to be going or not. Almost, it had seemed, he had preferred to stay where he was to nurse his misery.

'Don't trip over your liver, chum,' Beebe had advised cheerfully. 'It's hanging out this morning.'

Beebe was in a gay mood, glad to put Hahdhdhah behind him and looking forward to the perquisites of civilisation, and he stared about him through the open gates of the fort as though seeing the land around them for the first time. Through the archway, the Urbida hills looked like shelves of coarse-faced stone, joined to steep bare walls by narrow gorges and sandy paths, with the Addowara Pass into Khusar country like a knife-cut in the rock.

Nearby, Pentecost was giving final instructions to his party. He was dressed like a Christmas tree, with map case and binoculars hung about him, with all his equipment, revolver, pack and water bottle. For Christ's sake, Beebe thought, they were only going to get in the goddam lorries and ride across the Plain of Toweida to the River Sufeiya! He expected to be in Dhafran in three days and at the coast in another week.

He glanced in the direction Pentecost was staring, towards the cloud of yellow dust that was being stirred up by Minto's marching files of Scouts, Civil Guards and Toweida Levies. They looked smart enough but Beebe had thought they were all glad to turn their backs on the fort. Beyond them, he could see Lack's lorries just entering Hahdhdhah village. Behind him Fox was sitting in the scout car, his eyes on the marching men, his head bent over the radio which had suddenly begun a frantic squawking.

In the fort, watched by a Hahdhdhah boy, the garrison's herd of goats were bleating in their pen near the timber store. Tonight, they'd probably all be slaughtered by the Hejris for their celebrations. They'd been living in the foothills watching the fort for weeks now and they were probably growing hungry and eager for a few home comforts. Beyond the goats he could see the stacked timber, the corrugated iron and asbestos sheets, all the pens crammed with enough stores to make a man wealthy for life. If Aziz had any sense, he'd clap a guard on it and keep the lot for himself but, Beebe suspected, he'd never even think of it and the whole lot would be smashed up and probably set on fire in one wild lustful looting that would leave them all as poor as when they'd started.

He saw Pentecost glance again at his watch. He could just imagine Lack sitting in the other scout car in Hahdhdhah, impatiently waiting for Stone at the radio to announce that the final lorry had left the fort.

Fox looked up. 'We're last out, sir,' he said. 'Captain Jeffreys left Zereibat ages ago and Captain Howard's just started leaving Umrah. They're in contact with each other.'

'Bit early,' Pentecost commented, his eyes on the road.

'Normal enough for Captain Howard, sir,' Fox grinned. 'Always was a bit like a pram in a panic.'

He paused, listening to the radio and watching the plain. 'Hope they didn't pick 'em up in Dhafran, sir,' he went on. 'The Brigadier'll play hell if he hears.'

Beebe interrupted. 'Do we have to wait for the exact moment?' he asked. 'Isn't it just a goddam formality?'

'To me,' Pentecost said coldly, 'midday is midday, not eleven-thirty or eleven-forty-five.'

'Your watch might be wrong.'

'I don't wear watches that go wrong.'

Beebe grinned. 'Your buddy at Zereibat seemed to think his watch might be wrong.'

Fox looked up, his pencil starting to move across a signal sheet. 'Sounds like they're clear of Umrah now, sir,' he said. 'Captain Howard's reporting to Captain Jeffreys at Zereibat that tribesmen are heading past him to take his place.'

'No comment from Dhafran?'

'No, sir. No comment.'

Pentecost was frowning. 'Funny,' he said. 'Have you heard Dhafran at all this morning?'

Fox was frowning too, now. 'Come to think of it, no, sir. And since you mention it, Captain Howard sounds a bit fussed about it. Hang on a minute, sir –' he grinned '– here they are now! Sounds like a rocket for him. They're telling him to get off the air. They're telling him – sir!' Fox's commentary grew to a shout as his pencil leapt across the sheet. 'They're telling him he's – sir, for Christ's sake, it's coming through in clear! It's priority to all Dhafran stations! "Umrah, Aba el Zereibat and Hahdhdhah will be held." ' Fox spoke slowly, repeating the message aloud.' "There will be no withdrawal – repeat no withdrawal – from the frontiers or from the Toweida Plain." '

Pentecost's jaw had dropped and Fox looked up, startled. 'That's what it says, sir.'

Alarmed suddenly, Beebe saw the expression on Pentecost's face tighten. Fox was staring at him with bewildered eyes.

'The last bloody minute,' he said furiously. 'The eleventh bloody hour! There've been bomb attacks in Khaswe and at Dhafran. They've been off the air since last night.'

'Shut up, Sergeant!' Pentecost turned to snap at Fox. 'Tell him to repeat it. We've got to have it repeated. Make it "Most Immediate".'

There was a tense silence in which Beebe realised that they were all watching Pentecost, all of them aware of the sudden change in the situation. Then they heard the harsh cheeping in the headphones again. Pentecost bent forward as Fox's pencil whipped across the paper.

'Again, Sergeant! I must have that once more.'

The radio clattered again then Fox slammed the switch over and turned to stare at Pentecost.

Pentecost was still studying the message, then Beebe saw him straighten up and run, clanking a little in his equipment, to stare across the plain. He swung round on Fox.

'Sergeant Fox! The Very pistol! Fire a red, and then, for God's sake, raise Captain Lack!'

Startled, Beebe heard the pop of the pistol and saw the Very light soar into the air. Immediately, his eyes swinging to the plain, he saw the marching men half-way to the village come to a halt. For a while, they seemed to be in some sort of confusion down there, then he saw it was because the lorry was turning. Immediately, he heard

Pentecost speaking into the microphone, still calm, still surprisingly unruffled.

'Lack? Pentecost! Get your people back here! Repeat: Get your people back here! Double-quick!' There was a pause then Pentecost's voice rapped out again, hard and peremptory. 'Don't argue! Do as you're told!'

He swung round on Fox. 'Sergeant, wait until you see them, then get that car back inside the gates! Fauzan, close the side gate and get your men up on the walls! See that every man's in position to cover those people outside! I want a look-out on the tower and every man armed! Get the lorries inside the gate!' He turned to Beebe and the urgency vanished as he spoke in his usual mannered politeness. 'Mr Beebe, I'm afraid you're going to be disappointed.'

'For God's sake!' Beebe roared, his temper exploding abruptly. 'Just because that old fool in Khaswe doesn't know whether he's on his ass or his elbow, I'm not staying here!'

'You're very welcome to leave any time you wish, Mr Beebe,' Pentecost said icily. 'Though I don't recommend it until tempers have been allowed to cool a little. You might not make it to Hahdhdhah. Now, if you'll excuse me – '

He turned away and Beebe heard him issuing orders to the Iraqi foreman. A moment later Beebe was back inside the walls of the fortress.

As he jumped down, livid with rage, the other lorries of Pentecost's group were swinging through the gate, raising a cloud of dust, and Beebe, his face twisted with dislike for everything Khaliti, saw them roar towards him one after the other and their drivers jump from the cabins and run to the walls. Fox was the last to appear, driving the little scout car himself with the Toweida driver clinging to the rear.

'They're on their way, sir,' he shouted.

'For sweet Jesus' sake!' Following Pentecost to the ramparts, Beebe stood gesturing, almost speechless with rage ' – for sweet goddam Jesus' sake, you're not going to start a battle, are you?'

Pentecost, who seemed to be in half a dozen places at once, helping to set up a machine gun, driving the Toweidas and Dharwas on to the ramparts, directing the lorries away from the entrance, stopped for a moment.

'I'm not starting a battle, Mr Beebe,' he said stonily. 'But I'm afraid I'm going to be involved in one. You, too. So it behoves you to get your head down.'

For a second, Beebe stood staring at him in fury, then he glanced out through an embrasure. Out on the plain, he could see green banners and a few small mounted figures emerging from the hills. Then a shot echoed softly on the distant air and he dodged hurriedly back against the wall.

'For Christ's sake – !' Beebe stared about him, startled, bewildered and angry.

He'd done it wrong! For once he'd left it too late!

5

For a moment, he remained like that, his back against the wall, then, in a single movement, he swung round to the embrasure near his shoulder and stared across the plain, his mind shocked, hardly able to believe that what he was witnessing was really happening.

Minto's men were hurrying back to the fortress now as fast as they could move, surrounding the lorry that held the big transmitter with which they contacted Khaswe, and Beebe could see Minto standing on the running board, directing them to move faster. Then, as he watched, he saw the mounted figures he'd noticed emerging from the lulls begin to thunder towards the open gate of the fortress.

'Zaid Fausan!' Pentecost's voice came shrilly. 'Are you ready?'

'Ready, Abassi!' Fauzan shouted back.

Fox looked up from the scout car where he was still sitting with the headphones on. 'Sir! Dhafran again! More instructions from the coast. "Hahdhdhah garrison to remain in control. Evacuation instructions cancelled. No shooting unless attacked." '

Pentecost gave a shrill bark of laughter. He was standing on the rampart over the gate staring towards Hahdhdhah village, his eyes squinting against the sun. Fox joined him, quickly checking the machine gun the Dharwas had set up.

Beebe pushed between them, still savagely angry. 'See here,' he shouted, 'you can have all the goddam battles you want, but I'm an American citizen and I'm not involved in your baby war!'

Pentecost half-turned, still icily polite. 'Not just now, Mr Beebe,' he pleaded. 'I'm rather busy at the moment.'

'I'm leaving here,' Beebe snarled.

'How?' Pentecost still managed to be polite, in spite of the confusion and the noise, and Beebe could have murdered him for his calmness when he felt harassed and afraid himself. 'How do you propose to do it?'

'I've got a Stars and stripes in my lorry,' Beebe shouted. 'I'll wave it. That'll stop the bastards shooting at me.'

'It's not something I'd take a chance on, Mr Beebe.'

Beebe glared then he turned and, in his fury, almost fell down the steps from the rampart to his lorry. A burst of firing from above made him jump and, through the still-open gates, he saw lorries appearing one after another from the village and roaring towards the fortress in a group, the dust in clouds about them. From the middle of them came a series of faint frantic squawks from Owdi's bugle, then he saw the Hejri horsemen, joined now by the group which had emerged from the hills, trailing the lorries – almost like Red Indians, Beebe thought, shocked.

He had reached his own vehicle now and had climbed into the back. Sweating with rage and fear he rooted among his equipment with stumbling fingers for the flag he always carried in case of emergencies. He'd used it before now, tied to the aerial or fastened across the bonnet and it had always worked. Crowds had always parted and he'd been allowed to pass. He snatched it from under his valise at last and threw it from the lorry. The Iraqi driver picked it up.

As he began to unfold it, Beebe stared again through the gates of the fort. Lack's lorries were now approaching Minto's hurrying men and Minto halted and about-faced, and they heard the rattle of rifles, then, as the lorries caught them up, Minto's group doubled for the fortress, the lorries close behind them as a barrier. Pentecost's voice came as he started to count the vehicles.

'One short,' he said.

As Minto's Toweidas broke away, a flurry of horsemen charged down on them and Beebe saw Pentecost nod to Fox. As the machine gun chattered, Beebe saw the dust jump among the galloping horsemen. A horse went down and one or two figures fell from their saddles but he couldn't tell whether it was because they were hit or because they were sheltering behind their mounts, then the first of the Toweidas were hurrying through the gate, gasping and panting, several of them without their weapons.

As they flung themselves to the dusty earth of the square, Pentecost was among them like a small fury, kicking them to their feet so that they scrambled up in terror of him and began to hurry to the ramparts where Zaid Fauzan swung at them with his fists, hurling insults at them as they got into position. In spite of all the training Pentecost had given them, they hadn't much idea of shooting, and they began to fire wildly, their bullets flying among the running men on the plain. But Lack's lorries had now formed a defensive box round the rest of the Toweidas and Dharwa Scouts, and the whole group was beginning to move towards the fortress in disciplined fashion, keeping pace with each other while the horsemen circled them, making short nervous rushes, unwilling to come too close to the disciplined fire of the Dharwas or the ancient automatics Lack had got going.

As they came within range of the fortress the horsemen stopped and were drawn up, screaming insults, and as the firing subsided, Beebe became aware of the Iraqi still holding the flag and staring at him uncertainly. He realised he had been so absorbed in the manoeuvres on the plain, he had forgotten his own situation.

'Get out there and wave it!' he shouted, climbing into the driver's seat of the lorry. 'We're going!'

'Now?'

'Sure! Before they close the goddam gates!'

The Iraqi didn't seem very happy but he unfurled the flag on its staff and headed for the gate, waving it wildly in front of him.

6

The gesture was seen by the Deleimi rifleman with the cold eyes of a hawk who was holed up in a huddle of rocks not a thousand yards away. Majid the Assassin had the courage of a fanatic. He was a Tayur reim and a Deleimi, accepting allegiance to no one but Thawab, and he was one of the few Deleimis who had worked himself near enough to the fort to be able to shoot effectively.

His indifference to death was well known, and if he were to be wounded he hoped he would show no weakness, because he had no fear of wounds or mutilation – or even of death. If he had been told to do so, he would have run on to Fox's hot gun muzzle. Fanaticism was dying out in the northern tribes these days as young men grew more educated and owed their allegiances not so much to Allah and his prophet as to political or nationalistic creeds. But despite this, Majid was an old-fashioned man and had never quite outgrown the ingenuous belief that death in battle was the true way to enter Heaven. He was quite indifferent to his fate, hoping only that he would be spared long enough to take with him one of the white-skinned Roumis or a few of the whey-faced Toweidas, and the waving of the flag in the gateway caught his attention at once.

He pushed his Garand rifle forward slowly until the sights came into line. Through the V of the backsight he could see a small moving triangle of grey which was the Iraqi foreman's shirt. Beebe's lorry had moved forward and the Iraqi was standing in front of it near the gates.

The rifle followed him, the foresight moving up slowly, and pausing for a tiny instant of time as he steadied his breathing, Majid took the first pull of the trigger.

Occupied with his battle, Pentecost didn't notice what was happening by the gates until he turned and saw Beebe's lorry edging forward and the Iraqi foreman waving the flag in the gateway.

'What in God's name is that man doing out there, Mr Beebe?' he shouted in his high-pitched voice.

'He's stopping your goddam battle!' Beebe roared back in a fury. 'So that I can get the hell out!'

'Bring him back at once!'

Just at that moment, there was a lull in the firing and the single shot from the hills seemed to echo round the walls. The Iraqi had stopped dead and Beebe watched with horrified fascination as the flag appeared to drop in slow motion from his hands. The Iraqi leaned backward – so slowly he seemed to be hanging by an invisible thread – then his body buckled in the middle, and he sat down abruptly, and slowly, just as slowly, toppled over to lie sprawled on his back in the dust, a red splodge where the bridge of his nose had been.

While Beebe was still staring, the last of the panting infantry began to arrive in the fortress, stumbling past the body of the Iraqi without even looking at it. Lack's scout car appeared, with Owdi on the back optimistically trying to blow the 'Charge', and the final single figure of a small limping Dharwa private, then the plain was empty of running figures except for the horsemen and a lonely figure staring bewildered and angry at the gate whom Pentecost recognised as Aziz, his bannerman holding his green flag just behind him.

'Close the gates!' Pentecost shouted and Beebe, still unable to believe his eyes, saw Sergeant Stone and several of the Dharwas slam the huge gates and lift the heavy cross-bar into position.

'Shore it up, Sergeant,' Pentecost called, and Stone waved and sent several of his men towards the timber store. They began to return a moment later with lengths of timber.

The horsemen were still screaming their hatred as the solitary figure of Aziz rode slowly towards the Urbida Hills, followed by his bannerman, and Pentecost's heart went out to the old man, feeling a sense of guilt that didn't really belong to him and wondering how in God's name he could get a message to him to say it wasn't his fault.

Lack was standing by the scout car as he joined him, still cursing, his face thunderous.

'Who was that bloody fool waving a flag?' he shouted. 'What the hell was he trying to do?'

'Never mind that now!' Pentecost's face was full of cold fury. 'What delayed you?'

Lack drew a deep breath.

'Those bloody Toweidas,' he snarled. 'Usual left-foot right-foot trouble. Ran like a lot of bloody rabbits. Int-Zaid Suleiman with 'em. It couldn't have been worse. We were right in the middle of the narrowest street in the place with that bloody Owdi screeching in my ear to know what to blow. Int-Zaid Hussein would have gone, too, I reckon, if I hadn't flung him in the lorry. Why in Christ's name did they leave it to the last minute?'

'Bombs in Dhafran. Damaged the radio room. Go on.'

'We lost the lorry with the medical supplies. The bastards were standing about as coy as unmarried mothers and they let the bloody Hejri set it on fire. Not that you can do much to stop 'em with weapons that are about as much use as old box-tops.'

'How many did you lose?'

'I reckon about fifty altogether. Some coming back, some in the village. We couldn't turn round till we got to the Square and all the kids were crying and the women shrieking they were going to be raped by the Hejris. We lost some of 'em and their men went after 'em. What went wrong?'

'Nothing went wrong,' Pentecost snapped. 'We got a priority from Dhafran. They've changed their minds in Khaswe. We've got to hold Hahdhdhah.'

PART TWO

A Parallel from the Indian Wars

s i x

1

As the sun disappeared in a blaze of salmon-coloured glory behind the hills, the fortress seemed to stink of dust and smoke and the fading scent of fear. Down in the courtyard, Fox had brought order into the chaos and the vehicles were standing now in neat rows, with an armed guard on them. Above him the Dharwa Scouts, the Civil Guards, and the sullen Toweida Levies peered out of the embrasures at the fading light, and behind them in the living quarters they could hear the wail of women.

Their losses, apart from forty-three missing Toweidas, had been small. Two men including Beebe's Iraqi had been killed and five wounded, only one of them seriously, but the Toweidas had been shaken by the panic and by the loss of their comrades and by the fact that inside the fort there were still civilian clerks, storekeepers, drivers, and a few women and children, wailing over the loss of their men. They were left with eighty Dharwa Scouts – good soldiers if simple-minded, thick-headed and vain – forty-five tough Civil Guards, two hundred indifferent Toweida Levies, twenty-five civil servants, transport drivers and commissariat clerks, and twenty or thirty wives and a few children.

Studying the lists, Pentecost frowned. They were all his responsibility. Somehow he had to protect them or get them to safety. He had already ordered the rations to be reduced, and though there was plenty of ammunition he would have to make sure it wasn't blazed away without cause. For the time being, too, he knew he had to watch the Toweidas, and had instructed Zaid Fauzan that each post was to contain at least two Dharwas or Civil Guards.

The Hejris had stayed outside the fortress all day, waving their green banners and shouting insults, but not venturing too close. Occasional little rushes were made, but against the bare walls and closed gate they were half-hearted and were soon stopped by a burst from one of the out-of-date machine guns.

Pentecost had watched them, moving from one side of the fortress to the other, his eyes bright and narrow, so that to Beebe, watching him with a sick feeling of guilt at the Iraqi's death, he seemed to be actually enjoying himself.

During the night there was a series of explosions outside the walls which reduced the Toweida bazaar, brothel and mud huts to dusty rubble, and flurries of musketry between the fort and the infuriated Hejris who had been approaching to take them over as points from which to direct firing at the walls. A strong party of Toweidas and Dharwas under Int-Zaid Mohamed had already fortified the old stables and they had posted sentries, feeling that they had done all they could to make the place secure.

Curiously enough, by next day there was a surprising lightness of spirit in the atmosphere round the fortress – rather as though they'd all been expecting trouble and welcomed it now that it had come with a feeling of 'Oh, well, let's get it over.'

Fox had buried the bodies and got the goats safely into a sheltered pen near the wood store by this time and there appeared to be plenty of fodder with all they had been able to cut during the hours of darkness from the area near the gates.

An elaborate plan for defence, flanking fire and barricades had been produced and one of the rooms had been cleared of stores, and quarters arranged for the women and children, with water butts for washing which could be refilled during the hours of darkness when the courtyard could not be overlooked from the hills. Toweida craftsmen had been put into the armoury to make grenades, and the Khaliti blacksmith set to work to put metal shields on the scout cars so they could be used if necessary as makeshift armoured vehicles.

Chestnut had produced a proclamation on the ancient duplicating machine and it had been posted round the fort to let them all know what had happened, and field telephones were strung from one strongpoint to another. The cellars were full of grain, working parties were organised and the civilians recruited – women for the hospital, the men as labourers – and all spirits, whether arrak or brandy, had been impounded.

Black-outs, parapets, patrols and pickets had been organised, and a watch set against fire or the defection of the Toweida Levies. Even spears from the ancient armoury had been placed near loopholes in case anyone got near enough to try to shoot through them.

Sanitary arrangements, a wireless watch and a hospital had been set up. Cigarettes were rationed, and the well had been sandbagged and was now guarded in case of

Toweida treachery, and handmills were being constructed by Dharwa Scouts to grind corn. On Fox's suggestion, a Union Jack had been made by Bugler Owdi but, in his enthusiasm, he had incorporated a crescent and crossed swords, and it had hung, bizarre and ridiculous, under the flag of the Sultan until Stone had pushed up another one, 'Chelsea for the Cup', and Pentecost had drawn a line and had them all brought down except the Khaliti flag.

Despite his fury at being trapped and his own sick misery at the death of the Iraqi, Beebe couldn't help being impressed by Pentecost's professionalism. The books of verse had vanished and he had seemed to come to life. The old languid manner was still there, but there was a gleam in his eye suddenly as though this were what he had been born for and he were actually relishing it. He appeared to be everywhere at once, listening to the sergeants, the zaids, Minto trying to organise a sick bay, and the deputations of civilian drivers and clerks who insisted on being allowed to leave, despite the fact that the Hejris clearly had no intention of permitting them to. Barbed wire was laid in the gaps between the stony outcrops and the ancient mortars were taken from the lorries and placed where they could command the rocks. In addition, Lack had produced the rusty $1^1/2$" Martini mountain guns and a quantity of dubious ammunition that had been captured during some distant foray against the Hejris, and Fox had set to work to make them function.

A scale of rations had been fixed, though there was no bread because the civilian bakers had been on the lost lorry, and Pentecost had set Stone searching through the battered library for a recipe. Within twenty-four hours they were producing loaves of a sort. So that it couldn't be taken over in the event of treachery, he moved the officers' quarters into the armoury, and it was there they conducted their first conference, Pentecost at the head of the table in a smartly brushed uniform.

Lack seemed to think he was slightly mad. 'You can't hold a place like this, Billy,' he said. 'I'm all for biffing 'em for six but one good-sized artillery shell would bring the walls down! People just don't get besieged these days!'

'The French were,' Pentecost pointed out. 'At Dien Bien Phu.'

'For God's sake, we haven't the men! We should get out! Abandon the place!' Lack's face twisted sarcastically. 'With honour, of course, but if necessary without. After all, if anybody was let down, we were.'

Pentecost didn't appear to have heard. 'I'd like every room searched,' he said, 'and a list made of everything we have that might be useful.'

Lack stared at him frustratedly but he did as he was told and produced his lists that evening.

'Coffee, sixty pounds; sugar, five hundred pounds; tomatoes, two hundred and seventy-five cans; dried fish, forty pieces; olive oil, two hundred and fifty quarts...'

Pentecost listened to him carefully as he continued his recitation.

'...condensed milk, a hundred and fifty cans. There's wheat in the stables outside we can bring in, forty-five goats in the fort...'

'Weapons?' The word stopped him dead.

'We'll have to base the defence on small arms" Lack said. 'All we have are two mortars and those two old Martinis, together with eighty rounds of ammunition, all in a highly dangerous state.'

'I wish we had a few land m-mines,' Minto said. 'We've got pentolite for blasting,' Pentecost pointed out. 'What about the machine guns?'

Lack pulled a face. 'They've been a joke for years. They've been stripped down for instruction so often by those bloody clumsy Toweidas they shake to pieces when they fire.'

Pentecost seemed unperturbed. 'Never mind, they'll be useful. We'll have a guard put on the grain. I wouldn't like it to be filched. We ought to be able to hold out for around three months with luck.'

Lack exploded. 'Billy, we can't! When I think of what those rat-faced gnomes in Khaswe have let us in for I bleed internally, but – we – can't – stand – a – siege!'

Pentecost blinked. 'We'll negotiate as often as possible,' he pointed out.

'With those bastards?'

'While we're tailing, they're not shooting. All the same – ' Pentecost smiled, blandly indifferent to Lack's fury ' – we'll have the loopholes strengthened with wood and use the timber from the bazaar to make the stables stronger. And all fodder must be brought from the stables into the fort. We'll do that tonight as soon as it's dark. We'd also better get Stone to give some of the Toweidas a little more instruction in musketry. One of the Dharwas was hit by a Toweida bullet yesterday and we can't afford that.'

2

Beebe was still suffering from the bitter knowledge that for once he had guessed wrong and from the miserable awareness that no one but himself was responsible for the Iraqi's death. It had come as a shock, too, to discover that the Stars and Stripes meant nothing to the men outside the walls, and he had been carefully keeping out of the way, certain that Pentecost's fury when they met would be blistering.

He crouched on the ramparts, well away from everyone else, digesting his bitterness and guilt. The plain towards Hahdhdhah was empty and shimmering in the heat. There was a wild confusion of granite shards to the south, then the broad valley towards the village where the flat stones laid in the earth like flagstones had been polished by the passing of countless feet. Near the village there was a cairn of white rocks erected by travellers but it was falling down now because no one bothered to propitiate Allah these days,

Beebe stared at it with narrow eyes, angry with himself, angrier still with Pentecost at whose door, despite his own procrastination, he still somehow managed to lay his situation. Down in the courtyard, he could hear Chestnut's clipped Scots and Stone's harsh command. Everyone seemed to have a job to do except himself and the women, and it made his resentment even more bitter.

He jumped as he heard a footstep near him and he saw it was Pentecost. Beebe stared at him uncomfortably.

'I guess I owe you an apology,' he growled.

Pentecost was staring through an embrasure and didn't bother to turn his head. 'We all make mistakes, Mr Beebe,' he said calmly.

'I killed that guy.' Beebe was determined to scourge himself.

'It happens, Mr Beebe.'

Beebe stared at him, wishing to God he'd offer something in the way of comfort, something to set his mind at rest.

'I thought they'd let us go,' he went on.

Pentecost turned at last and gave him a twisted little smile. 'The first rule of siege warfare, Mr Beebe,' he pointed out, 'is that one must always stop anyone getting out who will otherwise be a drain on the rations.'

He offered the comment in the dry prim manner that Beebe had seen countless times on films where the cavalry had been held up by Indians and he wondered for a moment if in his own dry private way Pentecost was deliberately acting the part, pretending to be just what he was expected to be, carrying it a little too far even so that he had become a caricature. It would have explained a lot, because no one who was as purposeful, incisive and professional as Pentecost was now could be so completely unreal. But then he realised that Pentecost wasn't acting at all. His family history was so firmly written across his life he had come to believe that everything that was worth doing could only be done by such people as himself, and because of this the present situation made special calls on him and demanded sacrifices which, because he felt himself a member of a privileged caste, he had to make without hesitation or fear. He even seemed to consider belonging to his class a prerogative and in return tried to give it style in his own old-fashioned way.

Beebe was startled by his discoveries but he knew he was right, and he felt curiously at a disadvantage. He felt he had to try to make amends. He lit a cigarette quickly, his hands shaking.

'How long will it be before someone gets through to us?' he asked.

Pentecost shrugged and, in his correctness, his military precision, Beebe would have liked to have grabbed hold of his neat little figure and shaken it until his head rattled. 'I wouldn't like to say,' he said.

'Won't they send help from Dhafran?'

'I doubt if it'll be very easy. They've got to hold the Fajir Pass open and, if I know my Hejris, they'll have thought of that, too.'

'You mean the bastards are all round us?'

'That's exactly what I mean, Mr Beebe. I'm sure you can find a parallel from the Indian Wars in your country.'

Beebe already had. It was standing in front of him, clean despite the recent confusion, well-shaved, an example to everyone. He was the arch-commander from every Indian film Beebe had ever seen – dry, efficient, humourless, unloved – an example to his men. Beebe almost expected him to claim acquaintance with Custer. He could even smile, God damn him!

'And while you're at it, Mr Beebe,' he was saying cheerfully, 'I think you should hoard your cigarettes. It might be a while before you can buy any more.'

Guiltily, Beebe snatched the cigarette from his mouth and stared at Pentecost. 'You really mean we're here to stay?' he grated.

'Until help comes.'

'You mean, weeks?'

'I mean months, if necessary. One remains faithful to one's calling. We are at the moment only in the process of what the army calls "taking a grip".'

'Jesus,' Beebe said. 'All these kids!' He stared again at Pentecost, dislike strong inside him but driven to offer help. 'I can work a radio,' he said bluntly. 'It'd free Chestnut for other duties.'

'That's uncommon good of you, Mr Beebe,' Pentecost said in his out-dated way. 'We might need every hand before we've finished.'

'I'll get him to show me around and then I guess he's yours. I'll get my set in there and keep the watch. I've slept with headphones on before now. It's the safest place down there, anyway. There isn't even a window.'

Pentecost smiled. 'You'll be alone most of the time, Mr Beebe. I always think that makes the job twice as difficult. You have too much time to think.'

Beebe scowled. 'I'm not a thinking type,' he said. 'I never had the equipment.'

3

That night in the darkness, they heard the sound of a horse's hooves and the jingle of harness over the thudding of the motor that gave them electricity, and they all crowded to the ramparts, their hearts thudding, in expectation of an attack.

'Bin T'Khass!' Pentecost decided the voice wasn't that of Aziz but one of his lieutenants who had picked up the name from him. 'You are now shut in!'

Pentecost turned to Zaid Fauzan alongside him. 'Tell him that we wish to send out the women and children,' he said.

The voice from the darkness came back at once as Fauzan shouted the message.

'We are camped across the road to the south,' it announced. 'No one will leave. Neither woman nor child. Not sick. Not injured. Not the American. Feed them so that your men will go short. Toweida is Hejri country.'

There was a long silence then the Hejri horseman, unable to resist a little private hostility of his own, loosed off his rifle against the fortress. The bullet struck the wall, throwing up chips of stone, then, twisted shapeless, whined away into the darkness.

'Give him a burst, Sergeant,' Pentecost said to Fox. 'I don't suppose you'll hit him but it might encourage them not to come too close.'

The rattle of Fox's gun shattered the silence and the flash at the muzzle dazzled them for a second.

There was another shot that struck the wall above the gate, then they heard the horse's hooves clattering among the rocks. One of the guns in the stables opened up but nothing happened.

'That seems to be your answer, Mr Beebe,' Pentecost said with a smile.

4

Rather to everyone's surprise, the first few days were quiet, as though the Hejris, thwarted in their first attempt, were having to do a little thinking about their next move, and with the disgraced Toweidas repeating in manic detail every firing, loading and maintenance move after Sergeant Stone, when the next attack came they were all ready.

'Wish we had a rocket or two,' Stone whispered to Fox as they stared over the ramparts in the darkness. 'A Sidewinder in the middle of Addowara village'd send 'em back to Khusar – but fast.'

'You've a hope,' Fox murmured. 'The bloody Khaliti could never afford anything more than pea-shooters.'

Stone gazed into the blackness among the rocks. Behind them they could hear Chestnut sorting out his clansmen for an attempt to start work on a barbed-wire defence. Wire was the only thing they were short of and they hadn't enough men to patrol it, and the knowledge that it wouldn't take long for one of the Hejri horsemen to hitch his mount to it and tow it away in the dark, posts and all, didn't help Chestnut to feel enamoured of the Toweida Levies he was picking out to make up his party.

'– Forsyth,' he said. 'MacNab. Dowd. Murray –'

Stone grinned. 'The bastard'll have 'em in kilts, given a chance,' he said.

'Khaliti tartan.' Fox smiled. Then his smile died. 'I expect those bastards in Khaswe are having a great time arguing whose fault it was,' he went on, 'with Billy Pentecost and the rest of us eyeball to bloody eyeball with the Hejris.'

'Never mind,' Stone said softly. 'They'll always give you a bit of coloured ribbon to sew on your chest when it's over.'

'Don't you kid yourself,' Fox said realistically. 'Not for Hahdhdhah. They can't even pronounce it in England. They'll never get round that mouthful of bloody aitches. It looks the same either way and sounds like a cross between a sigh and a belch. There'll be no gongs for this little lot.'

Chestnut's party crept through the gate carrying the coils of wire and steel posts and mauls. There was only the sickle of a new moon to see by and they seemed to make a tremendous clatter, even before they started their work. Standing near one of the embrasures, Pentecost peered out in the hope of keeping them in sight. Above him, Beebe was stringing an aerial from the look-out tower and every now and then the flash of his unguarded torch swung round so that with every minute Pentecost expected a burst of firing to knock him off his perch.

When the firing came, however, it was not towards the tower but towards the wiring party. There were a few scattered shots, then a lot of shouting and the sound of running feet, and almost at once it seemed there were Toweidas outside the gate demanding to be let in.

Shooting was still going on, bewildering in the darkness, but nothing was coming near the fortress, then they heard yells and the sound of horses' hooves, and soon afterwards Chestnut reappeared with the rest of the Toweidas, a group of contemptuous Dharwas and a furious Fauzan dripping blood from one hand.

'Yon bastards lost their heids, sorr,' Chestnut said as Fauzan was led away by Minto. 'Just a few scattered shots. One happened to hit Fauzan in the hand, and yon bastards upped an' bolted. Fauzan did all right. He didna lose his head. He got his boys among the rocks gie'in' as good as they were gettin'. But we've lost a lot o' the wire, sir. Yon bastards oot there hitched their gees to it and towed it awa'.'

Pentecost shrugged. 'Well, it was sooner than I expected,' he admitted. 'What's left of it we'll use on the walls.' He gave a little troubled sigh. 'All the same, it makes a difference. What if they come at night? How are we off for lights?'

Chestnut shook his head. 'Bad off, sorr. Yon's a big drawback. We canna' see. But Ah reckon ah can fix somethin' wi' a couple of Aldis lamps.'

'Have a go, Chestnut.'

'Aye, sir.' Chestnut hesitated. 'I've had another idea, too, sir. I've seen yon Dharwas cookin' their grub. They don't use dung like the Toweidas. They keep pinchin' chips off yon zanhae wood we've got stored in the north corner. It flares. It's got natural turpentine in it, sorr. Burrns wi' a hot bright flame. How aboot gettin' some of yon spare drivers and clerks on the saw mill? We can mix it wi' straw an' bits of thorrn bush and soak it in paraffin, and wrap it aroond wi' one of yon plastic sheets. It ought tae gi'e us enough light tae shoot by.'

When daylight came, the reason for all the fuss during the night became apparent. The Hejris had built a sangar of stones and bundles of green branches in front of the fort, not more than two hundred yards away. Beyond, towards the village, they could see tents and horsemen alongside the road on both sides, their ranks marked here and there with green banners.

Pentecost stared at the breastwork with narrowed eyes. 'That's where they'll come from,' he observed to Fox, 'and we ought to knock it down. But I can't risk losing Dharwas, and the Toweidas are going to be no good outside the walls. We'll just have to let it stand and hope that before long someone in Khaswe pulls his finger out and sends a relief.'

5

What Pentecost didn't know, what his wife didn't know, what no one but Cozzens knew, was that orders didn't even include a relief.

'No rescues,' Cozzens had been told firmly by the British Minister in the privacy of his office. 'And no heroics. We back up the Sultan, and such borders as he's agreed upon with his neighbours, but we don't create any new ones or support artificial old ones. If the border's in dispute, we must wait for it to be settled by UNO.'

'What about Pentecost?' Cozzens had demanded.

'He volunteered to be seconded to the Khaliti army,' the Minister had said, frowning.

'Encouraged by the Government,' Cozzens had pointed out.

152

The Minister had sighed. 'We can't make distinctions for individuals,' he had said. 'For the purpose of the treaty, we have to regard him as a Khaliti soldier.' He had seemed to be squirming in his clothes with wretchedness at what he was having to say. 'We have to! We have no option and we can't risk involvement.'

Fortunately, thank God, Cozzens thought, the Minister had now gone so that at least he had room to move. With him had gone Forester Hobbins, cynically assured of a hearing when he got home, and only the Bishop of Harwick of his unwanted guests remained.

The Bishop had emerged from the Intercontinental Hotel to announce that he had made a change in his plans. He had stood before Cozzens, a tall ascetic-looking figure, playing for all he was worth the part of a man of God who was aware of earthly things.

'I have decided,' he had announced, 'despite my personal feelings, that I have a duty to those boys down there.' He had indicated a sandbagged post and a group of Cozzens' soldiers behind a machine gun. 'While what I have to say publicly might encourage the Khaliti it might not encourage them, and I have decided it should be kept back until things have resolved themselves a little. I shall stay here. It might help the women to be brave if they see me.'

Pompous bastard, Cozzens had thought. It wouldn't make a damn' bit of difference. He wondered cynically how much Harwick's decision was due to the fear of a bomb in his plane; because, immediately afterwards, he had driven to his hotel through streets that stank of burning, past huddled groups where British and Khaliti soldiers held the crowds back so that the ambulances could pick up the injured and the dead, and had hidden himself behind the boarded windows and locked doors. If any of the Khaswe wives wanted to see him, Cozzens thought, they'd have to drag him out by the scruff of the neck, and certainly the Bishop's presence hadn't done much to help Charlotte Pentecost survey her bleak husbandless future. When he had seen her last she had been full of the high hurt rage of youth.

In the shabby flat she occupied in the old town, Charley Pentecost remembered her conversation with Cozzens. Male talk of a lifetime had rubbed off on her and she knew enough about military operations to realise that Cozzens had been altogether too vague when he had claimed it shouldn't be long before the Khaliti army had her husband safely at the coast.

She had insisted on seeing him and she had been far from satisfied by his answers.

'They'll be sending fresh bods from England.' Cozzens had seemed to be writhing inside at the lie he was offering her. 'We need them, Charley, because we're too thin on the ground at the moment to move. Until we get them the Sultan won't dare send anybody north.'

She had not been slow to notice that he made no promises of relief. 'What happens when they arrive?' she had asked. 'What about Billy?'

'That'll be different.' Cozzens had still been careful to make no promises.

'But at the moment, nobody's doing anything?'

He had been unable to meet her eyes. 'I'm afraid that as orders stand the only person who can do anything is the Sultan,' he had admitted. 'A lorried force from Dhafran. Wintle'll nip in and fetch 'em out.'

'And the Toweidas? Without Billy?'

'They'd have to leave, too.'

'Surely that would mean the Sultan giving up the frontier?'

'Yes. That's what it would mean.'

'I can see him doing it.'

Cozzens had had the grace to look uncomfortable. 'Under the circumstances,' he had offered, 'would you like to go home? I'm sure I can arrange it quickly for you.'

She had stared at him bitterly. 'Not likely,' she had said. 'I'm staying here till Billy's safe.'

She shifted uncomfortably in her bed, wondering just how long it would be safe to go on occupying the flat. Pamphlets reminded her of her danger every day – 'Do not take the same route twice' – 'Avoid youths on bicycles' – 'When shopping do not face the shop' – and she knew that the airport had been closed since a BOAC Trident had collapsed on its belly as a neatly-placed bomb had blown out one of its oleo legs. It had not caught fire but it would take a long time to clear, and remained, crumpled and scarred, a monument to the failing grip of Sultan Tafas. Fortunately, no one had been killed but not long afterwards the front doors had been blown off the reception building and the bar in the lounge had gone up, scattering whisky and arrak and studding the walls with splinters of glass. Three buses and two cars had also vanished in flowers of flame and the VC10 flights from London and the Caravelles from Paris and the big Boeings from America had been diverted to Cairo; and the British Embassy now stood bleak and scarred with flame, where a mob of students had thrown petrol bombs through the windows. Because it was built of concrete they hadn't managed to raze it to the ground but they had done a great deal of damage and the British Ambassador was

155

now sharing a back room with one of his secretaries, while lesser mortals were crowded into bathrooms, kitchens and storerooms.

She drew a deep breath. She had a shrewd idea her husband was in a sticky spot and she longed to be shot of Khalit, out of the country with him and her children, and away for a while from the harsh world of political feuds. Yet she had not complained. She and Pentecost were more than merely wife and husband. They were excellent friends who cared for each other's opinions and she always felt a heel when she set her fears on paper. It had taken courage to embark on marriage at all, she remembered. There had never been a settled home, never any hope of proper and steady schooling for their children, always shabby furniture in someone else's flat, and always – because they were forever on the move – having to sell cars at knock-down prices and buy them in the next place on a sellers' market. As long as she could remember, they had reeled under the weight of their overdraft but, since every other Serviceman seemed to suffer from the same trouble, until Pentecost was tossed out on a pension or managed to reach the higher ranks where it was easier, she had endured it without feeling hers was a special case.

Curiously, though, it wasn't the discomfort or the penury that troubled her. Though it was fashionable to deride duty and to regard soldiers and their wives as stupid, people like her believed in such things, because their families always had. It was the loneliness that upset her and the jumped-up types who thought because she was married and alone she was fair game for their wandering hands.

Suddenly the futility of the whole thing hit her. After all they had endured, no one had the right to ask them to endure this latest insult to their intelligence without trying to do something about it.

6

The Bishop of Harwick was rather startled when a pretty young woman descended on his hotel in what was clearly a furious temper.

'My child,' he said in his most unctuous voice, 'I can hardly enter the politics of the affair.'

'Of course you can,' Charley snorted. 'What I want isn't tea and sympathy but practical help.'

The Bishop eyed the tray he had provided for her on her telephoned request for an interview and realised he had made a mistake.

'I've heard of you,' Charley said. 'I've read about you in the newspapers. I've even seen the things you've written and seen you talking on the telly. It seems to me, though, that protest isn't enough. I'm tired of people protesting. The whole world must be full of marching columns of half-wits carrying banners and placards, all driven on by people who aren't really involved. I want to see a few less protest marchers, a few less banners and a few less placards, and a bit more involvement by the people who say they're concerned.'

'But, I am involved and I am concerned.'

'How?' Charley demanded. 'Protesting? Seeing a Minister or two? How about offering to meet the Hejri holy men and discussing it with them? How about getting hold of a gun and going up there to fetch my husband out?'

The Bishop decided that perhaps she was a little overwrought. Carrying a gun would help no one. And as for meeting Hejri holy men – !

'You could even go home,' she went on, 'and find out what the Government's intentions are. You could start shouting about it on the telly. There are plenty of cameramen about. Alec Gloag would give you five minutes, I'm sure. You could even punch someone on the nose.'

The Bishop looked startled and she went on angrily.

'Why shouldn't a Bishop punch someone on the nose?' she asked angrily. 'You've announced you've decided to stay here to be of help to anyone who needs you. Well, I need you, and if the Bishop of Harwick punched a Cabinet Minister or two on the nose, the whole world would want to know why.'

It was irrefutable logic but the Bishop didn't see it that way. 'I'm a man of God,' he pointed out 'Not a pugilist.'

'There have been other men of God,' she said sharply, 'who weren't afraid to take up arms when they had to. All through history. There was one in my father's regiment in the last war – I've heard him talk about him. He thought the Nazis were such a lot of bastards it wouldn't matter if he joined the army and got hold of a gun. There was that parson at Pearl Harbour – the Praise the Lord and Pass the Ammunition chap. I'm tired of emotional blood-baths. I'd like to see someone put down his banner and pick up a club for a change. If you can't do anything for me, my lord Bishop, I'll try the Sultan himself. I'm told he likes pretty girls.'

7

The day had been tiresome and troubled and Pentecost's fear that the Hejri would soon notice how they could overlook the fortress from the spurs of the Urbida Hills had been correct and there had been a great deal of sniping. One of the Toweida Levies had been shot in the eye as he peeped through a loophole, and Pentecost's rat-like charger and two goats had been killed. They had had to set to work at once to build shelters along the ramparts, and one of the Toweidas had been killed and two more wounded before they had succeeded in hiding the men at the embrasures. Pentecost had got everyone – officers, NCOs and civilian – working with tents, canvas, timber, torn-off doors, rush matting, corrugated iron, boxes and sacks of earth. But while the men on duty could not now be observed, it was still possible to see into the yard of the fortress, and getting to the men's quarters still necessitated a frantic dash from one side to the other.

By the grace of God, their water supply was safe. The well was deep. It would have been a fatiguing business, however, hoisting enough every day for the garrison of over three hundred together with the civilians, women and children, but someone had seen fit in the past to build a tank and install a pump, so that it was possible to pump the water up, and allow it to run to the various taps about the fortress by its own weight.

As the iron legs were built into the wall of the fortress, though, they were as good as a ladder and, as they had half-expected, the attack, when it came, was directed at the water tower. There was a wild rattle of rifle fire and the sound of running feet in the darkness.

'Here they come,' Fox said grimly. 'Eyes down for the count!' As the alarm bell went and the firing started,

Pentecost went himself to the rampart by the tower. He was under no delusions and, unlike some of them, didn't underrate his opponents. Fox vanished to the main gate and Minto and Stone to the other two walls. Chestnut waited with the reserve, and Bugler Owdi, awed by the new responsibility the siege had laid on his shoulders, was blowing the 'Assembly' in the courtyard, his face shining with fervour as his eyes flickered over the running figures he had summoned.

It was hard to see where the bullets were coming from and they could only shoot back at the flashes of the Hejri rifles, and Pentecost walked round the ramparts with Fauzan, the old man cuffing the excited Toweidas as they fired at shadows. Beebe appeared alongside them from the radio room as they waited. He was basically a good-tempered man despite his outburst on the first day of the siege and he was still sufficiently troubled by the death on his conscience to feel that, with the radio silent, he owed it to Pentecost not to sit still and do nothing. Ever since the start of the siege he had sat alone in the little dungeon-like room where Chestnut had erected his equipment, silent and angry and still chafed by guilt.

'Anything I can do?' he demanded brusquely.

Pentecost blinked at him. 'I can't afford to have a foreign national killed to satisfy the pride of a Hejri sniper,' he said. 'I suggest you keep your head down, Mr Beebe.'

The faint pompous overtones of the speech – as though Pentecost felt he were only a nuisance – irritated Beebe.

'You've got another think coming, son,' he said. 'If those bastards out there are aiming to kill Luke Beebe, he's aiming to stop 'em.'

'Can you use an automatic weapon?'

Beebe's face fell. 'I guess not,' he said. 'But all Yanks know how to shoot.' He hoped he was right but he was none too certain because he'd heard that there were more Americans killed on the first day of the hunting season than there were deer.

Pentecost gave him a small tight smile. 'Then I suggest you see Sergeant Chestnut, Mr Beebe, and ask him to enrol you in the reserve.'

'That's not a trick to keep me outa the way?'

'Not for a moment. We shall need all Chestnut's people if anything dramatic develops. But, since they're not immediately involved, it'll give you time to pick up the rudiments of a Lee-Enfield rifle.'

'OK,' Beebe nodded. 'I'll see Chestnut. I hope I can understand him.'

As he vanished, the firing increased and bullets began hitting the ramparts. Chestnut appeared with a couple of Toweidas dragging one of his fireballs, a four-foot bundle of faggots, shavings and brushwood, all soaked with paraffin, and loosely wrapped in one of the plastic covers from the store.

'She's all ready, sorr,' he said as the Toweidas hoisted it to the ramparts.

The firing swelled up again then they heard the chink of stones outside the fortress.

'The bastards are coming up the legs of the tower,' Chestnut whispered. 'Now, sorr?'

'Yes, Sergeant I think now.'

'Right, sorr! You, MacNab! You, Doig! Over with it!'

Chestnut struck a match and the fireball flared into a livid flame and, assisted by the Toweidas, Makna and Dayik, he pushed it over the ramparts. The whole side of the fortress was lit up at once, and they could see the

Hejris scattered about the plain, shooting up at them. Immediately, firing broke out from the embrasures and they saw one or two shadowy figures fall.

It was obvious an attempt was being made to blow the tower down and Pentecost pulled the pin from one of their few grenades and, leaning out, tossed it down. There was a flash and an iron crash from below and they heard screams as they drove off the dynamiters, but almost immediately there was a tremendous roar and they saw the tower lurch and pieces began to drop off. Flakes of rust and old paint and fragments of wood came down on them with a shower of dust, and a small girder, torn loose by the blast, fell with a clang and a clatter of rusty bolts into the courtyard. They heard someone yelp with pain in the darkness below and when the smoke and the dust had cleared they saw that the tower, although it hadn't fallen, had canted heavily on one side.

'Didnae manage it, sorr,' Chestnut said cheerfully. 'Ah'll gae down to ma reserve, though, just in case.'

As they grinned at each other, they heard Minto's voice from the courtyard below them, and leaning over, saw him lying on the ground alongside the fallen girder with his left ankle at an awkward angle.

He was trying to pretend in the modesty of pain that he was all right, and they realised he'd been running up the steps when the explosion had occurred and the falling girder had hit him. They had just reached him when they heard the Hejris outside begin to scream.

'Hold it, Freddy!' Pentecost said, bolting for the stairs to the ramparts again. 'Back in a moment!'

Through the embrasures, he couldn't make out at first what had happened. He could see Hejris running towards the fort and firing had started from Lack's outpost in the stables. Then he heard Chestnut shout behind him in the courtyard.

'Sorr! Mr Pentecost, sorr! Yon explosion's blown a hole in ma radio room!'

Turning, he ran down the steps to the courtyard again, where Minto was painfully dragging himself clear of the steps. A Toweida Levy, his clothes covered in dust, was staggering through the open doorway of the radio room, his face dazed, and, beyond him, in the semi-darkness, Pentecost saw Chestnut and his men already firing. The door had been blown off and the shattered transmitter scattered across the floor. There was a hole in the wall where the window had been and already several Hejris were inside.

Chestnut seemed to have things well under control, however, and Pentecost waited in the background, letting him have his head. Beebe was there and Pentecost saw him pick up a rifle from a Toweida who had stumbled away yelping with pain, and fire into the radio room.

'Missed the sonofabitch,' he said furiously.

'Get yon heid o' yourn doon, Mr Beebe!' Chestnut screeched at him in his high mad voice. 'An' get oot o' ma way! Ye cannae keep the bastards back on your ain!'

Beebe backed away sheepishly, then Chestnut waved his men forward and they rushed for the door, firing as they went. Beebe, hanging on the edge of the fight, wondering what to do, saw Pentecost alongside him.

'Sandbags, I think, Mr Beebe,' Pentecost said quietly. 'Perhaps you'll help me scrape up a few of the drivers and clerks.'

The Martini on the rampart above them cracked twice on its improvised carriage and then it was all over, with Chestnut crouching among the rubble of the wall firing

163

out at the fleeing Hejris. There was a corpse wearing a battle dress and another in robes and one of the Toweidas holding his head in a corner.

They worked through the hours of darkness, with Beebe kicking and swearing at the reluctant clerks and drivers to force them to fill sandbags. Then Pentecost discovered metal lockers in the store which had once been used to keep the ants from the clothes of European soldiers and they were dragged out, filled with rock and soil from the courtyard and stuffed into the gap in the wall, with ammunition boxes filled with stones and even the ancient bound copies of The Illustrated London News and The Graphic from the garrison library which were thick enough to stop a bullet. Only when the hole was filled did Chestnut back away, his lean fanatic face grimy and covered with sweat. Pentecost passed him a water bottle.

'Thank ye, sorr,' he said. 'It's verra welcome.'

It was only then that they remembered Minto, and Pentecost found him inside the improvised hospital where, under his instruction, a couple of Toweida women and the Toweida interpreter were putting a plaster cast on his ankle.

'You all right?' he asked.

Minto looked up, his face pale and twisted with pain. 'Coping,' he said shortly. 'I think we've fixed it between us.'

He nodded at the two women who bobbed their heads nervously at Pentecost.

Pentecost said nothing for a moment and Minto went on.

'Sorry and all that, Billy,' he said.

Pentecost managed a smile, but he was a little shaken by the loss of one of his officers so early in the struggle. 'Better get some sleep,' he said.

Chestnut put his head round the corner as he turned away. 'Mr Lack on the field telephone, sorr!'

Pentecost picked up the instrument and at once Lack's voice came harsh and full of anxiety.

'What was all that racket about?' he asked.

'They were after the water tower,' Pentecost said. 'They blew a hole in the wall and nearly brought it down.'

'Anybody hurt?'

'Nothing to speak about,' Pentecost said, more lightly than he felt. 'Freddy got a broken ankle.'

There was silence for a moment from Lack then his voice came again slowly. 'That's bloody tough tit for Freddy!'

'Yes. How about you?'

'Keeping my pecker up. I got a few of the bastards as they went past.' Lack sounded pleased with himself. 'But I'm beginning to smell like a pigsty and I'm not sure I like standing here like a hen's bottom turned inside out.'

8

All round Lack's post in the old stables there was a great deal of noise but none of the Hejris seemed prepared to come close enough to try conclusions with the machine guns on the walls. It was impossible for either side to do much damage in the dark and for a long time Lack stared out into the blackness, aware of his own insignificance. His heart was thumping wildly and he was fully aware of what might happen to him if he relaxed.

No one was shooting at him now, though he was well aware that even if someone could stir up the Hejris enough to accept a few casualties, his small post in the stables was well fortified and able to hold them off. His only worry was the Toweidas. They had run for the main gate that first night when the wire had been snatched from them, but he had with him Int-Zaid Mohamed and half a dozen Dharwas to strengthen the uncertain Levies, and he felt reasonably secure.

He peered out again, aware that the firing had died away. Alongside him, one of the Dharwas was sneering at the Toweidas and he told him to be quiet in an abrupt manner.

Listening again, conscious that his fingers were trembling and sweat was trickling from his armpits, he decided that the Hejri riflemen who'd been peppering the mud walls of the stable had disappeared. No one had been hurt and they had not had much difficulty in hanging on to their position. Nevertheless, despite his bluster, he was not as confident as he pretended. He didn't look forward to more nights away from the main body of the men in the fort. Numbers gave him confidence and Pentecost so far had showed no sign of nervousness.

He already detested Hahdhdhah with all the fibre of his being. If he had disliked it before because it was comfortless, hot and a long way from luxury, he loathed it now because it had suddenly also become very dangerous, and he decided to recommend that the outpost in the stables be withdrawn. Then he felt it might look too much as though he were afraid and decided against it after all, because he was also afraid of appearing afraid.

'Abassi –' Int-Zaid Mohamed appeared out of the shadows ' – I think this is not a good place to be.'

His doubt curiously made Lack feel more sure of himself. 'Dry up, Mohamed,' he said. 'We're all right.'

As he stared through the sandbagged window, though, he wished he could feel as confident as he sounded.

'Abassi –' Mohamed was alongside him again ' – I think we are surrounded.' Mohamed was nervous. He was a Toweida and his wife was in Hahdhdhah village and Lack suspected that he was anxious to change sides.

Mohamed jerked a hand. 'I hear them over here, sir. I hear them on all sides.'

In the shadowy interior of the stable, Lack stared round him.

The Toweidas were clearly uneasy, but the Dharwa Scouts seemed unmoved, waiting with the placid imperturbability of hill men, their weapons – their fathers and mothers, they called them – in their hands.

He looked again at Mohamed. 'Are you sure? he asked.

'Abassi, I hear them.'

For a long time, Lack debated what to do, then they heard a voice outside not far away, calling softly.

'Tell Int-Zaid Mohamed that we have his wife and daughter,' it said.

Mohamed was silent for a moment, his eyes staring, then he groaned and sat down abruptly on an ammunition box, as though his legs had given way.

'We are thinking of giving them to the young men,' the voice continued, and Mohamed's agonised expression changed to one of fury and he snatched up his rifle and fired wildly through the slits they'd knocked in the walls.

Lack pushed him aside. 'Stop that,' he snapped. Mohamed dropped the rifle and collapsed again, turning enormous tormented eyes to Lack who stared back at him, aware of a new factor suddenly intruding, and began to be afraid again.

He glanced at Mohamed who seemed limp and exhausted with emotion, as if the spine had been drawn out of him, then the Toweida began to moan, rocking from side to side.

'I'm sorry, Mohamed,' Lack said awkwardly.

'Abassi –' Mohamed lifted his eyes as though they were heavy ' – my daughter is only thirteen years old. Let us give up.'

'Oh, God, Mohamed,' Lack said, 'we can't even think like that!'

Mohamed began to moan again and Lack began to imagine a frightened child in the centre of a ring of fierce Hejri reims who grinned and snatched at her clothing.

Jesus, he thought, always less of a brutal and licentious soldier than he liked to imagine, how much did the stable – or even Hahdhdhah – matter against a child's agony? What did anything matter? Who was going to benefit if they were all wiped out?

Awkwardly, nervously, his hand felt the door. It was barricaded and solid but Lack found his heart was thumping again and he wished Pentecost were there because he felt sure Pentecost would know what to do. Then Mohamed, his face tortured, lifted his head, listening. One of the Dharwas touched Lack's arm and pointed silently through the embrasure.

Lack stared, seeing nothing, but the Dharwa pointed again, as though he were aware that men were close upon them.

'Abassi –'

As the Dharwa spoke, there was a wild flurry of firing outside, and the Dharwas leapt to their embrasures and started shooting back. Occasionally, Lack saw flashes outside and his nostrils were filled with the smell of cordite, then a lighted torch was thrust through a window and the dry hay that remained on the floor flared immediately, filling the place with a red glare. Two of the Dharwas began to beat at the flames with blankets and for a while the interior of the stable was bedlam, then Int-Zaid Mohamed began to yell in a wild voice and, rushing to the door, struggled to open it. Seeing him, three of the Toweidas joined him, and before Lack could stop them, they had vanished into the darkness outside, and Lack was bowled over as more of them bolted for the door.

One of the Dharwas joined him and they tried to push the door to, but the Dharwa staggered back, a bullet in his throat, and as Lack fought on his own, a rush of figures from outside hurled him back into the stables.

seven

1

In the bar of the Intercontinental Hotel, the press were waiting for something to happen. It didn't pay to go wandering around on your own any more, because the terrorists couldn't tell the difference between a sympathetic newspaperman and a soldier in civilian clothes so they shot at anything that moved and asked questions afterwards. It was much safer to wait until Cozzens or one of his staff was prepared to give information, or to badger the army press relations office and demand that something be laid on. In the meantime, they criticised each other's work, drank the cheap liquor and, if they got a chance, slipped into bed with one of the few women left in the hotel.

At that moment, Mike Diplock, the UP man, was none too sober, and Fay Bulstrode, of Time-Life, who spent most of her time living on the fact that she had once parachuted into the jungle in Vietnam, was arguing fiercely with one of the London men on the merits of getting to the forward areas.

'We're not here to tell them at home how Sergeant Bloggs from Huddersfield ties his bootlaces when some wog's shooting at him,' the London man was saying. 'We're here to give them the overall picture.'

One of the French photographers was snoring in an armchair by the wall. He had chosen a corner sheltered from the window by a pillar, just in case one of the lunatics from the Wad area came screaming past in a fast car and slung a grenade through the glass. By the look of him he was drunk.

Arriving through the door from the street, Gloag stared round them all with jaundiced eyes, deciding he didn't like any of them much.

He found a chair and lit a cigarette, cynical about them all. He remembered Cozzens' press conference that morning, and the note of wariness the General had allowed to creep into his voice when he had announced that although Hahdhdhah was besieged he had every faith in its defenders. It had obviously been hard to announce the loss of Umrah and Aba el Zereibat, and Gloag had had a feeling that nothing Cozzens had said had disguised the fact that they had been lost through a mistake.

It had not been the most successful of conferences and Gloag had followed it with a boring tour of the town in a convoy of jeeps, well escorted by a Saladin armoured car, and a Saracen troop-carrier – load of infantry armed to the teeth, laid on by the Army Press Relations Officer. They had gone round the outposts where the units of the British Army were keeping back the hostile Khaliti youths simply by standing still behind barbed-wire enclosures and looking grim. Nobody had pulled a trigger. Nobody dared. The Khaliti because of what they might get in return. The British because of what they might start. It had been stalemate and while he had run off a few feet of film and made a snappy commentary for his programme, it didn't really make good TV coverage. His viewers expected him to produce the sort of thing other TV commentators didn't manage to produce.

He was just wondering what he could do about it when a Khaliti waiter approached him with the cringing humility of all Arab waiters, to announce that he was wanted in the lounge.

'Who is it?' he asked.

'A Mrs Pentecost, Abassi.'

Gloag wondered who the hell Mrs Pentecost was and had just let his mind drift idly into wondering if she were lonely and found the hot nights trying, when he jumped. Pentecost! Of course! The chap in Hahdhdhah!

'I'm coming now,' he said.

The lounge was crowded with bored people, most of them waiting for a plane out of Khaswe. A lot of them were drinking too much – they had invested money in businesses or property there, and most of them were already aware that they were considerably poorer than they'd been when they'd arrived.

Charlotte Pentecost was sitting alone near to the window, he noticed, as though she couldn't care less whether some clot threw a bomb through the glass or not. He noticed with satisfaction that she was pretty, young and just his type.

He sat down beside her, putting his hand on her wrist as she made to rise. She made no attempt to pull her arm away and he warmed to her. Plenty of women had offered themselves to him. Alter all he was Alec Gloag, worth a small fortune, famous, notorious even, and young and good-looking enough in a hard way to be interesting to women.

She didn't waste time beating about the bush and Gloag very quickly realised she wasn't interested in him. What she had to say, however, soon made up for the fact. What she was presenting him with was a ready-made crusade, the sort of thing he always dreamed of. Not just a news story, but something he could really go to town on. She wanted him to stir up pressure for her husband and she had facts that no one else had got.

'This is for your ears only, Mr Gloag,' she said, and he had a feeling that she knew she was being a traitor to her own side – that normally she would have regarded him as the enemy but that she was so concerned for her husband she was prepared to treat with anyone to help him. 'Please don't quote me and please be careful or they'll jolly soon track it down, and then not only will I be in trouble, but so will my husband.'

Gloag nodded. 'You can count on me.'

She gestured, her hands moving tiredly so that he realised what she was going through. 'It seems to me,' she said, 'that the British Government, despite their insistence that they're supporting the Sultan, is only giving him limited backing.'

Gloag eyed her cautiously. 'The place's full of troops,' he pointed out.

'Khaswe,' she said. 'Not the frontier. Hahdhdhah's no concern of ours and General Cozzens has to leave my husband to look after himself.'

'At this place up in the hills?'

'Exactly. And if he can't send troops up there, the only person who can help is the Sultan. I've been to see him.'

Gloag looked at her speculatively. 'And will he?'

'He told me he would. But I don't believe him. If they fetched Billy out, the Toweidas wouldn't stay. Billy told

173

me so – more than once. They'd have to give up the frontier, as well as the fort.'

Gloag frowned. 'I can't see the Sultan doing that.'

'Neither can I.' She gave him a tired smile. 'So no one's helping.'

Gloag was silent for a moment. 'Will your husband hang on?' he asked eventually.

She nodded. 'He'll try. But he's not the type to believe in dying for a lost cause.'

Gloag stared at his cigarette. 'It seems to me,' he said slowly, 'that the real story's not here in Khaswe but up in Dhafran.'

She gave him her tired smile again. 'That's what I hoped you'd feel,' she admitted.

He looked quickly at her, realising that for once it was he who was being manoeuvred. 'But I can't go up to Dhafran,' he said. 'They won't give us permission.'

'Army lorries go,' she pointed out 'It takes two or three days.' He began to catch the drift of what she was suggesting. 'And could I get a lift on one of these lorries?' he asked.

'So long as you keep it quiet and kept your head down. There's a Khaliti sergeant who fixes things. I've sent things up to Billy. He'll need bribing but I could give you his name and tell you where to find him.'

He studied her warily. 'This is all very useful, Mrs Pentecost,' he said. 'What are you wanting out of it?'

She looked him squarely in the eyes. 'Only that someone does something to make sure my husband's safe,' she said. 'You might say I'm trying to mount a rescue operation.'

Gloag grinned, suddenly liking her for her forthrightness. It made a change from the normal toadying he got from people who tried to persuade him to use his programme to make money for them.

They talked for a while then Gloag rose. 'I'll do what I can, Mrs Pentecost,' he said. 'How about dinner tonight? I could arrange a car to fetch you.' He still hadn't given up hope and she was a very pretty woman.

He guessed wrong again. 'I've two children to look after, Mr Gloag, and no Khaliti woman'll sit in for me. Come to that, neither will any army wife. They're all too scared of leaving their own children. And in any case, I'd much rather you were on your way to Dhafran.'

2

As the thin light of early morning increased and the pearliness vanished and turned silvery with the dawn, they were able to pick out the stable as it emerged from the darkness. With the roof burned away, it had a skeletal appearance, like a blackened set of ribs among the rocks where the Hahdhdhah had once scratched a living. The land and the huddled hamlet beyond looked parched, the colours strident browns, yellows, crimsons and purples. Beyond that the plain seemed empty and the silence thunderous, only the yellow grasses and thorny bushes moving in the gritty wind.

Brooding on the rampart above the gate, Pentecost frowned, his mind nagged by the disappearance of Lack. He felt sick with guilt about it. Yet the stable had been a sound and solid fortification and should have been held, and only Mohamed's forgiveable agony had started the chain of events that had caused it to fall. He had been icily furious with Mohamed, cold and deliberately cruel, but it was impossible not to be sorry for him, especially when a Hawassi frog pedlar from Addowara appeared outside the fort, with his tiny flayed wares strung on a stick like spread-eagled naked human beings.

'This is what your wife and daughter will look like after we've raped and killed them, Mohamed,' the chant went up.

Old Fauzan, his face grim, shot the pedlar between the eyes with a borrowed rifle and he vanished head over heels into the rocks, but no one was surprised when Mohamed vanished over the wall the next night.

It hadn't brought Lack back, either, and the sporadic firing from the trees it had started had driven them out of the courtyard into the shelter of the walls. Forty-eight hours had elapsed now since the loss of the stables and they were all waiting for daylight, knowing that when the sun rose and the night colours vanished they were once more reasonably safe for another day.

'I think, Sergeant – ' Pentecost stood on the ramparts, in the increasing light, watching the chattering Dharwas in the square below, and talking over his shoulder to Fox ' – that we'll have to set up a sortie to get one or two of those trees down. We'll make a note today which are the most troublesome and send a strong patrol out with saws.'

'Very good, sir.'

'And that leads me to another point. We can't spend the whole day crouching under the walls. There's got to be a better method of getting about the place. How about getting a few people to work with crowbars? The whole rampart's resting on the rooms below and the interior walls are only mud. Join them all up so we have a corridor, and make holes by the stairs up to the ramparts, so there's no running across the courtyard every time the alarm goes. How about getting Mr Beebe on to that?

Chestnut's going to be busy for some time getting us in contact with Dhafran again.'

When Chestnut arrived with his report, however, his bleak expression seemed to suggest that the damage to their communications was heavier than he'd expected.

'We're no' goin' tae get yon transmitter o' Mr Beebe's goin', sorr,' he said. 'Yon bang under the tower finished it when it finished mine. The receiver's working, though, but it means we can only accept messages. We cannae send 'em oot. Yon sets in the scout cars'll never reach Dhafran.'

'I see.' Pentecost's face was expressionless, despite the sick feeling in his stomach. 'What are the hours for transmissions to us?'

'Apart from emergencies, sorr, we receive from Dhafran in the evening. Khaswe in the morning. Emergencies any time either wavelength.'

Pentecost considered the situation for a moment. 'We'll make a point of listening out at all times,' he said. 'Can you arrange some sort of signal that would warn us if anything came through during the day?'

'Ah'll rig up a loudspeaker and keep the volume well turned up. We'd hear it OK.'

'Fix that will you, Sergeant? As for getting messages out of here, we'll have to send 'em by hand if we can find a volunteer. And while we're at it, do you think you and Mr Beebe could think up some means of alternative power for the lighting? Just in case something happens to the generator.'

Chestnut nodded, his face grim in the grey half-light. 'Aye, we can do that, sorr. We have a few ideas aboot a lot o' things.'

He vanished and Pentecost heard his high screech demanding Fahzait and Aliri, the waiters from the sergeants' mess who had been detailed to help him.

'Forsyth – O'Leary – where are yon wee scrounging bastards – ?' A moment later, Beebe appeared. Minto, under sedation from the drugs he had administered to himself, was still asleep in the hospital.

Beebe was weary. Rather to his surprise, he was still alive when he'd firmly expected to be dead. Though he had behaved with courage during the attack on the tower, reaction had set in later and he had found himself shaking and unable to stop it. He felt numb, larded with dust so that his body seemed flayed, and he was suffering badly from the knowledge that he was not as brave as he had thought. He was a strong man, burly and able, and he had always been well able to look after himself. But, in this new situation, his strength was of no use to him. He couldn't shoot and knew nothing about soldering, and he was intelligent enough to realise that so far he owed his life entirely to Pentecost's forethought. The smaller, frailer man had proved a master of his profession and Beebe had been caught by an unwilling admiration and a now obsessive desire to be of help.

Pentecost nodded to him as he stopped nearby. 'We've been hard hit, Mr Beebe.' He had showed no further sign of disapproval at what Beebe had done on the first day of the siege and made no bones about the disaster they had suffered, and the fact that he seemed to be taking him into his confidence soothed Beebe's ruffled feelings a great deal.

'Two officers gone,' he said. 'Three with Mohamed, and four with Suleiman who never reached us from the village on the first day. That's heavy casualties.'

'You're doing OK, son,' Beebe said grudgingly.

Pentecost shrugged. 'I wish I could do more for your safety, Mr Beebe.'

'Aw, forget it,' Beebe growled. 'Luke Beebe can look after himself. You're doing fine. So far you've guessed right all down the line.'

Pentecost permitted himself a grave smile. 'Luck,' he said. 'When intuition drives out logic, one decides to do things for reasons not altogether apparent at the time.' He paused, studying the American. 'Since you can't get out, Mr Beebe,' he went on. 'I might have to lean on you a little.'

'Lean away,' Beebe said. 'How long for?'

'When there's no longer any hope of relief, I'll pull down the flag and the Toweida Plain will fall into Aziz's lap. There's one other thing, though. I've been keeping a diary.'

'Your wife'll be pleased to read it.'

'It's not for my wife I'm writing it,' Pentecost said dryly. 'It's for posterity, you might say. Somebody's bound to get blamed for this little business here in Hahdhdhah – and, for her sake, I'm making sure it won't be me – or you – or poor Lack – or any of the others either.'

Beebe studied him. 'I'm right with you,' he said slowly. 'I'm way ahead, in fact.'

Pentecost paused then he went on with a faint air of embarrassment, as though to discuss his wife with a comparative stranger was simply not a thing a man should do. 'I happen to love my wife, Mr Beebe,' he said. 'And I'm making sure whatever happens to me, she'll be able to hold her head up afterwards.'

Beebe wondered why Pentecost was telling him so much and he decided it was because he suddenly felt the weight of his responsibilities and needed to talk a little, and because, with Lack missing and Minto out of action, he couldn't manage it with Fox and the NCOs. He'd heard of the loneliness of command.

'She's like you in many ways, Mr Beebe,' Pentecost went on. 'Sometimes she's a bit hot-headed and does things she feels sorry for later but –' Pentecost smiled ' – underneath she's got that same splendid warmth I've always found in Americans.'

Beebe felt touched and no matter how he tried to persuade himself he was being manoeuvred he couldn't quite manage it. From Pentecost what had been said was quite a compliment. 'Nice of you to say so,' he growled.

'But if I don't get out of here and you do –'

'Shucks!' Beebe felt embarrassed. Pentecost was putting on his besieged 7th Cavalry act again. 'That won't happen.'

Pentecost disagreed. 'It might, Mr Beebe. And if it does, I'd like you to see that my diary gets to the right quarters.'

'The General?'

Pentecost shook his head. 'I think not,' he said. 'I think it should be handled privately. I'm sure you and my missus could decide what's best between you.'

Beebe began to see where the discussion was leading and the old resentment at being manoeuvred rose again. Nevertheless, he still felt under an obligation.

'OK,' he said. 'I'll remember.'

Pentecost smiled and Beebe realised the interview was over. Pentecost was an expert at letting you know things like that without offending.

'Thank you, Mr Beebe,' he said, and Beebe noticed that even on this occasion he hadn't been able to unbend sufficiently to call him by his first name.

As Beebe turned away, Pentecost moved to an embrasure and as he stared across the plain, his eyes seeking the comfort of indefinite distances, he heard a cry from the tower. Against the lightening sky he saw the pointing arm of the Dharwa sentry.

'There, Abassi! There!'

Beebe had swung back to him and they moved together along the rampart until they stood below the tower, peering through the embrasure.

'To the left of the rock, Abassi!'

Then Pentecost saw what the sentry was pointing at. At first in the poor light it looked like a crude black cross, propped up on a wooden frame, then they realised that it was not black but red. He took it at first to be some sort of bloody sacrifice staked out there, some propitiation to Allah laid down by the superstitious Hejri – a skinned and slaughtered goat – then he realised just exactly what it was and why it had been placed there, and his whole stomach heaved.

'Oh, Christ,' Beebe breathed. 'It's Lack!'

For a moment, Pentecost said nothing and Beebe realised he was struggling not to vomit. Somehow, it had seemed to Beebe that he had been waiting for something like this ever since Mohamed's defection. They had heard the screams of the Toweidas who had run into the waiting Hejris and the following morning had been able to pick out the sprawled bodies of those who had been shot or cut up by the curved swords before they had reached the gates.

181

Pentecost himself had led the sortie that had brought in the corpses. Five Dharwas and seven Toweidas had been found crouching in a gully waiting to be rescued. The rest were all dead, lying in the ruins of the stable or along the path to the fort. Only Lack had been missing, and for the whole of the forty-eight hours that had elapsed since, Pentecost had been dreading something like this.

He felt desperately lonely. The loss of the only two other British officers threw a tremendous weight on his thin shoulders. Then Fox appeared and he caught hold of himself and stood upright.

'Sergeant!' His voice was steady and brisk and efficient. 'I'll want you and twenty Dharwas and Zaid Fauzan. I want a blanket and a stretcher, and see that we have men with strong stomachs.'

'Who'll be in charge, sir?'

'I shall.'

They brought in Lack's remains without interference, though they knew there were riflemen in the sangar. Fox would have liked to have led a raid on it and shot everybody he could find and he knew that Pentecost felt the same, but Pentecost had decided not to risk any more lives and they headed silently for the gate and, with their shirts stuck to their bodies in the oppressive heat, they buried Lack at the far end of the courtyard with the Toweidas and the Dharwas who had been killed.

There was no ceremony over the grave, not even prayers. It was as though, in face of the frightful cruelty Lack had been subjected to, prayers were useless, and they merely lowered the blanket-wrapped bundles into the hole in the ground, Pentecost standing in silence as the civilian clerks did the work.

For the rest of the day the fortress remained silent and brooding. It seemed extraordinary in the twentieth century, with all the sophistications of civilisation, that men could regard each other with such hatred that such an unspeakable incident could have occurred.

'They hadn't touched the poor bastard's face,' Stone said, his face hard. 'So we could see what he was feeling while they did it.' He swallowed, his eyes hard. 'There's one thing, though,' he decided. 'It'll make the bloody Toweidas think twice before throwing up the sponge again. It'll make 'em fight all the harder if they think this is what's going to happen to them if they don't. I bet that wasn't what Aziz intended.'

3

As it happened, Aziz had had no hand at all in the murder of Lack. Trembling with fury, he strode up and down before the camp fire, the shining Mannlicher in one hand, the other gesturing at the men seated around, their faces gleaming in the glow of the flames.

'We are not savages,' he grated. 'The days when captives were turned over to the old women are past! Where is the mercy of Allah and the dignity of the sons of the Prophet in such work?'

There was a lot of murmuring from the Hawassi and the Tayur, but an answering growl from the Hejri tribesmen silenced them.

'Perhaps it was Thawab's intention to frighten the Toweidas from the fortress,' Aziz went on harshly. 'I could have told him that Bin T'Khass cannot be frightened. All Thawab has done is strengthen his hold on the Toweidas. They will never surrender if they fear death at the hands of Thawab's torturers.'

In his position near Thawab, Majid the Assassin moved uncertainly. What he had done to Lack had been done with the clear knowledge of Thawab though not with his direct orders, and for a moment he was afraid that Thawab might repudiate him.

Thawab was not even thinking of him, however. He shifted uncomfortably, aware of the eyes of his men on him. What Aziz had said was true, he realised. The cold-blooded torturing had been a mistake, but it had seemed a good way at the time to show the men in the fortress that he meant business.

He moved uneasily again. They were all aware that they'd been slow on the day of the evacuation. It had been Aziz's intention to have his men drawn up near the fortress ready to slip inside the moment the last lorry had gone. It was a plan motivated partly by his wish to be present when Pentecost left, a wish to salute the young man in the way he had seen Western soldiers salute each other, but Thawab had spoiled it all by demanding caution and they had decided finally to hold their men in the hills until they were certain that the fortress was empty.

Aziz had not hesitated to make clear his disgust. 'If Thawab had been bolder,' he had said loudly, 'we would have had possession of the fortress and the plain. I warned thee that Bin T'Khass was not Jefeiri-sa at Zereibat. He is a great warrior, small as he is.' He was still angry and bewildered, and felt betrayed at the reoccupation of the fortress, but in his heart of hearts he still felt sure that whatever had gone wrong was not the fault of Pentecost. 'Next time,' he said, 'there will be no hesitation, and Thawab will do his share in the forefront of the line.'

The raid on the water tower had been led by Aziz's Zihouni reims but when they had fallen the attack on the smashed wall had been carried out by Hawassis, men of the Deleimi nation, and it reflected no credit on Thawab that this, too, had failed. There was only one grain of comfort for him from the last forty-eight hours and that was that the Khadari leaders had arrived in his camp from the south with the news that they and the Jezowi and the Shukri had thrown their lot in with the northern tribes and repudiated Sultan Tafas' treaties with them for guarding the Dharwa passes.

Their arrival had been a triumph for Thawab because he had seen the problems of a closed pass long since and had sent messages with hot nationalistic promises inviting the Khadari to talk, and he hadn't hesitated to let Aziz know it.

'The Khadari were always more of a burden than a help,' Aziz had retorted, though he had known that what he'd said wasn't true. The Khadaris were a sept of the Dharwas and good fighters and, at any other time, he might have been glad to see them in his camp.

But now it was different. Everything about the situation round Hahdhdhah was wrong. It smelled wrong. There were dozens of armed men swaggering about Addowara village and the tented camps in the foothills, and Aziz was aware of a sense of calamity and inevitability. There was an electric atmosphere he hadn't felt since he had been a child, with the Deleimi alert with the religious enthusiasm of a jehad, imbibing the red-hot doctrines of the politicians Thawab was trotting out thinly disguised as holy men.

The thing was getting out of hand and he didn't wish it to. He wanted Hahdhdhah but he wanted it on his own terms, with Pentecost unharmed. I am getting old, he had told himself. I am growing sentimental for brave young men. But there could be no going back, no half-hearted prosecution of the attempts on Hahdhdhah. Already his authority had been undermined by Pentecost's retention of the fortress and Thawab's suggestion that Aziz had treated with the enemy. Any hesitation now and one of Thawab's men – probably the Assassin, Majid – would take the opportunity to remove him from the scene with a bullet in the back.

Yet the appalling thing that had happened to Lack had shaken him to the roots of his being. Never in his life had he believed in cruelty for its own sake. He had killed men in battle but he had no time for the mentality of torturers and he had no hesitation in saying so.

Thawab shifted uncomfortably. 'We shall never break into the defences merely by rushing them.'

'Nor by torture!'

Thawab ignored the comment, sensing that he was beginning to gain ground. 'I have a scheme, Aziz,' he said. 'The Khadari are engineers. They build bridges over the gorges of the Ridwha and guard their families in caves against the winter winds that roar through the pass.'

'So?'

'They know how to use explosives. They will dig a mine under the water tower and blow it up. When it falls, it will bring down the wall. The Deleimi will be ready to rush.'

'As they did last time?' Aziz said coldly.

Thawab said nothing and Aziz stared at him with narrowed eyes. 'You have the explosives?' he demanded.

'The Khadari obtained them from Umrah. The English officer was careless.'

186

Aziz regarded Thawab's smooth face with hatred, aware that he had seized the initiative from him again. He tried to talk of the mine carelessly, as though he considered it of little moment.

'How can we be certain it will destroy the wall?' he asked.

Thawab sneered. 'The Khadari know how to bring the tower down so that it falls outward. The wall will come down with it.'

'And suppose Bin T'Khass discovers this mine?'

Thawab exploded. 'Bin T'Khass! Bin T'Khass! Bin T'Khass!' he shouted. 'This is all we ever hear! Who is this Bin T'Khass? Some mythical warrior?'

'He is a greater warrior than Thawab,' Aziz said coldly. 'He doesn't behave like a besotted sufi. One day men will sing songs of him as they do of El-Aurens and Owinda-el at Dhafran. But I will leave you to your miners. And I will leave your Deleimi to the job of guarding them. This time, though, they will carry banners so we can see where they are and it will be Hejri men who will lead the rush when the wall falls.' He was less concerned with insulting Thawab than with making sure that when the breach was made it would be assaulted by men he could control.

Thawab seemed to sense what was in his mind. 'Aziz is afraid that his friend, Bin T'Khass, might be hurt?' he sneered. 'He who talks with two tongues.'

Aziz's eyes glittered. 'Bin T'Khass is not Thawab. He does not talk of the killing of kings from the entrance to a rathole. He is a man of honour. And he can out-think Thawab.'

'Can he?' Thawab was goaded into another blast. 'I have friends in the north who promise me artillery! They can bring it into Khusar by aeroplanes from Egypt.'

Aziz glared. 'I have spent all my life attacking Toweida forts,' he snapped. 'There will be no need of artillery!'

Again he knew his motives were suspect. Artillery was too impersonal and always at the back of his mind was the knowledge that he owed a life. And it had become a life for which he found he still held a strange affection.

Thawab had risen to his feet, tall in the glow of the flames. 'Thou wilt delay until it is too late!' he snapped. 'The English will bring a column of soldiers.'

'Thawab has announced that the passes are held!'

'Very well.' Thawab backed down unwillingly before the force of Aziz's character and the hold he still had over the Khusar tribes. 'But let there be one sign of relief, Aziz, and the guns will come down from the north. Modern battles are not won with rifles.'

Aziz's expression didn't alter. 'It is agreed, and may the hand of Allah be seen in it. For the time being, I will ride to the fortress to correct Thawab's mistake over the white officer.'

'Perhaps you will even apologise?' Thawab sneered.

'Yes,' Aziz snapped, his head up, his eyes flashing. 'I shall tell Bin T'Khass that this was the work of a fanatic and that from now on we shall conduct our war as if we were civilised. Perhaps then the Toweidas might think more eagerly about surrendering.'

4

'You're going out there?' Beebe said. 'After what happened to Lack?'

Pentecost sighed. 'I'm going out, Mr Beebe,' he said.

'I think you're nuts, son!'

188

Pentecost eyed him mildly. 'Perhaps I am, Mr Beebe,' he said. 'But if talking to Aziz can save a few lives, then it's worth the risk.'

As he stepped outside and the gate was closed again, Beebe stared at Fox. Despite his resentment, despite his contempt for Pentecost's posturings, his admiration couldn't be denied.

'That's quite a guy you see when you look close,' he said unwillingly.

'I could have told you that,' Fox said coldly. 'Long since.'

Aziz was waiting where he always waited, but this time there was no sign of a banner or a ceremonial bodyguard.

'Bin T'Khass,' he said as Pentecost stopped in front of him.

'Aziz el Beidawi! I come in sorrow and in great anger. My friend did not die in honourable battle. He was murdered by your torturers.'

'Not my torturers, Bin T'Khass,' Aziz said slowly. 'They are Thawab's fanatics, and I come in grief that such a thing has happened. Death should be a poet's conception – clean, in battle, not obscene mutilation like this. While I live it shall not happen again.'

Pentecost nodded. 'So be it,' he said. 'Let us conduct ourselves like warriors.'

For a moment there was silence. Aziz had delivered his apology – and Pentecost knew what it had cost the proud old brigand – had made it clear that Lack's murder was an isolated incident which would not be repeated.

'I grieve also – ' Aziz spoke suddenly, breaking into Pentecost's thoughts ' – I grieve also that Bin T'Khass and

189

Aziz, both honourable men, should thus find themselves at each other's throats.'

'I also, Aziz.'

'And that Bin T'Khass goes back on his word and holds Hahdhdhah after promising it to me.'

Pentecost paused, searching for words. 'The men in Khaswe played us both false, Aziz,' he explained slowly. 'They did not tell us the truth. But I am a soldier and must obey.'

'There is no solution, Bin T'Khass?' The words came like a cry of anguish. Aziz was well aware what his insistence on talking to Pentecost cost him in the way of the loyalty of his men and he was in need of reassurance.

Pentecost shook his head. 'There is no solution, Aziz,' he said. 'I cannot leave my post. That also would not be honourable.'

Aziz's eyes were troubled. 'I see that. We are both committed. I to my people. You to your honour.'

The conversation was stilted and awkward as Aziz tried to grasp at the old habit of things, at the warm conversations they had had before. But things were different now. They were on opposite sides and Pentecost was holding himself stiffly aloof, and while it made the old man's heart ache that they should be so cut off from one another, it also gave him pride in his friend that he should behave so correctly. There was no enmity between them, only a strange sort of respect.

'How will it all end?' he asked.

Pentecost's face remained expressionless. 'As it began,' he said. 'I shall be still in Hahdhdhah and Aziz will still be outside.'

Aziz responded with a thin smile. 'Thou speakest bravely, Bin T'Khass,' he said. 'But I think that Aziz will be in Hahdhdhah and Bin T'Khass will be on his way to the coast. Thou canst not hold out for ever, and no relief column will get through the Fajir Pass. The Khaliti agents from Khaswe have been among the Jezowi and the Shukri and the Khadari tribes, and the passes of the Fajir and the Ridwha are closed. Only the Muleimat remain faithful to the Sultan.'

Pentecost didn't allow his face to change at the news, and Aziz was silent for a moment, regarding him sadly.

'If no relief came, Bin T'Khass,' he asked, 'wouldst thou accept defeat?'

'Defeat can be honourable enough, Aziz. I do not believe in dying unnecessarily. If hope faded, then I should surrender.'

Aziz smiled. 'If thou were to accept surrender, Bin T'Khass, it would be an honourable surrender. In the West, are not honourably defeated soldiers allowed to march from the field of battle bearing their weapons and carrying their flag?'

Pentecost smiled. Aziz had old-fashioned ideas. 'This is how it was, Aziz,' he agreed. 'Nowadays things are different. Men pass into captivity.'

Aziz frowned. 'I would allow thee, Bin T'Khass,' he said earnestly, 'to march out with thy flag and thy sword.'

Pentecost smiled again. 'Perhaps it will be not necessary, Aziz,' he said. 'Perhaps the relief will come first.'

Aziz's face changed. 'There will be no relief,' he said sharply, knowing he couldn't afford to allow a relief. His hope now was to send emissaries to the Muleimat to bring them round to the same side as the Jezowi and the Shukri and the Khadari. With the pass at Tasha closed, too, there would be no way over the mountains from Dhafran; and, with no hope, Pentecost could accept defeat and he, Aziz, could spare his life.

'I have no wish to see thee die, Bin T'Khass,' he said.

'Nor I thee, Aziz.'

'Thou dost not blame me for the murder?'

'Not now, Aziz. But I shall not fight less because of this.'

'Nor I, Bin T'Khass.'

Pentecost stepped back. 'God go with thee, Aziz,' he said.

Aziz's old eyes flickered. 'And with thee, my son.'

The strange interview over, Pentecost walked slowly back to the fortress, while Aziz moved to where he had tethered his horse. From his position above the gate, Beebe saw the slight figure returning, its wide shorts flapping in the breeze that lifted the dust. A few heads rose from the sangar but there was no shooting.

'What did the bastard say?' he asked as Pentecost appeared through the gate.

Pentecost frowned. 'He let slip that the Khadari and the Shukri and the Jezowi have joined them and that the Ridwha and Fajir passes are now closed.'

'Is that what he came for – to gloat?'

'No.' Pentecost was silent for a moment. 'He wanted us to know that what happened to Lack was none of his doing. He said he wants to conduct his war in a civilised manner.'

'Civilised!' Beebe snorted. 'With atrocities like that!'

Pentecost shrugged. 'All war's an atrocity, Mr Beebe,' he said.

eight

1

His mind filled with irritation, Brigadier Wintle stared across his desk at Alec Gloag.

The commentator stood before him almost like a soldier on a charge, but he showed none of the anxiety of a Toweida Levy in the same position. Covered with dust and unshaven, he stared back at Wintle, briskly defending what he'd done.

'I don't care if you're the chairman of the governors of the BBC,' Wintle was saying. 'I don't care if you're God Almighty himself even. You and your cameraman shouldn't be here and I can't do with you here.' He paused and his eyes gleamed. 'All the same, I'll say this: You've got guts. It takes courage to come up to this neck of the woods just now.'

Gloag nodded at the compliment. 'You can't send me back,' he said. 'I represent a major television network.'

Wintle's mood changed again – abruptly. 'And I represent the Sultan! And this is Khalit not England! I can do anything I damn' well like – even with you!'

Gloag wondered if with Wintle he'd guessed wrong in heading north, then he noticed that Wintle was studying him thoughtfully. He had placed his hands on the desk and was leaning forward.

'Mr Gloag –' he regarded Gloag shrewdly and drew a deep breath – 'since you are here, I'm not going to send you back. You can interview whom you like. I'll even lay it on. But this is my military district and, by God, you don't say one word that could jeopardise the chances of those people in Hahdhdhah.'

'If you put a ban on me,' Gloag replied, 'it could ruin my story.'

'If your story's likely to harm Pentecost,' Wintle said without hesitation, 'then I'll be happy to ruin your story – you, too! I hope you understand that. No matter how important you are. The great British public doesn't agree with its sons being butchered to make a Roman holiday for television stars.'

Gloag glared at Wintle. He wasn't used to being told what to do. 'No story of mine's likely to harm Major Pentecost,' he pointed out.

Wintle's eyes glittered. 'It might be fair, I think,' he observed, 'to say that it hasn't always been your practice not to harm people.'

'No.' Gloag had to agree. 'If I feel there's an injustice I'll trap fingers and enjoy it. But it seems to me Pentecost's been put in a hell of a position, and the public ought to be told. I'm not afraid of the Government or what they say.'

'Neither am I,' Wintle said. 'Which is why I had to seek employment with Sultan Tafas.'

Gloag inclined his head again in acknowledgement. 'The difference, though,' he pointed out, 'is that you don't have the ear of the public. I do. And when it thinks it's being done brown its indignation can bring down Ministers.'

Wintle smiled and it suddenly dawned on Gloag that behind his offer to help there was a collateral somewhere. He waited, wondering what it was, and Wintle went on slowly.

'This is one story you're going to tell with care, Mr Gloag,' he said. 'I hope nevertheless that you'll make a great deal of it so that it'll be known in England just what's resulted from this decision to hang on to Khalit.'

Gloag waited, knowing more was coming and guessing what it was.

Wintle was watching him closely. 'If what seems sense to me is done and the British Government gets out of Khalit,' he went on, 'then Tafas is finished and I'll be out of a job, so you can take it from me that what I'm saying doesn't contain any attempt at self-preservation. You'll already know that one of my officers was killed by the bomb that blew in the front of the mess here and that two of my British sergeants lost their lives, to say nothing of several Khaliti soldiers. Are you following me?'

'I'm way ahead of you, Brigadier.'

'I'm glad,' Wintle said, 'because I've just also learned that a British officer up at Hahdhdhah has been murdered.'

Gloag frowned. 'I heard their radio was cut off.'

'So it is. But I'm in touch with a few inspired sources. A Khaliti mule driver from the village there, as a matter of fact. He was thankful to be shot of the place. It's full of Hejris and he was scared they'd find out he was accepting pay from me. The officer was captured and tortured to death. His name, for your information, was Captain George Gould Lack.'

Gloag made a note of the name and waited for Wintle to continue. 'I'm not going to tell you exactly what was done to him,' Wintle went on. 'It would serve no useful purpose and would only distress his next of kin. I hope you'll play that part of it down.'

Gloag's head lifted. 'I can't omit it.'

'But you needn't go into details,' Wintle snapped. 'At the same time as he was captured by the tribesmen, sixteen of his men were also cut down. They panicked and ran. That's how good the Toweidas are, Mr Gloag.'

'Am I allowed to say that, Brigadier?'

Wintle nodded. 'I hope you will. The people at home need to know. The Government in England got caught with a hot potato. There's such a thing sometimes as being too bloody honest and this is one of the times. They should have repudiated the treaty and be damned to their reputation. There isn't a man in Khalit who's reliable just now. I've even warned Tafas of his Ministers. Because of this I doubt if anyone, from the General in Khaswe up to Pentecost in Hahdhdhah, sees the sense in staying on the border. Captain Jeffreys lost thirty-five men deserted on his way to Dhafran. Howard lost twenty-seven. All Toweidas. The Toweidas are ethnically Hejris and the whole northern plain is Hejri country. Is all this of any use to you, Mr Gloag?'

Gloag looked at the hard thin face of the soldier and nodded. There was a great deal of bitterness in Wintle's eyes and for the first time Gloag began to see why.

'We have been told to hold this northern border, Mr Gloag,' Wintle went on. 'But with trouble in Khaswe we don't have the men to do it. How do you work that one out?'

'I don't, Brigadier.' Gloag paused. 'Will there be a relief column?'

Wintle paused. 'At the moment,' he said carefully, 'I have enough trouble here. Especially as I've now been told that the Dharwa tribes have thrown in their lot with the Khusar people. That leaves only one pass to the north open – the Tasha.'

'Shall you use it?'

'Eventually, please God!' Wintle spoke with a simple faith that impressed Gloag.

'What about the relief then, Brigadier?' Gloag was aware that he was becoming more involved than he wished.

'That's the interesting part,' Wintle said. 'The British Government's rightly claiming that disputed frontiers are no part of their treaty with the Sultan, and that therefore they're not responsible for Hahdhdhah. The Sultan naturally takes the opposite view and claims that if the British Government is staying in Khalit, it should stay in the whole of Khalit. Including Hahdhdhah. He therefore says that since his own troops are tied down by the troubles in Khaswe, it's the British Government's duty to relieve Hahdhdhah. Which makes nobody responsible. I hope you have that clear.'

Gloag drew a deep breath. Wintle, like Charlotte Pentecost, wanted the power of television behind him – and for the same reason. Gloag's crusade was growing bigger by the hour.

2

Khaswe was worse now than it had ever been. Despite the soldiers standing on every corner, despite the sandbagged entrances to government offices, military headquarters and hotels, the city was virtually at a standstill.

Although the place was crawling with troops, a police officer had been murdered not far from the palace the night before and the road to the airport had been mined. The previous day even Group Captain Southey, the air officer commanding the small RAF unit at Carmel airstrip, had very nearly lost his life. A mine had killed a hurrying Khaliti businessman who had been foolish enough to pass his car just at the crucial moment.

It was at the city airport, however, that the rebels had scored their biggest success. A bomb in the control tower had destroyed all the radar and talk-down systems and now nothing could land until they were repaired. Khaswe was virtually cut off from the rest of the world because the surf outside had always made shipping difficult and no one had travelled by sea for years.

Sultan Tafas considered the situation bitterly. He had an uneasy feeling that things were slipping from his grasp. Up near the Dharwa Hills two village headmen had had their throats slit for allowing their young men to be used for road construction by the troops at Dhafran, and further north, the Khadari tribe, to whom he had been paying subsidies for years, had overnight gone over to the Hejris and declared for their traditional enemies to the east, the Jezowi and the Shukri. Between them they had closed two of the passes to the Toweida Plain, and now Rasaul, his Minister for the Interior, had resigned with a feigned illness. The Sultan guessed that he was just waiting in the wings until he felt it was safe to reappear – either at the Sultan's side, with the country well under control again and British soldiers guarding everything; or in his place, with the British gone. Either way he would be on the winning side. And certainly he would be alive. Which was something.

Despite his age, however, Tafas was far from lacking in courage. He looked up at the man standing at the other side of his desk. Brigadier Yani was a short sturdy handsome man, British-trained and commander of the Khaliti air force, whom Tafas had persuaded to step into Rasaul's shoes.

'With Rasaul gone,' Tafas said, 'can we trust the police?'

Yani hesitated then he shook his head. 'No,' he said frankly. 'We can't. Their ranks have been infiltrated by Havrists and National Front men.'

Tafas sighed. He had been bombarded with angry communications from England – from every civilised country in the world, in fact – and by furious messages from Cozzens. On the Sultan's orders, not a single press interview had been arranged by the Khaliti command and Cozzens was growing tired of bearing the brunt of the journalists' anger. He was also insisting that something should be done about giving up the Toweida Plain and releasing Pentecost and his men, but the Sultan hadn't the slightest intention of giving way. No final report had yet been received from the American oil expert he'd sent up there, and of all the places in Khalit where oil might be found, the Toweida Plain was the only one where he might have hoped for success.

Tafas frowned. The discovery of oil could make so much difference. There would be American backing and American power behind him, and wealth might bring about a vast change in the attitude of his people. Greed could unite them and a defence of the Toweida Plain could be acceptable if it were proved worth anything.

He sighed again. It would have been so easy to pack a bag and pick up the Sultanate jewels and leave for the

South of France. He had a yacht in the harbour and could live on it in luxury until such time as he could acquire a property in Italy or Spain or France. He would not be short of money. He had been putting funds into a numbered account in Zurich for years.

Despite this, however, he didn't for a moment entertain the idea. He had made a treaty with the British and he intended to see it implemented. He knew that if his country cut itself off from Britain or America, Russia or China would move in, and while it didn't matter much to the Sultan who supported Khalit, he preferred the British and the Americans because he was selfish enough to realise his own future was safer with them. His courage was the courage of stupidity, stubbornness and greed, and the fact that units of his forces, led by two or three young foreigners, were cut off in the north, actually cheered him a little because he saw political advantage in it. Hahdhdhah had to be held. If it were given up – even if only the British officers were brought out – the whole frontier would collapse. While they remained there – besieged or in control, it didn't matter – he was buying time.

He drew a deep breath. 'I had the wife of Major Pentecost to see me,' he said. 'She told me it was my duty to send a relief column up to Hahdhdhah.'

Yani said nothing and he went on slowly. 'It is a pity I can't help,' he said. 'She was a very persistent young woman. A very attractive one, too.'

Yard still said nothing. With both the British and the Sultan being difficult, it seemed that all the land north of the Dharwa range was going to have to look after itself. He wondered where they went next.

The Sultan enlightened him. 'If we do nothing to help,' he pointed out, 'the British will have to help. Their people in Hahdhdhah will suffer otherwise. They'll never allow that.' He paused. 'I'm told,' he went on, 'that there have been deaths already.'

'That is so.' Yani inclined his head.

'And that they have gone off the air.'

'My information is that they can still receive.'

The Sultan smiled. 'We must get them a new transmitter,' he said. 'We must not let them be forgotten. Especially by their own government. Couldn't we fly one in? By helicopter?'

'We haven't got any helicopters, sir. Only old Douglas transport planes.'

'I have one.'

Yani swallowed nervously. 'It would be difficult at Hahdhdhah,' he pointed out. 'The hills run too close to the fort. Your machine is old, too, sir, and not very manoeuvrable and the pilot would be under direct fire all the way in. It would look bad if he failed.'

The Sultan raised his eyes. He knew exactly what Yani meant. News of a failure in the north might easily mean failure in Khaswe. If the tribesmen around Dhafran learned there had been a minor victory at Hahdhdhah they would try for a victory in Dhafran, to – and in Haraa and Afarja and Khowiba. And that kind of victory would mean that the nationalists in Khaswe who were bent on ruling would go all out for victory on the coast.

He suddenly regretted all the cheese-paring he had insisted on in the past that had left his troops ill-equipped and low in morale, and his air force a sad organisation of elderly Dakotas and cast-off fighters. At that moment, with the only helicopter his own old machine, he would have been glad of a few of the newer and more sophisticated aeroplanes he'd more than once been offered and always turned down because he needed the money for other, more personal things.

He drew a deep breath. 'I still think we must try,' he said. 'A transmitter, medicines and comforts. Evacuate the wounded. It would encourage the garrison. It might also,' he added, 'encourage Mrs Pentecost.'

3

Majid the Assassin was the first to see the old helicopter. He was waiting among the rocks with a few of Thawab's men, his eyes on a small group of deer which had appeared from nowhere, and as he saw the aircraft he guessed at once what it was up to.

He jumped to his feet immediately and banged on the shoulder of the boy who was operating one of the few elderly walkie-talkies that Thawab owned.

'Warn everyone,' he said. 'Tell them to start firing when I give the signal. And tell them to be accurate. Then get hold of Lord Thawab.'

The boy nodded. 'Aziz too?' he asked.

Majid stared at the approaching helicopter. 'No,' he snapped. 'Not Aziz.'

From the fortress they could see heads bobbing eagerly among the folds of land as the helicopter approached, the thud-thud of its whirling rotors smiting the hills with the beat of the engine.

'I think he's going to find it bloody awkward getting in here,' Fox said.

'I think so, too,' Pentecost agreed. 'Get everybody out. We've got to keep a few of those heads down.'

As Fox disappeared, Chestnut slammed to attention beside Pentecost. 'Sorr, permission tae make a suggestion!' He gestured with one hand and as Pentecost turned he could see Beebe dragging up a long-armed contraption of wood and metal.

'What is it, Sergeant?'

'Catapult, sorr!' Chestnut stared at him, his eyes mad in his thin fanatic face. 'Made o' bedsprings. We can hit yon sangar wi' it.'

Pentecost looked startled. 'You've tried?'

'Aye, sorr. Last night. Wi' stones. Mr Beebe an' me have been working it oot for a couple o' days. We put extra weight into the pan tae gi'e the correct range, sorr. Permission tae demonstrate, sorr.'

Pentecost glanced at Beebe. 'Does it work, Mr Beebe?' he asked.

Beebe grinned. The knowledge that help was coming bolstered him up and he was eager to do some damage before the siege ended.

'Sure does,' he said, 'though I guess I'm not so goddam happy with live ammunition.'

Pentecost rubbed his nose. 'You'd better demonstrate, Sergeant.'

As Beebe bent over their contraption, Chestnut reached for a grenade.

'For Christ's sake, Mac,' Beebe breathed nervously, 'go easy with that goddam firework!'

'Awa' wi' ye!' Chestnut grinned his thin crazy grin and held the grenade at arm's length over the pan on the arm of the catapult, the firing lever held down with his thumb. 'Pin out! Into the pan! Now!'

As he snatched his hand away, there was a twang of springs and the arm flew up against its stop with a thump and the whole contraption leapt on its stand.

'Watch, sorr!' Chestnut screamed and they peered through the embrasures as Beebe counted.

'Three-four-five!'

There was a flash in the air over the distant sangar and the sharp crack of the exploding grenade. A howl of pain went up and Chestnut, looking madder than ever, turned to Pentecost.

'Shrapnel, sorr!' he said gaily.

As the Dharwas and the Toweidas and the few Civil Guards took up their positions, the walkie-talkie came to life and their eyes lifted to the helicopter again.

'Hallo, Hahdhdhah –' the English was overlaid with a thick Khaliti accent ' – I am now going to try to come in.'

Pentecost clicked the switch. 'We have cleared a space,' he said, his eyes flickering over his shoulder at the strips of cloth held down by stones in the middle of the courtyard. 'You'll see the white cross.'

'Can you give me support?'

Pentecost glanced at Chestnut and clicked the switch. 'We have arranged this already.'

'OK, I come in now.'

The helicopter was approaching the grey walls of Hahdhdhah when a flare went up from the hills and the firing started in a sudden concentrated fury that showed it was organised. Immediately the machine guns in the fortress opened up a counter fire with the Martini mountain guns while Chestnut's weird weapon sent grenades into the air one after another to keep heads down behind the sangar. For a while the racket in the narrow bowl of the hills was incredible.

As the helicopter began to descend, they could see the pilot's head turning from right to left as he tried to make up his mind what to do, then they saw bullets striking it and saw the plexiglass star. The machine seemed to hover for a second, tilted backwards, then lifted away from the fort again.

'Hello, Hahdhdhah.' The walkie-talkie clicked. 'I have been hit.'

Pentecost slapped the microphone into Chestnut's hand and turned to call to Stone waiting near the gate with the scout cars.

'Stand by!'

Beebe was staring through the ramparts. The sun was the colour of egg yolk and the brush of the grit in the wind against his forehead made him scowl with irritation. His high spirits of a few moments before had vanished. He had faced the humbling fact some time before that he was not as brave as he had thought and he had been looking forward to getting to safety, and the sight of the stricken helicopter choked him with disappointment.

'You won't need the cars,' he said heavily. 'The sonofabitch's too far away already.'

'Hello, Hahdhdhah –' the voice from the headset came faintly ' – I must pull out – I –'

The helicopter was well away from the fort now and suddenly they saw it plunge downwards and disappear into the low ridges of land in the distance. Immediately, a howl of triumph, clearly heard in the fortress, went up from the slopes, and a moment later they saw a column of smoke begin to rise in the air to drift over the fort.

The Hejris were screaming with triumph under their flags, shouting and jeering and firing at the fort, and Beebe found himself crouching with his head down next to Pentecost, whose small features were straight with a narrow kind of privacy that was scornful and detached. 'That helps nobody,' he said slowly. 'Only Aziz.'

nine

1

The grim mood at Hahdhdhah was reflected in Khaswe. Nothing had changed there, though the airport was open again and the RAF was flying civilians out of the city. No one wanted to fly in, because the bombs and the shooting had ruined Khaswe as a holiday resort for jaded Europeans.

Even the British forces gave no feeling of security any more. An officer and several men in a lorry had been trapped down a narrow street and hit by grenades, and three more men had been lost getting the wounded out. In addition, explosives smuggled into the basement in milk churns had blown in the front of the Sultan Khalil Hotel and set every sun blind on the facade clattering back into its box. Even the Palace had been hit by mortar fire from the Khesse district. They'd winkled out the Khaliti who'd been firing it and captured the weapon, but the thought of mortars worried Cozzens. When it had started, it had been simply rifles and pistols and men shot in the back.

Nothing had been released to the press about the Sultan's attempts to drop supplies to Hahdhdhah, but somehow it had reached the city, and, taking advantage of the concern with the frontier, the Nationalists had redoubled their efforts. The mob had been out on the streets again and the troops were still cleaning away the debris, the felled trees, the broken glass and the burned-out cars, and Cozzens' desperate request by telephone to Wintle at Dhafran for extra Khaliti troops had been turned down. Forcibly. The line was bad but there was no mistaking the explosion of anger at the other end. Wintle was no longer a British officer and he didn't have to defer to Cozzens.

'No!' he snapped. 'I'm holding everything I've got here in case I can persuade Tafas to let me go in and fetch Pentecost out! Why in God's name don't you get to work on London to put some pressure on the old bastard?'

Cozzens frowned, thinking of his orders. 'London's waiting for UNO,' he pointed out doggedly. 'They say it's your problem.'

'Tafas says it's yours.'

'My orders categorically forbid me to move.'

There was an angry silence on the line and the goaded Cozzens turned the idea of rebellion over in his mind. 'What if I managed to drum up some help from somewhere – from London or Tafas, it doesn't matter – could you mount a column?'

There was another silence on the telephone then Wintle's voice came back grimly. 'With someone to look after the shop up here, yes. I'd need a few days, though. We lost a lot of vehicles when those bloody bombs went off. We're trying to put it right but it takes time, and we can't fiddle about with penny numbers – not with two of the Dharwa passes closed.'

Cozzens drew a deep breath, knowing he was committing himself. 'Make your plans, Jem,' he said. 'I've been working on a few people. Have you anyone you can send in command?'

Wintle's voice came harshly in his ear. 'Pentecost's attached to me,' it said. 'If a column goes, I lead it.'

As Wintle rang off, Cozzens stared at the Havrist leaflet on his desk. It gloated over the death of Lack. He'd already had the unenviable task of seeing the widow of Captain Griffiths who'd been killed at Dhafran, and he thanked God that Lack had not also been married with a wife in Khaswe awaiting his return.

He sighed, knowing perfectly well that the trouble in Khalit was a result of military judgement being dominated by political factors. The Khaliti nationalists with their pamphlets were growing altogether too enterprising for the number of troops Cozzens had at his disposal.

He glanced at the instructions he'd been preparing to enable him to stretch his command to its limit. Traffic was to go one way only because it made it easier to discourage car-borne assassins, and mosques were to be searched in spite of being holy places, because they were being used to harbour dynamiters. But he was still working with one hand tied behind his back because in the hothouse atmosphere of the United Nations the British Government was even now finding it easier to explain away the death of a British soldier than a Khaliti terrorist.

Cozzens picked up his pen and scrawled in the margin, 'Bayonets to be used if necessary.' They looked menacing, he thought, and they weren't issued for opening tins of bully beef. Then he threw down the pen and frowned. None of this helped Pentecost up in Hahdhdhah, he decided bitterly, and Hahdhdhah was the place which still remained most in his thoughts.

On an impulse, he picked up the telephone and asked for Group Captain Southey. Southey's command consisted of only a half-squadron of Harriers, and they were in Khaswe really only as a threat.

He broached the subject that was in his mind at once. 'If you had to, Tom,' he asked, 'could you lay on a jet strike?'

Southey's voice came back, a little startled by his shortness. 'Of course I could,' he said. 'What do you want? Rockets? Guns? Bombs? Napalm?'

Cozzens responded brusquely to the sarcasm. 'The way things are shaping I might need the lot.'

Southey was a thin wiry man, not inclined to get excited about anything, but he sounded even more startled now than before. 'You don't mean you're serious, do you, for God's sake?'

'I might be,' Cozzens admitted grimly.

There was silence for a moment, then Southey's voice came again. 'I should look at your orders,' he advised. 'This is sheer suck-it-and-see.'

'I'm not carrying the can for the politicians, Tom,' Cozzens said. 'Not even if it costs me my job.'

'It might well.'

'I've never been ambitious. And we're supposed to be a band of brothers not a flock of sheep. You heard the news from the north?'

'Is that what you want the jets for?'

'That's it exactly. They lost a few men.'

'On top of the desertions when they first put the cork in?'

'On top of those. Mostly Toweidas. But one of ours, too. He was caught outside and tortured to death.'

There was silence for a while from Southey. When he spoke again his voice was heavier. 'Hang onto yourself, Alan,' he warned. 'A murder isn't supposed to affect people like you and me. We're supposed to sit here calmly drinking pink gins, being nice to the the terrorists and remaining unmoved when our chaps are knocked off. Can't you forget it?'

Cozzens paused. 'I've got some dark places in my soul,' he said. 'But not that kind.'

'Was it bad?'

'It was bloody bad, and I want to know how you feel, because Tafas is still standing firm on his belief that the frontier's our problem. If both sides are hanging back, things could get rather sticky for young Pentecost.'

There was silence for a moment, then Southey's voice came back briskly. 'We could doubtless get some lines crossed somewhere. I'd need convincing it was worth it, though. Especially after what happened to that Khaliti pilot. Hahdhdhah was no place for a chopper with the Hejri in the hills. Did you know he was going?'

'I never know what Tafas is up to. He either forgets to tell me or decides to keep his own council.'

As he put the telephone down, Cozzens saw that Colonel Steyne, his Chief of Staff, had appeared alongside the desk. 'I want all British wives brought together,' he said. 'Take over the Sultan Khalil Hotel. They're doing no business since they lost their entrance, anyway. We can arrange a school there for the children, and for God's sake, let's circularise everybody to go home.' He paused and looked at a note on his pad. 'Mrs Griffiths?' he asked. 'Is she still here?'

'Going tomorrow, sir,' Steyne said. 'She's staying with my family for the moment.'

'That's very civil of you. How's she taking it?'

'Pretty well, sir. They're really quite remarkable, these women, aren't they? They live with this possibility all their lives, I know, but it's still surprising how well they conduct themselves when it happens.'

'How about her belongings?'

'Not much, sir. The sort of stuff we all cart all over the world. They had an auction. Everybody was pretty noble. It raised quite a bit.'

'How about Charlotte Pentecost? How's she taking it?'

'Haven't seen her lately, sir. I thought you –'

Cozzens shook his head. 'I know her too well,' he said. 'And she blames me for Hahdhdhah. I don't think she'd welcome a visit from me.'

'I'll get my missus to call on her, sir.'

'Tell her to make it as accidental as she can. I don't think she's the sort to welcome an official visit – even by your wife.'

'I'll do that, sir.' Steyne hesitated. 'You'll have heard, sir, about the Khaliti chopper pilot?'

Cozzens looked up, aware that something unpleasant was coming. 'Go on,' he said.

'His body's been returned, sir.'

'Where to?'

'The Palace, sir. It was found in the road outside. Nobody knows how it got there.'

Cozzens felt his heart sink. 'Go on, Steyne,' he said. 'I'm sure there's more.'

'Yes, sir. He'd been beheaded.'

Cozzens was silent for a moment. 'Seems to show that the Hejris are in touch with our terrorists, doesn't it?' he said after a while. 'But it makes sense, because it was the Nationalists who pulled the Dharwa tribes over and closed the passes. Things aren't getting better, Steyne, despite what they try to say in London. They're getting worse.' He sighed and reached for his spectacles. 'Let's get down to that bloody report. Let's see if we can't concoct something that'll let 'em know quite firmly what sort of political stew Tafas has stirred up without sounding as though we're whining.'

2

Staring over his suffering capital, Sultan Tafas tried not to think of the young Khaliti he'd forced Yani to send north.

They had been kind to him when they told him but he knew what the boy would look like. What the northern tribes did to their enemies was common knowledge, and explained why the Toweidas were always unwilling to exchange blows with them.

As he thought about the incident, it occurred to him – as it had occurred to Cozzens that, to get the body down to the Palace in a matter of four days, there had been liaison between the terrorists in Khaswe and their traditional enemies, the Khusar tribes. There was a saying that when the Khaliti and the Hejri slept in the same bed it was time for the Sultan to watch out, and he began suddenly to see what it meant.

He stared again from the window, noticing that there was a new pillar of smoke hanging over the city near the sea. He was still angry after his last interview with Cozzens. Cozzens had clearly not been enjoying his job and both of them had become blazingly angry.

'How did this man Gloag get up to Dhafran?' the Sultan had demanded. He was a keen televiewer and knew all about Gloag and was particularly sensitive to the pictures Gloag had drawn of him. 'I gave instructions that newsmen were not to be allowed on the frontier.'

'There are always ways and means in Khalit,' Cozzens had said coldly. 'Men take bribes.'

'He is insisting that we mount a rescue attempt. I'm told he has a lot of influence in England.'

'Not with the Government, sir.'

'The people are the Government,' Tafas said, and Cozzens' expression had indicated that he was about to laugh in the Sultan's face. But Tafas had not equated his comment with his own actions and had gone on angrily. 'And he is persuading them that you should mount a relief column.'

'My instructions, sir,' Cozzens had said quite firmly – and Tafas had known he was squirming under the stupidity of the whole thing ' – are that within the terms of the treaty, the word "Khalit" does not mean the disputed frontier.'

The argument had seemed to go on for hours. Tafas was still boiling with rage. With both himself and the British holding off, the Hejris had gained control of the Toweida Plain as far south as the Dharwa Passes and only Pentecost stood between them and consolidation. And any moment now he expected to hear that the Muleimat had rejected the yearly subsidy he sent them to guard the Tasha Pass.

If only Cozzens would accept that what Gloag said was correct! Even though Gloag's reasons for wanting troops on the Toweida Plain were different from the Sultan's the end would have been the same. If only his officers were more experienced, he thought heavily. But warfare had never been a profession among the Khaliti and they would have been no match for the tribes from the north. The relief column Gloag was demanding, though it was demanded only for the rescue of Pentecost, could be enough to frighten off the northern tribes long enough for the elusive oil, which would solve so many of his problems, to be found. But it required a force stronger than Tafas could manage with his commitments in Khaswe, and he turned away from the window to stare gloomily at a map on the desk. Then, unexpectedly, unbelievably, he felt he saw the solution. If the British wouldn't take care of the frontier, he would do it, and the British could look after Khaswe. That was the treaty and they'd promised they would abide by it.

As a solution it seemed incredibly simple. He would withdraw every single Khaliti soldier from Khaswe and send them up to reinforce Wintle at Dhafran. It would mean an unholy row with Cozzens and there'd be a great deal of radio activity between Khaswe and London. But he could always answer that, since within the treaty the British wouldn't take care of his frontier, he would have to do it himself and leave Khaswe – still within the treaty – to the British. That would set them scraping the barrel in London and there'd be fresh British troops in Khaswe within forty-eight hours. They'd been telling him for ages now that Hahdhdhah was his affair. Very well, he would make it his affair, and let the British have red faces over the possibility of losing Khaswe. It was a calculated risk because the British, in their present mood of disillusionment, might just refuse and then the trouble might prove too big for all of them put together. But it was worth the risk, and would keep the Toweida Plain – and its oil – for Tafas.

He picked up the telephone and asked for Yani.

3

The news of the Sultan's decision was given out on Radio Khaswe that evening. Charley Pentecost heard it with a mixture of disbelief and delight. She was so sceptical about it she rang Steyne's wife to make sure it was correct.

Mrs Steyne was an inveterate gossip and was only too willing to discuss it.

'I've hardly had time to talk to Frank about it yet,' she said. 'I've been getting Estelle Griffiths and her family off, and you know what it's like when you have to get an escort to the airport. One grows so sick of seeing a Saladin just behind you if you want to go anywhere.'

'Penny –' Charlotte brought her back to the point firmly ' – Tafas says he's sending the whole Khaliti army. All of it! What happens in Khaswe if he does?'

'Frank says some of those people at home who thought this lot up'll have to pull their fingers out pretty smartly. He seems to think that old villain in the Palace's been a bit cute. He expects a couple of companies of Marines in on the very next plane.'

'Penny –' Charlotte could hardly speak for her delight ' – I can't believe it!'

'I can.' Mrs Steyne chuckled. 'Frank came home still shuddering after getting it straight in the face from Teeth and Trousers. Tafas has thrown the ball right back into his court.'

4

Whatever Cozzens thought of the Sultan's decision to send a relief force to Hahdhdhah, Wintle at least was delighted at the news.

He had been in a grim mood, occupied with trying to find sufficient serviceable lorries to pass his men through the Tasha when the time came. It wasn't easy, because the country was so bare they would have to carry all food, water and ammunition, as well as their own petrol. And it was pointless mounting a small column that would only be driven back. If the Tasha Pass changed hands, as it was rumoured it might, a halted vehicle would only ask for trouble. A column stopped in the Dharwas was a column in grave danger.

The news from Khaswe had changed all that, however, and gave him hope. He sent for Gloag at once.

'Mr Gloag,' he said, and Gloag could see he was fairly dancing with excitement, 'we're going in to fetch Pentecost out. I take it you want to come with us?'

Gloag grinned. 'My God, I do!' he said.

'Right.' Wintle rubbed his hands together. 'You'd better get yourself ready then. How about equipment? Is there much?'

Gloag grinned. 'Not more than we can carry.'

'Keep it as small as you can. We're short of lorries. I'm scraping the barrel all the way from Afarja to Khowiba and south to Haraa.'

'Who gave the OK?'

'Tafas.'

'He did?'

'He's decided that Whitehall can look after Khaswe and he'll look after the frontier. And he's got London by the short and curlies again because they've stated quite categorically that that's their policy. He's given 'em forty-eight hours. They'll do it.'

'And then?'

'As soon as the first Khaliti units arrive we can start assembling our column and head north.'

ten

1

For some time now, they had been kept awake at night by drumming from the direction of the stables, by shouting, and by serenades on a particularly lacerating instrument that sounded like an out-of-tune horn.

Since Minto's injury and Lack's death, Pentecost had begun to rely a great deal on Beebe, Zaid Fauzan and the sergeants, and as they listened to the racket going on from the direction of the stables, they discussed the reason for it in his office.

'Think it means an attack, sir?' Fox asked.

'Maybe it's because some of 'em have left for the passes and it's to make us think there are more of the bastards still here than there are,' Beebe offered.

'Could be.' Pentecost looked worried. 'Could be something else, too.'

It was hard to tell what the tribesmen were up to, and Pentecost was unwilling, without Minto or Lack, to take too many risks to find out. But, two nights later, when the racket from the stables had stopped, they heard a keening song in the darkness from the rocks near the side gate, as though one of the Hejris were bewailing the death of a

218

friend. At first the Dharwas jeered, then Fauzan cuffed them to silence and sent for Pentecost.

'Listen, Abassi,' he said. 'It's a message. It sounds like a warning.'

Cocking his head, Pentecost was able to pick out the Toweida words of the song clearly.

> 'Oh, my brother, Talal,
> Leave before it is too late.
> Bring your wife, Talal.
> It will soon be too late.'

Pentecost glanced at Fauzan and then at Fox alongside him. 'Who's Talal?' he demanded.

'Half the Toweida Levies are called Talal,' Fox said bitterly, as though he'd often found it a problem.

Pentecost turned to the grim old zaid. 'Fauzan, find out if any of our Talals has a brother with the Hejri – or a cousin or a nephew.'

Half an hour later a diminutive Toweida appeared before Pentecost.

'Talal Jad, Abassi,' Fauzan said. 'He has a brother-in-law outside.'

Pentecost eyed the Toweida. 'Is his wife here?' he asked. Fauzan nodded and Pentecost stared towards the rocks where the keening had now stopped. 'They're obviously going to try something,' he said. 'And they're trying to hide the noise. Pass the word there's to be no talking on duty. We want to hear what they're up to.'

'What might they be up to, Abassi?' Fauzan asked.

'Mining,' Pentecost said laconically. 'Under the wall.'

219

2

In the woollen tents in the hills, the feeling of victory grew more marked. Remarkably little success had attended their assaults on the fortress, but the arrival of the Khadari miners had begun to give them all increased confidence, and Thawab stared at Aziz triumphantly.

'Three days, Aziz,' he said. 'We blow the mine three days from now. I hope the Hejri men are ready.'

'We are ready,' Aziz growled. 'Make sure your Deleimi are taking care of the Khadari miners.'

'My Deleimi have guarded the stables well,' Thawab said. 'There's nothing to fear. The fortress will be ours.'

He indicated the men behind him and Aziz noticed a small mean-looking man standing among them.

Thawab caught his eye. 'This is Rhamin Sulk,' he said.

'And who in the name of Allah is Rhamin Sulk?' Aziz snorted. 'He looks the size of a mongrel and has the face of a rat.'

The little man with Thawab frowned and his eyes glowed dangerously. Thawab grinned. Aziz's hasty tongue was always a good ally.

'That is dangerous talk, Aziz,' he reminded him placidly. 'Rhamin Sulk comes from Khaswe. He is fighting the battle against Tafas.'

'I have heard of his men. They fight round corners. They are good at shooting men in the back.'

Thawab grinned again. 'They will remove Tafas before long. Aziz should remember this. Rhamin Sulk could be a dangerous enemy in the future.'

Aziz sneered. 'I am not afraid of Thawab's assassins,' he said.

'Rhamin Sulk has come to bring us news. The Muleimat have closed the Pass of Tasha. It is being kept secret. If Owinda-El can be caught in the gorges, they will never recover from it in Khaswe.'

Aziz was not displeased. With no relief force, there would be no artillery. He had Thawab's promise. He could still feel he controlled events and, God willing, Pentecost would be in another part of the fort when the mine went up.

A thought occurred to him and he stared sharply at Rhamin Sulk. 'If his business is with the Muleimat and the Khaswe assassins,' he demanded, 'why is he here?'

Thawab gestured. 'He brings greetings from the fighters in Khaswe. They wish us to work for the freedom of Khalit.'

Aziz glowered. 'Khalit is not my concern.'

'We are part of Khalit.'

'We have never been part of Khalit,' Aziz roared. 'Why otherwise do we fight for Hahdhdhah?'

Thawab eyed him contemptuously. Aziz knew nothing of the cross-currents of Arab politics or the high visionary enterprise of a twentieth-century alliance. 'This is a narrow belief, Aziz,' he said.

'I am doubtless a narrow man,' Aziz admitted, 'but I have always been a free man. I do not take orders from men who shoot round corners.'

'You are out of date, Aziz,' Thawab said softly, Aziz's discomfiture as heady to him as hashish, and there was an answering growl from the Deleimi. 'Times have changed. We are no longer tribes. We belong to a great whole. We are as one. We fight for freedom for our nations.'

3

The business of keeping silent was difficult, because the Dharwas were a noisy group, always anxious to fool about. For a long time they had even been making a jest of scuttling across the open space between the ramparts, dancing and weaving and even pretending to be hit, and they had always found it a painful business controlling their desire to chatter and gesticulate.

With no sound to break the stillness, the oppressiveness of the hills grew worse. The dominant note had always been the size and desolation and it always took time to recover from the depression which the stillness and the melancholy of the giant landscape brought on. All the colour was purged away by the glare of the sun so that the view looked as though it were an old faded photograph. Apart from the eagles circling the hills or the occasional vulture hanging in the sky, there was remarkably little sign of life. In the distance, in Hahdhdhah village or in the camp across the road to the south, they occasionally saw groups of people, and now and again, a horseman hotfooting it down the road. Once they saw several of them in the distance across the plain, chasing a buck, which had emerged from a gully, but for the most part Aziz's men kept their heads down and the landscape was empty, so that no sound broke the heavy stillness. In the fort, apart from the sentries, everyone was asleep or resting in the shade below the walls, and sometimes the unnatural silence became so oppressive an outbreak of firing and the screech of Owdi's bugle came almost as a relief.

Because he had no wish to alarm anyone, Pentecost had not told a soul except Beebe and Fox and Fauzan the reason for the silence, and during a dawn pause in the horn-blowing and drumming and the shouting from the sangars and the stables, Minto appeared, dragging his injured leg between his two improvised crutches.

'God, that hospital,' he said to Fox. 'Chap in there's going round the bend. Says he hears the Great M-Maggot burrowing beneath the soil to drag him away. Bit hysterical, shouldn't wonder.'

Fox's eyes gleamed. 'Or else he's heard digging, sir,' he said.

He gestured towards the water tower where, as they knew, there was little opportunity to provide flanking fire, and turned to one of the Toweidas nearby.

'Fetch Abassi Pentecost!'

When Pentecost arrived, he brought Beebe with him and they knelt on the floor of the hospital, their heads to the ground. Beebe looked up.

'The bastards are here somewhere,' he said. 'But I can't tell where.'

'Why not try a stethoscope?' Minto suggested. 'We've got one.' Pentecost gestured without tuning his head. 'Get it, Freddy,' he said.

With the stethoscope to his ears Beebe bent again to the earth floor, then he dropped it and bolted for the door. They heard the motor of his lorry start up as he reversed it across the courtyard, and a moment later he appeared carrying a coil of wire.

'I can probably get it to show up on the gravimeter,' he said. 'We ought to be able to pinpoint the sonofabitch.'

Tracing the digging to a point near the radio room, he sat back and looked at Pentecost. 'You can hear the goddam picks,' he said. 'You can even hear when they hit stone. They're after the tower again.'

Fox looked at Pentecost. 'What's the answer, sir?' he asked. 'A counter-mine?'

'How far away do you think they are?' Pentecost demanded.

'Ten feet,' Beebe said. 'That's all.'

Pentecost looked worried. 'They could finish it tonight,' he said. 'I don't think we've much time. We'll have to go out and blow it up. Pity we haven't Lack. He was our expert on explosives.'

Beebe sat back on his heels. 'I'm not so goddam amateur at it myself,' he said. 'I could make quite a mess with a coupla pounds of plastic.'

Pentecost's eyes shone. 'What will you need? We have pentolite in the cellar.'

'That's fine,' Beebe nodded. 'And I'll want a battery off one of the cars to set it off. Sandbags to damp it down and picks and crowbars to dig it in.'

Pentecost turned to Fox. 'How many men, Sergeant'?

Fox looked worried. 'No good arsing about with a few, sir,' he said. 'We've got to be able to hold off any rushes they lay on to try to stop us.'

'Forty?'

'We've got plenty of men, sir. How about sixty?'

'Very well. Sixty. Thirty Dharwas and thirty Toweidas. If we mix the Toweidas in with the Dharwas, they'll not dare desert. That ought to be enough. We'll go through the side gate. It's nearest. One group to give covering fire and act as reserve. Another to go for the stables. How about after dark, Mr Beebe?'

'I reckon that'd be tricky. We've got to be able to see what we're doing and we've got to make no mistake. We'd lose guys in the confusion and probably end up without the battery.'

'And the Toweidas could sneak off easier,' Fox agreed. He turned to Pentecost. 'It's got to be daylight, sir.'

4

Pentecost watched the preparations grave-faced. Outside in the courtyard Fauzan was going over their instructions with the storming party again and again.

'I think I'll lead this one, Sergeant,' Pentecost said quietly.

Fox looked up quickly. 'No, sir,' he said immediately. 'If anything happened to you, the whole bloody affair would fall apart.'

'That's right, I guess,' Beebe agreed.

'I ought to go.'

'No, sir,' Fox said firmly. 'If you got hit the Toweidas would be over the wall like a shot. They know who's holding this place together.'

Pentecost considered the suggestion then he nodded. 'Whom do you suggest then, Sergeant?'

'Mr Beebe to attend to the blasting, sir. Me and Sergeant Stone to handle the punch-up. I'll lead the reserve. Stone to go in and clobber 'em. He's young and he's fast.'

'We shall have to expect casualties, Sergeant. In daylight anyway.'

Fox stared gravely at him. 'We've always had to expect casualties, sir,' he said. 'That's what we're paid for.'

The drumming from the stables continued but it seemed that there were no large numbers of Hejris there, and the few there were conducted themselves with a great deal of arrogance, shouting and gesturing and waving their flags at the fort.

'How many do you think there are?' Beebe asked nervously.

'Not many,' Fox said. 'Thirty perhaps. There are a lot more further out, though.'

225

Another shout went up and Stone grinned. 'The bastards'll be yelling for another reason before long,' he said.

Carelessness, fatalism, arrogance, pride of race – all made the Hejris vastly underrate the men inside the fortress, and it was decided to make the attempt during the afternoon, when they might be growing slack in the heat.

As the men gathered under the wall near the side gate, armed with rifles, revolvers, bayonets and grenades, they all went over the instructions again.

'It's got to be done fast,' Stone was saying. 'We've got to get there quick and under cover.'

'Try not to get too far ahead, Mr Beebe,' Pentecost advised. 'An isolated man in front of the others would be a shot for a sniper.'

Beebe licked his lips uneasily. 'OK, I'll watch it.'

'And if you can manage it, bring us back a prisoner. We might find out what's going on outside then.'

Fox and Stone nodded. Fox looked thin and lean, as though he were a jockey ready for a point-to-point. Stone's square face was set and he seemed ready for anything.

Pentecost turned to Chestnut and the limping Minto and the zaids. 'Very well, gentlemen, let's have the whole garrison on the walls. And silently. We don't want anyone outside to suspect what we're up to.'

Beebe's group gathered under the screen they'd erected near the small side gate, hidden from sight, all of them silent, the Dharwas grinning all over their faces at the prospect of excitement.

With the sun still nailed to the sky, Beebe felt a little sick as he reflected how much depended on him. He still

226

wasn't sure what had made him volunteer, but the unbending rigid attitude of resistance that Pentecost showed had stirred in him an unwilling admiration that was growing daily, and he had committed himself almost without thinking.

From the ramparts, Minto, sitting in a chair at an embrasure near one of the Martinis, a rifle in his hand, raised his fingers to indicate they were ready. Pentecost looked at Beebe who nodded, and the civilian drivers they had recruited swung the gate back. There was a group of rocks shining metallically just beyond the arch and Beebe and Stone slipped out silently and waited there for everyone to emerge. Then Stone called softly, and the blasting party began running for the stables.

For a moment there was no reaction, either from the lulls or from the stables, then suddenly the Hejris came to life. A green flag went up and a blast of rifle fire burst from the ruins. Two of the Toweidas went down at once, rolling over like shot rabbits, but one of them leapt to his feet again and went after the others, limping heavily, his face twisted with pain.

There had been no attempts to fortify the ruins, and in no time they were against the wall and Stone was lobbing grenades inside the windows.

'OK.' He nodded to Beebe as the crashes stopped. 'Inside!'

5

From the ramparts, Pentecost watched as Stone's men began to throw out bundles of twigs and stones to form a barrier between themselves and the hills.

Behind them there were already three sprawled silent figures on the ground, and three more limping back

227

towards Fox's group among the rocks, their heads down to avoid the storm of bullets that had started from the hills and the surrounding folds of land. The silence of the afternoon had been split by the violent outbreak of firing from the walls; and from all sides, from ditches and gullies and the rock piles, men were seen running to reinforce the reims firing on the stables. Occasionally one of them stood and waved, clearly thinking that it was an attempt to cut a way out of the fortress, and a hail of fire was being directed at the gates, as though they expected them to open at any moment and a convoy of lorries to emerge.

The uproar was deafening, with everyone shouting and no one listening. Zaid Fauzan was flourishing a revolver at a loophole with wild gestures, laughing like a maniac, and Owdi was alternately blasting away on his bugle and firing his rifle. Next to him one of the Toweidas, overcome with the excitement, was shooting wildly at the ruins of the stables and Pentecost took him by the shoulders and directed his aim towards the rocks while he kept firing automatically. The wounded Dharwas from the hospital came crawling out with rifles and crept to the parapets, shouting with joy at the prospect of a fight after all the silence, but the Hejris were keeping up a remarkably well-sustained fire and soon there was a steady stream of wounded men heading back again.

In the stables, Stone and his group were crouched low behind the walls shooting towards the rocks, Stone cuffing the Toweidas as they fired wildly, their heads down. Still sickened by the sight of what Stone's grenades had done to the defenders, Beebe was searching for the shaft of the mine. He found it just outside the wall on the Hejris side of the stable.

'You've got to cover me,' he said to Stone. He signalled to his Toweida helpers but as they grasped their picks and crowbars and the explosives, the Deleimi guards began to appear from the hole. They were shot as they emerged by the Dharwas who by this time were dancing and laughing with excitement.

'OK,' Beebe yelled as they dragged the last of them out of the way. 'Let's go!'

Holding the haversack containing the pentolite, he jumped into the shaft, followed by the men with the battery and the wires. Immediately, out of the darkness a Khadari miner appeared and Beebe shot him with the revolver hanging from the lanyard round his neck. More came out, some with their hands up, and Beebe passed them up the shaft, but they were all killed and dragged away except one, his teeth ripped out by a bullet through the cheek, whom Beebe, remembering Pentecost's request for prisoners, managed to save. The Dharwas were now almost out of control in their excitement and he had to swing his fists to stop the butchery.

With the last of the Khadari miners hiding in a chamber at the end of the tunnel, Beebe got to work by the light of a torch held by one of the Toweidas. Sandbags, rocks, everything they could find was used to tamp the pentolite in place in the holes Beebe had dug out with a crowbar.

'Detonators,' he said, realising he was shouting in the sustained excitement.

The man with the detonators failed to appear, and Beebe found himself shrieking with rage. It was some time before they realised that the man had been killed, and it was Stone who clambered out of the shelter of the stable and dragged the body inside. He was hit in the upper arm as he did so but not disabled and he ignored the wound, searching the dead man's haversack for the detonators.

'For Christ's sake hurry!' Beebe shouted, in a panic of fear that they would be overwhelmed before they'd finished.

The detonators were passed to him at last and, forcing himself to be calm, he unwrapped them carefully. It was a job that demanded a steady hand, and the thought that they might at any moment be swept away by a rush from the rocks made it difficult to keep his head. He found he was sweating profusely in the stuffy atmosphere of the tunnel and had to keep shaking his head to blink away the moisture that filled his eyes.

He attached the wires at last and pressed the detonators firmly into the plastic pentolite, then driving the other men before him, began to pay out the coils, cursing and sweating every time they became tangled. At the top of the shaft, he attached one of the wires to the battery, his fingers fumbling and clumsy in his haste.

'The bastards are coming!'

Stone's words struck his ears but he forced himself to ignore them. The firing redoubled and a Dharwa fell against him, knocking him over, and he had to drag himself clear and paw about in the rubble under the body for the end of the loose wire.

The Hejris had left the sangar now and were running towards the stables with the green flags, aware at last of what was happening and determined to stop the demolition of their work. Firing increased from the ramparts and Fox's post among the rocks, and Beebe heard the crack of the Martini.

'For Christ's sake hurry!' Stone shouted. 'We can't hold 'em much longer!'

'Nearly ready,' Beebe shouted back, and he was aware of Stone clambering up the pile of rubble, a Sten gun in his hand. The chattering in his ear almost deafened him, and he became aware of men falling sideways. A bullet hit the ground near his head and whined away, then he looked up as he finally managed to find the end of the wire.

'OK,' he said. 'Stand clear.'

Then he realised that Stone had fallen backwards and was sitting among the rubble, still holding the Sten, his legs outspread, a thin trickle of blood coming from his mouth, a bewildered expression on his face, enamelled eyes blankly on the sky. For a second, Beebe stared at him, startled, then he remembered why he was there and clapped the second wire to the battery.

Near the wall of the fort he saw the earth balloon upwards in a cloud of blue smoke, then the blast, travelling along the tunnel and up the shaft, knocked him over on to Stone. Stone didn't move and it dawned on Beebe that he was dead.

For a second, shocked, he crouched near the body, trying to avoid the falling dirt and stones and small bouncing rocks, then he turned and jerked a hand towards the fort.

6

As the light faded from the sky, the Dharwas were still noisily excited and Minto cheered the shocked Toweidas by giving them all a tot of arrak and doling out cigarettes. As they had all been smoking a mixture of cloves, chopped straw and bark for some time, cigarettes from the store which they kept for the sick were a tremendous reward.

Beebe's prisoner had died and they lost four men killed and seven wounded but they soberly felt that, despite the loss of Stone, they had done a great deal of damage and still retained the initiative. The scattered corpses of the dead outside troubled them, but they were just beginning to recover from the shock of the fight when the alarm bell rang, and Owdi's bugle started in a tuneless fanfaronade.

Fox put his head round the corner of Pentecost's office.

'Main gate, sir,' he said. 'The bastards have got torches and what looks like tar barrels!'

'Cover the gate, Jim,' Pentecost said, reaching for his belt. 'And let's have the searchlight and some of Chestnut's fireballs ready.'

The firing burst out as he spoke, a sudden clatter from outside and the sharper, more disciplined, answer from inside.

In a fury at the loss of the mine, Thawab had flung his men against the gate with everything he possessed. But the attack was ill-organised, and though the tar barrels were fired, under the sustained fire of the fortress and a sortie led by Pentecost they had not been pushed hard enough against the woodwork and the hurriedly mounted attack was driven off. For ten minutes there was a frantic free-for-all and in the darkness one of the Deleimis actually managed to scramble into the fortress. Just as the infuriated Fauzan knocked him flying and was on the point of blowing his brains out with the revolver, Fox pushed up the weapon.

'Take him down to the cells,' he said. 'Billy'll want to talk to him.'

As the dazed and sullen man was dragged away by a couple of none-too-gentle Dharwas, sporadic firing was still going on at the Deleimis crouching among the rocks.

Still shuddering from the violence of the attacks, Beebe could hear a man wailing near the gate and he wondered if it were the prelude to another attempt at a mine.

'What's he saying?' he asked Fauzan who was waiting alongside him.

'He says, Abassi, that his brother has been killed in the fight and that as life means nothing more to him, he wishes to die also.'

He moved Chestnut's searchlight nearer and, cocking his head to listen, directed it carefully and hefted his rifle in his hand.

Beebe shivered. He was still overwhelmed by Stone's death that afternoon, still wanted to weep at the shock and horror of the killing inside the stables. The raging excitement of the Dharwas as they had returned, their boasting of their prowess as warriors, the ecstatic joy of fanaticism they had felt at the fight as they had exhibited their stained bayonets and blood-splashed clothes, had not touched him. He felt drained and lonely in his misery.

Fauzan glanced at him, guessing what was troubling him, and gestured at the searchlight.

'Abassi,' he whispered. 'Press the switch.'

As Beebe's hand moved and the light flared they caught a glimpse of a red Deleimi cloak and black headcloth among the rocks, then Fauzan's rifle cracked near Beebe's ear and the red cloak disappeared with a jerk.

'You can switch off the light, Abassi,' Fauzan said with a grim smile. 'We have helped him join his brother.'

When everything was quiet, Pentecost sent Chestnut to fetch the prisoner and Ali, the Toweida interpreter, from where he was cowering among the civilian workers, his head under a blanket. It was hard to say who was more worried. Certainly the Deleimi, a lean tigerish man with a

233

curled beard and a vast bruise on his cheek where Fauzan had hit him with his revolver, showed no fear.

'Ask him how many of the Hejris and Deleimis there are outside,' Pentecost said.

The answer came back quickly. 'More than Bin T'Khass can stop.'

'And where did the miners come from? The men who dug the mine?'

The Deleimi spat. 'They came from the Khadari,' he said.

'Does Wintle know?'

Yes, the Deleimi said, Owinda-el knew all right. A Khaswe official had been visiting the Khadaris in an attempt to negotiate their loyalty for another year and they had sent him back with a message that the Ridwha and the Fajir passes were closed to Sultan Tafas.

'Who else is with Aziz?'

A list of tribal names and leaders followed, quoted by the Deleimi with a fierce pride, as though he were determined to frighten them. Among them they noticed that of the Muleimat.

Minto looked at Pentecost. 'That m-means every bloody pass through the Dharwa range is l-locked up, Billy,' he said.

Pentecost frowned for a moment. 'Does Owinda-el know this too?' he asked the prisoner.

The Deleimi sneered. 'The Muleimat are cleverer than the treacherous Khadari,' he said. 'They have not told him. They have taken the Sultan's subsidy.'

Pentecost was silent for a moment. He had noticed the Deleimi's contempt for the Khadari. 'Many Khadari miners were killed when we blew up the mine,' he pointed out. 'This would not please the Khadari.'

The Deleimi sneered. 'The Khadari are cowards and turncoats. They have taken their dead and gone back to open their pass. They are going to take Tafas' money again.'

They were silent while the prisoner was led away, then Pentecost turned to Chestnut. 'Take his weapons and ammunition from him, Sergeant,' he said. 'Then give him a meal and turn him loose.'

'Loose, sorr?'

'Yes. But make sure his meal's a sparse one. And let Ali be profuse with his apologies. Let him feel we have few rations. He'll tell Aziz and they'll probably decide it isn't worth risking lives when we're likely to chuck our hand in soon. It might buy us a little time.'

7

The tower still stood. The wall still stood. The gates still stood. And a great many lives had been lost for nothing, and the Khadari, taking their dead with them, strapped across the backs of mules and donkeys, had started to leave the camp at Addowara to begin their long trek home. Once more Thawab's boasts had proved valueless, and he was merely more short of followers than before, and there were growls among his men that he was wasting lives.

'Thank God I did not commit the Hejri,' Aziz sneered. He gestured at the bruised face of the freed Deleimi. 'Bin T'Khass is more likely to starve than be defeated by Thawab.'

The infuriated Thawab's hand went to his gun but Aziz brought up the Mannlicher. 'I can shoot the eye from a rat,' he pointed out coldly and Thawab subsided.

'Aziz is a great leader,' he said, controlling his temper. 'But it is Thawab who does all the work. If the Khadari leave us, so be it. We do not need them. Rhamin Sulk is back with his offer of guns.'

'We do not need guns!'

Thawab flared. 'He also brings news that Owinda-el is soon on the move,' he shouted.

Aziz paused, disconcerted. He tried to appear unconcerned.

'You will have to hurry, Thawab,' he said slowly to give himself time to think. 'Bin T'Khass will defeat thee yet.'

Thawab exploded. 'We should bring in artillery!' he shouted. 'Owinda-el is coming!'

'He has not arrived!'

'Do we have to wait until he rides through the gate?'

'He can run backwards and forwards from Umrah to Zereibat for all I care,' Aziz snapped. 'Until he passes the Dharwa range he is none of my concern. Khalit is a whore of a country and Tafas is a shadow of a sultan. Let him rot in the ditch he has dug for himself.'

Thawab began to recover his control. 'Aziz is an old fool,' he said. 'He thinks only of his own back garden. The world has changed. A share of Khalit is ours for the taking. By helping the Khaliti to throw out Tafas we can demand land south of the Dharwas. Then it would be Khusar who controlled the passes and the plain beyond.'

'We are not farmers!' Aziz stormed. 'And Thawab gave his promise! No artillery until the plain was reached!'

Such was the power of the old man's personality and the threat of his anger, Thawab backed away and there was a muttering among the minor chiefs. Then one of them intervened. 'Let Thawab stick to his word,' he said.

'A gun could smash down the gate with a handful of shells. We have plenty of time. Let us destroy Owinda-el for good in the Tasha and finish off Hahdhdhah at our leisure.'

There was a chorus of agreement and murmurs from Aziz's supporters. But not enough to give him much comfort. Always he had hoped for a negotiated peace and the joy of seeing Pentecost march out unharmed. His mind was not subtle and, obsessed with old-fashioned things like honour, he had not known until Thawab outlined them what the aims of his nation were beyond the taking of Toweida. As he turned away into the shadows, his mind was made up. His own forcefulness had stopped the artillery but it was only a temporary check, he knew, and he must follow the defecting Khadari and bully them into keeping the Ridwha Pass closed to lock Wintle from the Plain.

As Aziz vanished among his followers, Thawab stood for a moment, lost in thought, his hand on his belt, his teeth gnawing at his lower lip. Then he saw Majid the Assassin standing alongside, staring after Aziz, his thin fanatic face twisted with hatred. For Majid there was never any question about who was right. He had been brought up since childhood to believe that a Deleimi was always right and anyone who belonged to any other clan was wrong.

He was a thick-headed man imbued with the red-hot doctrine of the holy men who had stirred his fathers to passion and blinded their vision. To Majid the whole of life was an electric atmosphere filled with the religious enthusiasm of ancient jehads. He was unafraid in attack and fed on hatred, living always with defiance, existing for no other reason than to continue his struggle against anyone and everything that was not Deleimi. His tribe was small and his views narrow, and his courage was a fervour that cost him nothing in steeled nerves.

Thawab watched him for a moment, then his eyes narrowed. 'Aziz is an old fool,' he said softly.

'Thawab speaks the truth,' Majid said automatically.

'He has the brain of the Toweida goat and is twice as stubborn. Deleimi men could be the rulers of Khalit. Aziz is nothing more than a stumbling block.'

'Nothing more,' Majid agreed.

'Without Aziz, Deleimi men could be powerful in Khusar councils. Even in Khaliti councils. It is a great wonder no Deleimi warrior has ever thought of this and removed him from the scene.'

Majid's head turned quickly and, as he stared at Thawab, Thawab read in the fierce unafraid eyes exactly what he wished to see.

'Could you remove Aziz, Majid?' he asked.

Majid spat and patted the Garand rifle. 'I could remove Aziz,' he said quietly. 'Whenever Thawab asked.'

eleven

Their sufferings were not measured by the number of killed and wounded, which so far had not been great, or even by sickness – though the list was growing. They were measured by confinement, overcrowding, and smells. Three hundred odd people – more with the civilians – were having to live in a space eighty yards square. Their sanitation arrangements had always been bad and, though they had improved them, they had still remained primitive and inadequate. They were verminous and a plague of insects like sand fleas, brown ticks that bored into the skin, had given them all itching sores.

Food had grown monotonous and scarce, and they were now eating a toasted wheat mash that could not sustain life – grain ground laboriously by the women with pestle and mortar or by a mill driven by the jacked-up driving wheels of a lorry. Their tobacco was gone and condensed milk was kept only for the wounded, so that dysentery was spreading and they dreamed and talked of food whenever they were off duty.

They were all tired now and only Pentecost seemed untouched by exhaustion. He had had a trench dug across the courtyard so that they could cross it without coming under sniper fire, and since the mining, had decided that silence was perhaps their most effective weapon and had given orders that no one was to fire except at specific targets. As they crouched behind the embrasures under the shelters of canvas and rush matting, the fort looked empty, with nothing moving for hours at a time. But it also looked ominous and if a Hejri or a Deleimi showed himself outside a rifle cracked, setting off a chain reaction so that hundreds answered in reply.

The weather had changed to cold winds and sleet and the sky took on the colour of ashes, and with their short rations they were chilled blue at night so that Pentecost had startled Beebe by appearing in a Persian sheepskin coat that made him look like a pop star posed for publicity. But the Toweida were growing nervous again and verses from the Koran had been stuck in cleft sticks on the ramparts as prayers for relief. They were all losing their sense of proportion as little irritations appeared mountainous, and small quarrels kept breaking out between soldiers and civilians, between Dharwas, Civil Guards and Toweida Levies, even occasionally between Dharwa and Dharwa and Toweida and Toweida. The zaids and int-zaids who were left were barely on speaking terms and it was only the loss of Lack – which had reduced the British officers to two, three including Beeb – that kept them from losing their temper with each other, because Minto was invariably occupied in the hospital and had even moved his quarters there. He had performed miracles with repulsive wounds and had sat night after night over the medical books and the bound journals from the library. He had even tried amputation, using the meat saw from the kitchen, and had emerged looking like a butcher. There was little anaesthetic left now, though, and it was never used for the lighter wounds and the worry over his patients made him irritable. As for Fox and Chestnut, they had little in common, but since one was on duty when the other was off, there was little opportunity for them to quarrel, though Chestnut's complaints about the refusal of Fox's men to understand him were growing daily more bitter and Fox's insults about Chestnut's ancestry were occasionally not entirely in jest. As for Beebe, he was preoccupied these days with his own thoughts.

Somehow, like Aziz, he had fallen against his will under the strange spell of Pentecost and several times he found himself wondering just what it was about the boy that held him. He was far from being a dynamic character. Placid as a stone Buddha, his habits were monkish and he would probably grow dry and dull with age; but, Beebe realised, he had the kind of courage that was probably the finest of all, the courage to keep on keeping on and on, far beyond all reasonable hope, never thinking of himself as ill-used, and never thinking of himself as brave. He was always a little stiff, always formal, rarely unbending or laughing, but always friendly. Yet underneath his odd personality there was a whip-cord-and-steel core. It had been Pentecost who had brought in Stone's body and attended to its burial.

Nobody argued long with him, yet he was always able to disagree with the greatest possible politeness, so that they began almost to apologise for their different opinions. He had his finger on everything that happened and never seemed to sleep. Sometimes, to Beebe's fury, he didn't even seem to be tired. He was always prowling about, chiding a Toweida, talking gently to one of the children, or managing to wring a grudging smile from its mother, soothing the angry civilian employees who blamed him for their incarceration, placating Fox over Chestnut, or Chestnut over Fox, sorting out quarrels between Dharwa and Toweida and, when they were serious, coming down with a bang on both contestants so that they were quick to realise it wasn't worth the effort.

He rarely showed his anxiety, but once Beebe had found him at one of the embrasures staring to the north. His whole body had been tense, wiry and alert like a terrier at a hole.

'Something worrying you?' he had asked.

Pentecost had turned, his face thoughtful. 'A little, Mr Beebe,' he said.

'Set my mind at rest.'

Pentecost's head moved slightly, in a small gesture towards the north.

'I don't understand it,' he said. 'Why don't they bring up guns?'

'Guns?' Beebe's jaw had dropped. 'Artillery, for Christ's sake?'

'Why not, Mr Beebe?'

Beebe found his throat was dry and he swallowed quickly. The young men in the fort had talked so casually about dying he had considered it all a load of crap at first. Now, vaguely, he saw that their understatements were only their way of equating a possibly violent end to their lives with a rather boring joke, and he saw that they did it because it helped them to avoid looking the fact directly in the face.

'Maybe they've got none,' he suggested.

'Maybe not,' Pentecost said slowly. 'But it wouldn't take them long to get some. They could fly guns into

Makhrash and have 'em through the Addowara Pass in forty-eight hours. Why haven't they?'

Beebe stared to the north, hoping that there was a damn' good reason why not. So far, it hadn't occurred to him that the northern tribes had not reached the limit of their resources.

'Think they'll try?' he asked.

Pentecost shrugged, his smooth face expressionless. 'I'd be surprised if they didn't,' he said.

The idea of artillery shells plunging into the fortress, striking haphazardly at men, women and children, worried Beebe and brought him more and more to consider a problem that had been concerning him for days now – that of getting a message to Wintle warning him that, contrary to what he believed, it was the Ridwha not the Tasha Pass that was open.

Messages continued to reach them. The British Government, thrown into a panic by Tafas' move north, had scraped up two companies of fire-fighters and flown them into Khaswe. The airport was under control again, but the shooting and the bombings continued. A British officer had been shot in the back and two more headmen had been murdered, one in the Dhafran area and one near Haraa, while tribesmen from over the borders to the east and west, taking advantage of the trouble in Khalit, were busily exchanging shots with the Muleimat in Umrah and the Khadari in Zereibat. The whole country was seething with unrest.

But the British had not called Tafas' bluff because they had not dared to, and with British troops flying into Khaswe, his army had moved north towards Haraa and finally Dhafran. Already the first scouting lorries were heading out of Dhafran towards the Tasha.

The news obsessed Beebe, particularly when none of the civilian workers, worried by the banners clustered in the encampment near the village, would offer to take a message south. Despite their professed desire to leave Hahdhdhah, they were terrified of being caught, and Pentecost was not eager to risk one of the stolid, cheerful Dharwas who were the backbone of the defence. There were only thirty of them still active and he knew he could never trust one of the Toweidas.

Time was of the essence, Beebe knew. They had already been besieged for forty-five days but, while the bleak courage of the garrison was still obvious, the unburied dead around the stables came back to plague them with their stench. Twice already the rations had been reduced and there was a great deal of sickness among the civilians who were not buoyed up by responsibility. They were living on a handful of meat and rice a day now, and Beebe knew that if Wintle was caught in the Tasha, nothing on God's earth would ever produce a second column of sufficient strength from the Sultan's indifferent army to get through to them in time.

Like the Fajir, through which he had passed from Dhafran on his journey north, the Tasha was narrow. Its sides were a limitless expanse of rock and crumbling hill, with vast slopes of shale and shingle. Its paths descended in zigzags, and it was a place of dry, windless silences. Down its roads the Muleimat warriors strode, their heads up, always armed; and the few guards, in fragments of Sultan Tafas' uniform, rode their thirty-two-inch-high donkeys, their rifles across their backs, their putteed legs hanging down on either side almost to the ground while their miniature mounts tottered along on twinkling feet. It was a place where bridges constantly slid away into gulfs in the rains, where there were always dead mules and donkeys which had not survived the journey, or burned-out lorries, their wheelless axles in the air like the amputated stumps of some strange metallic victim of a ritual murder.

It was an oppressive place and in Beebe's mind there was always the picture of Wintle's lorries caught beneath its crags. He had not had any particular fondness for Wintle when he had met him in Dhafran but, remembering how little fondness he had had for Pentecost when he'd arrived at Hahdhdhah, he now began to wonder if perhaps the fault were with him and not Wintle, because there was a great deal about Wintle that was repeated in the younger man. Though their characters were very different, they were both professionals in the best sense of the word.

Wintle deserved a chance. And, even more, so did Pentecost.

2

Resolutely, Beebe knocked on Pentecost's door. Pentecost was writing at his desk and outside the fortress was silent. An unexpected rainstorm had saturated the sentries and left them cold and wretched in the wind that followed.

There had been a lot of drumming during the day and Beebe had heard bugles among the rocks, and seen Deleimi tribesmen dodging from cover to cover. They had been expecting an attack after dark but the rain had come at the crucial moment and stopped them in their tracks, and Beebe had later seen the shadowy figures withdrawing towards Addowara, their shoulders bent against the rain, their garments soaked.

Pentecost waited for him to speak, a small smile playing across his lips. Beebe always felt awkward in his presence, even sometimes like a small boy up before his headmaster.

'You found anyone yet to get out to warn Wintle?' he asked bluntly.

Pentecost eyed him for a moment, then he shook his head.

'Wintle'll be going into a trap, with the Ridwha wide open,' Beebe pointed out.

'I'm aware of that, Mr Beebe. I'm also aware that the Khadari might still decide to wait and see which way the wind blows.'

'Somebody ought to tell Wintle. The Tasha's more dangerous than the Ridwha.'

Pentecost acknowledged the truth of this with a slow nod of the head and Beebe drew a deep breath.

'How's about me?' he asked.

For a moment, Pentecost said nothing and Beebe was half afraid he was going to laugh in his face. He ought to have known: Pentecost would never have done anything so impolite.

'You, Mr Beebe?' he said, and Beebe found himself wishing to God he'd do him the honour of just once using his Christian name.

'Yeah, me,' he said. 'Why not?'

'In principle, no reason at all why not, Mr Beebe.' To his surprise, Pentecost didn't immediately offer an objection. 'There are one or two small drawbacks, however. You don't speak Khaliti and you don't look much like a native of the state. There's an encampment guarding the road south and if they caught you wandering about outside the fort, they wouldn't be in doubt for long about where you'd come from.'

'I can disguise myself.' Beebe ran a hand over his face. He'd stopped shaving at the beginning of the siege and his heavy beard and moustache had grown rapidly.

'I suppose you could,' Pentecost agreed. 'All the same, I'm not entirely happy about it It's not your quarrel. You're not really involved.'

'All the more reason why I should leave,' Beebe said. 'Then everybody'll be able to say I shoved off just when it was getting dangerous.'

Pentecost stared at him. 'I shouldn't, Mr Beebe,' he said gravely.

He so sincerely meant what he said, Beebe found he was embarrassed. 'Yeah –' he grinned foolishly ' – why not? I'm not a soldier. I can't even shoot. Hell, you'd never miss me.'

Pentecost smiled. 'You did remarkably well when you destroyed the mine. Nevertheless –' he shook his head ' – I'm as responsible for you as I am for all those civilian drivers and clerks and store-keepers and their women and children.'

'For God's sake!' Beebe exploded.

'I can't let you go.'

'Why not?'

'Because they'd pick you up at once.' Pentecost frowned. 'You saw what happened to Lack. I'd need much more convincing that you couldn't be recognised.'

Beebe left the office not certain whether to be angry or humiliated; then, going back to the radio room, he saw the strip of red cotton cloth he had thrown over the receiver to protect it from the drip of water when the rain had driven against the cracked wall in the wind.

He stared at it for a moment, then he grabbed it and threw it on his bed and, pulling a roll of Khaliti money from his case, he went outside again to the cellar where the women and the civilians sheltered. An hour later, he returned with heavy sandals, a pair of the baggy cotton trousers the clerks wore, a yellow shirt, the blood-stained woollen cloak in henna-dyed wool that had been worn by the prisoner he'd brought from the stables, a brown girdle and a length of dirty grey-black cloth for a turban. Inside the prison he had occupied, the ammunition belt, dagger and battered Lee-Enfield of the man they'd captured at the gates still rested on the bed. The stock of the rifle was scarred and pitted, as though it had been used for a hundred and one domestic chores from breaking firewood to knocking in nails. Picking it up, Beebe carried it back to his room, and that evening, after dark, he smeared his face, hands and feet with shoe polish and began to dress himself in the garments he'd bought. It was some time before he felt satisfied with the result then, putting the ammunition belt over his chest and the dagger at his waist, he picked up the ancient Lee-Enfield and went along the corridor to where Pentecost lived.

Pentecost was on the walls and he waited nervously for him to return. After a while he heard footsteps on the stairs and straightened. Unfortunately, it wasn't Pentecost. It was Sergeant Chestnut and, as soon as he saw Beebe, his mad eyes flared and he reached for his revolver.

'For Christ's sake, Chestnut!' Beebe howled. 'Don't shoot! It's me! Luke Beebe!'

Uncertainly, the gun already in his hand, Chestnut stared at the shabby figure cowering against the wall, its hands clawing at the air.

'Beebe,' he said suspiciously, 'what are ye doin' in yon get-up?'

'Oh, for Christ's sake – ' Beebe almost fainted with relief as Chestnut thrust the gun back in the holster ' – I'm going to try to get down to Wintle! Somebody's got to go.'

'Does wee Billy know?'

'Not yet. He said I had to convince him I'd got a good disguise. Hell, I think I convinced you.'

Chestnut's crazy covenanter face stared at him with disapproval then it broke into a frosty smile. 'Ye sure as hell almost got a bullet in y'r guts,' he said. 'Ah reckon if ye can fool me ye can fool oor Billy. Ye might even convince Aziz.'

He stared at Beebe more closely, frowning heavily. 'Yon girdle's wrong, though,' he said. 'The Deleimi dinnae wear 'em like that. They twist 'em before they tie 'em, and they wear their daggers underneath. The murdering bastards dinnae like ye tae see what they're aboot tae stick in ye. An' mon, y'r headdress's a' wrong. Yon's an Indian turban. They wear 'em different here.'

Beebe grinned. 'Sergeant, can you fix it for me? And how about the colour?'

Chestnut grinned. 'Ye're a wee bit on the purple side,' he said.

3

Pentecost was reading the casualty figures with Minto when Chestnut appeared on the flimsy excuse of asking his advice about the Martinis. They were still talking when the door opened again and Beebe appeared.

Minto immediately reached for Pentecost's revolver which was lying on the desk near him and Chestnut had to jump forward.

'For Christ's sake, no, sorr!'

Minto's hand dropped. 'What the hell's he doing in here?' he demanded. 'Who is he? Some bloody spy from Aziz?'

'Yon's Mr Beebe, sir,' Chestnut pointed out, and Beebe saw their faces fall.

'I guess I've maybe convinced you I couldn't be recognised,' he said, and Pentecost came round the table to pear more closely at him.

'You look uglier than normal, Mr Beebe,' he said with a hint of a smile and Beebe's brown-stained face split in a grin.

Pentecost stared at him for a moment, frowning, then he raised a hand and adjusted the headdress, drawing the ends down to hang over Beebe's ear, and gave a twitch to the woollen cloak.

'Deleimi,' he said. 'You look like one of Thawab's men.'

'You reckon I'll do?'

Pentecost permitted himself the ghost of a smile. 'I think perhaps you might, Mr Beebe. You've produced a perfect complexion from somewhere.'

'Officers' boot polish, sorr, mixed wi' other ranks',' Chestnut said.

Pentecost stared again at Beebe, then he picked up the revolver from the table, and looked again at Beebe. 'I think it might be a good idea if you wore one of these under your night-gown,' he said.

'I can go?' Beebe asked.

'What happens if you're stopped?'

Beebe grinned. 'I grunt. I'm a bad-tempered Deleimi.'

Pentecost frowned. 'The Deleimi are a suspicious people,' he said. 'What's more, they like boasting. It's plain to them not to. I think we ought to work out something better than that. You couldn't have been wounded in the face, for instance?'

Minto grinned. 'I've got some rags I took off one of the Dharwas,' he said. 'They haven't been washed yet. If you don't object to dried blood and a few other things to go with the stains on that cloak. I could arrange for you to have been shot through the face.'

'I can take my teeth out,' Beebe said. 'I've got a plate. I got my front incisors kicked out playing football.'

Pentecost nodded. 'And let's get Ali to write him a letter,' he said. 'To indicate he's on his way to relatives near the Sufeiya to recover. From one of Thawab's minor chiefs – Taif el Heiridhin or Yasin or Abu Mauliyi. Something nice and florid. If anyone argues, you can point to your face and produce your piece of paper.'

Beebe was grinning now. 'I'm going then?'

Pentecost smiled. 'I don't think I could stop you, Mr Beebe.'

They were still laughing when Ali appeared with the laissez-passer he'd written. He'd borrowed a sheet of cheap notepaper from one of the civilian workers who'd bought it in Hahdhdhah village. The Arabic scrawl indicated that the bearer was Khallaf, a Deleimi rifleman shot through the face in the attack on the gate. Because he had lost teeth and part of his tongue, he was permitted to go to relatives to recuperate. 'Let no man call him coward,' it ended. It was signed Abu Mauliyi. With it, Pentecost handed over another folded paper.

251

'What's this?' Beebe demanded.

Pentecost smiled. 'You might call it instructions – to leave.'

'I don't need a written order, for Christ's sake!'

'You might,' Pentecost said gravely. 'There'll always be someone who'll try to suggest you slipped out because things were becoming unpleasant.'

'They wouldn't say that!'

'The world's full of grocers, Mr Beebe.'

They were studying him carefully now in a final check-up, adjusting his headdress and the bandages round his face, and rearranging his clothing. One of the few remaining goats had just been slaughtered for the following day's meal and the grinning Fauzan brought some of the blood in a clay bowl.

'I hope you haven't got a queasy stomach, old boy,' Minto said. Beebe grimaced. 'Go ahead,' he said. 'It's in a good cause, I guess.'

Minto splashed the blood literally over his clothes and bandages and head so that his beard and moustache dried stiffly and his hair stuck out in spikes under his headcloth.

'Hold your head up, Mr Beebe,' Pentecost said as he practised walking. 'A wound's something to be proud of. You're a Deleimi warrior and you've been well and truly blooded.'

They were still studying his appearance for mistakes when Fox appeared to tell them that the timbers and rocks had been removed from behind the gate.

'Dark as the inside of a cow, sir,' he said. 'They'll never see anything.'

'You know your way, Mr Beebe?'

'Hell, you can see the lights in Hahdhdhah. After that all I have to do is follow the road down to the Sufeiya.'

They shook hands all round, then while the sergeants went to the wall, Pentecost accompanied Beebe to the gate. Zaid Fauzan stood there, uneasy with the rocks and sandbags and timbers pulled away.

'Nothing moving, Abassi,' he whispered.

Beebe turned to Pentecost, suddenly terribly frightened by the silence and the darkness. Until that moment, he had never realised how much security he had found inside the crumbling stone walls.

'Hell,' he said, hesitating. 'I didn't realise it would be as scary as this.'

As he slipped outside, Beebe felt rather than saw the gate close behind him, and heard the low shuffling sounds of the rocks and timbers being replaced. It was then that he realised he was alone and that there was no longer an eight-foot-thick wall between him and the Deleimi murderers who had flayed Lack alive and exhibited Stone's remains.

For a moment, he found his knees refusing to bend and his limbs refusing the demands of his brain, then he heard a rustling sound among the brushwood on his right, and half-expecting to see one of the green banners that haunted his sleep appearing from a fold of ground, he dived away from the wall to where he knew the rocks huddled. It might have been only a small animal but it was enough to stir his paralysed limbs and he lay panting and shuddering for a while in the darkness until he could find his courage again, and moved away from the fortress in a low crouching shuffle in the direction of Hahdhdhah village.

4

After a quarter of an hour's stumbling in the shadows, barking his knees and skinning his elbows on rocks, Beebe stopped dead, suddenly aware how much more difficult movement was at night. Then, as his eyes grew more accustomed to the darkness, he saw the road on his right and made his way towards it. As he reached it he glanced towards the fort and realised that for the first time he was looking at it from the outside. He'd been half asleep when he'd arrived and hadn't even bothered to look up, and now he saw how low the walls were, how fragile the whole thing seemed.

After a while he heard voices ahead of him and, before he was aware of it, he had almost stumbled on to a low fire hidden behind a cluster of rocks. There were half a dozen Hejri warriors round it, and for a moment, Beebe stood motionless, staring at the men who had risen slowly to their feet as he emerged from the darkness, their hands reaching out for their weapons. His heart pounded in his chest and his limbs felt paralysed with fright.

One of the men approached, his rifle in his hand, and Beebe realised he would have to do something. As the man spoke, he made a grunting noise and pointed to the bloody bandages about his face and the matted hair of his moustache and beard. The Hejri peered at him in the dim glow of the fire, then he said something which Beebe failed to understand and turned his back on him indifferently.

The gesture was a tremendous boost to Beebe's morale. They were cruel men used to pain and wounds in their daily life and they weren't prepared to waste much sympathy on him. As they turned away and squatted again by the fire, Beebe stood for a moment, then he shuffled out of the glow of the flames, one hand to the bloodstained bandages as though the pain troubled him.

From that point on, he passed several groups of men carrying flags, and realised he was passing through the Hejri lines. The first groups all challenged him, reaching for their rifles as they spoke, and he realised they must be the outposts, but later he was ignored, and he saw he was in the middle of the Hejri encampment where it sprawled across the road to the village.

Here the men were bent over wounded friends, and a donkey with an injured man astride its back was heading out of camp. Almost without thinking, Beebe began to follow it. More wounded attached themselves to them and soon a straggling group had formed, heading across the plain.

Hahdhdhah village was a hive of activity. Men lounged in doorways and, through the openings, by the dim light of oil lamps, Beebe could see interiors with more men in groups, arguing loudly. Some of them wore bandages but they all carried weapons, and the women shuffled between them silently, while children stood in little clusters staring wide-eyed at the activity. There were a few horsemen trotting about and in the square he saw the remains of Lack's lorry. The houses alongside were black with smoke.

The shuffling group of wounded came to a halt. Beebe stopped with them, then he became aware that they were all excited. He couldn't make out what was agitating them so much, until he saw a man drawing on the walls of one of the houses. The crude picture he was forming with a stick of charcoal from a fire appeared to be a gun.

Then a youth, probably hoping to strut and swagger among the girls, tried to take the battered rifle from him and Beebe was so startled he almost let it go. Remembering just in time that he was supposed to be a warrior, to whom his weapon was another limb, he hung on to it, grunting fiercely and reaching for his dagger, and the youth released the rifle and fled. A little shaken, he hurried through the village and was marching head down when a horseman suddenly clattered across his path and halted his mount. The rifle in his hands was pointed at Beebe and a harsh voice snarled at him. His heart pounding, Beebe gestured at his bandages. The man snapped something else at him and Beebe continued to gesture. Still the man snarled and, still grunting, Beebe pulled away a corner of the bandage and showed the matted blood on his moustache and opened his mouth to show the gaps where he had taken out his dental plate.

Still the man stared at him suspiciously and, finally remembering the paper Pentecost had given him, Beebe fished it from his robes and handed it over. The horseman stared at it then he called to another younger man lounging in a doorway, dressed in trousers and shirt and draped with ammunition belts.

The newcomer stared at the blood-stiffened hair hanging over Beebe's eyes, then he thrust the paper back at him and spoke quickly to the man on the horse. Beebe caught the name, Abu Mauliyi, once or twice. The horseman growled something and gestured with his rifle that he was free to go. Almost sick with fear, Beebe grasped the old Lee-Enfield and marched past, his head up as he had been told, conscious of the horseman's eyes on him all the way out of the village, his back tingling at the prospect of a bullet in the spine.

It was growing daylight as he put the village behind him and headed across the dusty plain. There were still horsemen about, trotting towards the north or driving cattle before them, but he was ignored. There were one or two curious glances at the dried blood on his face and beard and on the bandages, and occasionally a sympathetic question to which he answered with a gesture at his mouth.

After a while, he came to a check-point, probably set up to guard against deserters, where he was challenged again. This time, however, the paper brought no comment. The sentry was smoking a cigarette and Beebe stared at it desperately, aware that he had not smoked for three weeks. The man saw the look in his eyes and offered it to him. For a moment, Beebe hesitated, then he nodded, took the cigarette and put it to his mouth awkwardly, as though it were difficult to get it between his lips.

The first puff gave him new life and the sentry grinned at his expression, slapped his shoulder and waved him on.

He began to feel he was safe at last. Horsemen still clattered past, the trappings of their mounts jingling, and occasionally a camel, its bells clonking softly, to mingle with the babel of voices. At every house there appeared to be roistering Hejris, some of them taking to prostitutes with henna-dyed fingers and toes.

Now that he was growing used to freedom it was a wonderful feeling to be out of the fortress, to be able to see beyond the wood-and-stone walls to the distance and know that nothing held him in. Occasionally, he caught the scent of blossom from the withered bushes, a harsh scent but, after the odours of Hahdhdhah, inexpressibly moving. He had no idea how far he had travelled. Soon he would have to cross the river and since his pass took him only to the village on the banks, anywhere beyond he would be regarded with suspicion.

In the early morning light, he met a boy with a herd of scraggy goats and, by signs and gestures, managed to convey that he wanted milk. The boy had a tin bowl out of which he appeared to eat his meals and he filled it with milk from one of the nannies and passed it over. Turning away, Beebe affected difficulty in drinking, and, because of the bandages, spilt a lot of it down his clothing. Then, giving the boy a coin, he marched on, weary now and moving more slowly.

He still met horsemen or riflemen, but there were not so many now and he realised he would have to be more careful. A single individual would rouse more suspicion than a straggling crowd.

During the day, growing tired, he decided to sleep and, finding a place among the rocks, curled up in as much shade as he could find. He awoke late in the afternoon, having slept far longer than he expected. He still had a long way to go and he was growing hungry now, so he ate one of the withered oranges he'd brought with him and gnawed at a hard biscuit, and drank from a thin sliver of sullen water moving between the stones.

As he followed the stream south, he realised it was growing broader, and he knew he must be approaching the Sufeiya and that this stream was one of the feeders from the mountains. Finally, he saw a gleam of water and a cluster of brown-yellow buildings in the distance and realised he had reached his second obstacle. Now there was only the river. Hahdhdhah was as good as saved.

5

From his scout car, Brigadier Wintle stared from under his Dharwa headdress at the entrance to the Tasha Pass. Behind him the huddle of buildings that made up Afarja village showed among the shrubby slopes of juniper and myrtle, and further along the road he could see the tower of Afarja fort, since the fall of Umrah the last eastern outpost of the Sultanate.

He glanced again at the pass with a jaundiced eye. Near him, staring through binoculars, was Zaid Yasin, the commander of the fortress, a small leathery little man, his figure draped with map-cases, revolver and binoculars. Wintle pulled the headdress lower, his eyes narrow.

The Dharwa Heights rose in front of him like a vast wall, patches of red shale interspersed with black rock. To the right the mountains curved round, climbing steeply, the peaks shining in the late sunshine against the pale blue sky.

Wintle was worried. There was something ominous about the stillness. The Muleimat had not sent their headmen down to meet him and he had a suspicion that somewhere, somehow, something was not as it should be. It smelled wrong. It felt wrong and, before plunging into the pass, he had halted his lorries to study the place.

Behind him, his men watched, sitting in their vehicles with their weapons, already covered thickly with the red-brown dust of the border, all a little bored despite the prospect of excitement, the Dharwa scouts wishing Wintle would get on with it so they could be among their hated enemies, the tribes to the north. Over the little column there was a smell of hot oil, metal and rubber.

The rest of Wintle's men were five miles back along the road. It had been Wintle's intention originally to head into the pass, with no other consideration but the relief of Hahdhdhah, but the strange intuitive feeling that all was not as it should be had halted him until the rest of the column caught up with him.

He was still wondering whether to take the risk and go ahead when he heard the sound of an approaching vehicle, its gears grinding noisily as it climbed the zigzag path up the hill.

'What the hell – ?' he said aloud. His instructions had been that there was to be no show of haste, no indication that they were heading for Hahdhdhah, in the hope that the owners of the prying eyes that he knew watched them all along the road from the mountain tops might think he was only trying to regain Umrah from the northern tribesmen.

As he turned in his seat, he saw another scout car hurtling towards him, throwing up the dust and bouncing harshly on its springs on the rocky track. The driver was a Khaliti subaltern from Khowiba, at the far end of the border road.

'What the hell are you doing here?' he snapped as the other scout car drew alongside. 'Haven't you enough to do at Khowiba?'

He stared at the other occupant of the car, wondering what the hell a blood-stained scruffy-looking Deleimi was doing aboard. He could tell he was Deleimi from the twist in his girdle and the way his turban was tied.

'Reimabassi!' The subaltern looked a little nervous. 'I was told to find you. Zaid Waouzzit thought it was important.'

The Deleimi had climbed from the scout car now and was standing alongside Wintle. 'I'm Beebe,' he said in an American accent. 'Lucas Beebe. I've just come from Hahdhdhah.'

Beebe had crossed the Sufeiya in pitch darkness aware of the increasing cold. The clear sky had filled with clouds in a matter of minutes, it had seemed, and as he had waited in a cluster of thorn bushes on the river bank for darkness to come, it had begun to rain, at first in a drizzle and then, unexpectedly, in a downpour that soaked him to the skin and left him chilled to the bone. The storm had brought a squally wind with it and he had crouched miserably on the bank of the river, wretchedly aware of his empty stomach and the weakness of his limbs.

As the darkness had thickened, he had slid down the crumbling bank, his feet unable to find a purchase on the thin soil that was being washed down by the rain, and the mud at the bottom was sticky beneath his sandalled feet as he moved forward cautiously among the white boulders that filled the bed of the river. On his right, he could see the lights of Sufeiya village and hear the roistering of the Hejris guarding the bridge, and the squeals of women. He was saturated now and frozen, but at least the rain was keeping the sentries on the bridge out of sight.

It was difficult finding his way forward because some of the boulders towered above his head and in the darkness he found he was terrified of losing all sense of direction. Trying hard to keep the lights of Sufeiya behind him, he headed out among the rocks, climbing one, skirting another, banging his knees in the darkness as his sandals slipped on the wet stone. Then a dog started barking from the bank, probably disturbed by the sound of his feet, and he saw a door open and a shot rang out, to send the dog yelping to safety.

Terrified that they'd shoot at him, too, he flung himself down among the boulders, aware that he'd skinned his ankle in his haste. After a while, he rose and continued, moving towards where he could now hear the murmur and rustle of water.

After a while, he was standing at the water's edge and saw that he'd come to the crisis of the crossing. According to Zaid Fauzan, the river was deep enough in its centre to drown him, and, because of its depth, there was a swift current after the rain. He stared at it for a moment, trying to summon up his courage, then he began to move forward. Coming from the mountains, the water was icy, far colder than he'd expected, and it took his breath away as it rose above his knees and embraced his stomach. The clothes he wore clung clammily to his body, heavy and sodden, but he struggled onwards, feeling his way cautiously into the stream. Then, abruptly, when he wasn't expecting it, the ground beneath his feet fell away and he disappeared beneath the water.

He came up, gasping and shocked with the cold, and struck out instinctively for the opposite shore. He was aware of the current carrying him towards the iron bridge and, terrified that he'd be borne beneath one of the sentries who would hear him splashing in the water, he almost lost his head. He was still fighting his way across when he barked his knees against a submerged rock and found he could put his foot down. But as he stepped forward, his foot slipped and he fell again. As he rose, spluttering and frightened, he realised he'd twisted his ankle.

He was in the shallow water at the other side now, trying to find his way to the bank. His knee felt as though he had scraped all the skin from it, and his ankle gave him sharp jabs of pain as though the sprain was worse than he'd thought.

Gasping, dragged to the ground by the wet woollen cloak he wore, he flung himself down to get his breath, aware that he'd lost the revolver from under his clothes. Oddly enough he'd hung on to the battered Lee-Enfield and he decided that perhaps it was safer that way.

Struggling among the rattling reeds at the far side, he found himself beneath a high earth bank and moved frantically along it, unable to find a way up and terrified he'd still be there, in full view of the sentries, when daylight came.

He found a narrow gully where water lashed down in a steady stream from the Dharwas towards the river bed, and managed to scramble up it. He was soaked and plastered with red mud and, as he reached the level of the road, he realised just how hungry and cold he was. He had lost one of the heavy sandals he had worn, so he kicked the other off and set off barefooted towards where he could see the vast shadow of the mountains against the sky.

Several hours later, sick with weariness, he realised he'd lost his way and sank down among the rocks to recover his breath before picking out the entrance to the pass. He soon found the road again, and headed up the slope, marching with a heavy limp into the mountains. It was still dark and he saw no one, though occasionally he glimpsed a light just off the track where some Khadari hut lay among the boulders or where some goatherd cooked his food for the night. Occasionally a dog barked but he moved warily round them, keeping to the side of the road so that if anyone appeared he could vanish among the rocks. As daylight came, he dragged himself lamely into a gully to rest.

When he woke, the sun was out, warming him with weak rays through the watery clouds. The road now was just a muddy track full of puddles, its edges running with noisy water. He was about to climb from his hiding place when he heard voices and, peeping carefully out, he saw groups of men in tattered robes and head-cloths, interspersed here and there by shabby green battledresses and peaked caps.

He remained there all day, trying to forget the emptiness of his stomach and the chill of his body as the wind howled through the mountains from the north. Only the thought of Hahdhdhah prevented him from throwing his hand in. From time to time more Khadari and an occasional Zihouni in a black cloak appeared, and in the end he decided it was safer to remain where he was until dark.

He waited until it was no longer possible to make out the rocks along the road before he emerged, then, limping heavily, began to head south again. His ankle had stiffened up by this time and every step was agony. The damp woollen cloak hung like a lead weight from his shoulders, impeding his movements, and clinging to his legs and arms as he walked.

How long he trudged on he didn't know because eventually he was moving in his sleep. Once he fell, and once he walked clean off the road into the rain gully that ran alongside the road, knocking himself half-silly as he crashed down. He climbed out, numb with misery, and found his way to the road again, conscious of the pain in his ankle and all the places where he had skinned himself in falling. He was shivering with cold now and frantic with hunger, stumbling, falling and weaving about the road in his exhaustion. Then, blinded by weariness, unaware of what he was doing, he suddenly realised someone was shouting at him and, as he pulled himself together, a dark figure seemed to rise out of the shadows.

A torch snapped on and, by its reflection, he saw that he was faced by a young man in a black Zihouni headdress. He wore a greatcoat, unbuttoned and hanging open, and over one arm was a rifle.

Immediately Beebe's exhaustion fell away from him and he lifted the old Enfield butt-upwards in his right hand as he gestured with his left at the soaked and bloody bandages round his head. The Zihouni didn't seem satisfied with his grunts and spoke to him in words he couldn't understand. In the end, he produced the safe-conduct pass purported to have been signed by Abu Mauliyi, and the youngster stared at it in the light of the torch, frowning heavily, weighty with officiousness. Then he pointed backwards and spoke again and Beebe realised he was telling him that the Sufeiya was behind him and that he had no right to be in the pass.

Beebe was a bedraggled, desperate figure by this time, and the boy grabbed him roughly by the shoulder and tried to turn him back. Beebe shouted incoherent words but the boy insisted, and as he let go and pointed again his head turned away, the angle of his jaw gleaming in the reflected glow from the torch. At once, almost without thinking, Beebe brought up the rifle with all that remained of his strength and heard the satisfying crunch as it struck the boy on the chin.

Even before the boy had fallen to the ground, he was weaving in a staggering run for the rocks at the side of the road.

6

'I guess it turned out I got on the wrong road after the
river and was in the wrong pass,' he said to Wintle. 'I'd
got into the Ridwha instead of the Fajir and I was nearer
the end of it than I thought. When it came daylight, I saw
a bunch of guys coming towards me. They looked like
Khaliti troops and, brother, was I pleased to see 'em! Only
I forgot what I looked like and they were just going to
plug me when I remembered I wasn't a wounded Deleimi.
Boy, did I yell? I threw away that goddam gun and flung
my hands up and started yelling for help. Fortunately, one
of 'em understood English. They had a lorry down the
road and they took me to Khowiba where the guy in
charge decided that what I had to say ought to be said to
you.'

Wintle eyed him. 'And what have you to say?' he
demanded.

Beebe moved round the scout car, limping heavily, and
Wintle saw that his feet were wrapped in rags which
appeared to have been torn from his clothes. 'This
goddam pass is closed,' he said. 'The Muleimat are
waiting in there for you with everything they've got.'

Wintle's eyebrows danced. 'Are they, by God?' he said.
'I had a feeling they might be.'

'The Ridwha's open,' Beebe went on. 'Or as good as.
The Khadari had enough at Hahdhdhah. We sent 'em
away with bloody noses. But Pentecost said not to trust
the bastards, all the same. He thought Aziz might send
someone after them to stiffen 'em and they might still wait
to see which way the wind was blowing.'

Wintle's face was grim. 'We'll knock the bloody
stuffing out of the sods,' he said, 'then next time they'll
think twice before changing sides.'

He studied Beebe for a moment. 'How do you feel?' he asked.

'I guess I'm fazed.'

Wintle handed him a brandy flask. 'I'll send you to Dhafran as soon as I've got this bloody column turned round.'

'No!' Wintle turned back as Beebe spoke sharply. 'You don't send me back to Dhafran!'

'You need medical attention,' Wintle said. 'Your feet look like hell.'

'They'll hold up a bit longer,' Beebe grimed. 'I guess maybe I can ride now.'

Wintle stared at him. 'Why the hell do you want to go back there?' he said. 'It's no joy ride to Hahdhdhah.'

Beebe considered the question. He wasn't sure himself. It certainly wasn't bravery. He didn't enjoy danger and he disliked discomfort. Somehow, he decided, it was connected with Pentecost. He had to be there when Pentecost emerged to greet his relief. There'd be a faint frosty smile on his thin features and he'd come forward, dressed immaculately as always, aloof, unapproachable yet strangely appealing. 'Hello, Mr Beebe –' there wouldn't even be a Christian name, he knew, but he found himself looking forward more than he could believe to being the object of Pentecost's gratitude.

He tried to explain. 'I guess I don't really know,' he said. 'Maybe it's because I was there when it started and I want to be there when it finishes.' He managed a weary grin. 'I guess also maybe I want to see that guy's face is all.'

'Which guy?'

'Young Billy Pentecost. Brother, you sure have a hot property there!'

PART THREE

Friends in High Places

twelve

1

Wintle was coming.

The news brought to Hahdhdhah by Wintle's radio message had produced an electric effect. When Chestnut had delivered it to Pentecost, they had stared at each other silently for several long seconds, then Pentecost's tired face had broken into a slow smile. It was cold now and the wind was lifting the dust and they were all growing weary of the monotony.

'That's good news, Sergeant,' he had said.

'Aye, sir,' Chestnut had agreed. 'It is, that.'

When it was passed among the Toweidas and the Dharwas, men had wept, then it had swept into the courtyard and up the stairways and down into the cellars. It was written out in English, Hejri and Khaliti for all to see and a single thought surged through the minds of everyone. They were saved! It didn't matter that Wintle was no closer than the road that ran along the south of the Dharwas from Umrah to Aba el Zereibat. If they could only hold out a few more days, Wintle would save them. His fame along the frontier was secure. No one – not even Aziz – treated him with impunity. He knew how the Hejri and Deleimi thought and knew their deviousness, their stubbornness and their vanity. There would be no stopping him.

Later in the day, Chestnut produced a bundle of pamphlets he'd printed on the ancient duplicating machine they'd used for proclamations. OWINDA-EL COMES, they announced. TAKE CARE, AZIZ. TAKE CARE, THAWAB. OWINDA-EL IS ON HIS WAY. Chestnut was very pleased with them.

'It'll help Billy,' he said as he showed them to Fox. 'Make 'em realise we've got friends in high places, mon. Ah thought it might be a guid idea to fire 'em fra' the walls.'

'What the hell with?' Fox asked.

Chestnut's humourless face cracked into a grin. 'Ma catapult,' he said. 'Me an' yon Beebe built a gey grand one, mon.'

2

Thawab was furious. He flourished the printed paper in front of Aziz's nose and glared round at his followers.

' "Owinda-el comes," ' he read aloud. ' "Take care, Aziz. Take care, Thawab. Owinda-el is on his way." Now what does Aziz say about his great plans?'

'The Khadari are holding the pass at Ridwha,' Aziz roared back. 'I have been myself to see them.'

'They cannot stop Owinda-el! He has guns and radios. The Khadari have nothing but rifles and their muscles and blood! And why did he not go into the Tasha? We were waiting for him there. There has been treachery.'

Aziz lifted the Mannlicher slowly. 'Dost thou accuse me, Thawab?'

There was a tense silence and Thawab controlled himself. 'No,' he said carefully. 'I do not. But we have waited too long and there has been too much talk of Bin T'Khass and not enough of Rhamin Sulk's guns.' He paused and stared round at the tribal chiefs who were watching them. 'We can have them here in twenty-four hours.'

Aziz stared at him, unable to speak, knowing in his heart that the one thing he had tried to avoid was now inevitable. With Wintle heading for Hahdhdhah he no longer dared put Thawab off. Hahdhdhah had become a symbol. It had no value either to them or to the Sultan and it didn't even stop the tribesmen swarming across the Sufeiya. But it did indicate whose authority covered the plain, and that was enough.

He suddenly realised he was an old man – tired, disillusioned, and conscious that he no longer held the Hejri tribes in the palm of his hand as he had in the past. Tragedy was a recurring motif of age and all he wanted at that moment was to go back to his lands in the north, taking his son and the Hassi girl from Addowara with him, and remain there quietly for the rest of his life. Events were out of his control.

'Very well,' he said quietly. 'Bring Rhamin Sulk's guns.'

He remained standing silently by the fire, still holding the Mannlicher, aware of defeat and heedless of the shouts around him as everyone leapt to their feet and began to hurry away. There was little he could do now, except to try to prevent a massacre.

3

Not far to the south, the Khadari had ambushed Wintle's truck convoy in one of the few savage gorges the Ridwha Pass contained, and the armoured cars could use neither their weapons nor their mobility and the column had taken casualties. They had withdrawn a little now, and Wintle had brought up mountain guns to blast the Khadari from their perches, and at the end of a bitter day's fighting the guns had gone into action and they had driven ahead another few miles.

Satisfied, they had halted for the night and fires had been lit and the cooking pots filled when they heard a heavy thud somewhere to the north. It made the air contract and the shock seemed to travel through the earth to where they stood.

Wintle looked round, frowning, but Beebe could see nothing that could cause them any immediate worry. Groups of Khaliti troops were preparing for their evening meal, and he could see the smoke of fires and the reddish-yellow colour of their vehicles among the rocks. The bleak landscape was empty. Ahead lay the mountains, the slopes touched with shadowed purple where the sun failed to reach, and there were a few mud houses at their bases where Wintle had established his headquarters.

Again the thud came and he stared round him, puzzled, but unable to see anything.

'That's a gun,' Wintle said. 'To the north.'

Then Beebe remembered the excitement he'd seen in Hahdhdhah and the man who'd been drawing on the wall of a house with a stick of charcoal snatched from the embers of a fire, and he knew what it meant. The Hejri had at last brought up the artillery Pentecost had been afraid of.

'They're firing at Hahdhdhah,' he said.

Wintle snapped round. 'Of course they're firing at Hahdhdhah,' he said.

He strode off, calling for his officers, and immediately the cooked food was issued and Beebe saw the Dharwas bolting it as fast as they could, while others began to throw equipment into the lorries.

Wintle returned. 'We move at first light,' he said. 'We can't do a damn' thing here in the dark. But we'll make a few more miles before we have to stop for the night.'

He paused again, staring up at the mountains, as though calculating what the resistance might be, and again they heard the thud to the north.

'Thank God they don't seem to have much,' Wintle said. 'Or else they're short of shells.'

Almost at once, there was another thud and the men climbing into the lorries paused, their heads lifted, their ears cocked.

'Well, that's four of the bastards,' Beebe said bitterly. 'I guess they're not that goddam short!'

4

The first shell arrived without warning, fired from the slopes near the Addowara Pass. The fortress was settling down to its evening routine of boredom, and the sentries, already beginning to shiver with their empty bellies against the increasing chill, had been placed for the night. Despite the discomfort, though, there were no complaints. Wintle was coming and they only had to hang on until he broke through the Ridwha, and even the Toweidas were beginning to think themselves great warriors.

The Dharwas were chattering on the walls on the dangerous south side where the ground sloped upwards and the walls were shallower, and Pentecost, his rounds made, was just sitting down to a spartan meal with Minto when they heard the shriek of a shell, and heard it whine overhead, and the crack as it exploded in the plain to the south.

'What in God's name's that?' Minto said.

Hurrying to the walls, they stared out over the plain. A puff of smoke near Hahdhdhah village was still hanging in the air and they could see figures running among the rocks and gullies like a lot of disturbed ants.

They were still watching when they heard another distant thud and another whine overhead, close enough to make them all duck. As they lilted their heads again, they heard the crack of an explosion and once more the puff of smoke, and rocks and dust were flung into the air to the south. Again the distant figures moved agitatedly and they saw a horseman galloping madly away and disappear into a gully. As the horse reappeared at the other side, still galloping at fall speed, they noticed its rider had vanished.

'Yon's a shell.' Chestnut had appeared on the walls now and was staring thin-faced and narrow-eyed towards the collapsing fountain of dust. 'Seventy-five or eighty-eight millimetre, or one o' yon Russian guns they've got.'

'Not very big,' Minto observed with studied off handed-ness.

'Wi' respect, sorr, big enough tae do a lot of damage tae the walls.'

As they watched, another shell screamed towards them and they ducked again. This time the shell exploded on the outskirts of Hahdhdhah and they saw fragments of timber hurled into the air as it demolished a hut.

'Direction's fine,' Fox commented dryly. 'Elevation's a bit out, though.'

There was a long silence broken only by the nervous chattering of the Toweidas around them, but no more shells, then they saw a horseman appear from the village and gallop at full speed across the plain towards the Addowara Pass.

'The mayor,' Chestnut grinned. 'Off tae register a complaint.' Pentecost was staring at Hahdhdhah village. 'I take it the artillery's arrived,' he said. 'I hope Wintle isn't wasting time.'

5

As it happened, Aziz's emissaries were doing better with the Khadari than anyone could have expected, and they had pinned Wintle down again five miles further on from his night encampment.

They were on a bare ridge now above the river and, no matter how carefully Wintle sited his lorries, it proved impossible to prevent the Khadari sniping on to the face of the slope. Aziz's threats had certainly put fear into the Khadari headsmen.

After the day's sun, the sickly smell of death hung over the place, and as they tried to move forward again, Beebe passed three mules lying in an open grave at the side of the road. The Khaliti troops had not had time to bury them properly but there had been some shallow excavations there, where rocks had been dug out for wall-building, and they had used them for the mules.

Something cut the air over his head with a sharp whip-crack slap and a moment later a dull smack and a high-pitched whine sounded from the rocks behind him. He glanced upwards, unafraid. After Hahdhdhah this seemed trivial.

Wintle glared at him. 'Get your head down, Beebe,' he snapped. 'You're not behind the walls at Hahdhdhah now.'

Calmly the sniper probed the convoy, firing twenty or thirty rounds, and a platoon of men went off to the left in an attempt to search him out. It was too easy for men riding in lorries to be picked off to allow him to remain hidden. After a while, there was a flurry of firing and a shout from above, and Beebe saw the platoon returning down the slopes among the rocks.

The column moved on again, passing the traces of the battle that had been fought by the vanguard. There were more dead mules by the road, their legs stuck out, stiff and ugly, and here and there the splash of blood on the white stones, and ridges scorched by the shells of the mountain guns. Eventually it started to rain and the Khaliti faces around Beebe became puckered with misery. Almost immediately, however, it stopped again, and the wind dropped and the heat in the gorge made the stones steam. Again they ran into hidden snipers, and had to halt the main column round the bend while the advance guard shot it out with them and another section made a detour up the slopes to get behind them.

They moved off eventually in full darkness, the pace painfully slow. Beebe was fidgeting with nervousness. His injured ankle had been strapped up by a medical officer and while it was painful it was possible now to walk. Although he had abandoned his turban, he still wore the rags in which he had escaped from the fort, and, with his unshaven face and the remains of the boot polish that clung to his skin, they made him a weird sight among the neat uniforms of the officers.

The column began to splash and rustle through a stream across the road. The wooden bridge had been destroyed and none of them enjoyed being wet. All day they had listened to the steady thud of the guns to the north, not a rumble so that they knew there were not many, but a regular thud so that Beebe had begun to grow worried.

'The bloody place'll be full of holes now,' he said. 'Can't they do anything to help from Khaswe?'

'Hold your water,' Wintle soothed him. 'I'm aware of what you're feeling.'

'Even a few goddam bombs would help.'

'Not here,' Wintle said. 'We haven't been fighting Aziz for twenty years not to know that. And in any case, I suspect they've got their hands full down there already.'

Wintle didn't know the half of it. It seemed to most of the people in Khaswe that the place was in flames from one end to the other again. The Intercontinental Hotel had also had its front blown in now and the press were camped in the rear dining room, a little shocked by the fact that two of their number had been killed by a mine. Cozzens had imposed a strict censorship when he had discovered that certain foreign newspapers were busily dispensing news of his plans and that they were being sent out from Europe to the Nationalist leaders by sympathetic embassies. He had also got rid of all extraneous people and had gladly shunted the Bishop of Harwick home at last, determined not to be responsible for his safety, and was now trying to get rid of the women and children.

By the grace of God none of them had yet been hurt, but he had withdrawn them all inside a compound controlled by the army, which included his headquarters and the palace. It wasn't possible to stop infiltration even into this, however, and there had been a little sniping, but he had the main points well guarded, though he was fully aware that, even with the extra men sent out from England, they were not gaining any ground. They were merely holding on and, despite what was being said in the House of Commons, their chances of remaining indefinitely were remote. The Khaliti Nationalists had not gained the initiative yet but they were encouraged by their successes and Cozzens was well aware that most of his own moves were only in answer to theirs.

He felt old as his problems crowded in on him. He had heard that the first messages from Gloag up near the Dharwas – and God alone knew how he had got there! – had been answered with a furious cable from his company demanding that he change his attitude. His later messages – their attitude unchanged – had been received in noticeable silence, however, because questions were suddenly being asked by responsible people. They had finally provoked a flood of new instructions from Whitehall and Cozzens was now fighting with his hands tied, knowing he couldn't hit back hard enough to discourage further incidents.

As the telephone rang, he almost jumped.

'Cozzens,' he snapped, snatching it up.

'Alan – ' it was Southey's voice ' – I think we've found a way round.'

'It's a pity we have to indulge in diplomacy to help young Pentecost.'

Southey's voice sounded harsh as he replied. 'I didn't make this situation and my orders state categorically that Hahdhdhah's no affair of mine,' he pointed out. 'For that matter, it's none of yours. It belongs to Tafas.'

'Tafas is saying nothing,' Cozzens growled. 'He's lying low. I think the old bastard's considering abdicating after all.'

'He is?'

'He got a report from that American oil expert he sent up to Hahdhdhah. He got out. He's with Wintle now and he sent down some preliminary notes. Besides, we're not going to win this battle, are we? No matter how we look at it.' Cozzens sighed. 'What have you worked out?'

'We have rockets. We ought to be able to land them right where they're wanted.'

'Are you going to fly them up?'

'Not on your life!' Southey's voice was full of determination. 'I've told you my orders and I'm sticking to 'em. But I've found a way round them. Some of them have been here a long time. We can declare half a dozen or so of them dangerous. It ought to be enough.'

'Go on.'

'Normally, the bomb-disposal people would attend to them but I'm quietly handing 'em over instead to Tafas' people. They can use 'em on Aziz.'

'Do they know how?'

'We've shown 'em. They've been practising.'

'When do they go?'

'About midday tomorrow. There'll be no shadow then and they'll be able to see more.'

'Very well. Can they do the job?'

'They'll blow Aziz's whiskers off without even singeing him. There's just one thing – '

'What's that?'

'They've asked for some information about where Aziz's people are. They want to make their fireworks count.'

'What do you suggest?'

Southey paused. 'What about this Yank who got out of the fort? He'll know. Can we contact him? Get him to identify a few points.'

6

Boots rang on stones, hooves struck sparks. As they had floundered among the rocky outcrops, several more animals had broken legs and had had to be shot.

The wind that blew from the north was cold now and as they probed further to the summit of the pass the shelter of the bushes and trees grew thinner. The snipers were still troubling the column and every single one of them had to be winkled out, and it was a slow and laborious task because Wintle knew as well as the Khadari that he couldn't afford to arrive at the other end of the pass with half his men casualties. There were reported to be ten thousand Hejri and Deleimi and associated tribesmen in the Toweida Plain and hostile Shukri and Muleimat and Jezowi in the Tasha and Fajir Passes who would turn round if he emerged weak and come down on him from behind.

As the bullets of a new flank attack began to ripple along the crest held by the Khadari, Wintle was called to the radio. As he read the messages, his lean face softened.

'They're laying on a strike,' he said to Beebe. 'Two aeroplanes with rockets.'

He spread a map of the Toweida Plain on the bonnet of a scout car. 'They want us to pin-point where the Hejri are,' he said. 'They want you to tell 'em.'

Beebe stared at the map, then his hand moved across it. 'Here,' he said, and Wintle marked the points where his finger jabbed with a pencil. 'In these folds of land here. In the Addowara Pass. And here.'

Wintle began to make out a message to Khaswe, glancing at the map, and they waited impatiently while the operator sent it.

'Christ knows where Tafas got the rockets,' Wintle said. 'He hadn't any when I was last in Khaswe.'

They had not heard the guns from the north for some time now, chiefly due to the noise their own column was making. A group of wounded came back, and a corpse lashed to a Khadari donkey, the body shrunken, its hands dark with dried blood. As it bounced past, a Dharwa rifleman at the side of the road shook one of the dangling hands, watched by his grinning comrades, and the corpse passed out of sight. Then a mountain sheep, bewildered by the shooting, appeared and rifles cracked. It fell as it was galloping flat out, down among the rocks, and a Dharwa sergeant requested permission from Wintle to fetch it in for cooking.

The radio began to chatter again and Wintle turned back to the operator who was scribbling on a pad. Eventually, he handed the pad to Wintle who stared at it, frowning.

'They say this isn't enough,' he said to Beebe. 'They're afraid of putting their fireworks into peaceful Toweidas. They don't want to stir up trouble for the future. Is there any way they can identify the Hejri, they want to know?'

'For Christ's sake,' Beebe said. 'What do they want me to do? Run ahead of the bastards and wave my arms?'

Wintle's grin died quickly. 'A good point,' he said. 'But you have to remember we have to administer this bloody frontier, even when Hahdhdhah's relieved. We don't want to make the Toweida hostile, too. We have to live with 'em.'

'They wear different clothes. Different colours.'

'You can't tell what colour a chap's wearing when you're flying at four hundred miles an hour five hundred feet up. You can't tell how he ties his turban or the way he twists his girdle. Isn't there anything else? Did he have his horsemen camped anywhere special? Did they have anything to identify them?'

'Yes, by Jesus!' Beebe remembered the green banners they had seen whenever the Hejri had appeared, the banner Aziz had always carried for his parleys with Pentecost, those banners that he had seen in his sleep. 'The bastards carry green flags.'

Wintle stared at him. 'They never carried flags before.'

'It was some stunt of Aziz's. He always carried one when he came to parley. There were dozens of 'em. Big ones.'

Wintle studied him for a moment then he turned to the signaller and scribbled the information on to the pad. As the set began to squawk again, he swung back to Beebe.

'Just keep your fingers crossed,' he said. 'We haven't heard those damn' guns lately. I just hope they aren't making life too much like hell in Hahdhdhah because we shall be through in two days now and up there in four, and somebody in Khaswe's finally pulled his finger out to hold Aziz off till we arrive.'

Beebe grinned. 'I'm glad I'm not Sister Hannah carrying the banner,' he said.

thirteen

1

The realisation that the siege had entered a new phase had come home to them with the first wildly directed shell from Addowara. They had not wasted their time, however, because Pentecost had been expecting artillery ever since the beginning of the siege and they were well sandbagged against blast and flying splinters, and all women, children, civilians and wounded had been removed to the cellar – even the last of their small herd of goats. It was dark and stifling down there but at least they could come to no harm.

For the rest of them, however, there was no shelter except in the slit trenches that they'd dug, or the sandbagged hides, and the first ear-splitting crack the following morning had rattled fragments of stone against the walls.

They were all well aware that a few direct hits would soon demolish the gates and their only hope was that ammunition was in short supply.

Out of the first shots there were a fair number of overshoots and undershoots, then a shell exploded to the right of the gate, and gouged out a huge chunk of stonework as though it had been bitten away by a giant mouth. The wooden supports splintered as the rocks flew into the air, and a great deal more of the wall rolled into the courtyard. One of the Toweidas was killed and two were badly wounded, but even as they were being carried away to Minto in the hospital, they were already struggling to push the rocks back into the wall and shore it up with timber and sandbags.

Fortunately, at that point the firing stopped, as though the tribesmen, having found their range, were sitting back for a meal. It started again three hours later, when six shells were fired. One of them struck the main look-out tower, killed two Toweidas and left the tower rickety on its supports; another chipped the top off the wall where they had repaired it, sending showers of rock fragments into the air; three whined over the fort to explode in the plain beyond; and the last struck the gate.

By this time, the fortress was surrounded by smoke from burning timber and the air was full of flying dust. A bucket stream from the well put out the flames, then they discovered that the rooms below the look-out tower had caught fire, and they struggled in sweating heat to get at the woodwork before it burned away and the place collapsed. As they worked, the Hejri outside kept up a steady fire, peppering the walls and any unwary head that appeared opposite an embrasure.

By the end of the day they had been bombarded three times and had counted eighteen shells. It wasn't many, especially as eight of them had sailed overhead or exploded among the rocks short of the fort, one of them even among the trees where the Hejris had massed under a banner for an assault. The screams of pain had not comforted them much, because they were busy with their own wounded, but at least the assault had not taken place.

Altogether the fort had been struck ten times and was clearly falling to pieces like a lump of wet sugar. One of the towers was down, the gate was splintered and, at one point where the shells had hammered at the same spot, the wall had crumbled until it was only six feet high. As night fell, they realised that the generator had been smashed and, as they waited in terrifying darkness until Chestnut linked up their emergency supply from the lorries, Pentecost mustered everyone on the wall where the gap occurred, half-expecting an attack.

But none came. The shell among the Hejris had unnerved them and they were sitting back waiting for the guns to do their work at longer range.

'There are two of 'em, sorr,' Chestnut said at their evening conference. 'One in the pass and one a bit tae the right. I got a line on the direction o' the shells.'

'No more than two?' Pentecost asked.

'Two's enough,' Fox said.

It was a strange little conference. Pentecost was the only British officer present now because Minto was fully occupied in the cellars with the new batch of wounded. They had had five men killed during the day and seven wounded and the morale of the Toweidas had slumped abysmally.

It was obvious that a great deal more of the shelling would make Hahdhdhah untenable. Eventually the Toweidas would reach the point when they would refuse any longer to fight, and without them there were not enough men either to hold the walls or repair the damage that was being done. They were all tired and weak through too long on short rations. Nerves were on edge and sickness was increasing, and even Pentecost had started to dream of food and freedom whenever he fell into a fitful sleep. The women, ashamed of their dirt, no longer appeared, and crouched in a huddled group in the cellar, keening their sad songs, some of them widows already.

The day when, after the first receipt of Wintle's message of hope, Pentecost had warned against over-confidence seemed to have long gone, and they were fighting for their lives again. It was now sheer luck whether Wintle or the Hejri arrived first.

For some time Pentecost had been debating whether to parley with Aziz. Fighting to the last man was no longer sensible these days, no matter what orders said, but, with Wintle almost through the Ridwha, there was no point in hanging on because if the Toweida Plain were lost now, it was gone for ever.

As the others offered their opinions Pentecost was sharply aware of the loneliness of his position. The responsibility was all his and he was never lonelier than now. With success or failure balanced on a knife-edge, the decision he was debating was a tremendous one. How long dare he hang on? Already they had held out beyond the point of reasonable endurance and no one could accuse them of cowardice. Without Wintle, the beginning of the shelling might have made the decision easy.

'I think we have to decide, gentlemen,' he said, 'just how much longer we can reasonably stay here. What do you think?'

They all offered their opinions, which varied from forty-eight hours from the youngest int-zaid, who was influenced by the fact that he was a Toweida and knew that if the Hejri broke into the fort they wouldn't show much mercy, through Fox, who gave them a week if the shelling continued, to Zaid Fauzan, who was a Dharwa and had spent his whole life on the frontier and hated the Hejri and Deleimi tribes with the hatred of generations. In Fauzan's world, there was no place for any arrangement and he would willingly have held the fort to the last man and the last bullet.

Privately Pentecost thought that the young int-zaid's was the nearest estimate. The others were too optimistic and Fauzan's idea of resisting to the last man was simply not worth considering.

'I think,' he said, 'we must play it by ear. So long as we can rebuild the walls and so long as the Levies don't start disappearing over the wall, we must keep trying. We have food for perhaps fourteen more days – and with luck Wintle will be here before then.'

The first shell of the next day smashed Chestnut's laboriously constructed searchlight, and the second finally brought down the water tower and a section of the wall with it, and had the Hejris been sufficiently daring, they might have got into the breach. As it was, they were able to replace the rocks, though the great iron tank made a wonderful barrier from behind which Hejri riflemen could snipe at the walls. The third shell knocked away a portion of the south wall and it was then that they realised that missiles were falling into the courtyard, and that the Hejris had somehow also acquired mortars.

During the day they lost two lorries and one of the scout cars and the courtyard became a chaos of running men as they moved the remainder of the vehicles to positions under the south walls, where they were less likely to be caught by a direct hit. They were becoming aware now of the Toweidas grumbling, and that they were refusing to leave their shelters to effect repairs, and though Zaid Fauzan kicked them into action, Fox knew that before long they would cease to obey him, and some surly soldier might even put a bullet in his back. It made him bitter at the thought of the people who had neglected them.

2

Unknown to Fox, their position had concerned Tafas for some time. Mortar bombs had started to land in the Palace grounds and the façade was pockmarked where bullets had struck. The Wad, Victoria Street and Khesse were scorch-marked by flames and every hundred yards there seemed to be a burnt-out wreck. Beyond Khesse, the students rampaged, in complete control, and the Nationalists were feeding them now with rifles and pamphlets demanding the end of the régime. Food and petrol were scarce, and the water and electricity supplies were only intermittent. There were no buses and no ferry across the harbour, and he knew that he was surrounded by treachery and that plans were afoot to catch him in his car with a bomb.

Listening to the occasional pop of a rifle and the distant rattle of a machine gun, he stared at Rasaul's heavy face with disgust. The Minister had suddenly re-emerged after his feigned illness, with advice that seemed to consist only of strong hints that he should abdicate.

'The Nationalist leaders demand more say in the running of the country, sir,' he was saying.

'They have their parliament,' Tafas snapped. 'The Dhofar has been sitting almost continuously since the emergency started.'

Rasaul shrugged. 'The country north of the Dharwas does not even send representatives any longer,' he pointed out.

Tafas scowled. 'What do the Nationalists offer?' he asked slowly. 'In return for this greater say?'

Rasaul shrugged. 'Nothing but a willingness to cease fire.'

Tafas exploded. 'Why haven't I advisers who have the courage to say what they mean?' he snapped. 'They want me to abdicate.'

Rasaul essayed a small bow. 'That would seem to be their wish, sir.'

'And what is your view?'

Rasaul coughed again and Tafas knew what was coming. 'I fear you'll have to go, sir,' he said.

'I thought some sort of treachery like that was contemplated. What about the frontier?'

'The Havrists have contacted Thawab abu Tegeiga and he has agreed that, in return for the Toweida Plain, he will remain in the north until Khaswe is settled. After that, he will make sure the Toweida Plain becomes Khusar country.'

'Isn't he growing too big for his boots with Wintle on the move?'

Rasaul's expression remained unchanged. 'I understand that Thawab has brought up artillery and is shelling Hahdhdhah,' he pointed out.

The Sultan paused. 'Do we still have radio contact with Hahdhdhah?'

'The American, Beebe, said they were continuing to keep a listening watch for instructions.'

Tafas knew only too well what the American, Beebe, had said. He had not forgotten why he had been sent to

Hahdhdhah in the first place and a preliminary report on his findings had arrived on the Sultan's desk. There was no oil beneath the Toweida Plain. Not a drop.

The frontier wasn't worth fighting for, after all. All his hopes that wealth would unite his people were ended. Everything north of the Dharwas seemed to be as good as gone, and, for all he could see, so was Khaswe. There seemed nothing left but to bow out gracefully and take his old bones to the South of France to await death.

'What about Cozzens?' he asked. 'What are his plans?'

Rasaul paused. He had learned of the rocket strike from contacts at Carmel airstrip but he had made sure that Tafas had not. Tafas was clearly hovering on the brink of abduction and the news that Cozzens was getting himself involved on the frontier after all might well change his mind again. Tafas' well-known secretiveness had played into his hands, and even Yani and the air force officers were complaining that they'd been unable to inform him of the way things were shaping. 'General Cozzens has his hands full with Khaswe,' he said.

Tafas sighed and walked to the window, catching the sickly scent of blown roses from the garden. When this dreary business had started they had been in full bloom. Despite his defiance, he knew he had come to the end of the road. He was too tired to counter the plots against him. He belonged, he decided, to a more graceful age, not one where the methods of bazaar hucksters had become normality. He had lost prestige. He was openly scoffed at and despised and anarchy reigned on every side. He suddenly decided to give it all up.

'Make your arrangements,' he said. 'We will begin by giving up the north. All it seems to require is a signal.'

3

For a moment, as Chestnut read the Sultan's message he thought he was seeing things, then he yelled for the Dharwa orderly outside in the corridor.

'Abassi Pentecost!' he shouted. 'Iggeri! Quick!'

Pentecost appeared within a minute, covered with the dust that seemed to fill the whole of the fort for hours after every bombardment.

'Sorr!' Chestnut jerked his head at the buff form he held. 'Read yon.'

The words seemed to leap out of the paper at them. They were clear, in English, and had come direct from Khaswe.

'HAHDHDHAH TO BE EVACUATED REPEAT EVACUATED STOP TOWEIDA PLAIN TO BE GIVEN UP UNDER TRIPARTITE AGREEMENT BETWEEN AL HAVRA NORTHERN LEADERS AND SULTAN OF KHALIT TO BE SIGNED IN NEAR FUTURE STOP ARRANGE TRUCE STOP ONLY CONSIDERATION MUST BE SAFETY OF LIVES STOP WILL REPEAT HOURLY FOR CONFIRMATION.'

It was signed Tafas.

'Do you think it's genuine, Sergeant?' Pentecost asked.

'Nae doobt aboot it, sorr! Came through on the regular channel at the right time.'

Pentecost's tired face twisted, the creases round his mouth cracking the layer of dust that covered his skin.

'Ours not to reason why, Sergeant,' he said. 'Though it begins to look to me as though a lot of people have died for nothing. Perhaps it's just as well, though. I don't think we could have taken much more.'

The north wall was almost down and the tower in the south-west corner was a mass of rubble. The hospital was a nightmare of groaning men and they had finally run out of space to bury the dead and were burying them in the outhouses.

They had suffered three bombardments during the day, every one worse than the last, though the tribesmen, short of ammunition, were still limiting themselves to their six shells per bombardment. In itself it was not a holocaust, but the loosely bonded rocks of the walls were cascading into the courtyard everywhere now and there were half a dozen breaches, hastily shored up by sandbags, and ammunition boxes and lockers stuffed with soil. They had torn down inner walls to obtain material for repairs but every three hours until dark the six shells came to fill the place with the dust which billowed chokingly into the cellars, setting the women wailing and the children screaming. They had put out a dozen fires, and the courtyard was now only a litter of rubble, fragments of roof and splintered timber.

Pentecost stared again at the message Chestnut had handed him. The whole thing suddenly seemed to have been pointless. Stone was dead. Lack was dead. Minto was dragging himself round on crutches. To say nothing of the wounds and death dealt out to the Dharwas or the humble Toweidas pulled into the Sultan's force by promises of pay.

He suddenly felt very bitter. 'What time is the next broadcast?' he asked.

'One hour's time, sorr. Tae be exact, fifty-seven minutes from now.'

Pentecost nodded. 'I'll be here. I must have it confirmed.'

When Khaswe came up again, Pentecost watched Chestnut's pencil travelling across the pad.

'HAHDHDHAH TO BE EVACUATED REPEAT EVACUATED STOP TOWEIDA PLAIN TO BE GIVEN UP UNDER TRIPARTITE AGREEMENT BETWEEN AL HAVRA NORTHERN LEADERS AND SULTAN OF KHALIT TO BE SIGNED IN NEAR FUTURE STOP ARRANGE TRUCE STOP ONLY CONSIDERATION MUST BE SAFETY OF LIVES STOP WILL REPEAT HOURLY FOR CONFIRMATION STOP TAFAS.'

There was no change in the wording.

As Chestnut put down his pencil, he looked round slowly to where Pentecost was reading the message over his shoulder.

'What happens the noo, sorr?'

Pentecost seemed to be absorbed with his thoughts.

'How much light have we left, Sergeant?' he asked.

'Aboot an hour, ah reckon, sorr.'

Pentecost considered for a moment, then he turned away. As he paused in the doorway, he swung back to where Chestnut was watching him.

'Be so good as to tell Sergeant Fox to find a white sheet that will do as a flag, and to run it up on the main tower,' he said.

4

Aziz was among the first to see the white flag.

He was standing among the rocks, staring at the crumbling outline of the fortress. For three days he had watched it reduced to rubble, his spirits sinking lower and lower as the shells had done their work. No one asked him for orders now and he had given up his grip on the northern tribes without a murmur. He belonged to the past, part of the lost glory of the Hejri, to the days when a rifle or a machine gun was all a tribal leader could hope to possess. Thawab belonged with Communism, Fascism, Leftism and Rightism and all the other creeds that nowadays had their place in tribal strife. Aziz's politics were the simple politics of have and have-not, and all his life had been based on one thing and one thing only – the possession of the Toweida Plain. Thawab thought on a scale which included world blocs and his eyes saw Khalit and Khaswe and even beyond, and his shrewder mind told him that when Sultan Tafas finally vanished, as he inevitably would, the new rulers would look round to see who had helped them.

Eventually, the tightly-knit nations of Khusar country would start quarrelling among themselves, and would become only a few troublesome units which had once been proud tribes, each fighting for a place in the sun, while their leaders involved themselves in international politics and the future of Khalit.

Aziz sighed, prepared now to go north to his lands in Khusar. He knew nothing of artillery, aeroplanes and radios, and nothing of political blocs. He was a simple man whose concern had always been the honour of the Hejri nation and the demands it made for the Toweida Plain, his ambitions simply to push the border south of the Dharwas and see the Hejri led by someone of his own flesh and blood. But his sons were scattered, several of them even sympathising with the hated Thawab. The Khusar nations would never again be led by one of his stock. He was a tired old man, disillusioned, sick of killing, and so certain that Thawab wanted his life he ate standing among his followers.

Out of the whole shabby episode, only one thing had emerged worth having – the glow of his strange friendship with Pentecost, and all his ambitions had crystallised into the simple hope that the boy would survive. All along, this was what he had worked for, why he had ridden down to the Dharwa Passes and threatened the Muleimat and the Khadari and the Jezowi and the Shukri, why he had constantly prayed that Wintle would not reach the plain, so that Thawab's guns should not throw their impersonal death about the fort.

As he stared at the ruined buildings, his eyes empty, the light catching the lines on his troubled face, he suddenly noticed a flutter of white and wondered what new device Pentecost was building for Thawab's discomfiture. Despite the breaches that had been made, there was no longer any wish to rush the fort, the tribesmen preferring to wait until the guns had reduced its garrison to nothing. Hejri reims were no longer as Aziz remembered them, willing to die for their beliefs.

He sighed. The white spot over the wall was motionless, but then, as a breath of the wind from the north touched it, it moved and he realised it was a flag, a white flag.

For a second, his heart leapt as he realised that Hahdhdhah was offering to surrender, than it sank again at once as he felt that this could only mean that Pentecost was dead. He stared again at the fort, tears pricking his eyes, then he turned and strode away to the camp.

Thawab was asleep, but other men besides Aziz had seen the flag and they were arguing loudly with each other as he passed between the tents.

'There is a white flag, Aziz,' one of them told him. 'The fortress wishes to surrender.'

'It is no longer my concern,' the old man said in a low voice, absorbed with his grief. 'Thawab leads the Hejri warriors now.'

'Thawab is asleep.'

Aziz stopped dead and whirled. 'Then, in the name of Allah,' he roared, 'wake him! Who is this Thawab that he must be allowed to sleep undisturbed when great events hang on his heels?'

The men backed away hurriedly, then one of them broke from the group and began to run towards Thawab's tents.

5

There was weeping in the fort as the flag went up, and the women began to emerge from the cellars, dirty, bedraggled, dust-covered and ashamed of their appearance. A few children began to move about the ruined courtyard. One or two of the wounded appeared, their faces drawn, shuffling and limping among the strewn timber and stone.

Fox and Chestnut and old Fauzan seemed slightly lost, as though the strain of the last weeks had left them numb, as though their emotions, under control for so long, still could not be relaxed. The int-zaids, however, made no attempt to hide their relief. There seemed now, their expression seemed to suggest, a chance that they would see their families again.

The place stank. Not much of it was left standing, but there were still, despite the frightened women and children and the thankful wounded in the courtyard, men crouching among the rubble, still behind their weapons, and the Sultan's flag still flew from the staff above the central tower.

Fauzan recovered from the first emotions quickly and began to walk round what was left of the walls, a grim old man, unrelenting and bitter-faced, furious that they had finally had to give way before the hated Hejri, a man of unrelenting honest courage, still jeering at the Toweida Levies though, God knew, they had done their duty.

He paused here and there, resighted a gun, threw a few stones into place, suggested the rebuilding of a defence post. From the courtyard, Pentecost watched him. Minto had appeared, dragging his broken ankle, pale-faced from his long vigil out of the sun, his skin grey-green like the belly of a fish, his eyes sunken with weariness.

What would the people in England think of the defence of Hahdhdhah, Pentecost wondered. Probably nothing. Hahdhdhah was a distant place in the middle of a dusty plain surrounded by bleak red hills, in a country most people had never heard of. It was an obscure little defence, in an obscure little war, with small casualties, no publicity and remarkably little excitement. Just a lost little place with a name no one could ever spell.

Probably some TV commentator had done a piece on it, he decided, a swift-talking résumé kept within the allotted three or four minutes so as not to interfere with the Wednesday play or the sports features. Doubtless, talking in that harsh machine-gun-fire style of TV talkers that made it sound a little like a cup final. The Hejri are attacking. The defence is there, though. There's a movement on the left but it won't come to anything, because Zaid Fauzan's well up. The ball moves to midfield...

Pentecost allowed himself a small cracked frosty smile at his own bitter imaginings.

'It'll be nice to get back to Khaswe,' he pointed out.

'It'll be nicer still to go home,' Minto said.

As he stared over the walls, Pentecost suddenly realised what a joy it would be to see a different view. His heart full of emotion and overwhelmed by a desire to see his wife and children again, he felt weak at the thought of them and had to fight to keep back the tears.

Then he jerked himself back to the present and braced his shoulders. They were not free of Hahdhdhah yet. They still had to negotiate their exit, though somehow he had a feeling that Aziz would behave like an honourable man.

Even as he thought about Aziz, Fauzan turned his head from where he was leaning against a chipped embrasure, his grim face gentle as he looked at Pentecost.

'A horseman comes, Reimabassi,' he said.

Pentecost nodded and crossed towards him. Fauzan was on one of the few fragments of undamaged wall that was left, and he realised that the orders to give up Hahdhdhah had arrived only just in time.

As he stopped, the horseman reined in close to the walls. He was a thin-faced, hawk-nosed man Pentecost didn't recognise, and he noticed from his turban and the twist in his girdle, that he wasn't a Zihouni.

'You fly a white flag,' he shouted.

'We wish to arrange terms.' Pentecost's voice came out cracked and high-pitched and he cleared his throat noisily. 'I wish to speak to Aziz.'

There was a pause, then the horseman shouted back. 'Aziz no longer leads,' he said.

Pentecost's eyebrows rose, and he was momentarily aware of a curious pang of regret. 'Aziz is dead?'

'He is not dead. He is as nothing. Thawab leads the Northern tribes.'

Pentecost's eyebrows rose. He had never dreamed that Aziz could be supplanted so quickly. Doubtless the siege had found the old man wanting.

'Aziz is no longer with you?' he asked.

The horseman's mount caracoled and for a moment they didn't catch his words, then he brought it under control and tried again

'Aziz is still with us, but Thawab commands.'

There was a touch of pride in the voice, and Pentecost realised that his red cloak and brown girdle indicated that he was a Tayur, one of Thawab's men.

He paused for a moment, thinking. Somehow he didn't trust Thawab. He was reputed to be devious. Then another thought occurred to him. Perhaps he could do old Aziz a good turn. He was aware how much his loss of rank would affect his pride. Perhaps he could give him back a little of it.

'I will not treat with Thawab,' he shouted.

The horseman stared upwards, startled.

'Thawab commands,' he insisted.

'I do not trust Thawab. I have spoken already with Aziz and I know him for an honourable man. Thawab does not have this reputation.'

'Thawab will want to come.'

'Then the defence will be continued. Many more men will die.'

301

The horseman considered for a moment, then he raised his hand. 'I will tell Aziz,' he said.

6

'I am in command,' Thawab shouted in a fury. 'It is I who should conduct negotiations!'

Aziz said nothing, allowing Thawab's anger to work itself out.

'Who is Aziz?' he was shouting. 'He is finished! He is out of date – a back-number! I shall negotiate!'

One of the Zihouni chiefs interrupted. 'Aziz at least has spoken with Bin T'Khass,' he pointed out sharply.

Aziz grinned at the words, beginning to feel more confident. Thawab would never risk a quarrel – not with Hahdhdhah almost within their grasp. And what warmed his heart above all was the knowledge that Allah, the Beneficent, the Merciful, had left Pentecost alive and he had not forgotten the friendship between them.

The Zihouni chief was speaking again now. 'Let Aziz go,' he said. 'There will be no fencing between them. They have already spoken together.'

'No!' Thawab roared the word. 'I lead the northern nations!'

The Zihouni gestured angrily. 'Thou hast not spoken with Bin T'Khass, and we are all sick of fighting! We need our women. If they are surrendering Hahdhdhah, we shall get the plain of Toweida. So let us get it over and done with. Let us negotiate and be rid of them so we can go home.'

Thawab glared, prepared to argue, then he noticed that there was no answer from his Deleimis and he realised that they, too, were sick of the siege. Aziz mustered more support than he had known.

Suddenly, Thawab backed down, his eyes glittering. There would be time later to remove Aziz. He was still a child when it came to politics, and far too honest for a leader. And, after all, if anything went wrong, if the Sultanate repudiated any arrangements they made, it would be Aziz who would be to blame.

'Very well,' he said unexpectedly. 'Let Aziz negotiate.'

7

'Sir!' Fox appeared in Pentecost's doorway. 'His Nibs is here.'

There had been silence for an hour, not a single shot, not a shout, not a movement except from the village where they could see activity in the camp across the road – a flock of goats, the children who minded them, and a slow-trotting donkey. For an hour the whole plain had seemed to be silent, and the women had gone back to the cellars, because they had been doing it for so long it had become the habitual thing to do.

Pentecost laid down his pen. He had been finishing his diary, bringing it up to date, setting down every single fact by which they might be judged.

'Aziz?' he asked.

'The man himself,' Fox grinned.

Pentecost allowed himself one of his bleak smiles. 'I'll come,' he said.

He had already washed and shaved carefully and dressed in his best uniform. Fox, too, was carefully dressed in an officer's uniform made up of fragments from Lack's kit.

'Let's make them think there are still enough of us to hold them off,' Pentecost had said.

There were also four Dharwas, dressed in clean clothing, their jackets, girdles and head-dresses borrowed from all corners of the fortress so that they presented a confident appearance. Fauzan had cynically picked the four fattest men he could find, so that they appeared to be in no danger of starving. Pentecost wished to give the impression that they could stay in the fortress just as long as they chose. With this in his mind and with Wintle almost out of the Dharwas, it would be wise for Aziz to negotiate quickly and give him what he wanted.

He rose from the desk and fastened on his belt and revolver.

'Do we carry a white flag?' Fox asked.

'No,' Pentecost decided. 'We go out looking as though we've won.'

Fox grinned. Outside, the four Dharwas were standing at ease, their uniforms brushed and hurriedly mended, their boots clean.

'Very good,' Pentecost said. 'Let's go.'

As the splintered gate creaked open, they slipped outside, forming up into a group, and as they moved forward down the dusty road, lined with all the debris left behind by the attackers – scraps of clothing, broken weapons, scattered cartridges and trampled bushes – they saw five men break away from the silent line of horsemen in the distance. Then they saw Aziz, dressed like Pentecost in his best clothes – black Zihouni headdress, green girdle, black cloak and decorative beads. He held up his hand, and his four companions halted in a small group so that Aziz advanced alone, the Mannlicher butt-foremost as in all their previous meetings.

He had stopped now and dismounted. He was holding his own banner and as Pentecost came to a stop in front of him, his grim face broke into a smile.

'Greetings, oh my son!' he said warmly.

It was as good as an embrace.

'Greetings, my father Aziz,' Pentecost replied gravely.

Aziz grinned. 'Thou art a mighty warrior, Bin T'Khass,' he said. 'Thou saidst thou wert great and indeed thou art. They will sing of thee around the fires in years to come as they do of El-Aurens and Owinda-el. Thou hast almost defeated the whole Hejri nation.'

Pentecost replied in the same tone, boastful, vain, in the way the Hejris understood.

'We still can, Lord Aziz,' he said. 'But I have received orders from Khaswe. The Sultan makes a treaty. He is willing to give up the Toweida Plain.'

Aziz tried to make the surrender easier. On any other occasion he would have gloated over his enemy, but now he was anxious to salve the pride of the young man opposite. He could see that Pentecost was thin and hollow-eyed. The polishing and brushing, and the appearance of Fox and the four Dharwas behind him might have fooled Thawab but they didn't deceive an old campaigner like Aziz.

His voice was gentle. 'Thou hast not been defeated, my son,' he said.

'No,' Pentecost's words were brisk. 'Only in Khaswe have they given up hope. The plain is yours, Aziz.'

Aziz's face was grave. 'I take it without much joy,' he said. 'I would have preferred to have defeated thee, Bin T'Khass, and then taken thee to my tents as a friend and as the great warrior thou art.'

Pentecost's face split in a smile. 'That would indeed have been a celebration, Aziz,' he said.

Aziz's face grew grim as they came to the business of the meeting.

'What do you demand?' he asked.

'Safe conduct south of the Dharwas. Not only for me, but also for my officers and men, and for the wounded and civilians, women and children.'

'It is granted. I wish thee well. Do you still have lorries?'

'Enough. My men will march out.'

'All this is granted.' Aziz was eager to be helpful and he remembered again how someone had once described to him the honours due to a defeated army. 'You shall march out like warriors. With your backs straight, your heads high, and your weapons in your hands.'

Pentecost smiled, touched by the gesture. 'You are a generous foe, Aziz.'

Aziz smiled back at him. 'When will all this take place? My people are impatient to see thee gone.'

'Tomorrow, Aziz. We have nothing to stay for. Tomorrow when the sun is highest.'

'This is well.'

'My men will form up outside the fort for all to see there is no deception.'

'The camp across the road will vanish and my Zihounis will line up across the plain to see thee go. They will tell their sons, "We saw Bin T'Khass leave!" '

'You do me much honour, Aziz.'

Perhaps, Aziz thought, remembering Thawab, I am out of date with my honour. Perhaps we are both out of date.

'The signal will be when I haul down the flag of the Sultanate from the tower,' Pentecost was saying, and Aziz thrust his banner forward.

'I would consider it an honour if Bin T'Khass were to raise my own standard. When I am old it will hang in my tent.'

Pentecost gave a little bow. 'I trust thee, Aziz.'

'There will be no mistake,' Aziz said. 'I am in control. Thou hast not only held off our warriors, thou hast also defeated Thawab. He sulks now in his tent.'

'Until tomorrow then, Aziz.'

'Until tomorrow, my son.'

His heart full, touched by the old man's affection, Pentecost stepped back and saluted – the best he could manage. Aziz stared at him and gravely raised the Mannlicher in a strange parody of a present arms. Then, without a word, they turned their backs on each other and headed back to their respective parties.

8

Tafas waited in his palace, a defeated man suddenly grown old, watching the pearly light over the city catching the tips of the minarets. He heard the muezzin's keening cry lingering in the air – 'There is no God but Allah and Mohamed is his prophet,' and he sighed as he caught the perfume from the garden below.

Rasaul stood before him, confident of his own power growing as that of the Sultan dwindled. The city was quiet, because the news of the Sultan's proposed departure had somehow spread to the Khesse area. Only the British still hadn't heard, because Rasaul had been careful to keep it from them in case a complaint of treachery should change Tafas' mind. With power almost in his hands, Rasaul had no intention of permitting any accident of that sort.

'Arrangements have been finalised,' he was saying. 'Hahdhdhah is to be turned over to Aziz tomorrow at midday.'

The Sultan eyed him sullenly. He felt he had been betrayed and there was no one now he could trust – not even in the palace. Even his meals were late and carelessly served because the servants, too, were waiting for him to go.

He sighed. 'Brigadier Wintle was informed, of course,' he asked.

Rasaul inclined his head in a way that was meant to be an assent, but Tafas' eyes narrowed.

'You did inform him, Rasaul?' he snapped.

Rasaul's hesitation was barely perceptible but Tafas stared at him angrily. 'I will send a signal,' he said. 'Personally. From the palace radio station.'

Rasaul kept his face from showing his annoyance. He had hoped the whole operation could be completed without bringing anyone else into it – in case outside influences changed things. He had long since made plans to prevent such an eventuality, in fact. He tried to turn the old man's attention aside.

'There is a motor launch waiting in the harbour,' he said. 'It will take you to your yacht. I have made all the arrangements.'

I'll wager you have, the Sultan thought, maliciously deciding that Rasaul would find it hard going against the hotheads of Al Havra. Rasaul was almost as old as he was himself and he couldn't imagine Al Havra allowing leftovers from the Sultanate to hold any of the power they coveted.

'There seems to be nothing left to do, sir,' Rasaul said. 'Perhaps I might shake hands. In memory of the great times we have seen together.'

Resolutely, the Sultan kept his hand at his side. 'I have few memories of such times, Rasaul,' he observed coldly.

Rasaul's eyes glittered and the Sultan went on, his mind already elsewhere. 'There is one last thing,' he said. 'I must also say goodbye to General Cozzens. Please tell my secretary that my car will be needed.'

When the telephone rang in Cozzens' office, it was Group Captain Southey.

'Bingo!' he said. 'They're away!'

'Good!' Cozzens smiled. 'They'll be glad of a bit of help.'

As Southey ran off, Cozzens put down the telephone and sat staring at it with satisfaction. It rang again almost at once. As he picked it up the door opened and one of his aides appeared. He looked shocked. He indicated the telephone.

'I think that'll be Colonel Steyne, sir,' he said. 'They just telephoned from the palace. They've got the Sultan.'

'Got the Sultan?' Cozzens sat with the telephone in his hand, conscious of the meaningless grating of a voice in his ear.

'Assassinated him, sir,' the aide said. 'A bomb as he left the palace in his car.'

fourteen

1

As they formed up outside the fortress, even the Toweidas, cuffed and kicked by the old Fauzan, had managed to make themselves look presentable.

'You skinny sons of pigs,' Fauzan had told them the night before. 'You will march out looking like the soldiers you never were. The whores who were your mothers will not recognise you when I have finished with you. You will get your snouts out of the mud and hold your heads up. Reimabassi Pentecost has said we shall march out looking as though we have not been defeated – as indeed we have not – and you will look like it. Do you all understand?'

They did. In fear of the grim old man they had set to work with brushes and thread and made their uniforms presentable, despite the fact that once the Toweida Plain was Hejri half of them would desert. That was in the future, though, and Fauzan was very much in the present, and by the time they lined up behind the few remaining Civil Guards and the group of grinning Dharwas still on their feet, they were looking like soldiers. Their headcloths were adjusted as Fauzan wanted them, and their girdles, underneath their pouches, were twisted within an inch of each other.

Still Fauzan wasn't satisfied. 'Sons of pigs,' he said, marching up and down the lines. 'You would not do credit to a whorehouse! Tighten that belt! Adjust that girdle! Up with that rifle! Reimabassi Pentecost will be proud of you when we march away or I will know the reason why. You may not realise it, you sons of hogs, but you have just won a great victory. A handful of you have held the whole Hejri and Deleimi nations at bay. When you are old and the treasures of your pleasures have shrivelled to nothing, you will remember Hahdhdhah and say "I was with Pentecost." '

He moved on, adjusting equipment, pushing rifles straight, watched by the grinning Dharwas. 'There will be no medals,' he said, 'because the politicians do not like defeats. But remember this: You were never defeated. Thanks to Reimabassi Pentecost and your old friend, Zaid Fauzan, together with a little help from the other officers and NCOs, you have become men.'

The tirade went on as the women and children climbed into the lorries with the wounded and sick. It was a tight squeeze because there were not so many lorries now as there had been and there were more people who had to ride. But there was no longer any equipment. They had taken care to destroy everything of value during the night, and all that was left were Chestnut's catapult and all the torn heaps of timber, corrugated iron and plastic covers. Gazing round the ruined fortress, Fox realised how close they had come to defeat.

He looked up at the crescent flag of the Sultanate still flying over the tower and Aziz's banner among the rubble out of sight. As the crescent flag came down the green one would go up. Fox had arranged it carefully, deciding that Pentecost would not wish to show any sign of defeat. He had attached the green banner to the same shroud as the red and white Khaliti flag so that they would pass in the middle and fly there for a moment together, before the green flag rose to the top. He knew exactly how he was going to do it. He had even arranged a little ceremony of his own, and Nalk Owdi, standing with the cold sun shining on his bugle, had been told to blow as the red and white flag came down. It was meant to be a tribute.

In his tough unemotional heart, Fox found a tremendous admiration for Pentecost. He had borne himself, as Aziz had said, as the Dharwas at a meeting the night before had told him, like a great warrior, and Fox knew enough about war to know that without him they would not have held out a week.

Pentecost had not yet appeared from his office and Fox knew he was collecting up his belongings. He and the wounded Dharwa who had been acting as Pentecost's orderly had been packing half the night. They had put the long report on the siege that he had written and the diary he had kept so carefully, into his bedding roll with his private belongings and his books of verse. With Pentecost out of the room, Fox had sneaked a look at them and discovered with gratification that he, Beebe, Stone, Chestnut, Minto, Lack and old Fauzan had been mentioned with credit, together with a number of Dharwas and a few Toweidas. Nothing at all had been said about Pentecost. It was as though he'd been there only as a spectator.

The women were beginning to chatter, realising at last that their ordeal was really over, and the children were hanging over the tailboards of the lorries, chirruping like little monkeys, shouting insults at the Toweidas and worse insults at the Hejri lined up across the plain to the south.

Aziz was there. Fox could see him with his black headcloth and cloak, and he seemed to have routed out all the surviving Zihouni. There seemed to be two hundred or more of them there, sitting their horses in a tidy line that reflected Aziz's control of them. There were no banners in evidence, as though Aziz had ordered their absence so as not to gloat over the departing garrison, and they remained silent, moving only slightly as a horse edged forward or a man shuffled to a better position to see.

Chestnut was standing by the gate, near the remaining scout car, white-faced and silent, a taut-faced lean man, his mad eyes flickering about him for any sign of treachery or carelessness on the part of the zaids.

'What'll ye do when ye get home, Jim?' he asked.

Fox frowned. 'I'll quit,' he said. 'I've had enough. Nobody's got much time for us these days. We're just political pawns. We've had it. We're out of date.'

Chestnut's crazy eyes turned on him and Fox gestured. 'It's true,' he said. 'How often have you had swaddies up for being drunk saying it was because the girls won't go out with 'em – because they have to have their hair cut? How often have you been called a Fascist pig by a bunch of students throwing bricks at you?'

Pentecost appeared at last, neat as the day they'd first arrived in the fort, and with a grin Fox saw he was sporting the headcloth of the Dharwas, and the girdle of the Toweida Levies over his uniform.

'Bit exotic,' he said with an embarrassed smile. 'But it's to let them know I'm proud of them. They've done pretty well considering.'

'They've done damn' well, sir,' Fox said. 'But they couldn't have, if you hadn't been there.'

Pentecost stared back at the older man, his pale washed-out eyes unwavering. He was a rum customer, Fox decided, always a bit different from the rest of them.

'Thank you, Jim,' he said quietly. 'I can say the same about you. Is everything ready?'

'Yessir. Thought you might give 'em a bit of an inspection. It'd please old Fauzan and it'll help 'em to march a bit better. Besides –' he gave a twisted grin ' – it'll make the bloody Hejri realise that we're going in our own time and on our own terms.'

Pentecost's smile broke through, surprisingly warming, and he walked ahead of Fox to where the troops were formed up, moving among them, nodding at a man here, complimenting another one there, doing it in leisurely fashion as though there were all the time in the world. At Fauzan, he stopped and shook the old man's hand warmly.

'Thank you, Fauzan,' he said. 'I don't know what I'd have done without you,' and the Toweida Levies, who were terrified of the grim old warrior, were startled to see his eyes were full of tears.

'Will you be riding in the scout car?' Fox said in a low voice as they stopped at the end of the lines.

'No,' Pentecost said firmly. 'I'll be marching at the head of the column.' He paused. 'I hope Wintle was informed,' he ended. 'I wouldn't want him to take unnecessary casualties.'

2

As it happened, Aziz's message from the north arrived at almost the same moment as the Sultan's.

The news that Hahdhdhah had surrendered, shouted from a group of rocks by a Khadari sniper, was carried by a startled Khaliti officer, hardly able to believe his ears after the hard fighting of the last three days.

'It's a blasted lie,' Wintle snapped. 'The bastards are trying to persuade us it isn't worth trying.'

But even as he spoke, the Khaliti signals officer from the radio van arrived. He looked startled.

'Reimabassi!'

Wintle gestured angrily. 'I'm busy,' he said.

'Reimabassi –' the Khaliti thrust forward a message form ' – this is important.'

Wintle frowned and snatched the message.

'HAHDHDHAH TO BE EVACUATED,' he saw. 'REPEAT EVACUATED STOP TOWEIDA PLAIN TO BE GIVEN UP UNDER TRIPARTITE AGREEMENT BETWEEN AL HAVRA NORTHERN LEADERS AND SULTAN OF KHALIT TO BE SIGNED IN NEAR FUTURE STOP HALT FORCES SHORT OF TOWEIDA PLAIN ONLY CONSIDERATION SAFETY OF HAHDHDHAH GARRISON.'

314

'Who the hell sent this?' Wintle snarled.

'It's originated by the Sultan, Reimabassi,' the Khaliti pointed out. 'It's come from his office.'

'It's a fake,' Wintle said at once. 'Have it checked.'

Suddenly worried, he turned and walked slowly towards the front of his column where the armoured cars were hammering away at a group of Khadari rifle pits on the last slopes of the Pass. The stream of lead was smashing into the rocks and the cold sun was burning the hillside. The Khaliti soldiers were crouched on either side of the road.

As Wintle lowered himself to the ditch behind the Khaliti officer in charge, a shout came from above.

'Owinda-el! Hahdhdhah has surrendered! They are marching out now. The Sultan is giving up the Plain.'

'The bastards are persistent, aren't they?' Wintle said. But he frowned, wondering again if there were really something in it and that they were too late, and that Hahdhdhah had fallen and all its garrison been murdered.

'Hahdhdhah is finished, Owinda-el,' the shout came again. 'Aziz has negotiated terms.'

While Wintle was still trying to sort this one out, the Khaliti officer appeared from the radio lorry once more, and dropped into the ditch. He still looked a little startled.

'It's genuine, Reimabassi,' he said. 'It came from Tafas. It's from his private signal station. It was sent to Hahdhdhah last night.'

'Good God!' Wintle said. 'What's the old fool up to? Why have we only just heard? Why didn't the operator pick it up last night? He must have heard it.'

'It was when the sniping was at its worst, Reimabassi. We were having to move the radio van at the time. And the message was not addressed to us.'

Wintle scowled and the Khaliti went on, looking shaken. 'That's not the worst, Reimabassi. The Sultan has been assassinated.'

Wintle twisted quickly in the ditch to stare, then, realising he had exposed his head, ducked quickly.

'He was on the way to see General Cozzens, Reimabassi, it seems, with the news of Hahdhdhah. It's in the message.'

Wintle snatched the message form and, as he read it, his eyes glowed with anger. The thing stank of treachery. With Tafas assassinated Khaswe would go and Khalit would soon follow. He might just as well save his breath, because with Khalit in turmoil, no one, not the Duke of Wellington, Robert E Lee and Napoleon, aided by Lord God of Hosts, would be able to hang on to the Toweida Plain.

Then he suddenly remembered something he had discussed in signals with Cozzens and he glanced at his watch.

'For God's sake,' he said. 'I wonder if Tafas ever got around to telling Cozzens! If Pentecost's out of the fort, a few rockets among the Hejri just at this moment might stir 'em up enough to make a disaster.'

3

By the gate of the fort, Fox paused, waiting for Pentecost, and it suddenly occurred to him that it might be a nice gesture if Pentecost himself took down the flag. He had done so much to keep it flying, it seemed only fair to ask him.

He coughed.

'Sir! Occurs to me, you might like the honour yourself of lowering the flag. Something to keep when it's finished with – trophy, so to speak, to hang over the fireplace in Mrs Pentecost's dining room, along with Aziz's muzzle-loader and that ceremonial sword he gave you.'

Pentecost smiled. 'It had occurred to me, too, Jim,' he said.

'If anybody has the right to make a cushion cover of that flag, sir,' Fox said, 'it's Mrs Pentecost.'

Pentecost smiled again. 'Uncommon thoughtful,' he said, 'but it's a bit battered for a cushion cover.'

Fox grinned. 'Have to hang it in the hall, then, sir. Make it look like the regimental chapel.'

'Mrs Pentecost's not much of a one for military glory. She prefers help with washing up.'

They had reached the bottom of the rickety tower now. There wasn't much of it left but the staircase, and Pentecost stopped and stared across the courtyard. Behind him, the gates hung lopsidedly on their hinges, splintered where the shells had struck and the flying shards of metal had torn into them. The pillars that held them were pitted and scarred with bullet holes, and to right and left the wall had crumbled where it had been hit. Nearby, there was a long gap where several shells had torn it away and they had struggled to shore it up and rebuild the parapet with sandbags. The south-east tower was a mass of rubble, and the water tower, lying on its side, had wrenched part of the south wall down. There were several burned-out lorries at the far end of the courtyard, and the walls were charred and blackened where flames had roared along them. This was where Beebe had charged up with a borrowed rifle and almost shot Chestnut, where Minto, his ankle broken by a falling girder, had dragged himself away, and where Lack and Stone had waited to leave the fort on their fatal sorties.

Pentecost sighed. Matshed roofing was slapping in the breeze that blew through the gate, whirling fragments of scorched rushes over the pitted surface of the courtyard. Torn and charred records and documents fluttered about, and the splintered timber, the torn corrugated iron and the shed where the plastic covers were kept were all marked by the last bombardments. The place was a wreck, littered with scraps of clothing, empty tins that had once been used for drinking or eating, cartridge cases, Chestnut's lopsided searchlight surrounded by splintered glass, odds and ends of uniform and equipment, and here and there a coiled bloody bandage that had been stripped off by a man determined to march off with the rest. And it was full now of a graveyard silence that was vaguely oppressive.

Pentecost's eyes met Fox's and the sergeant looked up at the flag. 'You'd better go first, sir,' he said.

4

Wintle was almost dancing with agitation. Watched by Beebe and Gloag, he waited alongside the radio lorry, slapping his boot with his cane and smoking cigarette after cigarette.

'The bastards have already left,' he announced. 'We're trying now to contact Khaswe to call 'em off.'

Beebe's horror broke out. 'You've got to contact 'em!' he said. 'We had this thing made. If it goes wrong at this stage –' he almost choked with disgust.

The Khaliti signals officer appeared. 'Nothing yet, Reimabassi,' he told Wintle.

'Keep trying.' As Wintle turned away to light another cigarette, he jerked a hand at the Khadari positions. 'And let those bastards off the hook for the time being,' he told his second-in-command. 'One thing at a time. Let's get this sorted out first.'

As he spoke, a sound above him caught his ears, and he snatched the cigarette from his mouth and threw it away. One of his Dharwas saw the gesture and bent to pick it up. Wintle didn't notice. He was standing with his head in the air, looking towards the south, his dark eyes fierce and angry under the headcloth. Gloag, too, was staring upwards, and beyond him, Beebe, his face grey with horror. The sound increased rapidly, swelling until the whole sky seemed to be full of it, a great iron roaring that echoed in the narrow valleys. A mule neighed and the sharp high laugh of one of the Dharwas sounded above it, but they were sounds that were remote, as though the iron noise from the sky filled the whole of their existence.

'Where are they?' Beebe said in a low voice. 'Where are the bastards?'

The signals officer jerked a hand. 'There they are, Reimabassi! Swinging round the end of the plain.'

'They're coming in from the north,' Wintle said. 'For Christ's sake,' he burst out desperately, 'can't you contact them?'

The signals officer's face was pale. 'Not a chance, Reimabassi. They use air force frequency.'

They were all silent again as the iron roar of the two jets filled the Ridhwa, ricocheting backwards and forwards from the cliffs like a ping-pong ball in a narrow passage. Then they saw the aeroplanes pass between two peaks, two small shining machines laying over in a steep bank as they wheeled into position.

5

In the narrow cockpit of the leading machine, the Khaliti pilot studied the ground unrolling below him like a map.

The plain seemed empty at first, then he realised that outside the fortress of Hahdhdhah, there were two lines of men and several stationary lorries. Beyond them, lying back by the foothills near the village, there was another row of men who looked as though they might be Hejri horsemen.

He stared down at the horsemen as the machine banked. He had been told to look for green banners and there were no green banners there.

Then he saw a flutter of green on the tower of the fortress, whipping in the wind among the wreckage and the rubble. His hand reached for the switch of his radio to call his wing man.

'I think the Hejris are inside,' he said. 'That's a green flag on the tower, isn't it?'

There was a crackle of static in his ear and the other pilot's voice came back.

'I see a green flag.'

'That's our mark then. Let's go in.'

6

Fox watched the two jet planes calmly as they wheeled over the Urbida Hills.

'Bit bloody late in the day, sir,' he shouted up to Pentecost. 'We could have done with them yesterday or the day before. I expect they've come to pay a bit of a tribute for what we've done.'

He was rather annoyed with the two aeroplanes for spoiling his ceremony. As he had seen Pentecost go up the stairs, he had raised his hand to where Bugler Owdi was standing in front of the Dharwas, his face shining with fervour, his instrument on his hip. As Pentecost had lowered the Sultanate flag, the notes had rung out, sweeter and purer than Owdi had ever managed in his life before, only to be drowned immediately by the approaching iron din of the planes.

From his position on the tower by the flagstaff, Pentecost had smiled at Fox's little ceremony. Fox was always trying to work British ceremonial into the Khaliti army which, with its head-dresses and girdles, didn't really take well to it. But it pleased Fox and he suspected also that it pleased Fauzan.

A pity the din had drowned Bugler Owdi's tune, he thought. Bugler Owdi wasn't the best bugler in the world, but even though he occasionally hit the wrong note, at least his fervour was strong, and he was at one with Fox in his love of ceremony and for once hadn't made a mistake.

Owdi was lowering the instrument now and replacing it on his hip, his back straight, his head up, small and square, stern-faced as became a Dharwa bugler in front of a lot of half-baked Toweidas and Khaliti Civil Guards, and more than a little annoyed at the way the best thing he had ever done had been ruined.

The noise of the aircraft was growing louder now and Pentecost saw that they had banked above the Addowara Pass and were heading straight for the fortress. He could see two straight lines centred by dots and he assumed they were going to dip their wings over them.

Everyone was being uncommon sentimental today, he thought. Then, with a frown, he noticed that the noses of the machines were pointing directly at him and realised that the two aeroplanes, one behind the other, were not flying over the fort but were coming in, in a long slanting run which, continued to its end, would land them right alongside him on the tower.

At once, he knew what it meant. They had assumed that the green banner on the tower meant that Aziz's troops were in control. Immediately, he began to lower the banner.

From below, Fox saw him hesitate and stare towards the Hejri horsemen to the south, and instinctively he knew what he was thinking. If he hauled down the banner, if any of the horsemen were hit, there would immediately be shouts of treachery and, standing outside the fortress as they were, there would be no hope for the survivors.

'Sir, for Christ's sake!'

Fox's voice rose to a shriek as he saw Pentecost hurriedly raise the green flag again, then his ears were full of the iron sound of engines and he began to run for his life.

fifteen

1

What went wrong?

The first thing that went through Fox's mind as he cowered beneath the shower of debris was the thought, what went wrong? Everything had seemed so straightforward. Aziz was on their side. Wintle was waiting in the Dharwa Hills. There was to be no more killing. Yet, at the last moment the whole place had erupted in destruction.

He crouched in a tight ball, his arms over his head, his ears assailed by the shriek and clang of the explosions, aware of his body being struck by falling timbers and stones and a shower of pulverised dirt. Vaguely he was aware of the tower tilting slowly on the ruined remains of its broken supports, and the crash and quiver of the earth as it fell. Then, as he lifted his head, he saw vaguely through the pall of dust the open gate and all the people by the lorries flinging themselves to the ground, crumpling like wheat before a scythe, the Dharwa Scouts and the Civil Guards and the Toweida Levies lying in two long lines, with Zaid Fauzan, and Minto and Sergeant Chestnut still on their feet shaking their fists into the air. Beyond them, down the valley towards Hahdhdhah, the Zihouni horsemen were scattering wildly across the plain, their robes flapping as they rode.

Then the second batch of rockets arrived and Fox, just rising to his knees, flung himself down again, fully convinced by now of the most appalling treachery somewhere and the certainty that he couldn't possibly survive.

But he did. For a while, his eyes were full of flaming light and his ears were hammered by the smack of the bombs, and his body was lifted from the ground in a series of jerks as the explosions occurred; then once more he was holding his head, deafened, half-blinded, stupefied by the clamour, trying to dig down into the ground with his fingers away from the shower of bricks, stones, rubble, splintered wood, flying fragments of matting, and pulverised dirt.

Gradually, as the ringing in his head died, he became aware that the din had stopped and that the air, a moment ago full of the iron sound of aeroplane engines, was still again, as though a vast man-made squall had passed swiftly over him and moved on, leaving him shaken, stupefied and shocked by the violence.

He rose to his knees, dust in his hair and eyes and between his teeth, his head ringing with the racket, his body pounded and assailed by debris and noise and blast. But he was alive, filthy with dirt, his hair matted with dust, his face caked with it, spitting it from his tongue as he tried to draw breath in what seemed the airless vacuum of the ruined fortress. Stumbling to his feet, he glanced through the gate and saw that the soldiers outside were also scrambling up unhurt and finding their lines again, and that the lorries remained where they were, overhung by the wailing of women and the shrieking of children, and the furious shouts of men. The planes had vanished, the sound fading to an iron-throated rumble as they disappeared over the Dharwa Range.

Then he turned. The courtyard of the fortress was a ruin. It had been a wreck before but now the tower lay tumbled in a heap of stones, its splintered timbers sticking out of the rubble like broken bones – stones and matting all flung in incredible confusion across the courtyard like a child's pile of bricks scattered by an indifferent hand. Flames were licking at the matting and he saw the green banner lying on the stones, already alight.

He turned on unsteady legs, blinking and gasping for breath, seeking Pentecost. At first he thought he'd vanished, then he saw him lying among the stones some distance away. He seemed unhurt, only unconscious, like Fox his body layered with dust and small stones, his head to one side, his expression serene, flung headlong by the fall of the tower. Then, stumbling towards him, Fox saw that a shard of metal flying with snake swiftness through the air, had whipped away life. Across his feet, as though it had been laid there deliberately, was the crescent flag of Khalit.

Fox stared dry-eyed at him, feeling all the world's pain. He bent awkwardly, stiffly, to twitch the flag across the small shape like a pall, then, stooping, his head still ringing, his legs and arms still trembling, he got his hands under the body and lifted it to his chest.

As he moved towards the gate, his feet stumbling over the scattered stones and the baulks of timber, Chestnut and Fauzan appeared, and immediately he saw the tears streaming down the leathery, lined face of the old zaid.

'For God's sake,' Minto said, stumbling awkwardly behind on his crutches. 'What happened? What went wrong?'

They stopped in front of Fox but he wouldn't let them take the body from him and went on marching towards the lorries, his face expressionless, like a ghost with all the dust plastered across his features and clothes.

Then he became aware of the thud of hooves and a horseman swung across in front of him, flecks of foam flying as he hauled his mount back on its hind legs. Aziz's brown face was twisted with fury.

'Treachery!' he hurled in English at Fox, and Fox stopped dead and lifted his own furious face.

'Treachery be damned!' he roared back, unconcerned whether Aziz could understand him or not. 'He left the flag there when he saw them coming! So you'd know there *wasn't* any treachery! I saw his face! I know what he was thinking! I've always known what he was thinking! I know what he was doing and why he was doing it! It was him or the rest of us! It was him or – !'

Fox stopped and then at last the tears filled his eyes so that he couldn't see, swelling over and running down his face to make muddy runnels across the dust-caked skin.

Somehow Aziz seemed to understand exactly what he meant, and realising at last what Fox carried in his arms, his haggard face became tragic, every line and hollow looking as though he had lost a favourite son, his large eloquent eyes, like black velvet, agonised in his sorrow.

Another horseman appeared and now Fox saw that the Zihounis had drawn closer and that, running from the Urbida Hills were dozens of other men, some in robes, some in modern battledress, all flourishing rifles and yelping with rage.

Aziz gestured to his men, and Fox saw them whirl their horses and gallop away, to halt in a rigid line between the group by the lorries and the advancing men. The runners came to a standstill, and Fox saw the Zihounis lift their rifles. Though the men from the hills continued to shout, they made no attempt to advance.

'Go,' Aziz said brokenly over his shoulder. 'Take him away. I gave my word. Take him from Hahdhdhah and bury him like a warrior.'

For a second, Fox stared at the old man. Aziz's mouth was working with misery, the lines deeper than ever across his cheeks. Then he turned, stiff-legged as an automaton to one of the lorries.

There were women in there with children, and he stared at them with unparalleled ferocity, certain in his mind that there should be some gesture, some act of reverence.

'Out!' he said.

The women stared at him and began to protest.

'Out!' Fox roared. He turned furiously on Chestnut and Minto and Fauzan. 'Get 'em out,' he shouted. 'Get the buggers out! Shove 'em in the other lorries! He's having this one to himself! He's going to ride out of Hahdhdhah as he should do!'

Fauzan rapped out a few words and the women scrambled down, frightened, and Fox, still holding the body, the blood dripping down his trousers, waited, unaware of its weight, only vaguely conscious of Minto and Chestnut pushing the women into the other vehicles. Then, with Fauzan's help, he got the body into the lorry and laid it reverently down, still draped by the Khaliti flag.

Fauzan watched, his face twisted, his eyes full of tears, as Fox twitched the flag straight. Then without speaking, he lifted the tailboard of the lorry and shoved the steel pegs home. Fox straightened, aware of the stuffiness with the heat of the sun on the canvas top, and sat down near the cabin.

He sighed, drawing his breath as though it were painful, then he nodded to Fauzan, who was still watching over the tailboard.

'Let's go,' he said.

2

'What went wrong?' Beebe shouted, noisy in his grief, unaware that the assassination of a stubborn secretive old man in Khaswe was the key to the puzzle. 'For Christ's sake, Aziz was letting 'em go! The whole goddam thing had been called off! All they had to do was march out!'

His misery was overwhelming. Until a few weeks before he hadn't known Pentecost, and hadn't even liked him very much when he had got to know him. Then in the days of the siege he had come first to admire him and finally to feel that he had no fault. He had a texture and finesse, it had seemed, that had been given to him by tradition and pride. The ancient deeds and responsibilities of his family were imprinted over his whole character, as if they were stamped indelibly about his person; and all his beliefs, all his actions, all his temperament stemmed from them, inherited with his small neat frame, his features and his long delicate hands. He was not a clever man outside the calls of his profession, and narrow in his views, but he had always believed that he belonged to a small group who were the only people who mattered. In return for their birthright of privilege they were held to their duty by the chronicles of their ancestors and, guided by their pride, they considered themselves separate from the rest of the world, so that emergencies and disasters made special demands on them because they felt they had so much more to give than normal beings. What he had had to do had always been crystal-clear to him and, bound by his duty, he had been father, mother and brother to his men.

At any other time, Beebe knew, men like him would have been paid by Pentecost to do his repairs. Yet Beebe knew who was the better man. Obsolete, old-world and faintly ridiculous with his stilted sense of right and wrong, Pentecost had seen danger as clearly as anyone but he had also seen duty as a greater impetus than fear and he had drawn on his past, as though the dead of his family had strengthened him, and had fought his bloody little battle with dignity and compassion. It had not been physical bravery that had borne him up but a different kind of courage plain, old-fashioned, out-dated honour.

In his grief, Beebe was stupefied, thinking again and again of Pentecost's wife. What would she do now, he wondered wildly. How would she cope, with two kids to bring up? He'd *have* to find her, have to do what he could with all his power, if only to work out of his system some of the pity he felt.

Standing among the rocks, his grieving eyes were only vaguely aware of Wintle making arrangements to turn the column back on itself towards Dhafran, only barely conscious of men and machinery hurrying past towards the south, of the crunch of boots on stones, and the rumble of heavy tyres, and tired dusty faces as the Khaliti troops clumped back the way they had come. Then he saw Fox standing near him, holding a file of papers. He had recovered a little now, but his clothes were still torn and dirty, and his face was still covered with caked dust.

'He kept a diary, Luke,' he said.

'Yeah.' Beebe nodded numbly. 'I know. He told me. He told me I've got to see his wife about it.'

'He wasn't after money,' Fox went on. 'Though God knows, he was like the rest of us and didn't have much.'

'Yeah.' Beebe nodded again heavily, almost as though he were shaking off a blow. 'I know what he wanted.'

'Luke, I've read bits of it. I think it makes good reading.' Fox paused and went on with a profound bitterness that was shocking. 'Just the sort for the folks back home to enjoy when there's nothing exciting on the telly.'

Somehow his last words got through to Beebe and he knew then what he had to do. He had to see Charlotte Pentecost first and foremost and, certainly for the time being, dedicate himself to making everything all right for her. Then he had to persuade her to get this diary published.

'I'll see that guy Gloag,' he said. 'He'll help. He's said he will.'

He took the diary from Fox, holding it reverently, and turned away to follow the marching men. Behind them, in a silence that was sorrowful and austere, Dharwa Scouts were piling rocks on a patch of disturbed earth, watched from the hillsides by the Khadari riflemen. Now that the fighting was over, one or two of the snipers had come down to see what was going on, and their headman, a short blunt-featured man with a heavy beard, his eyes almost hidden by the brown Khadari headcloth, his body swathed with bandoleers of bullets, spoke to Wintle.

'Have no fear, Reimabassi,' he had said, rigid in his own cruel code of courage. 'Where he lies will never be disturbed. He was a great warrior.'

3

What went wrong, Aziz asked himself as he rode north.

Behind him the Hejri – the Zihouni, the Hassi and the Dayati – and the Hawassi, the Tayur and the Dayi of the Deleimi nation, were in the fortress. They had forgotten his defiance and the way he had set one tribe against another in his determination to see the convoy of lorries safely off the plain, and they had rampaged through the ruins, uncertain whether to be elated that Toweida was Khusar country again or enraged because the fort which had symbolised their sacrifices had ended as a mere heap of rubble, its walls no longer even high enough to give shelter to a caravan traveller heading north.

Aziz sighed and settled in the saddle. Less than half a mile behind him, he knew, there was another man on a horse, moving cautiously in his footsteps, a thin-faced, fanatic-eyed man with a red Tayur cloak, a Garand rifle across his saddle. He had been there a long time now and Aziz had known of him the whole time. He had entered the Addowara Pass within a quarter of an hour of Aziz himself, moving warily, never closing the gap between them, yet never allowing it to grow greater.

Aziz knew why he was there. The black camel of Islam was approaching his door but, his heart shrivelled with misery, he was quite indifferent. He had done everything to ensure the safety of Pentecost. They had acted like brothers towards each other. And then – then – something had happened. The old man in Khaswe, who he saw, now that all the facts of the news had been pieced together, had been the keystone of all their elaborate plans, had died. Dead, Tafas had brought down the whole edifice. Aziz could not think of it without a stab at his heart. Some fool had made a mistake and all the things he had done to save Pentecost, all the things other people who loved and admired him had done, too, had rushed together, it seemed, as the elements of a storm rushed together, and destroyed them both. He had been destroyed by Pentecost as surely as he himself had destroyed Pentecost.

Numbly, he had tied his few belongings across his saddle, said goodbye to the Hassi girl, whose eyes had studied his face with the heartbreaking innocence of youth.

'Lord Aziz,' she had said. 'Ayesha desires thy hand on her bosom and on the curve of her thigh.'

But she had only spoken instinctively, he knew, and he doubted if she had meant it, and he had turned his horse's head firmly towards the Urbidas. As he had left the camps in Addowara, he had heard the Zihouni musicians' high keening cry and he knew that in their strong love of courage they sang of Pentecost.

Though he rode with a straight back, his head high, his grey-streaked beard jutting like a battering ram, his eyes were stony and dead. His history, the history of his family, the history of the Hejri nation filled his mind like a heroic story, its tradition and pride not allowing him to show his grief with tears. Yet he was caught in a mortal sadness that cut through the pride written indelibly across his thoughts and character, in his strong head and the deep lines that ran down his face, in the carved scimitar nose and black emotional eyes.

He had nothing to be ashamed of, he knew. He had laid his greatness and his honour across the whole Urbida range, across Khusar country and the Toweida Plain, even into the Dharwa Hills. He knew that men like him gave all that was best in Hejri tradition and he had talked with warriors, had tasted the sweet wine of the Gods and enjoyed the soft kisses of golden girls.

The Addowara Pass was silent as he crossed into Khusar, its gorges still and empty. Occasionally in the silence, he heard the sound of a horse's hooves behind him, carried by some trick of the wind to his ears. But he paid no attention. Despite his straight back, he was an old man now, with eyes for nothing but the road ahead.

He rode past a goatherd sitting on a rock with his flock of flop-eared, yellow-eyed animals, their jaws moving drowsily right and left as they chewed at the tough grass. The place seemed as dead as a tomb. The goatherd, his young body wrapped in a woollen cloak against the growing cold, his head covered by the felt skull cap that marked him a Khusari, lowered the reed pipe on which he'd been playing and watched as he began to descend into the Khusar plain. As he raised the flute to his lips again, another horseman appeared, a fierce-looking man with a red Tayur cloak and a thin fanatic face. He was hurrying over the stony road, and there was a rifle across his crupper. Soon afterwards, there was a single shot beyond the bend of the road. It rattled on the mountain-side, thrown backwards and forwards by the silent crags, until it finally died away like a train disappearing into the distance.

JOHN HARRIS

CHINA SEAS

In this action-packed adventure, Willie Sarth becomes a survivor. Forced to fight pirates on the East China Seas, wrestle for his life on the South China Seas and cross the Sea of Japan ravaged by typhus, Sarth is determined to come out alive. Dealing with human tragedy, war and revolution, Harris presents a novel which packs an awesome punch.

A FUNNY PLACE TO HOLD A WAR

Ginger Donnelly is on the trail of Nazi saboteurs in Sierra Leone. Whilst taking a midnight paddle, with a willing woman, in a canoe cajoled from a local fisherman, Donnelly sees an enormous seaplane thunder across the sky only to crash in a ball of brilliant flame. It seems like an accident... at least until a second plane explodes in a blistering shower along the same flight path.

JOHN HARRIS

LIVE FREE OR DIE!

Charles Walter Scully, cut off from his unit and running on empty, is trapped. It's 1944 and, though the Allied invasion of France has finally begun, for Scully the war isn't going well. That is, until he meets a French boy trying to get home to Paris. What begins is a hair-raising journey into the heart of France, an involvement with the French Liberation Front and one of the most monumental events of the war. Harris vividly portrays wartime France in a panorama of scenes that enthral and entertain the reader.

THE OLD TRADE OF KILLING

Harris' exciting adventure is set against the backdrop of the Western Desert and scene of the Eighth Army battles. The men who fought together in the Second World War return twenty years later in search of treasure. But twenty years can change a man. Young ideals have been replaced by greed. Comradeship has vanished along with innocence. And treachery and murder make for a breathtaking read.

JOHN HARRIS

THE SEA SHALL NOT HAVE THEM

This is John Harris' classic war novel of espionage in the most extreme of situations. An essential flight from France leaves the crew of RAF *Hudson* missing, and somewhere in the North Sea four men cling to a dinghy, praying for rescue before exposure kills them or the enemy finds them. One man is critically injured; another (a rocket expert) is carrying a briefcase stuffed with vital secrets. As time begins to run out each man yearns to evade capture. This story charts the daring and courage of these men, and the men who rescued them, in a breathtaking mission with the most awesome of consequences.

TAKE OR DESTROY!

Lieutenant-Colonel George Hockold must destroy Rommel's vast fuel reserves stored at the port of Qaba if the Eighth Army is to succeed in the Alamein offensive. Time is desperately running out, resources are scant and the commando unit Hockold must lead is a ragtag band of misfits scraped from the dregs of the British Army. They must attack Qaba. The orders? Take or destroy.

'One of the finest war novels of the year'
– *Evening News*